P9-EEI-701

3 1833 04400 7315

Duets™

Dear Reader,

Duets was first launched in May 1999 and has proved to be a fan favorite. Each month we set out to bring you four sparkling romantic comedies in two separate volumes. You met many new authors in the lineup and revisited longtime Harlequin stars. Your letters and e-mails told us how *much* you enjoyed Duets!

Here at Harlequin we are always striving to reinvent ourselves, and so is the case with Duets. This is our last month of publication. Beginning in October 2003, look for Flipside, our brand-new romantic comedy series. In response to reader interest, we will be publishing two single books a month that are even longer than Duets novels. Look for #1 *Staying Single* by *USA TODAY* bestselling author Millie Criswell. Joining her in the launch month is Stephanie Doyle with #2 *One True Love?*

I think you will love these stories and all the fun books in Flipside in the months to come. Don't forget to check us out online at eHarlequin.com for news about all your favorite authors and books.

Yours sincerely,

Ms Birgit Davis-Todd
Executive Editor
Harlequin Books

SEP 2 3 2003

ROMANCE

"It's that biker party—I can't sleep."

Kirk huffed as he stepped into Bree's motel room. He speared his hand through his hair....

And froze in that position as his gaze swerved to Bree. "Oh, sorry," he murmured thickly, staring at her standing there in her underwear.

"I'm covered."

"Barely," he muttered.

"I'm wearing *more* than a bathing suit!"

Kirk wanted to say something, but he had the gut sense that if he opened his mouth right now, the only thing that would emerge would be a garbled string of incoherent sounds.

Look away. Be a gentleman. But his eyes were rarin' to roam free.

And roam they did. All over her long, lean, strong body.

"Are you all right?" asked Bree.

"No," he croaked.

"If you'd feel better," she said softly, "I'll slip back into bed, get under the covers."

Better? He doubted her in bed would make him feel any better....

For more, turn to page 9

"There's something in my sleeping bag!"

Louie opened his eyes at Alicia's screech. He'd thought she'd calmed down about this hammock thing after he'd made a big deal over checking out her sleeping bag and declaring it bug free. "Go to sleep, Bonbon."

"How can I sleep when I'm on the ground with the spiders and you're in the hammock?" She huffed something under her breath, followed by a flurry of thrashing and rustling sounds. "I want to sleep with you!"

His groin tightened at the thought of her curled close to him in the hammock. "I don't think it's a good idea—"

"Oh, we'll be fine," she said cozily. "I promise we'll only sleep. No hanky-panky."

The way she said hanky-panky made his skin prickle.

"I'll stay on my side of the hammock," she whispered as she climbed in. The hammock swayed gently. Then she made little needy, mewling sounds deep in her throat as she got comfortable.

He felt himself go hot. Yeah, sure, no hanky-panky.

This is going to be a long night. Long long long...

For more, turn to page 197

If you purchased this book without a cover you should be aware
that this book is stolen property. It was reported as "unsold and
destroyed" to the publisher, and neither the author nor the
publisher has received any payment for this "stripped book."

HARLEQUIN DUETS

ISBN 0-373-44173-8

Copyright in the collection:
Copyright © 2003 by Harlequin Books S.A.

The publisher acknowledges the copyright holder
of the individual works as follows:

LET IT BREE
Copyright © 2003 by Colleen Collins

CAN'T BUY ME LOUIE
Copyright © 2003 by Colleen Collins

All rights reserved. Except for use in any review, the reproduction or
utilization of this work in whole or in part in any form by any electronic,
mechanical or other means, now known or hereafter invented, including
xerography, photocopying and recording, or in any information storage
or retrieval system, is forbidden without the written permission of the
publisher, Harlequin Enterprises Limited, 225 Duncan Mill Road,
Don Mills, Ontario, Canada M3B 3K9.

All characters in this book have no existence outside the imagination of
the author and have no relation whatsoever to anyone bearing the same
name or names. They are not even distantly inspired by any individual
known or unknown to the author, and all incidents are pure invention.

This edition published by arrangement with Harlequin Books S.A.

® and TM are trademarks of the publisher. Trademarks indicated with
® are registered in the United States Patent and Trademark Office, the
Canadian Trade Marks Office and in other countries.

Visit us at www.eHarlequin.com

Printed in U.S.A.

Colleen Collins

Let It Bree

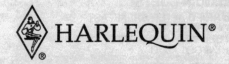

HARLEQUIN®

TORONTO • NEW YORK • LONDON
AMSTERDAM • PARIS • SYDNEY • HAMBURG
STOCKHOLM • ATHENS • TOKYO • MILAN • MADRID
PRAGUE • WARSAW • BUDAPEST • AUCKLAND

Dear Reader,

True story: A few years ago, a bull escaped from our regional stock show and found its way to a local highway where (until it was captured) it merrily galloped along with traffic. Being a romance writer, I read the story in the paper and found myself wondering, "What if a heroine was riding that bull?"

And so was born *Let It Bree*, where the heroine, Bree Brown, does indeed ride a Brahman bull out of a stock show to save it, and herself, from some thugs…one of whom becomes the hero in the sequel, *Can't Buy Me Louie*.

So kick back and enjoy a rollicking road story where a girl and her bull are rescued by a handsome scientist, the two of them (well, three) on the lam, on the road and falling in love! To read about my upcoming books, as well as enter contests for prizes, please visit my Web site at http://www.colleencollins.net.

Happy reading!

Colleen Collins

Books by Colleen Collins

HARLEQUIN DUETS

HARLEQUIN TEMPTATION

To Ruthann Manley,
wonderful friend and talented Webmaster

Acknowledgments:
Carl Rugg of Bovine Elite, who kindly helped
this city girl better understand Brahman bulls, and
Dr. Kirk Johnson (curator of paleontology at the
Denver Museum of Nature and Science),
who graciously answered my questions about his
research on the Cretaceous-Tertiary (K/T)) boundary
and for whom the hero is named.

1

BREE CUPPED Val's face between her hands. His mug was so huge, so hairy, it was like gripping a fur-covered volleyball.

"Val—" She stopped and frowned. She lifted her gaze to meet his, but her head remained dipped. Being six feet tall, she was accustomed to lowering—or as she preferred to call it, *dipping*—her head. Usually it just reinforced that she was different—bigger, taller, more athletic—than other females.

But today, ready to say something that meant life or death—which to Bree meant Europe or Wyoming—dipping was okay.

She stroked his chin, grappling for words. She'd never been a great talker. Action was more her style. "It's your moment," Bree finally said. Darn, she'd found the words and now her voice was quavering. She eased in a calming breath. "*Our* moment," she continued. "When you walk into the ring, be proud, majestic." She lowered her voice. "We both know you're just an oversize puppy, but keep that part buried, *deep,* because right now, you're tough. Awesome to the max. You're gonna blow them out of the stands—" She caught herself from adding, "and get me out of Chugwater.'' But even without saying the words, she imagined Val understood what was in her heart. He was her one-way ticket to freedom.

Emotion clogged Bree's throat. She swallowed hard, stuffing down the reality that escaping Chugwater also meant losing Val. She shifted her gaze to his expansive chest so he wouldn't see tears were threatening to spill. She *refused* to cry. That was for girls who played their emotions—and their charms— to manipulate people. Men, in particular.

Not Bree. She prided herself on cutting to the chase. Raising her head, she patted Val's massive shoulder reassuringly. ''Come on, Hot Stuff, let's make you a star.''

She led the way, her shoulders thrust back, her chin high. She wanted to look like a winner already—after all, the stock show was getting radio and TV coverage throughout the Midwest.

The tang of animal sweat and hay saturated the air. As they headed into the arena, the crowd's buzz intensified, reminding her of the time her crazy cousin Rupert stuck a twig in a hornets' nest, triggering a buzzing fury. Before those ornery critters had a chance to attack, nine-year-old Bree was pumping her long legs, running for her life. It hit her how, today, she was running again for her life. *A new life.* One where she could finally escape stuffy, small-town Chugwater, Wyoming, and discover the world.

Behind her, Val pounded the dirt floor in giant, Olympian strides. Oh yeah, awesome to the max. Af-

3 1833 04400 7315

ter all, Valentine Bovine was a major contender for the big prize—the Grand Champion Brahman bull.

Squinting against the glare of the overhead lights, Bree searched the stands. Under one of those Stetsons was Carlton Rugg from Bovine Best, the internationally renowned cattle breeding organization. They had a stellar reputation, and were known for their humane treatment of bulls, so she'd given them her verbal permission—an implied contract, not a written one—to bid aggressively for Val should he win the championship.

And if he won, she'd win three hundred grand—maybe more! With that kind of prize money, she'd fly out of nowhere, small-town Chugwater faster than a full-court slam. And Val would ease into the life of a full-time Romeo, making love to lady bovines for the remainder of his days. They'd both be happy…just happy in different parts of the world.

"Stepping into the arena, ladies and gentlemen," announced a baritone voice over the loudspeaker, "is Valentine Bovine." Chuckles rippled through the crowd. Fighting her sadness, Bree forced a smile. She'd named her bull Valentine because of the small white heart on his rear flank, and then she couldn't resist making his last name Bovine because of its lilt. Her name, Bree Brown, lacked any lilt whatsoever, and she hated it. Her mother had named her after the French cheese, brie, her grandmother had told her, but it wasn't until Bree was six months old that her mom had realized she'd misspelled it. And Brown? That was about as boring and ordinary as Chugwater itself.

"Valentine, the fourth and last finalist, represents the senior bull champion division," continued the announcer, his baritone voice reverberating through the speakers.

The crowd's incessant chatter prickled Bree's ears. She wiped at her suddenly hot, moist face and for a dizzying moment, she thought she might keel over. She'd never been this freaked out in a volleyball competition—but then, no single game had ever meant fulfilling her dream.

But in a sense, this was like a "single game" considering she'd only helped Mr. Connors, her neighbor back in Chugwater, show his bulls in competition before. This time, with Val, was Bree's first solo showing, all on her own.

Keep it together. Stay focused. Bree tightened her hold on Val's leather halter, needing something to grip to quell her adrenaline-crazed nerves. Just as she used to do in high-stress volleyball games, she took a few moments to distract herself. In her mind's eye, she envisioned Mr. Connors, who'd bequeathed Val to her in his will last June, seven months ago. It wasn't a surprise, really. After all, he'd let her name the bull the day it was born two and a half years ago, when she was barely twenty-one. Mr. Connors's death hadn't been a surprise either, but she didn't want to think about that now.

She swung her thoughts to Grams, with whom she'd

always lived a few miles outside Chugwater. She had vague memories of her father, who'd deserted them when she was two, and of her mother, who'd died when she was five.

The rest of Bree's family consisted of Aunt Mattie, Uncle Scott and three over-testosteroned cousins who lived next door. But even with a large extended family, it was old Mr. Connors who'd become her best pal. He was the one she'd entrusted with her most secret dream—one day to ride the Orient Express, the exotic and romantic train, through Europe. A fantasy she'd never dared confess to anyone, *especially* not her Aunt Mattie, who still fretted that Bree had earned a degree in art history rather than in something practical like accounting.

The announcer's voice jarred her thoughts. "Ladies and gentlemen, Doctor Marshall from Yuma, Arizona," he said, reintroducing the grand-champion judge.

To a smattering of applause, the livestock veterinarian strode across the arena, his leather boots kicking up dirt. The overhead lights sparked off his gray hair, the shine competing with his fist-size silver belt buckle.

"Slow, boy," Bree murmured. She barely tugged the strap and Val halted, standing stock-still. Brahmans were known for their smarts, but Val was exceptional. Not only did he understand her vocal and physical cues, Bree swore sometimes he could read her thoughts, too.

The vet began scrutinizing Val, running his hands expertly over the bull's back and sides. Val will live the rest of his life as a breeding Casanova, Bree reminded herself. But the justification felt hollow. If she hadn't been so busy these last few days hauling Val down to Denver, registering into the stock show, prepping him for the competition, she might have taken a few moments to ponder if winning your dream was worth losing your roots.

Finally, Dr. Marshall straightened, eyed Val one more time, then walked over to one of the 4H helpers who offered him a microphone. Taking the mike, the vet turned to the crowd. "Valentine," he began—his drawl making her bull's name sound like "Vaaalentiiiine"—"walks freely with good placement. He's got excellent thickness, depth of body, spring of rib, straight topline. Superior Brahman character." He paused.

Bree's insides lurched. This was the moment.

The next thing she knew, someone was shaking her hand. She looked into the judge's twinkling gray-blue eyes, vaguely aware he was congratulating her. People rose to their feet. Stetsons flew. Amid the shouting and whistling, the announcer's voice yelled, "It's Valentine Bovine, Brahman Grand Champion of the first Denver Stock Show Brahman Competition!"

People flooded the arena. Flashbulbs. Somebody motioned Bree to bring Val to an adjacent pen where she received a small bronze statue. More flashbulbs. A teenage girl wearing braces on her teeth and a rhinestone tiara on her head—who someone introduced as "Miss Livestock 2003"—joined Bree in another picture. Bree dipped her head a little, painfully aware she towered over the stock-show princess.

The princess disappeared. Several stock show officials joined her for another photo. Carlton, watching from the side, gave her a thumbs-up, a sign that his company was already outbidding other breeders for the rights to own Val. Carlton pointed toward the neon exit sign at the south end of the stadium, mouthing he'd meet her there.

And as Bree smiled shakily for yet another set of pictures, she noticed two cowboys standing to the side. One tall and somber, the other short and confused-looking. They looked ridiculously out of place, like Abbott and Costello gone bad in one of those old gangster films her Grams so loved.

Then the tall, somber cowboy sidled next to Bree, congratulating her in an east-coast accent, mumbling something about needing to get some stats on the bull. As he took the leather strap from Bree's hands, she noticed a large diamond ring on his pinkie finger. Had to be one of the owners of Bovine Best, a business worth millions. With that kind of money, maybe even his shirt buttons were diamonds.

But before she could check his buttons, the cowboy was leading Valentine away. Val jerked against the leather harness to look over his shoulder at her. As she stared into those big dark eyes for maybe the last time, waves of pain and loss washed over her. After two and a half years of grooming Val for this moment, it had all happened so fast—the trip, the competition, the win—and now her beloved bull was leaving her life forever.

She dropped her head so no one would see the blobs of tears. Honest to God, she felt her heart breaking.

Then, through her blurry vision, she caught sight of something wrong. She swiped at her eyes.

Mr. Pinkie Ring wore brand new turquoise boots.

Come·on, she thought. Okay, so maybe he had money to burn and wore diamonds, but fresh-out-of-the-box boots at a stock show? *Turquoise* ones? And why was he leading Val toward the west exit, when Carlton had pointed to the south?

She scanned the west, a mass of people, pens, cattle…but no sight of Carlton or any of the Bovine Best crew she'd met earlier.

Panic tore through her. *Are they stealing Val?*

She'd heard of such scams…criminals who'd kidnap, then sell, a prize bull on the black market to some dealer who'd claim he'd leased the bull and procured its sperm before the theft—and have forged records to prove it. These black-marketers made millions selling prize semen to ranchers eager to mix grand-champion genes with their herds. Unethical as hell, but it would take a small fortune in legal fees for the original owner—in this case, Bree—to prove her stolen bull's semen wasn't procured before the theft.

A small fortune. Every single penny of her prize money lost in legal fees.

And then there was the heart-killing image of Val, penned in some desolate location, unloved. No lady bovines around…nothing but a fake hind end to induce him…

No! Not to Val! Just as on the volleyball court when she felt an opponent was ready to strike, Bree had to make a decision, fast.

She darted, clawing her way through the mass of people. To her right, a Navajo blanket lay across a beam. Probably for someone's horse. Bree snatched a corner of the coarse fabric and pulled it with her.

Crazy ideas slammed through her mind as she picked up her pace. Maybe she'd toss the blanket over Pinkie Ring's face to distract him? It'd buy her a few moments to wrestle Val's strap from the man's grip. And then what? A guy with a pinkie ring, turquoise boots and a bad attitude might do something *really* crazy.

And sure enough, as soon as she spotted him, his jacket flapped open, exposing a gun holster.

Now she knew what that something crazy *and* workable might be. *He probably won't pull a gun with all these witnesses.*

She paused. *Wait a minute—is he talking to that cop?*

She shuffled in place. Weird. What did Pinkie and a cop have in common? There'd been a rash of internal police investigation stories in the Denver papers recently. Cops on the take. Black-market deals. Maybe some of those bad cops were in on this, too?

Can't go to the police. I'm on my own. Through a whirlwind of fear and fury, she fought to think what to do. *I could flash Val the signal to act tough, to charge, but that'd be dangerous with all these people and livestock around.*

Pinkie began walking again, away from the officer, Valentine firmly in tow.

It took Bree three giant steps to catch up. She slowed to a walk alongside Val, knowing instinctively he knew she was there. Eyeing the neatly creased, spotless Stetson on Pinkie Ring's head, she held up the blanket, ready to…

"Hey, girlie! Whatta ya doin' with my blanket?"

A man's angry voice behind her. Had to move. *Fast.*

She swung the blanket in an arc over her head.

Pinkie Ring jerked around. "What the—?" As he raised his hands to thwart the blanket attack, the lead shank to Val's halter fell free.

Behind her, more yelling. Feet pounded the dirt floor.

She swung the blanket in a wide, whooshing arc and flung it at Pinkie. As he stumbled and fell, she crouched and jumped—just as she would for a volleyball spike—using her body's momentum to hurl herself over the back of Val. They'd done this before, but always in open fields, not in a building!

"Go!" she yelled hoarsely, hoisting her leg over the animal's back as she grabbed a horn for balance.

Val snorted and lurched forward.

A woman screamed.

Bree held on for dear life as the massive beast broke into a trot.

THE MAMMOTH-SIZE VAN lurched and sputtered. Kirk Dunmore cursed under his breath and stared at the dashboard with its myriad buttons, switches and knobs. It reminded him of the spaceship panel in the sci-fi book he'd been reading lately. It starred a mighty warrior, Tarl Cabot, in the strange counter-Earth planet of Gor.

Only this wasn't Gor, it was Nederland, the funky counter-Earth mountain community an hour outside Denver, Colorado. And Kirk wasn't a mighty, solitary warrior trying to save the galaxy. He was a frustrated, soon-to-be-married paleobotanist trying to analyze the problem with this damn van. If he was in his old trust-worthy Jeep, he'd know *exactly* what to do.

But no, his future mother-in-law—with too much time and money on her hands—had had this state-of-the-art van delivered to Kirk on his excavation site yesterday outside Allenspark, Colorado. She called it a wedding gift, but Kirk knew it was really an expensive reminder that he was saying "I do" to her daughter Alicia in forty-eight hours, preceded by a rehearsal dinner in twenty-four hours, and he needed to get his dirt-caked, fossil-loving self home.

He stared at the dashboard and its myriad gadgets and buttons. So many, not even a scientist knew what to poke, prod or punch.

Honk. Honk.

Kirk glanced in the sideview mirror and caught the reflection of a blue pickup. It was early evening, the world glazed gray with winter, but he could discern that the hood ornament was a tarnished peace sign.

Honk. Honk.

"Give peace a chance," muttered Kirk.

Honk. Honk.

He scanned the dashboard one last time. So what if he had a doctorate and was on the verge of a major scientific breakthrough—right now, he was having one hell of a time figuring out this space-age dashboard. "Best option is to treat this contraption like I do my Jeep when it stalls. Pop it into second and let the good times roll!"

Kirk opened the door and jumped out, the impact of his six-one, two-hundred-pound body spraying January slush on his shoes and pants. Screw it. After countless hikes and digs, his boots and clothes had been caked with everything from Patagonian granite flakes to Arctic ice slivers. A little Colorado snow was nothing.

The chill bit his face. This part of the road was on a decline, so he ran a few steps, one hand against the open door, the other on the steering wheel. His footsteps sloshed. His breath came fast. The white van, covered with dirt and slush, rolled forward. Kirk jumped back into the driver's seat, popped the clutch and punched the gas. The van lurched, sputtered and stalled.

Rolling silently down a dark curving road, he eased the van onto the road shoulder. He set the brake and cut the engine. He recalled the gas gauge showing there was *some* fuel, so it couldn't be out of gas.

In the Rockies, on these mountain roads with no streetlights, night settled quickly. Kirk fumbled along the dashboard and pressed a button with the image of a light. The headlights blazed to life, cutting two tunnels of white through the descending darkness.

"Help!"

He looked up. In the haze of headlights stood a woman.

"Help!" She pumped her hands wildly up and down as though yelling the word wasn't enough.

He threw open the door and jumped down. "What's wrong?" he yelled, jogging toward her. She wore tattered jeans, scuffed leather boots, a blue-and-white checkered shirt. She didn't appear to be physically hurt.

"My—" She gasped a breath. "My friend and I need a ride."

He halted. "You're hitchhiking in these mountains at *night?*" The heat of his breath condensed into frozen particles on his mustache. Damn. It was too cold to be chatting with some hitchhiking cowgirl.

And too cold for her to be dressed in nothing but a shirt and jeans.

He started to take off his jacket to offer her when an instinctual warning shot through him. "Friend?" He looked around.

"Pe-pet," the street girl said softly, waving her hand dismissively as though she'd simply misspoken. "My *pet* and I are...lost."

A strength shone through her big, gray eyes. In his gut, he trusted that look. She wasn't helpless, but she needed help.

He unzipped his jacket and tossed it to her. "Put this on. Let's get you and your—" he looked around for a puppy or a dog "—pet into the van before all three of us turn into icicles."

Her smile was so appreciative as she slid her arms into the jacket that, despite the cold, his insides melted. Alicia had never given him a look of such sweet gratefulness.

Forget sweet looks. You're almost married.

"Your pet can sit on your lap in the front seat." There should be enough fuel to get them to a gas station. He'd traveled this stretch of mountain road plenty—around the bend was the Sundance Lodge and Café, a few miles farther was a place to fill up.

"He's, uh, too big to sit on my lap."

He? Oh, yeah, the pet. "Okay, option two." Kirk walked briskly to the van's rear doors. "Back here." What did this girl own? A Saint Bernard? Great Dane?

He opened the doors, figuring he'd drop this girl and her dog at the station, where they could call for a ride home and have a warm place to wait. He'd fill up and continue into Denver.

His thoughts were interrupted by the thud-thud-thud of steps punctuated with heavy, beastly snorts.

Kirk's stomach clenched. His mouth went dry.

Staring him down, heaving breaths of steam, stood a ferocious-looking bull with a hump on its back the size of a small mountain. The moonlight, gilding the beast in a surreal silver, added to the monstrous effect.

"He's gentle," the girl said, as though hanging out with ferocious animals was an everyday sort of thing.

Kirk glanced around—where had she hidden this creature? Spying the clusters of trees that hugged the road, he had his answer.

"His name's Valentine," she continued.

"I—I don't care if his name's Sweetheart," Kirk said, finding his voice, "that's one big mother of a—" This was not the time for conversation. This was time to *move*. Run like hell. Unfortunately, his body had other ideas. Like remaining frozen where he stood. If only he hadn't tossed her his jacket, part of him would be warm enough to flee, encouraging the rest of his body to follow.

The girl blinked, obviously realizing the terrifying effect of her "pet." "Oh, I'm sorry." She grabbed the brass ring in the beast's nose. "See, he's under control."

A street cowgirl holding a ferocious bull by the ring in its nose. Oh yeah, that would definitely stop the animal from charging and pummeling Kirk Dunmore into a grease spot.

"I'll take him to the back of the van," the girl continued breezily. "I'm sure Valentine can fit easily inside. He can lower himself onto his knees and scrunch down. He's special that way.''

He's special that way? Kirk had to put a stop to this, now. What would Tarl Cabot, the mighty, solitary hero of Gor do at a time like this?

The beast raised one mighty hoof and struck the road, the sharp thud reverberating through the chilly air.

"No ro-room," Kirk stuttered. "Va-van too small." He held up his gloved hands, the flattened palms parallel to each other, indicating what "small" meant in case she didn't know.

But she ignored his visual clue. Pulling on the halter, she led the bull to the back of the van. "What is this—about twelve by six?''

"Probably less," he said quickly, following at a safe distance.

"No, it's definitely twelve by six.''

Her confidence was irritating.

She continued talking as though this was nothing more than an evening stroll. "I used to put Val into Mr. Connors's small cattle trailer and it was twelve by six.''

Three cheers for Mr. Connors's cattle trailer.

"How are its shocks?''

"Excellent. I cart heavy tools." Damn. This wasn't the time to tell the truth. Unfortunately, lying had never been a skill he'd learned.

The cowgirl opened the back doors. "What's back here?''

"Some pickaxes. Shovels. Box of fossils."

"Fossils?"

"They're in a metal crate up front."

"Metal. They're safe. Valentine is a pussycat, trust me."

Damn irritating, that confidence of hers.

"Come on, Hot Stuff, let's get inside," the cowgirl said, followed by some kissing sounds.

Before Kirk could suck in another brain-numbing breath, the beast had placed one mighty hoof then another on the van's carpeted floor. Then, with the grace of a meaty ballerina, the beast disappeared inside as the van creaked and lowered with the added weight.

The girl shut the doors carefully, as though she'd just loaded the back with china, then walked back to Kirk. "You saved our lives." Her voice was soft with appreciation. It was too dark to see her face, but he imagined her having that same grateful look she'd flashed him earlier when she'd stood in the headlights.

And for a sweet moment, he knew how Tarl Cabot, the mighty warrior of Gor, felt when he'd rescued a damsel.

The cowgirl damsel slapped Kirk on the arm, one of those good-pals gestures that wiped out his Tarl Cabot fantasy.

"Let's go—or we'll freeze our you-know-whats out here!" She trotted toward the passenger door.

Stunned with the occurrences of the last few minutes, Kirk walked stiff-kneed toward the driver's door. As he sloshed through a chilly puddle, he experienced literally the meaning of ''cold feet.''

Was the anxiety he felt due to his impending marriage or the adventure he'd stepped into?

2

"NEDERLANDER HIGHLANDER RANCH," Louie repeated for the umpteenth time, rolling the words in his mouth as though tasting them.

"Some Scottish guy?" asked Shorty, taking a last drag on his cigarette and flicking it out the window. The lighted stub seared a thin orange flame through the darkness.

Louis slugged Shorty on the arm. "There's an ashtray in here."

"Oh." Shorty stared straight ahead, looking like a basset hound that had just been severely chastised. "Sorry, Lou."

Louie sighed. He hated guilt trips. Reminded him of his ex-wives. The first two, anyway. He also hated being stuck with an imbecile like Shorty on a critical job, but Shorty was the nephew of Clancy "The Neck" Venuchi and if Clancy said Shorty was working a job, only a bigger imbecile than Shorty said no.

"Forget it," said Louie. "We need to figure out where this Nederlander Highlander place is."

After a little boy hanging around outside the stock show had told them he'd seen a girl and her bull trot into a cluster of rundown nearby buildings, Louie and

Shorty had driven around that area for several hours. They'd waved money in winos' faces, until one swore he'd seen two people loading a buffalo into a big yellow truck with the words *Nederlander Highlander Ranch* on it.

The buffalo had to be the bull.

But Nederland Highlander?

"Shorty, get the map book. Look up Nederlander."

Shorty reached underneath his seat and retrieved the thick *Denver Regional Area* guide they'd purchased at the Tattered Cover.

"Right." Shorty flipped open the book and stared at a page.

"What're you lookin' at?"

"A map."

Louie bunched his fist, fighting the urge to smack some sense into his partner. "There's over a hundred pages in that thing. Check the frickin' index."

"Right." Shorty flipped to the back of the book. "Ned...er...lander," he muttered under his breath. "Ned...er—"

"N-e-d-e-r-l-a-n-d-e-r." Louie loved books, especially detective novels, so he had an affinity for words and their spelling. But he had a feeling this street map was the first book Shorty had cracked open in years.

Shorty made a smacking sound as his finger slid down a page. "Dere it is!" He brought the book to within inches of his face. "Ne...der...land." He looked up. "No e-r."

"Good." If it was in the book, it was close to Denver. So the girly and the bull had hopped a ride to a nearby town. Sweet. "Check which highway leads to it."

"Right." After a pause filled with more smacking, Shorty announced, "Twenty-five north to thirty-six to one ninety-three to one nineteen."

"I said which highway, not how high can you count." No sweat. They'd spent a chunk of today on the I-25 highway, and Louie remembered signs to highway 36. The rest was chump change.

He started the engine.

"Lou?"

"Yeah?"

"I'll use da ashtray next time."

If Louie has his way, there'd be no next time with Shorty. Fortunately, this job would wrap up soon. All Louie had to do was steal the frickin' bull and cart it to a rendezvous point outside Lubbock, Texas. There, they'd hook up with a go-between who'd pay them their dough and take the bull off their hands.

Louie'd never messed with a bull before, but after being told his take would be a cool half a mil, he figured he could dance with the beast if he had to. Besides, he'd done some studying. Brahmans looked tough, but were for the most part temperate-like.

Sorta like himself, he figured.

Louie turned the wheel and steered down a side street. He could almost smell his cut of the loot, a scent sweeter than his mama's spicy grilled sausages and peppers. With his take, Louie would fulfill his dream to escape Trenton and buy a boat in the Keys. Spend the rest of his days catching big fish, drinking strong whiskey and loving lusty women. Big, tanned, lusty women. The kind who overfilled a bikini and overloved a man…

Feeling a rush of rare benevolence, Louie finally answered Shorty. ''Yeah, just 'member we got an ash-tray.''

A match sizzled as Shorty lit his cigarette, making a great show of tossing the blown-out match in the ashtray.

Louis held out his hand for a cig.

''Thought you'd quit.''

''I did.''

''Then why you want a cig?''

''I need to chew something.''

A bit too quickly, Shorty tossed a cigarette which Louie caught in midair. He ran his nose along the white cylinder, inhaling the pungent scent of tobacco. Squeezing the spongy filter between his teeth, he said, ''We're on our way to findin' Mr. Money Bull.''

''Mr. Money Bull,'' Shorty repeated, blowing out a stream of smoke. ''I won't letcha down, Lou. We'll get that bull to Texas, wrap up da deal and never have to work again for the rest of our lives.''

Louie grinned, enjoying a whiff of secondhand smoke. Never have to work again. He could smell the sea breezes now. Could feel the hot sun on his skin, the sweet sting of whiskey on his tongue. And when he got tired of the tanned, lusty women, maybe he'd invite wifey number three down for a visit.

Hell, if Shorty did good and helped pull off this job without any more glitches, maybe Louie'd give him visiting rights, too.

"WELL, I'll be dam—"

"I didn't hear that!" Mattie stuck her head out the kitchen door.

Ida didn't look. Being seventy-five years old had its prerogatives, and one of them was enjoying words of the bluer variety. But forget explaining that to her daughter Mattie. Hell, it was still a mystery to Ida how she'd raised such a rule-fixated puritan as Mattie. Good thing she lived next door and not under the same roof with Ida and her granddaughter Bree.

"Hush!" Ida held up a gun barrel, motioning for silence. To the TV, she said, "All right, muffin, let's have a dose of straight talk."

Mattie stepped into the living room, wiping a dinner plate with a dishrag. "You watch too many gangster flicks," she continued. "You sound more like a gun moll than a respectable senior citizen. And how many times have I told you not to clean your pistols in the living room! What if company dropped by, saw weapons strewn all over and told the deputy sheriff? After that incident in the Buffalo Lodge, you swore you'd never again—"

"Hush!" Ida waved the gun barrel again. "They're talkin' about my granbaby."

"My niece Bree's on the news?" Mattie clutched the chipped china plate she'd been drying to her chest. "Did...Valentine...win?"

The pert, auburn-haired newscaster talked earnestly to the camera. "...reportedly the bull was stolen after winning the grand champion prize, which is worth hundreds of thousands of dollars to the seller—potentially millions to the buyer. This story is about more than a big bull. It's about big money."

The TV reporter checked something on a piece of paper. "Police say the alleged thief was wearing brown boots, blue jeans and a blue-and-white checkered shirt."

Mattie gasped. "That sounds like the outfit Bree picked out for the competition—"

"Police have issued an all points bulletin," continued the announcer, "for the alleged thief and the bull, which has a white heart on its right rear flank—"

"That's our Valentine, all right!" Ida blurted, standing. "They think my granbaby *stole* Valentine! What's wrong with those city slickers in Denver? Big-city smog go to their brains?" She mulled this over for a moment. "Ya know, Bree had a verbal agreement with that Bovine Best outfit...wonder if that implied contract is being misinterpreted by these media jerks. They're conveniently forgetting the word *implied* and making it appear Bree broke a contract and stole Val." After barking a few choice expletives at the TV, she said, "I gotta go find Bree—clear up this mess!"

Ida snapped the revolver chamber into place with a click. "Gotta grab my coat and boots—it's butt-freezin' cold this time of year."

"What in God's name do you think you're doing?" asked Mattie, her face pinched with irritation.

"While I'm getting dressed, find my keys, wouldja?" She glanced around the room. "I'll need my holster, too."

"Mother! You're not driving that…that death trap to Denver!"

"My pickup ain't no death trap. Just fixed the brakes last year. Where'd I kick off my boots? Oh, there they are."

"You can't get the bull into the pickup—"

"Hell, I know that. Bree 'n' I'll figure out how to get the bull home." Ida slipped her tiny feet into a pair of cream-colored boots with purple trim.

"I'd…I'd go with you, but I have three sons to look after."

"I know, honey pie. Now stop frettin' and help your sweet ol' mama get ready."

Mattie made an exasperated sound. "Does my sweet old mama *have* to carry a gun?"

"Yes."

"Why?"

"To shoot people with, sweetheart."

"We're in a family crisis and you're quoting from those…those bad-guy videos!"

"*The Fallen Sparrow,* 1943, John Garfield. Who wasn't a 'bad guy,' just a lost soul." Ida paused.

"And them's not just 'flicks.' Them's words to live by." She headed down the hallway. "Grab that bag of chips and a few apples. Meet you at the pickup," Ida yelled over her shoulder.

"VAN WON'T START," Kirk said, trying to sound calm. One hell of a feat considering a beast's massive, horned head nearly hung over the front seat, mere inches from the right side of Kirk's face.

Kirk reminded himself, again, that the girl said this animal was "intelligent" and "sweet-tempered."

"We're stuck?" asked the cowgirl. "We just got in!"

The bull released a hefty snort as though seconding her comment.

Man, that bull had bad breath. "I thought we had enough gas to make it to the station, but I was wrong."

Wind whistled past. Clouds were creeping across the night sky, blotting out part of the moon. Kirk swore a coarse bull whisker brushed the side of his face. Was this monstrous thing *hungry?*

"Uh, when did your beast last eat?" he asked.

The girl made an indignant sound. "It's a Brahman bull, not a beast. And it's a vegetarian, so it won't take a bite out of you. Unless you tick him off."

Tick him off? "I thought you said he was sweet-tempered."

"He has his moods, like anyone else."

Wonderful. A moody bull. Worse, one that occasionally got "ticked off." Kirk had never *ticked* anyone off. He was always Mr. Reasonable—the result of growing up with a wild, flamboyant mother for whom he had to constantly intervene. Once he'd had to mediate between her and a department-store Santa who his mother swore had propositioned her. Wouldn't that be Kirk's luck, after all these intervening, mediating years, to piss off a *bull?*

"Where were you headed to?" he asked.

"Chugwater."

"As in Wyoming?"

"You know another Chugwater?"

"What are you doing several *hundred* miles away from home?" He probably shouldn't ask. Alicia could make the story of a broken fingernail last a day...he couldn't even fathom how long a lost-with-a-bull tale might take.

"So, now what do we do?" she asked, ignoring his question. "Any ideas?"

"Ideas? Too many," Kirk muttered. He was accustomed to excavating and viewing the fossils of long-dead plants and beasts, not driving real live ones around.

He took in a deep breath and looked at the sky. Those clouds didn't look like snow clouds, but in Colorado, one never second-guessed the weather. He itemized his priorities. First, he needed to find shelter and food. Second, tomorrow morning, he'd deal with their travel logistics.

"There's a lodge up the road," he finally said. "A few minutes' walk. We can stay there tonight."

"Lodge?" She sighed heavily. "I, uh, don't have any money."

"I have a credit card. I've stayed there before. The area behind the lodge backs right up to a mountain. Good resting spot for your bull." He'd ask for one of the rooms at the far end from the main lodge. Considering it was January, high in the mountains, he seriously doubted anyone would be staying overnight at this out-of-the-way place. Stashing a bull would be the least of their worries.

He hoped.

"Do you have a cell phone?" she asked. "I'd like to call my grandmother."

"Service is maxed out." He'd tried calling Alicia earlier and discovered he was too far into the mountains to get a signal. "But I'm sure there'll be phones in the rooms."

"Think they'll have oats or hay?"

For Valentine. "There should be some grass, bushes outside...and we can order twenty bowls of cereal on top of dinner." He buttoned his top shirt button, anticipating the chill outside.

"Let's go," he said, opening his door. "Tarl Cabot, watch out," he murmured under his breath, jumping to the ground.

TWENTY MINUTES LATER, Kirk flicked the switch of room number one, located at the farthest end of the

Sundance Lodge. Although he'd assumed the place would be mostly empty, a gang of Harley riders—seen year-round in these parts of Colorado because of the scenic mountain roads—were staying overnight. Fortunately, there were two adjacent empty rooms available.

Bree followed him inside, checking out the far window through which she could see her bull tethered to a pine tree. "This room's perfect for me. I can keep my eye on Val."

He nodded. "Fine. I'll leave our sandwiches here while I check my room, make a call." He placed two butcher-paper-wrapped packages on a chipped wooden coffee table.

"Funny how they didn't question your wanting to buy five boxes of that oat bran cereal, too," said Bree.

Kirk chuckled. "Nederland's filled with free spirits—I could have asked to buy one of the tie-dyed T-shirts off their backs and they wouldn't have blinked an eye. The community is filled with former hippies or hippie wanna-bes. You know, peace and love and all that."

"Well, I like peace, but I can do without—" Bree huffed a breath and looked around the room, feeling a little stupid for her slip of the tongue. Just because she wasn't interested in love and marriage and all that nonsense, didn't mean she had to announce it.

"You're probably wondering what I was doing hitchhiking in the middle of nowhere," she said quickly, switching topics. "I, uh, missed my ride from the stock show and a really nice truck driver said he'd give us a lift to Nederland so I said okay but I didn't want to be dropped off in the middle of a town, so I told him just to leave us off on the side of the road. Figured we'd get a lift somehow to Chugwater, but nobody was stopping, so I jumped out in front of your stopped van…'' She sucked in a breath, hoping the story sounded relatively sane and plausible, and it should considering she'd left out the parts about the gangsters and guns.

As he stared at her sorta stunned like, she realized this was the first moment she'd had a chance to really see him in the light. His hair was thick, blond. And he was solidly good-looking. Put him in a double-breasted suit and a gray felt hat, he could star as one of those hunky, hard-boiled detectives in one of Grams's gangster flicks.

But she doubted this guy even owned a suit. He looked extremely comfortable in his faded jeans and blue-and-gray flannel shirt. Hard to fit his down-home look with that fancy van, though. The two didn't mix.

He finally broke the silence. ''Well, you're safe now. That's what matters.''

She hoped that was true. Thanks to this guy, she was, for the time being. Tomorrow, she'd figure out how to get back home, clean up this ''alleged theft'' confusion, and get back to leading a normal life.

''What's your name?'' asked Bree. She'd hovered next to the door as he'd filled out the registration stuff in the lodge lobby, so she hadn't overheard any information, such as his name or where he lived.

"Kirk Dunmore. Yours?"

"Bree Brown." She eyed the TV, knowing in her gut that the story of a Brahman bull trotting out of the Denver Stock Show would be on the news. Escapee livestock was big news. Last year when those llamas had bolted free and run down the I-25, it'd been on all the stations.

She'd check the TV later, when she was alone.

Then she thought, with a sickening realization, that chances were Grams, who watched the news religiously every evening, would have seen a story about Bree and Valentine riding out of the coliseum and be worried sick.

Bree looked around the room for a phone. "I need to call home."

"Yeah, I need to phone my fiancée, too."

Fiancée?

Bree pushed her hand through her curly hair, unsure why her stomach felt as though it had just flipped upside down. Couldn't be because of Kirk's remark. Like she cared. She eyed the sandwiches Kirk had purchased. *My insides are flip-flopping because I'm hungry.* After she'd eaten something solid, she'd feel lots better.

But when she looked at Kirk, her stomach did another somersault.

The way he stood—legs spread, arms crossed solidly over his chest—he looked like a rough and rugged explorer, the kind of guy who fearlessly tackled anything in the world.

What did he say he had in the back of the van? Pickaxes. Shovels. Oh yeah, this man treated life like an adventure. Only a man like that would understand Bree's own yearning to strike out on her own and discover the world.

She dipped her head, rubbing her chin against the slick rayon of the jacket he'd loaned her. She caught a whiff of scent—*his* scent. Male. Musky. Inside her, the curl of heat ignited, spreading through her like a small fire.

Kirk scraped his hand across the stubble on his chin. "I'll go check my room now, call Alicia, then come back for that sandwich."

Alicia? Had to be the fiancée. Bree nodded absently, slipping off the jacket so she didn't accidentally sniff any more of his lethal male muskiness.

He left, the room door clicking shut behind him. She'd do the same with her reactions. Shut them down. Tight. After all, he was just a nice guy who'd helped her out of a jam. By this time tomorrow, they'd both be back in their separate worlds, never to see each other again.

3

BREE RAN BAREFOOT through a jungle, crowded with vibrant green leaves, birds, hanging vines. Her feet slapped hard against cold, damp earth. Pounding footsteps followed, tracking her. She glanced over her shoulder. Dense foliage blocked her assailant's face. Her gaze dipped. He wore turquoise boots.

Bang-bang-bang.

Bree jolted awake. Cold perspiration slicked her body. She blinked into the dark, her gaze following a stream of moonlight from the window next to her bed.

Outside stood a massive, dark shadow close to the tree line.

Valentine.

She released a shaky breath. *I'm in the lodge. We're safe.*

Bang-bang-bang!

Swiping a shaky hand across her brow, she glanced at the digital clock next to the bed—3:00 a.m. Who would be knocking on her door at this time of the morning?

The thugs?

Her stomach curdled. *Could they have traced me to this lodge in the middle of the mountains?* Maybe not such a far-fetched idea considering they were determined to get Val, which meant big money for them, bigger money for whatever breeding outfit illegally sold Val's sperm. And for that kind of money, the thugs would go through anything, do anything, to get the prize.

Even take my life.

Hairs stiffened along her arms. *Don't start spooking yourself.*

Hell, if they're that smart, all they'd have to do is look behind the lodge and see Val plain and clear in the moonlight. No need to knock on any doors and alert people that they're stealing a bull!

Anyway, it was probably just some happy drunk, home from one of those rowdy Nederland bars, knocking at the wrong door. If the knocking continued, she'd call the front desk. Let them know some poor drunkard was knocking at random rooms.

She swung her feet over the side of the bed and edged through the dark across the thick rug, trying to remember where she'd put that phone after calling Grams earlier and leaving the message.

"Bree?" Bang-bang-bang. "It's me, Kirk."

She stopped in her tracks. "Kirk," she whispered. With a burst of pent-up energy, she ran to the door and threw it open.

A blast of frigid night air assaulted her. Shivering, she hadn't thought about how she was dressed, or *wasn't* dressed. All that stood between her and the freezing mountain night air was a spaghetti-strap pink T-shirt and matching undies.

Wrapping her arms around herself, she scooted back as Kirk stepped inside and shut the door behind him.

"A-anything wr-wrong?" she asked through chattering teeth.

"Don't you hear them?"

"Th-them?"

In the distance, a bottle crashed, followed by raucous laughter.

"It's that damn Harley party," Kirk huffed. "Those bikers have been going full steam ever since I went to bed. Haven't slept a wink."

Despite the cold, she smiled. With three wild teenage boy cousins living next door, she was used to all kinds of racket, day and night. If she could sleep through beer keg parties, band practices and a bunch of teenage boys screaming and whooping it up, it was *nothin'* to sleep through some drunken biker party.

"Where's the light?" Kirk asked.

She fumbled along the wall behind the door and flipped a switch.

The overhead light flickered on, casting the room in a warm, yellowish glow. Fortunately, the room heater was quickly warming things up, erasing the night chill.

Kirk, disheveled in a pair of worn jeans and a partially buttoned flannel shirt over a dark blue T-shirt, blinked and looked around. It hit Bree that he looked

kinda cute all sleepy and disoriented. He speared one
of his tan, roughened hands through his rumpled
hair...

And froze in that position as his gaze swerved to
Bree. "Oh, sorry," he murmured thickly, staring at
her underwear. He quickly turned away, his hand still
stuck on his head.

Having grown up in the country, Bree wasn't hung
up on what showed or didn't show. Besides, any es-
sential "body stuff" wasn't showing at all. And even
it if was, *big deal.* Ever since she was a kid, she and
her buddies—girls and boys—had often skinny-
dipped at the Connors pond.

"I'm covered," she said.

"Barely," he muttered.

"How long you gonna keep your hand on your
head?" she asked.

He dropped it, holding it stiffly at his side.

She laughed. "I'm wearing *more* than a bathing
suit, for gosh sake!"

Kirk wanted to say something, after all, his verbal
acumen covered the gambit from lectures to theoreti-
cal discussions, but he had the gut sense that if he
opened his mouth right now, the only thing that would
emerge would be a garbled string of incoherent
sounds.

And Kirk Dunmore, always articulate, with an IQ
topping 170, was at this very moment reduced to a
brain-damaged, blithering idiot. And not just *once* in
one night, but *twice.*

Okay, okay, even Einstein's brain might have turned to mush if he'd been faced with a Brahman bull.

But would Einstein have turned to brain mush face-to-face with a striking, partially clad woman of Amazonian proportions? Hell no. Rumor had it Einstein turned into a damn playboy when he crossed paths with the likes of Marilyn Monroe.

While all these thoughts collided in his head, Kirk realized he'd been staring openmouthed at Bree over his shoulder.

Look away. Be a gentleman.

But his eyes were behaving as though they'd been penned up for a lifetime and now were rarin' to roam free.

And roam they did. All over Bree's long, lean, strong body as though the most exquisite sights of nature had been molded into one mighty fine package.

The sheen of her tan reminded him of the warm, golden sands on New Guinea beaches. The curve of her breasts mimicked the lush, rolling hills of the Argentine pampas. And those red glints in her dark curls were like the fiery, predawn rays of the sun as it rose over the Himalayas.

But when his gaze dropped to her legs, no geographical reference could do them justice. Those achingly long, sensuous legs reminded him of the libido-searing Rod Stewart song "Hot Legs."

Was that a tattoo on her ankle?

At first he thought it was a flower unfolding, then

realized it was a chocolate being unwrapped. A chocolate kiss. He licked his lips, aching for just a drop of that chocolate to whet his parched soul.

"Are you all right?" asked Bree.

"No," he croaked.

"If you'd feel better," Bree said softly, "I'll slip back into bed, get under the covers."

Better? He doubted he could feel any better except...if...

Whoa, boy, put a lock on it. You're getting married in two days. Forty-eight hours. Two thousand, eight hundred and eighty minutes.

This had to be the result of the week-long dig he'd just finished. All that time alone, with nothing but prairie dogs and lizards for company, a man was bound to go whacko for a little chocolate drawing on an ankle.

In the silence, Kirk heard her tread softly across the carpet. Then the squeak of the bed as she settled in. And he tried to keep his mind trained on the lodge's wooden walls, upon which crookedly hung a framed print of a bear pawing a stream for salmon.

But no matter what he tried to focus on, his just-turned-bad-boy mind kept returning to the image of those long, tan legs and chocolate-tattooed ankle, stretching and twisting in the warm dark under those seductively soft covers.

Why had he been born a paleobotanist? Oh what he'd give for a moment as a plain ol' blanket conforming to the shape and warmth of Bree.

Breeeeee. The sound of her name was like the wind. Bree. Breeezy. With a soulful lilt, like in that Beatles song "Let It Be." Let it Bree. Let me lick that little chocolate on your ankle for the rest of my life...

Bree tucked the blanket under her chin and peered at Kirk. He seemed oddly off balance, as though he might topple over any moment.

"Kirk, you look a little unsteady. Need some water?"

"Chocolate."

"What?"

He coughed. "Uh, water. Right. Need water."

"Okay, I'll go grab a glass in the bathroom, get you—"

"No!"

He still stood with his back to her. "I'll get it. Stay put. And cover up."

He returned a moment later, downing a glass of water like a parched man, staring at her with wide blue eyes. He was so flustered, so red-faced, she suddenly got it.

"Don't tell me you're nervous about seeing me in my undies. We've already been through this."

"Not nervous. Not anymore."

Maybe he said he wasn't nervous, but he looked positively mortified. "Aren't you used to seeing naked women?" She almost said, aren't you used to seeing your fiancée naked? but figured that was getting into overly personal terrain.

"You weren't naked—just nearly naked."

Maybe Kirk was a throwback to another century where men were polite, discreet, and the wedding night was the first time they…

Wow. She didn't know men like that existed in today's world. And to think she, small-town girl from even smaller-town Chugwater, possibly knew more about the birds and the bees than Mr. Big City!

"Well, I'm all covered now, so it's a moot point," she announced.

Kirk put the glass aside, shot her a feeble smile, then backed up to the couch and fell into a sitting position. Avoiding looking at her face, he scraped his hand across his stubbled chin as though he'd just finished an incredibly long and exhausting journey.

"Wish I had a glass of warm milk," he rasped. He looked at her, his eyes burning as though he were running a fever.

"Maybe that café's still open?"

"At 3:00 a.m.?"

"Maybe those Harley people have some."

"Very funny. Obviously *one* of us has gotten some sleep."

Bree jerked her thumb toward the window. "Two."

Kirk looked outside at Val. "Okay, Val's gotten some sleep-eye too, lucky bull." Kirk narrowed his eyes, thinking. "Hmm, maybe I should take your bull to those bikers' rooms, position him behind me while I ask if they could please keep it down."

"That'd work," Bree said with a smile. "Val has a reputation for clearing out places. Once he accidentally kicked over a vat of chili at the Chugwater Chili festival—that sent people running! But his kicking was my fault. I'd accidentally brushed against his back left leg, which is our signal for him to kick out his right leg. It's a little trick I taught him. Another time he got loose in downtown Chugwater and tore into Mary Jane Tock's beauty parlor. The street was instantly filled with shrieking women in hair curlers and blue face masks.'' Bree giggled.

Kirk chuckled, shaking his head. ''Yeah, that's just what the Sundance Lodge needs in the wee hours of the morning. A bunch of hysterical bikers running amok in the parking lot.''

Bree laughed louder, liking how the two of them were sharing a fun moment. This sure beat the hell out of Kirk's mortification…or her paranoia that thugs were knocking at her door.

Speaking of which…

''Hey, you know what?'' she said, trying to sound as though she'd just had this great idea. ''Why don't you stay on the couch in here tonight? That way, you'll hardly hear those bikers.'' *And I'd have a built-in bodyguard.* She looked him over in his rumpled hair, flannel shirt and threadbare jeans.

Too bad those pickaxes are still in the truck.

Well, still, he'd be an extra body in case those thugs showed up. And two bodies, plus a bull, were better odds against two thugs.

In the distance, something crashed, followed by the syrupy sound of drunken laughter.

Kirk blew out a puff of air as he looked toward the far wall. "Think I'll take you up on your offer. At least the sounds are more muted in here."

Bree snuggled down in her bed, bunching up the pillow under her head, feeling the happiest she had in hours. She wasn't alone, she had a roof over her head, she and Val had a place to sleep, and tomorrow, ah sweet tomorrow, she'd be back home in Chugwater. Kirk had mentioned that his buddy in Denver, a guy named George who owned a cattle trailer, could drive her and her bull back home.

"Turn out the light when you're ready," she said sweetly. "And don't worry about me if you feel like staying up and reading or watching TV."

Oops.

Earlier, she'd switched on a local news channel and had watched, openmouthed, as some newscaster reported an alleged bull theft. Bree's name wasn't mentioned, but the newscaster described her clothes, right down to her scuffed boots. It had to be because of that damn "implied contract" that the media was insinuating she was a thief!

Bree shoved herself up on one elbow and stared wide-eyed at Kirk. "Uh, nix the TV idea! It would, uh, be too loud, keep me awake."

"No, I wouldn't watch TV at this hour," he answered calmly. "Might read, though." He rummaged through the stack of old paperbacks on the coffee table. "If it wasn't so cold out, and if the van wasn't parked down the road, I'd dash out and get *The Priest Kings of Gor,* which I left in the glove compartment.''

Bree blinked at him. ''The what of what?''

Kirk glanced up. ''Book by John Gorman. Science fiction.''

''Oh.'' She lay back down. No TV. Life was good.

Kirk rummaged halfheartedly through some books. ''What do you like to read?''

''Historical romances.''

''Really.'' He flashed her a look, then resumed his rummaging.

''You sound surprised. By which part? The historical or the romance?''

''I…just didn't envision you as a romance reader.''

''Really,'' she answered, mocking his droll tone.

He cocked an eyebrow, obviously catching her mimicry. ''You just don't strike me as the truffle-eating, pink-satin-slipper type.'' When she stared at him in silence, he finally asked, ''Something the matter?''

''Yours is a typical clueless-male response about romance novels. Double-dare you to find even *one* truffle-eating heroine in one of those novels. They're too busy flexing their stamina and intelligence in the face of adversity.''

His eyes glistened with amusement. ''I always love a challenge. So, I accept.''

Well, *that* response took her aback for a moment. She'd never met a guy who'd seemed eager to explore something new and romantic. Well, in a book anyway.

But then Kirk Dunmore was an explorer, she realized now, in more ways than one. A warming feeling washed through her as she realized she was starting to like the guy. Okay, she'd already known he could jump-start her libido with one whiff of his masculine-drenched jacket, but it was a bonus to realize he had an open, intelligent mind with just the right touch of feminist leanings as well.

Was he even from the planet Earth?

"So why the historical part?" Kirk asked, thumbing through one of the books.

"Well, I'll read about almost any historical era. But my preference would be the Roman era. First or second century B.C."

He was busy scanning the back blurb on the paperback. "Why?"

"My major was art history, with an emphasis on ancient Roman art. For my senior thesis, I wrote a paper on conserving ancient sculpture, focusing on a second-century statue of Marcus Aurelius."

"Very interesting," Kirk set the book down and met her gaze.

"My aunt Mattie doesn't think so. She's still stewing that I didn't study accounting."

Kirk chuckled. "Well, I must disagree with your aunt because I find your choice of study *very* impressive. Surprising, but impressive."

"I found your van rather…surprising, but impressive, too."

"Surprised me, too. It's a prewedding gift. My

mother-in-law—well *almost* mother-in-law—is always over-the-top. Too much money and time on her hands. Nice lady. Just too rich.''

He's getting married, Bree reminded herself. Of course, she'd known, but it didn't stop a tremor of disappointment rippling through her.

Murmuring she should go to sleep, Bree closed her eyes, determined to think about anything other than him. Like, where was Grams when Bree tried to call earlier? And should she have left the message on the answering machine that she and Val would be back in Chugwater, she hoped tomorrow? With the local news describing Bree's alleged theft, what if the sheriff or FBI had staked out Grams's and her home, listened to the answering machine and knew she and Val were on their way back to Chugwater?

She stared up at the ceiling. Sheesh, didn't anybody in authority check that maybe Bree was the innocent one in this mixed-up fiasco?

Well, I'll just have to be clever when I get back to Chugwater tomorrow. I'll pen Val in the south corner of Mr. Connors's field. Then I'll sneak into town and, from the back windows of Mary Jane Tock's hair salon, catch up on the latest gossip. Then I'll know what steps to take next.

''Thought you wanted to go to sleep.''

She shifted her gaze to Kirk. ''Thought you were reading.''

''Couldn't find any historical romances.''

Kirk liked Bree's smile. Her big dimples created

the cutest shadows in her cheeks. And when she smiled, her gray eyes twinkled as though they housed little stars.

Plus she was pretty without a dot of makeup. Her face had a clear, rosy freshness about it.

Funny, he couldn't recall the last time he'd seen Alicia without makeup. Or even what she looked like without makeup. For the two years he'd known her, her face was slathered and painted and God knew what else. She even had colored contacts. If someone were to ask him his fiancée's eye color, he'd have to say either emerald green or cobalt blue.

Not that makeup was a bad thing. After all, Alicia Hansen was a born-and-bred Cherry Creek girl, from the ultraexclusive section of Denver. Maybe Alicia had the money to preen and primp, but thanks to her family's wealth, she also used her money connections for good causes, like raising money for research and exhibits at the Museum of Nature and Science. Which was where they'd met when she'd hosted a fund-raiser two years ago. Thanks to Alicia's efforts, the museum had raised the money to build the current replica of the Minotaur's labyrinth which was gaining national recognition for its study of ancient mythology.

Yes, he appreciated and even admired Alicia. But most important, the two of them shared a common dream to have roots—a family, children—the kind of roots he'd never had as a kid.

He stared at Bree with her twinkling gray eyes and wild mass of curly brown hair. She was just the opposite of Alicia. Where Alicia was polished, Bree looked wild. Untamed, uncontrollable like the elements. Part wind, part sun, all soul and energy. He'd never met a woman like her.

And maybe it was late, but he wanted to know her just a little more…after all, after tonight and tomorrow, they'd never have the chance to talk again.

"So where'd you go to college?" he asked.

"In Laramie, on a volleyball scholarship. Started out as a psychology major, but after attending a traveling tour of Roman art, I switched majors to art history. Loved ancient art. Those ancient carvings were so raw, so passionate…so unlike anything I'd ever seen growing up in little Chugwater."

"What did you plan to do with the degree?"

"Escape Chugwater. Travel the world, see all kinds of *real* ancient art, not just pictures in books and on the Internet."

He'd never escaped anywhere. Never wanted to. Probably because he'd moved so much as a kid, and traveled over half the globe as a scientist, the last thing he wanted was to escape to somewhere else.

"So," he said, mulling over her response, "are you escaping Chugwater?"

"Almost did," she whispered. "Still might."

She was quiet so long, he figured he'd change the subject. "I love ancient art, myself. Leaf art."

She raised her eyebrows. "Excuse me?"

"I study ancient fossils of plants, especially the period between sixty to one hundred million years ago."

She emitted a low whistle. "Now *that's* ancient. And I was pretty proud to love first- and second-century art."

He smiled. "My area of expertise is the K-T boundary. The era when the dinosaurs went extinct." He paused. "Typically I stop here unless I'm chatting with scientists or other leaf whackers. I'm accustomed to other people's eyes glazing over about now."

But Bree's twinkled. "K-T boundary?" she prompted.

He smiled. "It's the layer of iridium that indicates that an asteroid—about the size of Denver today—hit the earth, which caused the dinosaurs to go extinct." Her eyes *still* twinkled. "So, by excavating fossils from that era, I'm also studying the traces of the K-T boundary and pinpointing when, exactly, the dinosaurs disappeared from the earth."

"Wow! Very cool!"

He grinned. Alicia *never* got this excited over his work. "Why, thank you. I think so, too."

"So, what's a leaf whacker?"

"We—paleobotanists and anybody else who joins our excavations—whack rocks to discover embedded fossils, which typically contain ancient leaves. Hence, leaf whackers."

"This K-T boundary…where is it?"

"Sections are all over the globe. The challenge is to find the thread, the link-to-link layers of iridium that prove my theory."

Her eyes grew wider. "Does that mean you've traveled all over the world?"

He nodded. "Many places, that's for sure."

She clasped her hands together like a little kid. "You are one lucky guy, you know that?"

"Lucky to love my profession, yes. But my personal dreams are more simple," he said quietly. "I've seen the big world. I want the smaller one. I want roots."

"Not me!"

"So," he started, piecing together her dream with her current situation, "when do you plan to see the world?"

"Don't know. Right now I just need to get back home…"

Her eyes moistened and she turned her head away.

When she stayed that way for several long moments, he got up and headed to the bed. Looking down at her, he reached out, hesitated for a moment, then gently patted her hair. He liked how the silky curls spiraled around his fingers.

"I'm sorry," he murmured, not sure why he should be sorry, but wanting to comfort her.

"It's been a long day," she whispered. She slid him a glance, her gray eyes filled with such a gentle sadness, he wondered what exactly she and her "pet" had gone through. And why.

Were they running from something?

Up to now, he'd bought her story that they'd been left on the side of the road. After all, this was Colorado, cow—and bull—country. But looking into her eyes, clouded with hurt, he knew, just *knew,* something more was at stake. Not wanting to dig, or upset her further, he simply stroked her hair, comforting her.

Minutes later, her eyes closed and she fell asleep.

4

"THERE IT IS." Louis turned off the headlights and eased the trailer down a side street off the main drag of Nederland.

"Dere what is?" asked Shorty, leaning closer to the windshield as though that would help him see better.

"In front of us, forty or so feet," Louie said, jabbing his thumb at the big yellow truck with Nederlander Highlander Ranch in red and blue doughnut-shaped letters on its back doors. "It's big and yellow and says exactly what that wino said was written on it."

"Oh yeah?"

"Yeah," Louie said between his teeth. "It's right frickin' in front of us or are you frickin' blind?"

"Don't need to get so sensitive, Lou," muttered Shorty. "I sees it."

"Sorry," muttered Louie, not really meaning it but needing to say something sorta nice so Shorty wouldn't go all sloppy sad and blow their chance to nab the bull—which meant nabbing a cool half a mil each.

"Hey, that truck's so yellow," said Louie, trying

to sound super friendly-like, "it's like followin' a moving block of butter."

"Yeah, a block o' buttah."

"You and me, Shorty, we were pretty damn smart getting a big black trailer 'cause we blend into the night." He didn't really mean that, the part about Shorty being smart, but compliments usually cheered people up.

"Right now," Louie continued, sounding as breezy as the winds over the Keys where he'd soon be living, "we're blending into the night like chocolate frostin' on chocolate cake. That dude would hafta be glued to his side mirror to realize he's bein' tailed."

"Chocolate frostin' on chocolate cake," repeated Shorty as he took a last drag on his cigarette and flicked it out the window. The burning embers flamed in the darkness.

Louis slugged Shorty on the arm. "Nice move. Next time, why don'cha set off a flare?" So much for being friendly-like.

Shorty rolled up his window. "Flare? Wha—?"

"We're on reconnaissance. We just found our mark—" Louie nodded toward the yellow truck down the alley ahead of them "—and you toss a lighted cig out the window! How many times I gotta tell ya there's an *ashtray* in here! But did you use it? No, better to signal the guy with a *miniflare* that we're *tailin'* him!"

"I'll use the ashtray next time, Lou."

"So you've said. Now shut up. I'm concentratin'."

Louie drove slowly, keeping some distance behind the truck.

"He's movin' awful fast for hauling a bull," commented Shorty.

Louis had thought the same thing when he'd seen the truck turn down this side street.

Suddenly, the Nederlander Highlander truck lurched to the right and parked in a well-lit spot between a scooter and a compact car. Louis did an ultra-smooth glide into a neighboring parking lot, conveniently dark with no streetlights.

"Primo lookout spot," he murmured, killing the engine. Damn, he was good.

They were sweetly hidden in the night gloom. And, between two Dumpsters lined up between the lots like some kinda green metal barricade, they had a clear sight of the parked Nederlander Highlander truck.

Louis breathed a small prayer to Saint Anthony for the strategically placed streetlamp that acted like a spotlight on the truck.

"Why'd he stop there?" asked Shorty, fidgeting with the pack of cigarettes in his jacket pocket.

"Look at the frickin' flashin' neon sign." Over the back door of the brick building that Mr. Nederlander Highlander would probably soon be entering was an orange-and-purple neon sign flashing Ned Head Ed's with a dancing beer bottle.

"Ned Head Ed's?" repeated Shorty, squinting at the sign. "What's a Ned Head?"

"Ned's an abbreviation for Nederland. If you'd

been looking as I was drivin', you'd have seen Ned-this and Ned-that on almost every frickin' store we passed."

"But Ned Head?"

Louie blew out a gust of air. "Ain't you ever heard of the Dead Heads? Jerry Garcia? The Grateful Dead?"

Shorty was quiet for a long moment. "Oh!" he finally said. "It's a play on da words *Dead Head*. Ned Head. Hey, dat's kinda cute."

This gig better end soon. Two more days with Shorty and Louis would remarry wifey number three, who not only applied less guilt and asked fewer questions, but figured stuff out faster.

"Dere he is!" Shorty pointed at the ponytailed guy shutting the driver's door of the yellow truck. With his hands stuffed into his jeans pockets, the guy slouched casually toward Ned Head Ed's back door and disappeared inside the bar.

The truck sat unattended.

"Go check if there's a bull in there," ordered Louie, flicking the overhead switch so the dome light wouldn't go on when they opened their doors.

"Me and what army? Did you see the size of that mother back at the stock show?"

"Just sneak up and look in the truck's back window."

"It's butt-freezin' cold out."

"You gotta coat on."

"So do you. Leather, too."

Louie'd known this topic would come up sooner or later. A week ago, when they'd got this gig, he'd had to do some fast shopping for Colorado winter weather. Shorty bought some butt-ugly wool and canvas coat, while Louie went for a fur-lined leather jacket. After they'd got to Colorado and put on their coats, Shorty kept flashing little jealous looks at Louie's jacket.

But Louie'd been accustomed to such looks all his life. Dudes givin' him those little jealous glances over his clothes, his cars, his dames…hey, it wasn't easy being a classy guy.

"I'm drivin'," Louie said, "You're sittin'. Now go!" He fisted his hand, ready to smack.

Shorty made a disgruntled sound and hopped out. Hunching over like some kind of chubby troll, he skittered through the opening between the Dumpsters. Just as Shorty reached the yellow truck, the back door of Ned Head Ed's reopened. The driver and several guys carrying boxes headed toward the truck.

Shorty, about ten feet from the truck, halted midstep as though stung by an invisible cattle prod. Slowly, he straightened, then began whistling and sauntering as though he were out for an evening stroll. Which might be convincing if it wasn't colder than a meat locker outside.

Louis sighed heavily. "You coulda acted like a wino or hidden behind a Dumpster," he said out loud, "but no, you act like you're out taking a frickin' stroll in a frickin' parking lot on a frickin' freezin' evening.'' He slammed his fist against the steering wheel, wishing it were Shorty's thick skull.

Fortunately, none of the people exiting the building seemed to notice Shorty's nonchalant strolling act. They opened wide the truck's back doors.

Louie strained to the left, peering into the back of the truck.

No bull.

He smacked the steering wheel again. ''Frickin' A. We fly all the way out to bohunk Colorado, rent this frickin' bull-size trailer piece of junk, only to lose what we had stole, clean and clear!'' That girl had balls. Stealing back the bull by mounting it and riding it out of the stadium like some kind of rodeo bull queen. And that was the last time Louie paid off a few cops for their ''support''—they'd watched, bug-eyed, as she rode away.

Shorty had navigated an elaborate U-turn and was whistling as he sauntered past the truck, heading back to Louie. ''Are you frickin' crazy?'' Louie muttered. ''Walking right past the people we're tailin'? Like they need extra help to ID us?''

A few minutes later, the passenger door opened and Shorty hoisted his chunky frame inside. ''No bull.''

''No kiddin'.''

''How'd you know?''

''I was sittin' here, looking at the truck as they opened the back doors. I was also lookin' at you—'' he shook his fist ''—walkin' past them not once, but twice! Why didn't ya just yell 'hi there' and introduce yourself?''

"They didn't notice me, Lou.'' Shorty's voice was getting all whiney again.

Wifey number three was looking better and better. Louie hunkered down, watching the people stash the boxes in the back of the truck. "We'll sit here, wait for the guy's buddies to leave and then we'll have a little chat with our ponytail friend.''

"What for? There's no bull.'' A match sizzled as Shorty lit his cigarette, carefully hiding the flame behind his cupped hand.

"He might not have the animal in the truck at this very moment, but he knows where he dropped our Mr. Money Bull.''

"Mr. Money Bull,'' Shorty repeated, blowing out a stream of smoke.

Louie grinned, enjoying a whiff of secondhand smoke. Enjoying even more the word *money*. Oh yeah, once this gig was up, life was gonna be sweet.

A few minutes passed as boxes were loaded in the back of the Nederlander Highlander truck, then the guys, except for the ponytailed one, returned to Ned Head Ed's bar.

"He's alone.'' Shorty made a great show of stubbing out his cigarette in the ashtray.

"Let's go have us a little chat,'' said Louie, tugging the collar of his leather jacket up around his ears.

"You carryin'?'' asked Shorty.

Louie shook his head no. "Don't need no gun to

convince Mr. Nederlander that all we need is a little information. I have a feelin' he'll sing with very little persuasion. Just like a little canary.''

''Tweet tweet,'' said Shorty, opening his door.

KIRK YAWNED and blinked open his eyes.

In front of him, like two burnished columns, were a pair of bare legs.

Long.

Shapely.

Sleepily, he gazed up those legs, past the thighs, daring to look farther...

She moved and a blast of sunlight hit him smack in the face.

He squinted, his eyes aching from the white brightness.

She moved again, her body shadowing his face.

He dared to open one eye, then the other, and stared at a very curvy bottom in a pair of creamy pink undies.

She bent over and the very curvy bottom widened provocatively, stretching those creamy pink cotton undies until the pink became sheer...so sheer, the color looked more fleshy than pink.

Kirk licked his suddenly dry lips as his pulse kicked up a notch. That was no fleshy *color*.

That was *flesh*.

His stomach muscles bunched. His face flamed hot.

Kirk blinked rapidly, amazed at the physical reactions he was having. He, who prided himself on his intellect. Dr. Dunmore, global expert on the late Cretaceous period, recipient of prestigious paleobotany awards, the discoverer of the new dinosaur species Saurexallopus lovei...

Was suffering from libido fever.

Struggling to breathe, Kirk watched as Bree pulled a pair of jeans over that tan, pink-clad rump.

"Checking me out?"

Caught.

He jerked up his gaze. "No, I, uh, was, uh, watching the sun coming up." Hell, he was getting married in less than forty-eight hours. Whoever named prewedding jitters "cold feet" was too subtle. This was out-and-out body freeze.

She turned and faced him, her hands on her ample jean-clad hips. "You really are from another planet, aren't you?"

With great effort, he maintained eye contact and whispered hoarsely, "Gor."

"What?"

He cleared his throat. "Gor, the counter-Earth planet." Which was pretty much the truth because Kirk Dunmore sure didn't conform to most of the stupid guy-stuff on Earth. He didn't play pool, swig beer and had long ago decided "nailing" a woman was despicable and demeaning for *both* the woman and the man.

So if Gor was good enough for Tarl Cabot, it was good enough for Kirk Dunmore.

Bree flashed him a quizzical look. "Is Gor where

you paleo-paleo-whatever-you-guys-are visit to dig up fossils?''

''No, it's what we paleobotanists say to cover moments when we're caught gawking at a woman's body parts. Very lovely body parts, may I add.''

Was she blushing?

His gut did that funny clench again and he wondered for one insane moment, if maybe, just maybe she felt the same things he was feeling.

With a swivel, Bree turned and headed back to the bed where she sat down and began pulling on her socks and boots. ''I know we've been playing a bit with each other, but the fact is, you're almost a married man, Kirk,'' she said quietly.

Almost married. Kirk could feel that damn body freeze creep from the tips of his hair all the way down to his toes. Okay, okay, his best buddy George, who was blissfully married and had two great kids, had admitted even *he'd* had a bad case of cold feet right up until the moment he said ''I do'' five years ago.

Kirk expelled a slow breath. *That's all this is. A little cold feet, or in my case, a complete body freeze.*

He reflected on why and how he'd fallen for Alicia in the first place. At the time, his dating life was more in danger of becoming extinct than the dinosaurs he researched. And when he'd talked to her about his recent discovery of the five-lobed Macginitiea leaf from the Tertiary period nearly forty-five million years ago, he'd loved how her cobalt-blue eyes stayed glued on him, immensely fascinated.

And when she'd murmured that she'd always wanted a smart, prestigious man in her life, he figured this Cherry Creek trophy number was hot for him.

After a few dates, when they were discussing their mutual desire to settle down, have roots, family and children, he did the first spontaneous thing he'd ever done in his life.

He asked her to marry him.

And when she said yes, it wiped out his years of growing up as a lonely kid, moving from town to town, calling at least six different men Dad. Finally, Kirk Dunmore was on the verge of having what he'd always wanted—roots, family, children.

And that had all seemed well and fine until…

Well, until meeting Bree.

Waking up in the room with her this morning, looking at Bree's freshly scrubbed face, and her "naked confidence" as she strode around in those pink cotton thingies, shook him up like he'd never been shaken before.

He didn't remember ever feeling that shaken up with Alicia. Maybe if she wasn't always slathering goop on her face or talking on a cell phone that seemed permanently wedged next to her ear, maybe he'd feel more shaken up.

Or maybe it had nothing to do with goop or phones. Maybe it was simply that Alicia didn't seem to give a hoot about his research anymore. Months ago, he'd chalked it up to her being preoccupied with the wedding plans, but he sometimes wondered what she'd be preoccupied with after the wedding…

"I'm gonna check on Val," said Bree, interrupting Kirk's thoughts.

"Okay," he said. "I'll join you after I think through a few jigsaw pieces."

Ignoring her questioning look before she exited, he rubbed his eyes. He had a lot on his plate today.

First, he needed to get gas.

Second, he needed to get back to Denver.

Third, he needed to contact George, ask him to give Bree and Val a ride to Chugwater. He'd call George now, but knew George and his family did their shopping on Saturday mornings, so Kirk would wait to phone.

Then there was the dreaded rehearsal dinner at Alicia's family's tony Cherry Creek estate. Monkey suits and small talk. Had Alicia said four or five o'clock? Well, one of those times should work. The family never expected Kirk to be punctual, blaming his absentmindedness on his being a scientist. Whether he was late, lost or just plain forgetful, they cooed and excused the "famous scientist."

He dragged himself off the sofa and staggered into the bathroom where he splashed cold water on his face. Somehow, in the midst of today's activities, he needed also to check the I-25 excavation site. He sensed he was close to unearthing some rare fossils there. Plus he'd accidentally dug up that strange, exotic engraved stone last week…very unusual, at least two thousand years old. He couldn't wait to show it to George.

"Hey!" Bree yelled from outside the bathroom. "You comin' out, or are you gonna primp in there all day?"

He grinned. Kirk, primp? Sounded like something he'd say to Alicia.

A few minutes later, he walked around the back of the lodge to where Val was tethered to a pine tree. The animal had a cozy spot, hidden from prying eyes, between Bree's lodge room and the back of the forest. Plus Val had plenty of grass and brush to munch on.

Bree was scratching Val's head, which looked as big as Bree's whole torso, while she talked to the animal.

"It's gonna be okay, Hot Stuff. You 'n' me, we're gonna get back home today. Maybe I didn't get to Europe, but that'll come in time." She rubbed the bull's back. "After what you've been through, we need to get you home where you can eat all the oats and grass you want in Mr. Connors's field. Meanwhile, I'll contact Bovine Best, clear up any confusion over the 'implied contract' fracas, see if they're still interested in purchasing you..." She sniffed.

Bree, crying?

Kirk stood, unsure what to do. Should he leave? Let her spend a few moments alone with her animal?

But just as he half turned to go, Bree said sweetly, "Mornin'."

He turned back. "Good morning." He observed

how the sunlight played tricks with her hair, highlighting strands of gold and maroon in those rich brown curls. Just like Bree, he thought, seeming so solid and strong on the outside, yet inside, harboring such sweet, tender secrets.

"Val, lookee who's visiting. Our hero, Kirk," she said in that velvety tone that twisted Kirk's heart. "Remember how he picked us up last night? Thanks to him, you had this safe, comfortable spot to sleep...and I had a safe, comfortable bed. Come on, let's say 'thank you' to this nice man."

"Oh, that's quite all right," Kirk said, holding up both hands.

But Bree just giggled, a fun, girlish sound that sent a crazy thrill zigzagging through him. "Come on," she coaxed, "let Val thank you." She crooked her finger at Kirk in a come-here gesture, those dimples in her cheeks turning him to putty.

He stepped forward, ready to do her bidding.

"Scratch him here," Bree said softly, taking Kirk's hand and placing it on a section of coarse fur between Val's horns.

Kirk tried to concentrate on the scratching, but he was far more aware of the warmth and softness of Bree's hands. And her fingers. So long, they didn't just interlace with his fingers, they coiled around them. Even better, he liked how their fingers moved in tandem. So natural, as though they'd done this a hundred times before.

For the next few minutes, he and Bree stood side

by side, scratching and stroking Val's head. Feeling and stroking each other's hands, accidentally of course.

After a few minutes of bull-loving, Kirk turned to Bree. "I told Alicia I'd call her this morning, let her know when I expected to be in—"

"She must be worried about you, running out of gas 'n' all."

"Actually, Alicia doesn't worry about things like that." She worried if Kirk would be late. Or not dressed properly. Or had lost his way.

Bree looked at Kirk, her eyes filled with something he couldn't decipher.

He meant to turn and go, but he wanted a few more moments to see what sunlight did to Bree's hair, how her skin glowed in the fresh air, the way her lips curved when she spoke. And if he was lucky, maybe he'd get another flash of those killer dimples.

They stood so close, he could almost sense her heat, almost hear her beating heart. And he ached to know how it would feel to take her into his arms, hold her close, mold her body to his...

Something nudged him from behind.

He looked over his shoulder at Val's massive head, rubbing against his back.

"He likes you," said Bree.

"Maybe he does, but I'm worried about those horns of his..."

Bree giggled. "Trust me. He wouldn't hurt you

with those. He's just nudging you with his nose, checking you out.''

''Gotta call Alicia,'' Kirk said quickly, backing off. He didn't mind scratching a bull, but being nudged by one was a far different matter. Even Tarl Cabot would agree, Kirk was sure of it.

A few minutes later, Bree walked back into her room to find Kirk on the phone. It occurred to her he could have used the phone in his room, but no big deal. Nobody in Chugwater locked their doors, so people were always coming in and out of each other's houses…finding Kirk here was almost like being home.

And for a moment, she missed being home. Home, the very place she swore she was so anxious to escape. How many times had she said she wanted to split Chugwater and see the big world? Yet sometimes…at crazy moments like this…she couldn't help but wonder again if fulfilling one's dreams was worth losing one's roots.

''Yes, dear, I'll call you from the gas station so you'll know when I'm leaving,'' Kirk said. ''No, I won't be late.''

Wow. Does his fiancée always need to know his every move? Maybe most married people were like that. Just another reason why Bree had zero desire to settle down. She wanted the free life, no constraints, not having to answer to anyone.

''What?'' Kirk suddenly said, straightening. ''Oh, no.'' He dropped his head in his hand. ''Poor Robbie.

What happened?'' Pause. "Broke his what?'' Pause. "That's called a *femur,* not a *female* bone. Alicia, stop fretting. So my best man is holed up in an L.A. hospital and can't make the wedding. Worse things in the world have happened. What's important is that Robbie is okay.'' He looked up at Bree. "Look, I need to go.'' Pause. "Me, too. Yes, dear.'' He hung up.

"Sorry to hear about your best man,'' said Bree.

"Broke his leg doing some fool stunt at a Raiders game.'' Kirk looked at Bree. "Thanks for your good wishes. I suppose Alicia feels bad about Robbie's health, too, but she's more concerned with the wedding plans...'' His voice trailed off.

"Well,'' said Bree, trying to alleviate the gloom that had suddenly settled over the room. "It's almost nine. If we get gas now, we can get to Denver by ten or eleven, then you said your friend George can help Val and me get to Chugwater—which means we'll be out of your hair and you can proceed to do all that fun getting-married stuff!''

Kirk stood, giving her a look that seemed almost sad.

"No need to check if the coast is clear,'' he finally said. "Even if someone sees us walking a bull, they'll just think they're having a sixties flashback.''

"But it's the twenty-first century.''

"Not in Nederland. Here, the sixties live eternal. Let me get my keys...''

He pulled them out of his shirt pocket. "Let me check how much cash I have for gas...'' He patted his back jeans pocket. "Funny, my wallet's missing..." He looked around the room. "See it anywhere?"

Bree jerked her gaze out the window, fighting a rush of dread. "Val," she whispered.

"What?" said Kirk.

"Val was nudging you."

"Yes. And?"

"And..." Bree swallowed, hard. "He may have nudged things out of your pocket and..."

"And...what?"

"And...snacked on them."

Kirk stared at her, realization dawning in his eyes. "You mean...your bull...might have *eaten* what was in my back pocket?" Kirk shook his head slowly, back and forth. "My wallet, my credit cards, my cash..."

Bree blinked rapidly. "I'm sorry. Really, really, sorry."

Kirk held up a hand, palm out. "Let's look at the problem, put together the pieces." He stared into the distance for a moment. "We can coast into town because the road is downhill into Nederland, but I'll have to call Alicia and ask her to wire money or maybe contact one of her wealthy friends in the area who can give us a loan..."

"Sounds like a plan," Bree said encouragingly.

"Yes, a plan that includes Alicia getting royally..." He groaned again. "If Alicia finds out I spent the night with..." He flashed Bree a look.

"Are you upset because Alicia will think we slept together?"

He nodded.

"So it's in your better interest if we can get money without Alicia knowing," said Bree. She mulled it over for a moment. "Would thirty, maybe forty dollars be enough to fill that gas tank?"

"To get to Denver, we could maybe do it on fifteen, twenty."

"Great!" Bree's eyes twinkled. "I have the solution!" She rolled back her shoulders, a big proud smile creasing her face. "We'll coast into town, find a bar and..."

Kirk waited. "And...what?"

Bree grinned gleefully. "I'll strip!"

5

"STRIP?"

It was the first word Kirk had said after his and Bree's trek, with Val in tow, down the road from the Sundance Lodge to where they'd left the van the night before. He hadn't talked the entire time, not even as they helped Val into the back of the van. But now that he and Bree were again sitting in the front seat, about to coast into Nederland, he was ready again to broach the subject of stripping.

"Yes, strip," Bree said sweetly, as though she were talking about butterflies fluttering about flowers and not naked bodies gyrating on tabletops. "Heck, my best girlfriend did it in a coffee shop outside Butte, Montana, last summer and made a fast twenty dollars…enough to buy a bus ticket home."

"Coffee shop? I thought places like that served coffee and doughnuts, not naked bodies."

Naked. He shouldn't have gone there. His mind started reeling with the sneak peek he'd gotten through those overstretched, ultrasheer pink undies.

Bree made an exasperated sound. "You know, being naked is *not* a big deal, not to a country girl anyway. When you think about it, we all strip every single night of our lives. So, that's all I'm going to do. Strip like I would for bed. Well, with a little dancing thrown in."

"Stripping," he said, his voice cracking, "is a...*sexual* act."

"Sexual?" She mulled that over. "Yeah, under the right circumstances, you're correct. But nobody's going to touch me. Well, except to shove money down my—"

"This conversation is officially over." Kirk thrust the gearshift into neutral. Avoiding eye contact with Bree, he more or less announced to Val, whose head hung partially over the front seat, "I'm going to jump out, get this baby rolling, then we'll coast into Nederland and figure out..."

Hell, he didn't know what to figure out. He had a wanna-be stripper, a buddy bull and a de-gassed van on his hands and *no* time to properly disassemble and analyze this problem to see the big picture.

This was a Tarl Cabot moment. Time for action, not thoughts and words.

He opened his door, hopped out, and holding onto the door, jogged a few feet to give the van some momentum. As the vehicle began rolling downhill, Kirk leaped back inside, slammed shut his door, and held the thought that at least the humans in the van were still clothed, for the time being...

Ten minutes later, after a very silent ride downhill on the narrow mountain highway 119, the van slowly coasted into a gas station in Nederland.

Kirk glided across the asphalt to a phone booth and stepped on the brakes. The van stopped. There was no way they'd start again without a tow truck or gasoline…and at the moment, he had no means to obtain either.

"Well," he said, shoving the gear into Park, "time to call the princess." He started to open his door when Bree grabbed his arm.

"Look," she said, not sure exactly what to say, but his calling Alicia didn't seem the better of any options. "Let's talk for just a minute, okay?"

Kirk shot her a glum look. "One minute."

"Remember last night when I walked in front of you in my undies and T-shirt?"

He made a strangled sound, his face turning a ruddy color.

"Well," continued Bree, talking faster, not wanting to waste even a second of her minute. "That's more than I wear when I go swimming at Mr. Connors's lake."

Kirk made another strangled sound.

"I'm not hung up on being natural."

"Stripping isn't natural," he said in a strained voice.

"It isn't? Then what do you call it when you take off your clothes at night?"

He cleared his throat. "We've already had this discussion."

"Humor me. What do you call it?"

"I call it taking off my clothes."

"Same thing."

Kirk released a tormented breath. "No, it's not. When I take off my clothes at night, I don't do it to entice women."

"Not even Alicia?"

He shot Bree a look. "That's personal, but for the sake of argument, I don't strip to entice my fiancée."

"What a shame…"

"Minute's up!" Kirk started to get out.

"Wait!"

He looked over his shoulder at Bree, cocking an eyebrow.

"Look," she said, pleading, "I don't want Alicia driving up here and finding you with me and Val." Bree was worried about Kirk and some flying princess fur, but even more than that, Bree was worried sick that someone from the "big city" would have seen her face splashed on TV. Maybe funky mountain people didn't watch TV, or maybe they thought splashing faces on TV was a groovy sixties thing, but Princess Alicia, after finding her man with another woman, might do something very unprincess-like and turn Bree and Val over to the police.

Which was a wild card, because Bree still wasn't absolutely certain that there were no "bad cops" in on the bull scam. Surely no Nederland police were…but if they called in "the girl and the bull" over some network-wide police radio…and some bad cops heard about it and pinpointed their location in this mountain town…

"So," she said, fighting the urge to give in to an utterly un-Bree-like hysterical moment, "let's you and me cut a deal. Give me ten minutes in a bar. If I don't have gas money after that, you can call Alicia."

Kirk flashed her a no-way look.

"Ten minutes!" she urged, "could mean money for gas, a drive to Denver where your pal will give me a lift to Chugwater. And ta da! I'm out of your hair and you're at the rehearsal dinner. Easy. Simple."

Bree looked around outside. "Plus, this is a pretty little mountain community, not some hole-in-the-wall. And it's barely, what, ten in the morning? Sleazy types don't go into bars at this time in the morning—"

"How do you know?"

"I'm from Chugwater, population two hundred. Well, almost. What you find in a small-town bar at this time in the morning are some wholesome, good ol' boy cowboys who're drinking coffee, a beer maybe, and they'd have one hell of a fun time throwing a few bills at a good ol' country girl kicking up some hotcha."

Kirk frowned, assimilating the string of words into some kind of sensible statement. After a moment, he repeated slowly, "...one hell of a *fun* time...throwing a *few* bills...at a good ol' country girl kicking up some *hotcha?*"

"Heck, this whole stripping thing is more a joke than a problem. And best of all, Princess Alicia would never know you'd spent the night before your wedding rehearsal dinner sleeping in a motel room with another woman.''

Kirk leveled her a look. "That's low."

"But truthful."

"You're blackmailing me."

"Yep, guess I am."

He stared out his driver's-side window at a gas station attendant dressed in a tie-dyed shirt with the words Buy Hemp, Be Free written in loopy purple script across the back.

"Could be there aren't even cowboys in this town," Kirk murmured. "You might be stripping for some hemp-loving Dead Heads."

"What?"

Kirk stared off into the distance, imagining the days, weeks, months of listening to Alicia whine about his "Nederland fling" with another woman.

"Okay," he finally said, sounding anything but okay. "You can attempt this cockamamy strip thing for ten minutes *tops* on the condition I'm sitting front row, right where I can protect you."

Bree's heart swelled a little at the thought of Kirk playing the protector. At six foot, she'd never had *any* guy play protector. If anything, guys made jokes about her height or how *she* could protect *them*.

But not Kirk Dunmore. It was as though he ignored the obvious and saw right through to her true self. That she was a little scared, a little ballsy and willing to take a risk. And suddenly she felt even braver, knowing he'd be right there, watching out for her.

"Sure," she said softly. "You can sit front row."

"And *nobody* touches you."

She nodded her head in agreement.

"And you only strip down to…" His eyes grazed over her body, his face turning that ruddy color again. "…to, uh, your pink undies and T-shirt."

She took a moment to ponder that. "Undies."

"And T-shirt."

"No, T-shirt goes, too."

"Stays. You don't wear a bra under that thing."

She fought the urge to smile. "So you noticed?"

"T-shirt stays," he repeated emphatically.

"Goes," she said authoritatively, defying him to one-up her again. "*If* I haven't made at least twenty bucks by that point."

He stared at the sky as though the answer lay somewhere in the clouds. "Deal," he finally muttered, adding something under his breath about not believing he'd just negotiated a stripping contract.

TEN MINUTES LATER, they walked to the front door of a wooden storefront building that advertised pool, grub and beer. Mainly beer. A wooden sign, hung crookedly over the front door, said Neder-Brewsky's.

"This is it," said Bree.

"I know," mumbled Kirk, who'd picked this bar after doing a quick reconnaissance around the area surrounding the gas station. He'd thought just he and Bree would jog down the back alley from the gas station to this bar, slip in the back door, but no. She'd *insisted* they slip Val down the alley, too, because she didn't want him cooped up in the van close to a busy street.

Kirk had reminded her this was only going to be ten minutes.

Bree had countered, in that authoritative voice she got when determined to get her way, that if a group of Harley partiers roared into town, Val might get spooked and *kick* his way out of a certain superfancy van.

So, just as she'd won the T-shirt argument, she won this Val argument, too.

After they'd safely tied Val to a fence behind Neder-Brewsky's, where the bull was nicely concealed, Kirk and Bree entered the bar.

It was mostly dark with some hanging lights positioned over several pool tables. More light was emitted by a variety of neon beer signs placed randomly around the room. A group of people, all wearing cowboy hats, sat at the end of the bar. Some guy with braids, wearing what Kirk had decided was the regulation Nederland tie-dyed T-shirt, was wiping glasses behind the bar.

"Be right back," Bree whispered.

Kirk grabbed her forearm before she took off, images of her wildly ripping off her clothes tearing through his mind. "First, tell me *exactly* what you're doing." He closed his eyes, then reopened them. "Okay, okay, I know what you're doing, but can we please discuss the *plan?*'' Did this girl ever weigh options, prioritize her actions?

''Plan?'' She sighed heavily and brushed his gripping hand off her forearm. ''I'm gonna tell the bartender what I'm up to, offer him a kickback—''

''Kickback? Good God, we're sounding like goons doing a shady deal.''

Bree rolled her eyes. ''You are such a worrywart. Do you do that with your fossils, too?''

''Fossils are a lot different than stripping.''

''Don't you dust them off, check them out, put them on display?'' Observing Kirk's openmouthed, silent response, Bree winked and whispered, ''Be right back.''

He remained standing in place, his feet bolted to the floor, stunned by Bree's comment…and her determination to play stripper. He'd had plenty of buddies crow about their trips to Vegas and how they threw wads of bills at strippers and lap dancers as though doing so earned them macho badges of honor. Kirk had always thought it ludicrous to pay a woman to expose herself…and told his buddies in so many words that only Neanderthals—or in this case, Nederthalls—paid for false love or lust. *Real* men never paid because they *earned* a lady's gifts.

Yet here he was, damn near playing pimp for a sweet country girl!

He took a step forward, ready to tell Bree to can the plan, but she was already leaning way over the bar, her firm, blue-jeaned bottom seductively outlined in neon red from one of the beer signs, while she whispered something to the bartender.

The bartender looked over at Kirk, back to Bree, and nodded.

Good God. She'd just negotiated herself a gig as a ten-minute stripper. This woman could probably negotiate anything.

Bree waved Kirk over.

He strode toward her, a hundred thoughts crowding his mind. Okay, okay, she was doing it, but looking around, there were only a few cowboys at the bar, some drinking coffee, some beer—just as Bree had said. And this early in the morning, he seriously doubted anyone would be soused and do something stupid.

A muscle twitched in his jaw. But if they did, Kirk would deck the sorry sonofa—

Bree was grinning like a schoolgirl, twiddling her fingers at Kirk as though this were some kind of talent show tryout. She pointed to a stool, indicating he should sit there.

He straddled it, glaring at the backs of the cowboys sitting several feet away.

"You want somethin' to drink?" the bartender asked.

"Yeah," Kirk answered in a low, mean voice he didn't even recognize. "Cola. With lots of ice in case I need to toss it at someone and cool them down."

The bartender did a double take. "Whatever, dude."

The bartender set the drink in front of Kirk, then put on some tearjerky country song with a guy crooning forlornly about the beautiful girl he'd left behind.

Kirk tried not to listen to the words—but they seeped through his brain and settled right on his heart. As the guy bemoaned losing the girl of his dreams, analytical, pragmatic—and since he'd walked into this place, badass macho—Kirk Dunmore realized he was getting a little choked up.

Because the words made him think of Bree.

Soon she'd be part of his past, just the memory of a naturally beautiful girl he left behind…and in his gut, he knew he'd always think of her, always wonder about her, always hope her life had turned out happy…

His thoughts ground to a halt when Bree jumped up on the bar and started doing what he could only describe as a hopping dance step.

Hopping?

He winced as she did a little turn in those boots, half clog, half bunny hop, while yanking and tugging her blue-and-white checkered shirt out of the waistband of her jeans.

Is *this* how she undressed at night? It looked more like a battle than an unveiling.

Someone laughed.

A vein throbbed in his temple. It was one thing for *him* to wince at Bree's bunny hop, but *no* man was going to make fun of her!

Another laugh. But this one sounded more like a raspy giggle.

Kirk felt the hairs bristle on the back of his neck as he realized that raspy giggle was...female laughter.

He squinted at the group gathered at the end of the bar. When he'd first walked in, before his eyes had adjusted to the gloom, he'd assumed the group to be cowboys.

But now that he could see better, he recognized them to be...

Five or six crusty old cowgirls.

One of them looked over her shoulder, her face tan and weathered. Wisps of white hair fluttered from underneath a Stetson that had a peacock feather stuck in the headband.

She smiled; one of her teeth was missing.

Being a polite sort of guy, he smiled back.

She winked. And nudged one of her cronies, who looked over at Kirk.

Bree, oblivious to the little drama taking place beneath her on the bar stools, was hopping her heart out on the bar, struggling to get her partially unbuttoned shirt over her head, though it seemed to have gotten stuck somewhere between her chin and her nose.

The only person watching her was the bartender, who was shaking his head as he wiped his glasses.

Meanwhile, the entire group of toughened cowgirls were eyeing Kirk as though he were a side of steak. The one who'd first eyed him reached deep into her well-worn jeans pocket and extracted something.

Grinning that missing-tooth grin, she waved a bill at him.

Another pulled out a bill, tonguing a toothpick between her lips. "I'll add a five to her five, sugar boy," she said in a gravelly voice, "if you'll get up there instead."

Sugar boy?

Bree, who'd finally wrestled the shirt off and could see what was happening, stopped her hopping. "Get the hell up here!" she yelled at Kirk. "We're up to ten dollars and counting!"

The group of cowgirls whistled and clapped, more of them waving bills at him.

Kirk looked at Bree, giving his head a shake. He was a scientist, not a stripper, and was about to say as much when Bree gave him the evil eye and mouthed "Princess Alicia."

He stomach plummeted. He looked again at the senior-citizen cowgirls, who were waving so much money, he could almost feel the breeze.

Bree, in her jeans and pink T-shirt, with that blue-and-white checkered shirt tossed boldly over one shoulder, stood wide-legged on the bar and gestured broadly to Kirk. "Ladies," she said loudly, "may I introduce Doctor 'Feelgood' Kirk, whose moves can cure your ills for just a few bills."

If Bree hadn't stunned him before, she did now. At what point did she evolve from good ol' country girl to stripper-carnival-barker?

The cowgirls started whooping even louder. "I wanna feel *real* good, Dr. Feelgood!" one yelled.

Another stood and did an up-and-down shoulder-shimmy, exposing a flash of massive cleavage that put the fear of God into Kirk.

Over the din of hollering cowgirls, Bree yelled at the bartender, "Put on some music! This man's gonna get down!"

Get down?

Next thing he knew, the frenzied mass of senior citizens had half pushed, half lifted him onto the bar. Damn, who would have thought women that age were so strong?

Soothing, soulful music began playing. A Beatles tune about times of trouble.

Oh, Kirk could *relate* to the words of "Let It Be." Odd the tie-dyed bartender hadn't put on "Truckin'" or some other Grateful Dead song. Maybe there were rival factions in Nederland between lovers of the Dead and of the Beatles.

"Hell, no!" yelled a wizened cowgirl. "Put on some hot Wynonna!"

The bartender, looking bored, ambled over to the CD player while Paul crooned, "Let it be, let it be."

Let it Bree, thought Kirk, wondering how in the hell she'd gotten him into this mess. New music started playing. A woman's husky, sultry voice oozing heat and sin. Had to be Wynonna, whoever she was. But if he didn't know, these old gals certainly did. They began thumping the bar in time to the music, whistling and whooping at him to strut his stuff.

He glanced at Bree. She had to put a stop to this nonsense.

But no, she was now straddling the same bar stool he'd just been at, thumping and whistling and whooping just like the rest of the tribe.

Traitor.

Bree grinned at him, those dimples clear even in this shady bar. She mimed rolling her shoulders and swiveling her hips.

Oh great. He was getting stripping lessons on the fly.

But when Bree mouthed "Alicia" one more time, he was willing to roll…a little. As Wynonna struck a prolonged, sultry note, Kirk rolled back one shoulder.

The cowgirls screamed.

He rolled back the other shoulder.

They screamed again.

Hey, maybe all he needed to do was a few shoulder rolls and they'd be home free…

"Take it off!" a short, plump cowgirl bellowed, waving a bottle at him. She was one of the girls who obviously liked beer for breakfast.

"I need some healin', Dr. Feelgood," another yelled.

Kirk glanced at Bree, who nodded her encouragement, pointing surreptitiously to the bills being waved in the air.

Taking a deep breath, which caused another surge

of screaming, Kirk started unbuttoning his flannel shirt. Bree, who had moved so she stood a little behind the group of crazed seniors, did a swivel-dip thing with her hips.

Oh great. He was supposed to be doing some complicated hip action along with the unbuttoning. He jutted his hip out in one direction, then the other. With every hip thrust, the women screamed in unison. Hell, how long had they been out on the range?

A five-dollar bill was waving somewhere near his groin. "Get the top off baby, and this is all yours," shrieked some frizzy gray-haired woman with a cigar butt hanging out the side of her mouth.

He quickly unbuttoned his shirt, trying to remember to hip swivel simultaneously. Bree was pressing her hands into the air, indicating he needed to slow down.

Slow down? Oh, *she* was one to talk. His life was on the line up here—if he took this *too* slow, these sex-starved geriatrics might swarm the bar and have their way with him. He'd heard of people being consumed by packs of wild beasts…he wondered if that was more or less painful than a pack of wild…

Don't go there.

He undid the last button on his shirt. Maybe if he turned his back to them, those leering, lusty looks would be less frightening.

He turned around. Keeping his back to them, he pulled down his shirt, sort of slowly, over his shoulders.

They started that screaming thing again.

He let the shirt drop to the floor.

A couple of fives fell on top of the shirt. *Ten dollars*. Maybe he'd better shift to some hip action again.

He rotated his hips once. Someone screamed. Another rotation. More screams. Damn, he was starting to feel like a one-man scream machine. Was it like this for Elvis, too?

Fingers shoved another five onto the bar, between his legs.

Hell, three five's was enough to get home... almost...

He turned around. In one swift movement, he yanked off his blue T-shirt. One woman let out an ear-splitting yelp and started unbuttoning her shirt.

Oh no.

The troops weren't just getting restless, they were getting rabid. It didn't help that Wynonna was groaning about taking her man and getting what she needed...

Bree waved her hands over her head. "Keep going!" she yelled, doing that hopping-dancing thing to the music.

Easy for her to yell "keep going." He was dog meat if these overstimulated seniors got any more aggressive.

Dancing and swaying to the music, Bree checked out the top of the bar. All right! Fifteen buckaroos! Hmm. But carrying a bull meant extra weight...they should probably have at least thirty, forty for gas just in case.

Wouldn't hurt to have a little eating money, too.

Yeah, she'd encourage Kirk a bit more. Get him to give the ladies what they wanted...then the ladies would give them what they wanted. *Money.*

Positioning herself behind the girls, as though she were one of them, Bree yelled, "Take off the pants! We want to see the goods on Dr. Feelgood!"

He tried to toss an evil look at Bree, but she acted as though she didn't see it.

He undid his jeans top button.

"More!"

"I wanna feel better, Dr. Feelgood!"

He popped the next button. And the next.

Bree was having trouble dancing. And she was an athlete, accustomed to playing sports for hours. But after a few minutes watching Kirk strip, damn if she wasn't out of breath, panting as though she couldn't get enough air.

She stared at his tan and sculpted chest, smothered in more chest hair than was legal. Oh yes! As her Grams would say, "This guy can eat crackers in my bed anytime!"

Bree had never dreamed a scientist could look like a hottie hunk. But she should have realized that any man who spends most of his time outdoors, sweating and digging for fossils...man oh man, of course he was in better shape than a construction worker and a ditch digger rolled into one.

Plus Kirk had brains.

"Oooweee, mama," Bree whispered. She wasn't

just dancing anymore, she was writhing in pleasure. This guy wasn't just a stud muffin...he was a stud muffin with smarts.

Bree's thin pink T-shirt was sticking to her chest. She glanced down at the sweat that soaked her top, which now molded slickly over her very pert boobies. Whoa. She'd never, ever gotten this worked up even in the heat of a fierce volleyball competition. Damn. This man was body-melding hot.

His pants were now completely undone, revealing a pair of white briefs.

White briefs? Bree winced. Hardly the Chippendale variety of underwear, but these ladies were so worked up, they'd probably go berserk over a pair of extra-large plaid boxers at this point.

She glanced at the bar. Still only fifteen bucks.

"Take it off!" Bree screamed. Or meant to scream. But when she opened her mouth, all that came out was a steamy, needy sound.

Didn't matter. The senior cowgirls were doing plenty of screaming themselves. One had crawled up onto the stage and was on her knees, a twenty-dollar bill stuck between her teeth, her face at eye level with Kirk's groin.

Kirk looked mortified.

Bree waved frantically at him, mouthing, "She's got a twenty!"

He nodded slightly, the tension in his eyes relaxing slightly, and started pulling down his jeans.

Another cowgirl scrambled onto the bar, a bill stuck

between her teeth. At this angle, Bree couldn't tell if it was a five, ten or twenty, but one look at Kirk's face and Bree knew it was twenty, minimum.

Oooweeee, they were almost on their way home!

"Give it to 'em!" Bree shrieked, suddenly finding her voice. "But take off your boots first!"

With a sharp look at her, he doffed his boots. Then, sucking in a deep breath that made his pecs double in size, Kirk lolled back his head—probably to hide his look of embarrassment and terror—and pulled down his jeans, down, down, until he stepped out of them.

Wynonna's sultry, siren voice escalated, along with the cowgirls' whines, moans and yells.

Bree clutched a nearby chair for support. Oh yes! He made tighty whities look like Mighty Tighty Whities.

Bree had had her share of back-seat moments. She wasn't an innocent when it came to men or their bodies.

But at this moment, this blood-boiling moment, she felt as though she were staring at the first *real* man she'd ever seen. He had a little age over those homeboys, and it looked damn appealing. Bunched up biceps. Masses of chest hair. Legs with muscle.

And a pair of briefs that should be bronzed for posterity.

Kirk looked down at the two ladies on their knees, then glanced up at Bree as though to say, *They're not giving it up.*

Bree blinked, trying to feel sorry for the guy, but

actually feeling so damn excited herself, she was ready to hop on the stage and rip those Mighty Tighty Whities down with her bare teeth. Hell, if her bank was nearby, she'd empty her entire savings account for a glimpse of…

She sucked in a deep breath. *Stay focused. Stay calm.* After all, she was his manager here…she needed to help him get this show on the road so *they* could get on the road.

She mimed pulling down his waistband…just a tad. *Tease 'em a little, Kirk,* she was thinking, willing her thoughts to him. Damn, didn't his fiancée *ever* play *any* hottie games with Kirk or was it just…well…that was none of Bree's business.

Even from this distance, she saw the blood drain from his face.

She nodded assertively, silently encouraging him to "Do it!"

While Wynonna did another groan about getting it from her man, the little old lady cowgirls were swaying in unison, some waving money, the others raising their hands as though at a revival meeting. Of the two on stage, one still had the bill between her teeth, the other had folded hers lengthwise, indicating she was ready to do some serious money-dipping.

Kirk closed his eyes, put his thumbs into the waistband of his briefs, and ever so slowly, pulled down the waist of his briefs an inch…

Bree tightened her knees, suddenly fearful she'd topple over. Heat rose in her like licking flames.

The little old lady with the folded twenty-dollar bill shook it over the teasingly opened briefs.

Kirk pulled them down an inch more.

Bree swooned out loud along with all the other ladies. Dark curls of hair peeked over the edge of the briefs...

The cowgirl eased her bill into his briefs while the other ladies screamed their approval. One of them thumped the bar so hard, Kirk's cola toppled over.

Kirk looked at Bree.

Bree motioned toward the other little old lady, still with the bill in her teeth.

Kirk did a subtle "no" shake with his head.

Bree shook her head "yes."

He turned himself toward the other lady, holding his briefs a bit open...

The Wynonna song came to an end, a heavy guitar chord vibrating through the air.

The room turned silent.

The little old lady inched closer to Kirk, rubbed the bill against his stomach, then dropped it, the way a dog drops a bone, into his slightly opened briefs.

The room burst into applause and cheers.

6

"THERE'S OUR BABY," said Louie under his breath. Down the alley, almost completely hidden by a brick wall, was Mr. Money Bull tethered to a chain-link fence.

"It's the bull!" Shorty suddenly exclaimed, pointing at the Brahman.

"That's what I meant by 'baby,'" muttered Louie.

After Mr. Ponytail had told them he'd left a girl and a bull on a nearby road, Louie and Shorty had spent the night at a motel close to the Mountain People's Co-op, a New Age food store where Louie had purchased a tofu-and-green-chili burrito for breakfast. He was still trying to figure out what the hell tofu was.

Since breakfast, they'd been trolling around Nederland checking out streets, alleys, yards...the town was so small, they'd covered most of it in twenty minutes.

After hitting the main drags, they'd started cruising side streets and alleys—and that's when they found Mr. Money Bull.

Louie murmured another prayer of thanks to Saint Anthony.

"I'm gonna pull over," he said, "not too close to the bull, but close enough for you to jump out and untie him—"

"You crazy, Lou?" Shorty was nearly jumping in his seat. "That animal might charge me or bite me—"

"Shut up. 'Member how I just walked away with that animal at the stock show? Just do what I did and quit complainin'. By the time you lead him to this trailer, I'll have the back doors open, and bada bing, we load him up and we're outta here."

Louie eased the van to a very smooth stop about thirty feet away from the bull, who kept nosing a tuft of grass, unfazed that he had visitors.

Louie smiled to himself. *Damn, I'm good.*

Beyond the bull, at the far end of the alley, was a gas station. They'd driven around this frickin' town enough for Louie to know that after loading the bull, all they had to do was drive straight down this alley, swing a left out of the station, and take the 119 to Denver. After that, it'd be chump change to find the main highway to Texas.

Then a whole helluva lotta chump change to live the rest of his life in the Keys.

"Get out," ordered Louie.

Shorty shot him a sullen look, then opened his passenger door.

Louie killed the engine while Shorty skulked toward the rump of the bull. "He's got the common sense of a cue ball," muttered Louie. "Approachin' a wild beast's butt…"

Louie had just opened his door when he heard a blast of thunder. He looked up. The skies were blue, barely a cloud…

A wild, piercing scream.

Followed by more thunder, although now it sounded like sheet metal being banged with a dozen hammers.

He looked down the alley and saw Shorty, a few feet from the bull, flailing his chubby arms and shrieking as the animal's back feet wildly kicked the chain-link fence.

Louie slammed his fist against the steering wheel. "Damn fool," he barked at Shorty, who couldn't hear him.

Louie jumped to the ground, slamming shut his door. Thanks to Mr. Smarts up there, Louie was gonna have to do some *serious* damage control.

Sirens screamed.

Cops. Muttering a string of expletives, Louie jogged a few feet, grabbed a still-shrieking Shorty by the collar of his jacket, and dragged him back to the trailer. After shoving him back into the passenger seat, Louie waved a fist under Shorty's nose.

"Be quiet or this'll make you quiet."

Shorty clamped shut his mouth, his eyes bulging.

Louie jogged to his side, got in. Starting the engine, he pulled away as calm as you please, passing the bull who'd stopped all his kicking and just stared at the passing trailer.

"Oh, *now* you act nice," Louie muttered. He

checked his side mirror. A police car careened down the alley behind them. "Pretty damn smart," he said to Shorty, who was shaking so hard, he could barely light a cigarette, "creating such a frickin' ruckus that people call the cops."

Louie gritted his teeth. "Get me a cig. I need to bite somethin'."

"I CAN'T BELIEVE we're in jail," muttered Kirk, looking through the bars at the small, cluttered office. A police officer sat behind a desk, reading the paper while eating his third doughnut.

"This is no jail," murmured Bree. "It's a cage in the middle of a store-turned-police department."

Kirk nodded. Nederland was so small, the police department was actually a rented storefront in an old strip mall up the hill from the town. Next door was some kind of senior citizens' center, which almost unnerved Kirk more than any cop shop after his earlier experience with frenzied geriatrics.

"Sorry," said Bree for the umpteenth time.

Kirk checked his watch. Eleven-thirty in the morning. He looked forlornly through the bars, reminding himself again that at least he was dressed. About an hour ago, dressed only in a pair of briefs with some twenty-dollar bills sticking over the waistband, he'd been interviewed by an officer of the law, who'd responded to a citizen's call that there was a bull in the alley behind Neder-Brewsky's...then, looking for said bull's owner, the officer had stumbled upon a stripper inside the bar.

Stripper. Interviewed in nothing but his briefs. *Those* were experiences Doctor Kirk Dunmore never wanted to repeat.

"Want to call Princess Alicia?"

Kirk slid Bree a look. "You can just call her Alicia, you know."

"Sorry."

"Enough with the sorrys." He blew out an exasperated breath. "We're in such a sorry mess, no need to remind ourselves about it."

He pondered, again, whether to call Alicia. When he and Bree had been escorted into this police station, they'd been informed they could make one call.

In a quick, whispered conference, Bree had confided to Kirk that she'd tried calling her Grams twice this morning, once at the lodge room, then at Neder-Brewsky's while the officer questioned Kirk, but both times there'd been no answer.

Kirk had contemplated calling his pal George, but after checking the time, he had realized George and his family still wouldn't be home.

Now here it was pushing noon, and he was running out of time. No, not running, avoiding. He was avoiding a very unpleasant "one phone call" to Alicia. But with the rehearsal dinner in, God help him, four to five hours, he had to let her know what was happening...

Kirk prided himself on never second-guessing his

decisions. But right now, he couldn't stop mentally beating himself for not calling Alicia at the gas station. If he'd just called her and admitted he'd lost his wallet, the worst he'd have had to deal with was her discovering he'd spent the night with another woman.

But no, he'd let the situation escalate until now he'd have to explain why he being held on indecent exposure charges for stripping. And when Alicia asked why, it was inevitable the topic of spending the night in the lodge with a strange woman would come up. And then there were the additional charges he'd racked up, something about violating some municipal ordinance about livestock on a roadway, but he doubted Alicia would even *hear* this third part because she'd be so busy shrieking over the first two.

Roots, family, children. Someday this fiasco would be far behind him, a distant thing of the past, and he'd have what he always wanted. Roots, family, children. Yes, that's what mattered.

Bree reached out and lightly touched Kirk's leg, not knowing what else to do. This was all her fault. This poor guy had stopped to help her and Val—and now look at the mess he was in.

He raised his head and gave her another I've-gone-to-hell-in-a-handbasket look. She bit her bottom lip, trying not to think that his tortured look, and that darkening stubble on his face, added immensely to his already rugged handsomeness.

Or maybe he just looked better because she'd seen all of him. Well, maybe not *all*. But enough that every time she looked at him, tickling waves of desire swept over her.

She eased in a calming breath that didn't calm her down at all. Poor Kirk didn't look at all calm, either. Well, maybe she could lighten the mood a little. Take some of the angst out of his torment.

"Too bad you didn't strip longer," she whispered.

Kirk gave her a sidelong glance. "Why?"

"Because you could have made enough to pay our bail."

Kirk snorted, sort of like a laugh. A gloomy, death-row kind of laugh. "Did they set a bail?"

"No. But if they did, I bet it'd be a thousand bucks."

"And you think I could have made a thousand dollars off those old broads?"

"Two thousand, easy."

His lips compressed, as though fighting the urge to smile, then he gave in. It started out small, a bit forced…then grew into a big ol' who'd-ever-believe-this grin. She hadn't really noticed before how his eyes crinkled when he smiled. Or how the laugh lines framed his full lips.

His blue eyes softened. "Thanks for the vote of confidence. But since I didn't make a grand—or two—looks as though I need to make that one phone call and call Princess Alicia."

Bree smiled. "You can just call her Alicia, you know."

"No, it's Princess Alicia because she's going to be

royally pissed when she gets wind of all this…'' Kirk let his voice trail off as he rubbed the back of his neck. ''Well,'' he said, standing, ''no use putting it off any longer.''

He took a step toward the bars. Gripping them, he called out, ''Officer, I'm ready to make that phone call.''

Suddenly, Bree couldn't stand the thought of Kirk having to tell all this craziness to Alicia. Bree didn't know the woman, but the way Kirk was acting, she hated to think of him having a full-blown lovers quarrel the day before his wedding. He'd been through enough already!

Bree had to do *something*.

''Officer,'' she chimed in, jumping up to stand next to Kirk. ''Can't you cut this guy some slack? He's getting married tomorrow, tonight's his rehearsal dinner, and *I'm* the one who got him into this mess.''

The officer, who looked as though he should have bought a bigger uniform several meals ago, ambled over and looked at them. ''Getting married, eh, buddy?''

Kirk nodded.

The officer brushed some powered sugar off his chin. ''This your fiancée?''

A funny thrill curled inside Bree. He thought *she* was Kirk's fiancée? She'd never wanted to get hitched, hated the idea of being bound forevermore to someone…but being mistaken for Kirk's lady felt different…felt good…

Kirk shook his head no.

Bree swallowed back an odd disappointment. She was probably going into these bizarre fantasies because she hadn't eaten yet...yes, that had to be it. After all, her dream was to escape her small, predictable life and explore the world! And she'd never grab that golden ring if it was tight around her finger.

The officer shook his head. "Pretty brave man to be hanging out with another girl on the eve of his wedding."

"He is brave—he came to me and my bull's rescue," Bree blurted.

The officer gave his head a shake. "And what were you doin' needing to be rescued with a bull?"

Bree's heart thumped wildly. Amazingly, this Nederland policeman, who appeared to be holding down the entire police department all by himself, was clueless that she and Val were "on the lam." Maybe he'd been too busy eating jelly doughnuts to do whatever policemen were supposed to be doing, like maybe checking most-wanted news bulletins on their police radios. And fortunately, there were no TVs around this station, so he wouldn't have seen any news flashes about "stolen" bulls.

She'd lucked out earlier, too, back at Neder-Brewsky's. After the arresting officer had finished interviewing Kirk, he'd started to talk to Bree when he'd gotten an emergency call on his portable radio. Something about a break-in at the Bear Necessities store.

Then things had happened fast. Because the arresting officer needed to respond to the emergency at Bear Necessities, he'd allowed Bree and Kirk to load Val back into their van and get gas, then the officer had called an animal control vehicle to escort Bree and Kirk to the Nederland police department.

On that drive, she and Kirk had wondered what the Nederland police—or this animal control person— would do if they swerved off the road and made a run for the highway. But obviously they couldn't drive fast with Val in the back, so they agreed that rather than risk Val's and their well-being, not to mention the slowest high-speed chase in the history of Nederland, they'd just do as they were told.

After reaching the strip mall, Val was first "impounded" on a little grassy area in front of the station, tied to a flagpole with a rope. The animal control person, some young kid in overalls with the words Question Authority stitched across his chest, seemed totally freaked out just to *look* at the bull, much less do something with it. So, Bree had tied Val to the pole, a spot she picked because there was plenty of grass there for him to munch.

"So what was I doing needing to be rescued with a bull?" she said, repeating the officer's question. Damn, she'd been lucky avoiding such questions so far. "Well, Officer, I was, uh, taking a bull break by the side of the road when my ride took off—"

The front door burst open.

In strode a different policeman, one whose uniform had three upside-down silver chevrons on his sleeves.

"What the hell is a bull doing tied up in front of the police department?"

The doughnut cop licked his lips. "Sergeant, it's impounded."

"A *bull* is *impounded?*" The sergeant looked seriously miffed. "And...there's a reason for this?"

Mr. Doughnut Cop motioned toward the holding cell. "Bradley, uh, Sergeant, these two are being held on multiple charges. Indecent exposure. Violating the municipal ordinance about livestock on a roadway—"

"We get several indecent exposures every weekend, so what's the big deal. But since when do we tie a *bull* outside the *police department* to a *flagpole?*" The sergeant strolled up to the holding pen and glared at Kirk and Bree. "Which one of you owns this bull?"

"Me," answered Bree, dipping her head a bit because she realized she was a good foot taller than Bradley.

"You two got transportation for this animal?"

"Yes," she answered. The van was outside, parked in front of the senior citizens' center.

"Drop these charges," said Bradley to Doughnut Cop. "We have better things to do than keep them here." He shook his head, muttering something about more bull inside this place than outside. "You're free to go," he said to Kirk and Bree.

Ten minutes later, Kirk and Bree walked somberly out of the station, not saying a word as they untied Val and loaded him into the back of the van. They were starting to get this bull-loading routine down to a science, they'd done it so many times. Then they quietly got into the van, which Kirk started and drove slowly away from the station.

When they reached the stop sign, Kirk shot a wry look at Bree. "No 'one phone call,'" he said calmly.

"You're a lucky guy."

"We're both lucky...can you believe how cool that sergeant was? Dismissing the charges, letting us go?"

Bree's stomach growled loudly. "Are we lucky enough to stop and get some food, too? I know you're under a time constraint, but I'm famished."

"Me, too." Kirk pulled a wad of bills out of his pocket and winked at Bree. "On our way to Denver, wanna grab a burger with a former stripper?"

KIRK TURNED the van back down the main road toward Nederland, from where they'd catch one of the highways to Denver. They'd stop for a burger outside Nederland—they'd seen enough of this town, thank you—where he'd also give George a call and set up a rendezvous point for him to pick up Bree and Val.

Bree and Val. Gone.

About time. His life had been a nightmare ever since he'd played the good Samaritan on that dark mountain road. Thanks to Bree, he'd lost his money, he'd damn near bared his most private of privates, he'd spent time in jail...

A cold fist squeezed his heart.

Who was he kidding? This hadn't been a nightmare...this had been the most alive, most exhilarated he'd ever felt with a human being...no, not just a human being, but with a woman…an exuberant, sensuous, wild-at-heart woman…

Damn, his insides were aching the way they had in the bar when that country singer had crooned that touchy-feely song about the girl who got away. Bree gone. Suddenly, Kirk didn't want to let her go. Ever.

Roots, family, children.

He squeezed the steering wheel, thinking back to those lonely years growing up, his mom at work or on a date, Kirk heating up a TV dinner, watching some sitcom for company. He'd sworn, even way back then, that he wouldn't grow old alone. That he'd be surrounded by a wife, kids, scattered toys, maybe a dog or two. He was on the threshold of that dream…

Wasn't he?

"What time will we get into Denver?" asked Bree, staring out the window at the mountains.

He glanced at his wristwatch. It was almost noon. "Including stopping for a quick burger, I'd say one, maybe one-thirty."

After dropping off Bree with George, Kirk would make a beeline to the I-25 excavation site. Quick check to see if there'd been any new fossil findings, and to pick up that old stone engraving. But now it had an additional purpose. He could focus on his work, cleanse his mind of Bree, then drive to Alicia's family's home in time to get ready for the frou-frou dinner.

"Watch out!" yelled Bree as a black cattle trailer on the opposite site of the highway veered across the divider line straight at them.

Kirk swerved the wheel and turned off the highway onto a dirt side road. "Crazy driver," he muttered, passing a sign that said This Way To Caribou.

Bree looked over her shoulder. "That trailer is still following us."

"What?" Kirk checked the rearview mirror and saw a hand with a gun emerge from the passenger side of the van. "We got some crazies on our tail," he yelled, competing with the pulse roaring in his ears and the thumping, banging sounds of the van tires navigating the bumpy road. What was it with Nederland? If some geriatric wasn't forcing you to strip, some trailer-driver was playing stick-'em-up?

A sharp ping sounded against the side of the van.

Bree grabbed his arm. "They're shooting at us!"

"Stay calm," Kirk yelled, feeling anything but.

Another ping.

Yet the van kept rolling. He glanced over. Bree looked ashen, Val looked...well, like Val. Kirk glanced at the spaceship dashboard. No nick marks there.

So whoever these nuts were, it appeared they weren't shooting to hit anybody inside the van. A thought raced through Kirk's mind. *They're just trying to scare us, not hurt us.*

Holding that thought, he quickly assimilated his options. He could keep driving down this dirt road farther into the wilderness, which only meant they'd be farther from help.

Or he could pull a U-turn, nothing too quick because he didn't want to hurt the passengers, but their best option was to get back to the main road, pronto.

Risky, considering they'd have to drive past the gun-wielding trailer crazies, but still, it was their best option.

He slowed down.

"What are you doing?" Bree squeaked.

He tilted the wheel. "Turning."

"Turn—?" Bree clasped one hand around Val's head, the other to her chest. "There's not enough room! They'll hit us!"

Kirk quickly glanced at the side mirror. He was still midturn, directly in the path of the trailer that was barreling down on them.

Time slowed down.

He turned the wheel a bit more sharply, sending the van into a sideways skid. Loose dirt and rocks flew, the smell of smoke came from the grinding brakes, but he held the wheel firm...kept the van turning. They were almost facing in the opposite direction.

The direction they needed to drive to get back to the highway. To safety.

The black trailer loomed closer, a gun pointed out the passenger side.

"Do something!" screamed Bree.

The bull bellowed.

Kirk punched the gas.

Too soon.

The van slid off the road and shuddered to a stop against a pine tree.

7

"WE WAS PRETTY LUCKY, Lou, seein' this van with the bull's head hanging over the front seat," said the squat guy, exuberantly waving his gun as he spoke.

The taller thug didn't answer. Wearing a sullen look, he kept pacing in those god-awful turquoise boots.

At least the rest of him no longer looks like a Vegas cowboy, Bree thought, recognizing him as the guy who'd try to steal Val back at the stock show. No, the rest of him now looked like the stereotypical bad guy. Zipped-up black leather jacket. Black chinos. Raven hair, slicked back. And that sullen expression that was the darkest of all.

The other guy had zero fashion sense. Stiff new jeans. A heavy brown cloth jacket. Alligator loafers.

These guys have serious shoe issues.

Bree released a weighty sigh into the bright red bandana tied around her mouth. And to think that nearly an hour ago, she and Kirk were driving away from the jail, free of charges, on their way to the rest of their lives.

They'd enjoyed that fantasy for all of…oh, five

minutes…before these goons had run them off the road.

In the moments following, the goons—by brandishing their guns—convinced Kirk to drive the van farther off the road and convinced Bree to move Val from the van to their cattle trailer.

Then the thugs had sat them down face-to-face, gagged them and tied Kirk's and her wrists behind each other's backs so they were pressed together like some kind of people sandwich. Their feet were tied separately.

During the whole tying-up episode, while the tall thug seemed to be pissed over every rope-tying technique the shorter one attempted, Bree had a momentary fantasy about getting her feet free, then realized it didn't matter. Even if she managed to get free and make a run for it, with her wrists bound behind Kirk's back, she'd still have to lug him wherever she went.

Which, she realized, was probably why these guys had tied them up in this face-to-face, huggy fashion.

"Should we plug 'em, Louie?" asked the squat guy, waving a gun in their general direction.

Bree's insides twisted. She'd kept it reasonably together up until now—maybe because she figured they just wanted Val and no other complications.

But now she had the gut-sick feeling that she was personally starring in one of her Grams's gangster flicks. And this was the scene where the camera swerved away while the pop-pop-pop of a handgun told the audience the bad guys had just done the ugly deed.

Silence.

The only sounds were the whispering wind through the trees and the crackle of leaves under those pacing turquoise boots.

Bree shifted her gaze to Kirk's squinty, now-what-the-hell-are-we-into look. Regret stabbed through her. If only she'd told him the truth about her and Val, Kirk could have made the choice about whether he wanted his life turned upside down for a total stranger and her bull.

But Kirk, being a good guy—no, a *great* guy—had never had the opportunity to make a choice. No, he'd acted like a real hero. Rescuing them, supporting them, hell, baring almost everything but his soul for them.

And now his life and her life were on the line.

Some way to repay a hero.

She held Kirk's gaze. For once, she was glad to be so tall because they were at eye level. Even if he was thinking she was the craziest, most dangerous woman who'd ever crossed his almost-dead path, she kept giving him her most heartfelt "I'm sorry" stare and prayed he understood she'd never meant things to get this out of whack.

But the way he glared at her, it didn't appear he was anywhere near buying into her "sorry" look.

"So whatta ya think, Louie?" asked the short thug. "Shoot 'em?"

Bree's insides twisted tighter. And for a crazy, edge-of-dying moment, she imagined Princess Alicia on the eve of her wedding discovering her fiancé's body gagged and tied to another woman, Bree.

No wonder Kirk was glaring at her.

"When'd you get so gun-happy?" barked Louie, taking the unlit cigarette he'd been chewing from between his teeth. "We ain't shootin' anybody or anything, Shorty, 'cause it'll only attract the wrong kinda attention."

Louie walked right to Shorty and jabbed the unlit cigarette in his face. "Like when you sneaked up on the bull's rump and somebody called the cops. *That* kind of attention. 'Member?"

Shorty nodded so briskly, his jowls jiggled. "You're right, Lou." He blinked rapidly. "Maybe let's just drive off with the bull and leave them two out here as bait for wild animals."

Louie made an exasperated sound. "And if some wild beast doesn't snack on them, then what? In a day or two, some tofu-eatin' love-in type comes hiking up here, unties 'em, and they squeal to the authorities about what happened."

Louie shot a look at Bree and chuckled. "Although the authorities already think the girly stole the bull, so maybe we can play that in our favor…" He continued to stare at her, his eyes narrowing.

Kirk frowned at her, his blue eyes glistening with questions.

Bree blinked at Kirk apologetically. Okay, so now

he knew the "authorities" thought she'd stolen the bull, *her* bull, which only added more chaos to the confusion undoubtedly swirling in Kirk's mind.

"Maybe we can stick 'em furder back in the forest?" suggested Shorty.

"And, like, drive that van down steep ravines and fly it over boulders into the forest, too?" Louie stared up at the sky and shook his head as though only he and God knew the burden he bore.

Looking back at Shorty, he continued, "Right now, their frickin' fancy van is a frickin' signal that people are here, off the road, in the woods. Sure, vehicles driving by can't see us, but like I said, all we need is one of those tofu-hikers reportin' a fancy van in the woods and, bada bing, we get a special visit from a ranger or sheriff. So, we gotta clean up this party, *fast,* get rid of both the van and them."

Get rid of them? Fast? Bree's body stiffened. She never got emotional, but if somebody pulled this gag out of her mouth, she'd wail to the high heavens over the god-awful mess she'd gotten them into.

She felt a movement in Kirk's body.

Blinking back stinging tears, she met his gaze, which had turned soft with concern. *Thank God. I won't die tied to a man who's thoroughly pissed at me.*

He shifted forward, almost imperceptibly, so that his chest pressed hard against hers. And he blinked once, slowly, as though to say, "Take it easy, we'll get out of this."

She held his gaze. It was the only thing she had right now—that reassuring look in his eyes that said to trust him. That he'd get them out of this mess.

She'd never been the weak one. *Never.* She was always the big, tall, strong girl who never broke.

But at this moment, Bree wasn't the strong one. And for the first time in her life, she welcomed it.

She slumped a little against Kirk, sinking into the shelter of his warmth and comfort. He was maybe an inch taller, but right now his strength made him bigger than life.

"Lou, what we gonna do?" Shorty asked, his voice growing whiney. "It's after one in de afternoon and I ain't eaten since that coop place."

"It's co-op, not coop, and shut up," Louie muttered. "I'm thinking, I'm thinking."

Kirk pressed his hip, slightly but firmly, against her.

Her first instinct was to tip her pelvis away, but he grew insistent, pressing harder. And that look in his eyes…he was commanding her to go along.

He slid a look at the thugs, paused and thrust once, hard, against her.

She glanced at the nearby thugs, wondering if they saw what was going on, but they were too busy pacing and grumbling to each other about guns, beasts and tofu.

She looked back at Kirk, her eyes widening silently saying, "Are you crazy? Just because we might die, doesn't mean we sneak in a quick hump!"

But Kirk's blue eyes flickered like gas flames, hot

and demanding. He glanced again at the thugs, waited a beat, then thrust again, hard and fast, against her. And again. And again. Her body molded tighter against his rock-hard body, the sensations building...

Liquid fire rushed down deep between her legs and Bree succumbed to its heat.

Suddenly she didn't give a damn if he humped her in the middle of Coors Field in front of thousands of spectators. Her body was on fire, the flames licking higher with each of Kirk's confined, tight thrusts.

She shifted a little, stifling a groan as his hard member aggressively nudged her nerve endings *just* right.

She pressed her pelvis forward, opening herself to him, barely suppressing the needy reverberations in her throat.

Hell, if I'm on the doorstep to death, better to die burning than be shot.

Angling her pubic bone so their groins were damn near soldered together, she pumped a little in tandem with his thrusts, stroking, rubbing, working him in small, hard movements through his jeans...

Now Kirk's eyes widened.

Anchoring her feet to maintain balance, she kept her controlled movements going while pressing her swollen, needy breasts against his chest, willing him to feel her hardened nipples through that musky-scented rayon jacket, through his shirt, down to that muscle-bound brown chest.

Her mind reeled as she fantasized how deliciously

sinful it would feel to bury and rub her hard, needy nipples into that thick mass of chest hair...

She whimpered into her gag.

In some corner of her heated consciousness, she sensed this was more than just sex. She'd always been an adventurer, and she was going out of this world tasting and exploring every single moment she could wring out of it...

And if this damn gag weren't in her mouth, she'd whisper all this to Kirk. And more. She'd tell him he was the first man who aroused more than just passion within her—that he ignited her dreams, her yearnings to be part of a bigger world. The two of them were explorers...they were meant to be together.

This last thought slammed through her, startling her.

She paused. A stream of sweat rolled down the side of her face. She'd never, ever felt this way about a man before...*meant to be together?*

She met his gaze, saw his arousal in those simmering blue eyes. She slid another quick look at the thugs, who were still busy griping to each other.

She looked back at Kirk, emotion moistening her eyes, her mind chanting, "Meant to be together, meant to be together..."

You belong to me, she thought, her mind yelling the truth to the world. Powerful sensations of love and lust roared through her. *You're the man I was meant to share my life with. And if I can't have that, I can have these moments...*

Sensations rocketed through her. She arched a bit onto her toes and gasped around the gag. Her need was building, her insides aching, ready, ready...one more push and she'd be...

Brring. Brring.

"What's that sound?" Louie called out.

All motion came to an abrupt halt. Her breaths catching raggedly in her throat, Bree stood stock-still.

Kirk stared into her eyes with a look filled with longing...and surprise.

Surprise? Probably because his damn cell phone had decided to ring just when they were ready to...

Louie strode over and stared at them accusingly. "What are you two up to?"

Brring. Brring.

He looked them over. "One of you got a phone hidden on ya?"

Kirk nudged his head, indicating he wanted to talk.

Brring. Brring.

Louie tugged down the bright blue bandana just enough for Kirk to speak. "It's...my...cell phone," he said hoarsely, catching his breath. "In my... front...jeans pocket." He sucked in a deep breath, obviously trying to regain some post-thrust equilibrium. "My fiancée drove to Nederland to pick me up...I'm not there, so she must be calling."

Bree's heart stopped cold. *Kirk was making love to me, knowing Alicia was nearby, waiting for him?*

Fury tore through Bree. Mainly at herself. Okay, she was no saint for getting carried away with the

near-death-let's-go-for-it fevered moment, but if she'd
known Alicia was just down the road, Bree would
have tempered her response! But had Kirk? Nooooo.
If a thug wasn't standing right next to her, a gun in
his pocket, she'd rip loose of these ropes and hook
the meanest right to Kirk's cheating, lying face before
he could say "princess."

Brring. Brring.

"And she won't stop calling until she gets an answer," Kirk added.

Bree glared at Kirk. Her meanest glare. The one she
used when she was ready to spike the ball for a killer
point.

"Fiancée?" Louie's dark eyes darted from Kirk to
Bree. "What you doin' hanging out with one dame
when you're set to marry another?" He shook his
head, reaching into Kirk's pocket and extracting the
still-ringing phone. "Take it from me, buddy, I've
done 'I do' three times…can the wedding. Just keep
havin' fun." He winked at Bree.

Angry heat flooded Bree's cheeks. Fun? At the moment of her impending death, she'd been some guy's
"fun"?

Oh, if they survived this, Kirk Dunmore was gonna
wish these thugs had finished him off after Bree got
through with him.

"Says Out Of Area," Louie said, reading the digital
display. He cocked an eyebrow at Kirk.

"Always says that in remote locations," answered

Kirk. "But it's Alicia. This is when she said she'd call."

"Where's she at?"

"Small church down the road. It's a convenient place to meet, we know the minister, parishioners…"

Brring. Brring.

"Reminds me of wifey number two," muttered Louie. "Nag, nag, nag. Okay, lover boy, I'm gonna let you talk on the phone 'cause I don't want no crazy-minded broad driving around lookin' for you and that fancy van." Louie looked at the phone. "Guess I press Talk, right?"

"Yes, that's correct," answered Kirk, trying to figure out why Bree was looking so pissed.

Louie paused, his finger poised above the keypad. "How d'I know you aren't playing me for a stooge?"

Kirk gave Louie a dead-on stare. "If you'd feel better, answer the phone yourself. Tell Alicia I'm busy and take a message."

Louie stared at Kirk for a long, drawn-out moment. The phone kept ringing. "Yeah, and all I need is for her to ask some personal-like question about you and I'm screwed. No, you can answer this call."

Louie punched a button and held the cell phone up to Kirk's mouth.

"Hello?" said Kirk. He paused, listening. "I'm, uh, tied up at the moment."

Louie smirked and shot a look at Shorty.

"What's that? You can tell by the phone signal that I'm in the mountains?" He rolled his eyes. "No, don't come looking for me! I don't care if you think a picnic would be fun..." He shot a can-you-believe-this look at Louie.

Louie mouthed, "Tell her you'll be right there."

Kirk nodded. "Honey, stay where you are. I'll be right there."

Bree envisioned smearing honey all over Kirk's body and tying him down near an ant farm.

"That's right," he repeated, "I'll be at the church in—" He looked at Louie, who held up five fingers.

"Five minutes, honey. You stay there, okay? Love you, too." He nodded to Louie that the call was over.

"I hit End?" mouthed Louie.

"She's already hung up, so it's okay to talk. Yes, hit End," said Kirk. While Louie was busy hitting the button, Kirk flashed a victorious look at Bree, who returned an I-hate-your-guts look.

Women. He'd never figure them out.

"Okay," Lou announced, holding up the phone, "we're off the air. You were smooth, Kirk. I owe you for that. I'll let you have this phone back in case missy calls again, but don't even *think* about pulling a fast one and calling for help 'cause Shorty here has a twitchy trigger finger. Got it?"

Kirk nodded.

Louie gave Kirk another long, drawn-out stare. "I'm letting you go meet your fiancée, buddy, 'cause I've been in love..." He looked at Bree. "...*and* in lust, and I don't want to deny you a long, lovin' life. I'm a simple guy. All I want is the bull, not a bunch

of dead bodies I gotta deal with. But you make one
false move...just *one*...and you can kiss your lovin'
days good-bye. Got it?''

Kirk nodded.

''What am I doin', Lou?'' asked Shorty, holding up
his gun.

Louie dropped the cell phone into Kirk's shirt
pocket. ''You're gonna escort Mr. Almost Married to
the church in the fancy van. Say you were helpin' him
with somethin'—'' He looked at Kirk.

''He, uh, was helping me locate fossils in the forest,'' said Kirk, taking his cue.

Louie frowned. ''Fossils?''

''I'm a paleobotanist. I collect fossils.''

Louie looked at Bree, then back to Kirk. ''Sure.
You collect *fossils*.'' Louie crooked a finger at Shorty.
''Come over here and help me untie these two.''

''What're *you* gonna do, Lou?'' Shorty asked, scurrying over.

''Me and girly are gonna drive the trailer down to
that Mountain People's Co-op 'cause there's every
type of frickin' vehicle imaginable parked around
there so a fancy van will blend in real nice. That's
where I'll wait for you.''

''Wait? How do I get there?''

Louie puffed out an exasperated breath. ''This town
is so small, you can walk its entire length in half an
hour. You walk from the church to the co-op. It'll take
you ten minutes, max.''

''May I make a suggestion?'' asked Kirk.

Louie, looking a bit surprised, nodded.

"If I tell my fiancée that he's my friend, it would look odd if I let him walk to the co-op. She and I will give him a lift."

Bree's eyes were burning with so much rage, Kirk swore next he'd see steam rising off her body. What was her problem, anyway?

Louie thought a moment. "Yeah, I like your thinking. You give Shorty a lift." Under his breath, he added, "Too bad you and I aren't teaming for this gig."

Louie turned to Bree. "You and me, we're gonna buy some bull food at that co-op. If they got tofu, they gotta have *something* your bull will eat. And you're gonna give me some bull-handling lessons, too, real quick-like."

Bree made a muffled noise behind her handkerchief.

Louie sighed heavily and pulled it down so she could speak.

Bree's face was redder than the just-released bandana. "Where are you taking Val?"

Louie looked heavenward for a moment, then back down. "None of your frickin' business. Now, I can leave you out here to be a beast-snack, or you can be a good girly and go shoppin' with me. Your choice."

"Bree," said Kirk, but she cut him off with a go-to-hell look.

"I'll go shopping," she said tightly. "And give you quick bull tips, on one condition."

Kirk held his breath. Damn, he knew this lady could

negotiate—but with killers with guns? Was she out of her mind?

He took another look at her thoroughly pissed-off face, inches from his own. Yes, she was out of her mind. It was almost more frightening to be tied to a woman with looks to kill than to have real killers around!

But even though she was temporarily insane, and for some reason hated his guts, he had to stop this negotiating madness. He pressed his knee against hers.

"Oh, don't start that with me again, buster," she said icily. She turned her attention back to Louie. "Here's the deal. I help you, you let me go free afterward."

"How do I know you don't go squealing?" asked Louie.

"Because *I'm* the one who's wanted by the law. I'd be an idiot to call the cops."

Louie nodded, a slow smile creasing his face. "That's for sure." He eyed her, chewing his bottom lip. "Okay, you got a deal. Let's get this show on the road."

MINUTES LATER, Kirk and Bree were untied, and Shorty and Kirk were walking toward the "frickin' fancy van."

Bree, rubbing her wrists from where the ropes had dug into her skin, followed Louie to the trailer. "Bull lessons, then co-op?" she asked.

"Yeah," said Louie, "that's the order." He turned

to Shorty, who was getting into the passenger side of the van. "'Member, Mr. Fossil is dropping you off at the co-op. I'll meet you there."

Someone coughed. Bree looked up and caught Kirk shooting her a knowing glance.

She countered with a "screw you" look and continued following Louie to the trailer. A moment later, she heard the van drive off. "Good riddance," she muttered under her breath. Almost-married, two-timing, thigh-rubbing Romeo…and she'd thought this was the man she was meant to share her life with?

Being on the verge of death definitely clouded one's thinking.

She was now alone in the clearing with the trailer, Louie and Val. And for the first time since the van had been run off the road, she wasn't scared one bit. *Men.* She suppressed a snort. No wonder she never wanted to get married…you'd have to "share" your life with one of them!

Louie was fussing with another cigarette, nipping at the filtered tip. He glanced at Bree. "Tall for a girl," he commented.

"Got a problem with that?" What was he gonna do? Shoot her before bull lessons? He *needed* her.

Louie smirked, then looked serious. "I like you. You got moxie."

Bree glanced at the trailer that housed Valentine. The sides had slats for ventilation, and she knew Val could see her through those openings. She also knew Val knew she was in danger. He was probably standing still, listening, waiting for her to tell him what to do.

Listening…waiting…

She suppressed a smile. Oh, yeah, Louie was gonna see just how much moxie she had…

"First," she said, pitching her voice in an ultra-girly friendly range, "do you want to learn how to make him lie down or do you want to learn how to lead him out of the trailer?"

Louie gave her a quizzical look. "What do I care if he lies down? If a situation comes up, I'll need to lead him out of this trailer."

That's exactly why she phrased her question that way. Men. Easier to lead than bulls.

"Okay, let's open the trailer doors," she said sweetly. Louie followed. Together they opened the doors. Val was standing there, his backside to them.

"Now," she said, dripping just a little more honey into her voice, "Val—that's my bull's name—is a little sensitive about your standing *directly* behind his rump." She stepped a little to the side of Val's left back leg. "What works best is if you stand to my right, just a *tad* on the outside of his right leg." She motioned to the exact spot she meant.

He hesitated, rolling a cigarette between his teeth.

"Don't worry," she said. "He knows it's me back here, so he'll just be a big ol' pussycat. And anybody standing with me, he trusts, too." She fluttered her eyelashes. "It's a total win-win."

Louie stepped forward just as Val's tail swished his face.

"Oh, how cute," Bree cooed. "He's swishing you. That means he likes you."

Louie muttered something unintelligible about wifey number something.

"Okay," said Bree, "keep standing *right* there. I'm going to give his leg a rub, which is a signal for him to start backing out…"

"WHERE IS SHE?" asked Shorty for the sixth, maybe seventh, time. He was smoking a cigarette, the gun tucked in his belt.

Kirk wasn't sure how long he could play this out, pretending Alicia was supposed to be waiting for him at this exact spot in the church parking lot. He'd passed this church earlier on his trek to the police station. But now he was spending his time gazing back and forth at the lot, Shorty's gun, the lot…

"She's always doing stuff like this," Kirk muttered, as if irked that Alicia wasn't here. "She seems to think punctuality is the thief of time."

"Eh?"

Kirk paused. "She's always late."

"Oh." Shorty took another drag on his cigarette, scanning the lot. "Well, we can kill a few minutes, what with girly giving bull lessons 'n' all…"

Kirk hated Bree being called girly, but he stuffed that thought down as he continued assembling the pieces of the puzzle in his head, trying to figure out how to put this damn picture together. Bree, Val and Louie would be at the co-op soon, Bree and Louie inside shopping. Should Kirk fake another call from Alicia, say she's now at the co-op…he groaned inwardly. Right. Two thugs, him and Bree and a bull at the Mountain People's Co-op. A Marx Brothers movie would be less crazy.

"Hey!" said Shorty, straightening in the passenger's seat. "Dat her?"

A plump woman with curly frosted hair was ambling across the parking lot. She was walking toward Shorty, who faced her, his head turned away from Kirk. Kirk gave the thugster a once-over, summing up that there was more gristle than meat on this guy. Kirk, however, was accustomed to being outdoors, working hard…

This was a Tarl Cabot moment. *Act, don't think.*

Kirk lunged across the seat. With one hand, he smashed Shorty's cigarette-smoking hand against the thug's neck. Flesh sizzled.

"Ow, you mutha—!"

With his free hand, Kirk reached for the gun. They grappled for the firearm, Shorty cursing, his neck bleeding from the cigarette burn. As they struggled, the barrel pointed wildly out the window, at Kirk, at Shorty.

"You crazy mutha—" Shorty yelled.

The woman in the parking lot stopped, stared at the two of them wrestling for control of the gun and ripped loose with a scream.

Shorty glanced over his shoulder.

Kirk took the opportunity to shove his foot against the passenger-door handle.

The door flew open.

Kirk shoved his foot against Shorty, who flew outside, the gun in his grasp.

With the woman still screaming, Kirk started the engine, punched the gas and lurched out of the parking lot, ducking in case Shorty decided to play target practice. He saw the woman run toward a fence on the perimeter of the church lot and disappear behind it. Good. She was safe, although Kirk seriously doubted Shorty wanted to shoot anyone but him.

And in the rearview mirror, as he saw Shorty jogging behind him as though he could catch the van, Kirk *knew* Shorty wanted to shoot only him.

SIX MINUTES and two stop signs later, Kirk turned down the street where he'd played stripper earlier this morning. Somewhere on the opposite side of the street from Neder-Brewsky's was the Mountain People's Co-op…sure enough, there it was, awash in a sea of tie-dye doing their grocery shopping.

He slowed down, looking for the black trailer.

Bingo. At the far end of a line of parked cars, bicycles and one Shetland-pony-drawn wagon sat the trailer.

"Damn," muttered Kirk under his breath, slowing down. He was tempted to pull a U and get off this street, but if Louie saw the van turning around, he'd get suspicious. If they flagged him over, how was Kirk going to explain the missing Shorty?

The missing Shorty who was bound to show up soon, running down the street...

Taking deep breaths, wondering which one might be his last, Kirk's concentration was momentarily shattered by a shrill, high-pitched whistle. He kept driving, avoiding looking directly at the trailer as he passed it. Maybe if he acted as though he hadn't seen them...he could buy time to explain where Shorty was...

Another prolonged, ear-splitting whistle.

He frowned. That was hardly a Nederlander kind of sound. He doubted these people ever raised their voices, much less whistled as though calling farm animals.

Farm animals.

He knew someone who knew how to call farm animals.

He looked in the rearview mirror. There was Bree, just like that first night he'd picked her up in the mountains, her hair a wild mass of curls, standing in the road waving her arms.

He slammed on the brakes, shoved it into Reverse, and backed up. Maybe Louie was in the store and she'd escaped?

He had to get to her, save her.

He skidded to a stop as she jogged the few feet to his driver's window. "Where's Louie?" he asked.

"Tied up in the mountains after Val kicked him

unconscious." She looked around the front seat. "Where's Princess?" she asked sarcastically.

"Where's—?" Kirk shook his head. "Are you crazy? We need to discuss our best option to save our lives, *not* discuss Alicia—"

"You *make love* to me while your *fiancée* is right down the *road?*" she said, her voice growing louder with each word.

Across the street, a young couple in denim overalls with red and yellow stars painted on their faces glanced at the commotion Bree was causing. Kirk smiled, flashing them the peace sign.

"I was getting my phone to auto-ring," Kirk said tightly, still smiling at the couple. "*You*, on the other hand, were doing something else."

Bree gasped loudly.

"Shorty's going to show up any minute, waving that gun of his," warned Kirk. "So here's our best option. You take the trailer and drive to Chugwater. I'll drive the van to Denver."

Bree paused, her attitude shifting to all-business. "But those thugs, not knowing which vehicle has the bull, will most likely call in *your* van license plate first rather than the trailer *they* rented. All they'd have to say is you've already been booked in Nederland on several charges, which that doughnut cop would verify, then the thugs might make up a few more things like seeing you drinking while driving..." Bree bit her bottom lip, obviously playing out the scenario in her mind. "Which means you *might* be pulled over on your way to Denver and booked *again.*'' She lowered her voice. "Of course, you'd get that *one* call…"

Images of a hysterical Alicia flashed through Kirk's brain, as though there was room for *that* hysterical image among all the others running amok through his mind.

He looked at his wristwatch. Nearly two. "Shorty's going to be here any moment," he muttered.

"Look," said Bree urgently. "Our best bet is to stay together, take the trailer. You told me you've traveled all over the state—you must know some back roads that lead to Denver…"

He nodded.

Her eyes glistened, the words rushing faster. "Great. So even if they do risk calling in their trailer as missing, the cops will be on the major highways, and we'll be on the back roads. You'll make it to your dinner on time…and on the way, we'll figure out a plan to get Val and me safely back to Chugwater."

A fragment of a Beatles tune played in his mind. "We can work it out." This could work. "I'll park the van," Kirk said. "Get in the truck and open the passenger door so I can jump in."

8

"HI LOU."

Louie peered up at Shorty leaning over him, that woebegone look in his eyes. Behind Shorty's head was the same damn blue sky, fringed with the same damn swaying pine branches, that Louie had been staring at ever since coming to.

His last memory was that big bull hoof flying toward him. Now his head pounded like a construction crew had taken up residence in his brain.

Coldcocked by a bull. This frickin' gig better wrap up soon.

"I'll get the gag and ropes off ya," said Shorty, crouching down and beginning to untie the bandana.

When he was finally freed from his bindings, Louie sucked in a lungful of fresh mountain air. "My frickin' head," he rasped. Pound-pound-pound. "Is there blood?"

Shorty did a quick survey. "No, but your hair's all messed up on one side, like somebody blow-dried it the wrong way."

Blow-dried? Louie squinted past Shorty's head at a circling hawk. *Hoof must have slammed against the side of my head. I'm lucky that beast didn't hit me directly—otherwise I'd be paying a personal visit to Saint Anthony.*

With some effort, Louie propped himself up onto his elbow and surveyed the area. "Where's the trailer?"

Shorty stood and shuffled back a few feet. "I, uh, think the girly and the guy got it."

"What?" Louie squeezed shut his eyes. He couldn't yell until his head stopped pounding. *Aspirin. Need aspirin.*

"Help me stand."

"You gonna slug me?"

Louie rolled his eyes. "That would sorta defeat my purpose, don'cha think?"

With Shorty's help, Louie righted himself to a standing position. After brushing pine needles and dirt off his pants and jacket, he caught a flash of bright yellow through the trees.

No. It couldn't be.

"Is that a *taxi* parked over there?" Louie had the answer when he caught the sheepish look on Shorty's face.

"You took a frickin' *taxi* all the way up here!" Louie rubbed his temples, willing the construction crew to take a break. "What happened to their van?" he asked quietly.

Shorty looked up with that basset-hound expression. "They, uh, parked it at the coop—I mean co-op. They took da keys."

"They got the keys," Louie said, forcing his voice

to remain calm. "They got the trailer. They got the bull." He paced a few feet, his head pounding with every step. "What else they get?" he asked through clenched teeth. "Your brains?"

Shorty's chin quivered. "You ain't one to talk," he said defensively. "You let that girly slug you and tie you up—"

"The bull kicked me," Louie said, lowering his voice into that manly range that defied any bastard to question what happened.

"Oh." Shorty fidgeted, glanced at the waiting taxi, then back to Lou. "The meter's running."

Louie held out his hand, waggling his fingers. Shorty fumbled in his jacket pocket for the box of cigarettes. Hitting the box once, hard, against his other hand, he extracted a cigarette and handed it to Louie.

Propping the cig between his lips, Louie began walking toward the taxi. "Good thing the cab's parked far enough away they didn't see me lying all tied up in the forest."

Shorty caught up with him. "That was my idea, Lou," he said exuberantly. "I told da cabbie to park a bit aways from where we was. Wasn't sure what was goin' on, but I knew you hadta still be up here."

"I don't like some guy being able to ID us."

"Lou, the cabbie's just a sweet kid. He moved up here to get away from the illnesses in society, to get back to the earth and rediscover peace and love. He's been playing some Phil Lesh, The Other Ones. It's groovy."

Louie stopped and removed the cigarette from his mouth. "You played spiritual advisor to some tofu cabbie?" He started to shake his head, but the movement only worsened the pounding. "Don't go soft on me, Shorty. We got a job to finish."

Shorty shook his head so hard, his cheeks jiggled. "No, Lou, I won't. Promise."

They walked in silence for a few moments, the only sounds the soft hush of mountain breezes and the twittering of a bird.

"Here's the plan," Louie finally said, stepping over a broken branch. "We'll take the cab to the van. Check the vehicle registration—get ourselves an address."

"Okay, Lou."

"You still talented at hot-wiring?"

"Sure thing, Lou," Shorty said, getting that exuberant edge to his voice again.

They reached the cab. Louie offered a small smile to the young kid behind the wheel, wondering how the hell he breathed with his nose pierced like that.

"Mountain People's Co-op," Louie said politely, preparing himself to get an earful of society's illnesses all the way there.

"WE'LL USE the service entrance," said Kirk, "pull in that brick driveway." He pointed at what looked more like a red-brick *road* than a driveway, the intricately laid-out bricks leading to the largest, most opulent home Bree had ever seen.

Not that the other homes along this street in Denver—an area Kirk had referred to as Cherry Creek—weren't awesome, but this home looked like one of those European castles she'd seen pictures of. Maybe it was the rock exterior. Or the turrets and balconies. She squinted. Was that a gargoyle? She blinked. Yep, nestled on a corner of the roof was a gargoyle.

Kirk's marrying into megamoney. Well, Bree could have guessed he was marrying into *money* from his fancy van, which he'd told her was a "wedding gift" from his future mother-in-law, but seeing this palatial home cinched Bree's understanding just how *much* money was in Kirk's new life.

But, he doesn't seem like the kind of guy who cares about money. Not to this extent. The Kirk she knew had heart and guts and passion. From what he'd mentioned of his digs around the world, she knew Kirk cherished wild habitats, the feel of soil in his hands, the sweat of honest exertion.

Such a man didn't need *wealth* to better experience life.

Alicia must be very special. Bree concentrated on the driveway, on her hands gripping the steering wheel, trying to deny the squeezing hurt in her heart.

"Head toward those open security gates," said Kirk, pointing toward a set of ten-foot-high black wrought-iron gates down the brick driveway. "We'll stop right before them, behind that row of bushes, and review our next steps."

"I don't think those bushes will disguise this cattle trailer," said Bree.

"There are so many people and service vehicles here, we won't be noticed."

That was true. Several big white trucks, the words Cherry Creek Catering stenciled on their sides, were parked on the far side of the gates. And within the gates were numerous other cars and vehicles, people scurrying about carrying trays and chairs and pots of flowers.

Bree parked alongside the row of green bushes.

Through an opening in the greenery, she peered into the backyard and gasped. It was like peeking into a fairy tale. A bridge, adorned with twinkling lights and flowers, led to the grandest tent she'd ever seen. Even bigger than the circus tent she'd seen in Cheyenne last year.

Bree suddenly felt small in the midst of all this grandiosity. She never felt small. And her dream was to explore the world? Right now, she felt overwhelmed just staring into a Denver backyard.

"Three-forty-five," Kirk said, checking his wristwatch. He blew out a gust of breath. "Wish I knew if it's four or five this shindig starts."

"Sorry those side roads took so long. And that we stopped for that burger." She'd been so famished, she'd thought she'd keel over if she didn't get something into her stomach. Kirk had been just as hungry—she still wasn't sure if they ate or inhaled their food.

"Thought we had a deal that you'd stop apologizing. Maybe the ride was long, but at least I got to hear how Val knocked out Louie." Kirk chuckled, shaking his head at the memory.

"Yeah," she concurred, "and I got to explain why I don't want to go to the police, just yet. If there are bad cops in on this scheme, who are they? So now you understand my best bet is to get home and contact Bovine Best. They specialize in breeding Brahmans, and have probably dealt with crazy situations like this before. They'll know best how to get me out of this jam."

She took a deep breath. "And although we didn't discuss this last thing…" She crossed her arms and pointedly looked away.

"What last thing?"

She cleared her throat and slid Kirk a look. "When we were tied up, I thought you were bumping me…to, uh, bump me…"

Kirk's face suddenly grew ruddy. "Oh. Well, uh, like I said, I was trying to trigger the auto-dial button on the cell phone…"

"You did a good job," Bree agreed, her voice growing breathy. Licking her lips, she added shakily, "And I, uh, was trying to help you trigger…" Well, that was sort of the truth, if one gave the word *trigger* multiple meanings. A self-conscious heat flooded her cheeks.

Kirk touched her arm. Currents of electricity crackled and flashed through her body.

"Don't explain," he whispered. "I loved your helping me trigger." He paused, his eyes heavy-lidded as he looked at her.

At that moment, Bree realized with a startling clarity that he'd felt every triggering moment she'd felt, too. Mutual passion, a love of adventure…they truly were meant for each other, weren't they? Her heart pounded with renewed hope. Maybe it wasn't too late…

"We only have a few minutes, Bree," Kirk said. "We have to go over our plans."

Minutes. *These are our last few minutes together.* Of course it was too late. Just because they were alike and shared common dreams and could generate more heat than a power plant didn't mean he was going to change his plans to get married to another woman…

Bree gazed at Kirk for the last time. She'd miss the blue of his eyes. Maybe they'd only known each other a day, but after what they'd been through, she felt as though she'd known him forever. She knew when those baby blues turned azure, he was happy. And when they darkened to cobalt, he was mad. Bree eyed the rough stubble on his face, then the cowlick at the crown of his head that gave him an air of boyish innocence.

And his lips. Full, sensual. *I wish I'd kissed those lips.*

Her heart wrenched again. *Let him go.* Their meeting had been by chance. A crazy encounter between two fellow adventurers, nothing more.

"As we discussed, I think you should ditch this trailer in that warehouse section in Commerce City," Kirk said.

On the ride here, she and Kirk had agreed that although they were willing to risk driving the trailer to Denver, she should lose it once she and Val were safely with George. Although Kirk hadn't yet spoken to George, just left several messages on his phone machine, he felt confident George could drive Bree and Val to Chugwater this afternoon. As Kirk had explained, he and George often spent Saturday afternoons exploring local excavation sites, so this would be sort of like that. Besides, after his and George's travels to primitive, remote areas of the world, they had an unspoken pact always to help each other.

"Anything else we discussed that we need to go over again?" asked Kirk.

She was willing to accept that it was too late for something more between them, but she still wanted to know if maybe, just maybe, he'd ever thought the two of them could have been more. After all, he wasn't married *yet*. It was asking a still-single guy a simple question…

Otherwise, I'll always wonder.

She cleared her throat. "Before we part ways, I have one thing I'd like to ask you."

"All right." He shifted his body more toward her, his eyes turning azure. "I'd like to ask you something, too."

She blinked. "You would?" She swallowed, hard.

After her overreactive, overheated bump-and-thrust in the mountains, she didn't want to be the one going out on a limb first again. "You start."

"Me?" When she nodded emphatically, Kirk smiled. "All right. Why do you have a chocolate kiss tattooed on your ankle?"

That's what he wanted to know? She fought a stab of disappointment, but it was better to know now that he wasn't curious about something deeper than a tattoo—like her feelings for him. "After a volleyball tournament in college, a bunch of us on the team dared each other to get tattoos. The choices were limited. I was torn between a skull with flames or a chocolate kiss."

"I thought maybe you were a chocoholic."

"I wouldn't push it away," she answered softly, thinking more of Kirk than chocolate. "Actually, I liked how the foil was starting to unwrap around the chocolate. It made me think of a new adventure being unveiled."

Kirk nodded. "I know that feeling. Now, your question."

Bree bit her lip, hesitating. "Kirk—"

"Kirk!" squealed a feminine voice, overriding Bree's voice.

Bree and Kirk jerked their heads toward his open passenger window where a thin, older woman smiled broadly, her teeth whiter and straighter than any Bree had ever seen.

"What's the almost-groom doing in a trailer?" the woman asked.

"Adrianne!" said Kirk, "What are you doing here?"

"I, uh, was invited?" She laughed casually, playing with a diamond pendant around her bronze neck. "Figured it'd be easier to park on a street behind the house, which is why I'm using the service entrance."

"Right. Damn."

"Damn?" repeated Adrianne, eyeing his beard and unkempt hair, then sliding a glance over at Bree.

"I just realized that Alicia probably invited others from the museum to this dinner."

"Oh, she did," Adrianne agreed. "While you were on your dig at Allenspark, Alicia phoned and invited us. Said she knew it was a bit last-minute, but she wanted to include everyone for the happy occasion."

"Us?" Kirk asked.

"Some of the fund-raisers, like myself. Also, Ralph, John, Isabella—"

"George?"

"Must have. I just walked past his parked car."

"I'll see you inside," Kirk said abruptly, obviously wanting Adrianne to scoot.

"All right." She flashed him a funny look, then headed toward the gates.

"Wonderful," murmured Kirk, sounding as though it was anything but. "George is inside, which means I won't be able to get to him for a while..."

"I have an idea," Bree said. "You go to your party,

and I take my chances driving this trailer to Chugwater.'' When Kirk shot her a no-way look, she continued, ''This is getting too complicated and, besides, it's your rehearsal dinner and you need to ditch that *Raiders of the Lost Ark* look.'' *And I need to leave you before my heart breaks.*

''No,'' Kirk said tightly. ''Same scenario we discussed before. What if those goons call the police and claim you stole the trailer? You'll end up in another holding cell, and in the midst of more insanity, those thugs will do their best to resteal Val.''

''You're going to be late to your party,'' Bree whispered. *Let me go. Let me learn to live without you...*

''I'll say I forgot what time it started. Everybody thinks I'm a bit absentminded, anyway.''

''I know differently.''

He paused. ''Yes, you do know me well...''

Kirk stared into Bree's eyes. They were wide and dewy right now, filled with unspoken words.

Funny how often they'd communicated without words. Through their eyes, their bodies. The grateful look Bree had flashed him that first night when he'd picked her up. The way she'd mimed what he should do as he stood on that bar, stripping. And the way her body had pressed and writhed against his when they were tied up...

His groin tightened remembering that last one...

He looked into her eyes, losing himself in their locked gaze. Her gray eyes shimmered with an emotion that permeated the air, penetrated his skin, wind-

ing its way around his heart, squeezing it, infusing him
with a fiery warmth that both exhilarated and tormented him.

No woman, not even Alicia, had ever affected him
like this.

Am I falling in love with Bree?

"Kirk! Darling!" called out another woman's
voice.

He looked out the windshield. "Damn," he muttered, watching the big-breasted woman in a cashmere
ivory dress sashay through the wrought-iron gate,
twiddling her fingers at the trailer.

"We have company," whispered Bree.

"My almost mother-in-law," he said under his
breath.

A young man sauntered behind her, his hands thrust
into the pockets of his pants, acting as though the
world couldn't be more boring.

"And my almost brother-in-law," murmured Kirk.

And following him was a lithe blonde in a creamy
orange dress, the chiffon skirt floating on the air with
each of her mincing steps. She was arm-in-arm with
an older gentleman who was guffawing loudly, probably over one of his own jokes again.

"And my fiancée and her grandfather."

"Princess Alicia?" Bree exclaimed, straightening.

"Yes, royalty is paying the cattle trailer a visit.
Adrianne must have clued them in...they probably
think I'm out here, cleaning fossils, forgetting what
time the rehearsal dinner starts..."

Rehearsal for the rest of my life to another woman.

Kirk reached over and squeezed Bree's hand. She squeezed back.

And in a startling flash of realization, Kirk realized he never wanted to let go of Bree.

The entourage fluttered around the truck like a flock of overdressed birds.

"Kirk, sweetie, that beard has got to go!" said Alicia, looking up into his open passenger window. "And no doubt you're wearing some dirty, fossilized clothes, which we should burn." She giggled. "Mommy has a gorgeous tux all laid out for you in the guest room…" Alicia touched her hair, which was sleekly pulled back in a chignon.

He gave Bree's hand one last squeeze, then released his grip. An irrational sadness washed over him—had he just released the best thing that had ever walked into his life?

Reaching over, he opened the passenger door.

Alicia waved her hand in front of her face, wrinkling her pert nose. "Euuuu! It smells like…"

"Bull," said Kirk.

"What?" said Alicia, fluttering her eyelids.

Kirk stared at her as though seeing her for the first time. Did all women wear eye shadow and lipstick that matched the color of their clothes? "It smells like bull," he explained, deciding this wasn't the moment to add that a real live one was in the back.

"And who is…?" asked Alicia, tilting her head to get a better look at Bree.

"Kirk, darling," chimed in Alicia's mother, having walked up behind Alicia. "You really must hurry and get ready. Guests are arriving." She glanced over her daughter's shoulder at Bree. "Are you delivering the extra tables and chairs we asked for?"

"No," said Bree quietly.

"Kirk, m'boy, how the hell is the returning warrior!" The grandfather reached up into the cab and slapped Kirk on the leg. "Is this one of our guests?" he asked, looking at Bree, his eyes twinkling underneath bushy white eyebrows.

Kirk grinned at Alicia's grandfather, Bart, with whom he'd shared a warm camaraderie since the day they'd first met. Bart was the heart of the family, a man who'd built a department-store empire from a one-room hardware store in Illinois.

Alicia's brother stood behind his grandfather, sliding a questioning look from Kirk to Bree.

Kirk's stomach clenched. They were all staring at Bree, wondering who she was.

"Hey, you're all wondering who this is," he said, buying time. Right. How the hell did he explain Bree? *She's on the lam with a Brahman bull. This is the woman I've stripped for and wrestled thugs to get here safely and where the hell's George?*

Nowhere. That's where. Kirk was on his own with this one. And considering George was inside, dressed in some monkey suit, his wife undoubtedly thrilled that a baby-sitter was watching the kids while she and hubby had a big night out, Kirk had a sinking feeling ol' George wouldn't be able to help out until tomorrow...

Which meant Kirk had to find a way for Bree to stay here tonight. He *needed* her to stay here tonight, *needed* to know she was safe, cared for. They could easily keep Val in the trailer...all Kirk had to do was convince them that Bree needed to stay in the house, in one of the guest rooms...

He smiled tightly at the staring, questioning faces of Alicia's family.

Suddenly, he reached back, threw his arm chummily around Bree's shoulder, and tugged her close. A big ol' buddy hug, although he'd have to be a dead man not to feel Bree's feminine curves molded against his side. And did he smell roses? She must have touched some in the mountains, the scent lingering on her skin. He squeezed her shoulder, vaguely aware of the strength of her muscles.

Curvy, rosy, strong. A sizzling combination of femininity and strength.

"She's..."

Curvy. Rosy. Strong. Curvy. Rosy...Rosy...

Robbie.

An image of his best pal clicked in, along with Alicia's comment that there was now no best man. "She's..." Was he crazy? Could this work?

"She's my best man!" Kirk announced.

9

BREE STARED into the dirt pit, her ego still smarting from being called Kirk's "best man."

Kirk stood next to her. He hadn't really combed his hair this morning, probably because he'd rushed to squeeze in this quick visit to the excavation site. The golden sun blazed the tips of his unkempt hair, giving it the appearance of a tangled halo.

Her hurt ego took a back seat as she observed Kirk. Damn, she loved it when the man looked primitive, unconventional. It was his truest nature, a reflection of his love of the raw, ancient world.

Very different from last night at the rehearsal dinner.

She suppressed a sigh looking at his clean-shaven face. That wasn't Kirk's doing, it had been Alicia's, who'd insisted he shave prior to the dinner. Not that it wasn't eye-pleasing to see his strong jawline or that sexy cleft in his chin. But Bree missed the roughened beard that gave him that *Raiders of the Lost Ark* look.

He was speaking, but she had to strain to hear him over the sounds of I-25 traffic rushing behind them.

"...it's been a major benefit excavating at the city's construction sites because it saves the museum the expense and effort of digging,'' explained Kirk, gesturing at the hole, which looked to be about twenty-something feet deep. ''Most people don't know that Denver is located *right* on top of one of the world's most fossil-rich layers. In this particular spot, we've documented sediments that date to the end of the time of dinosaurs.''

Her mood was definitely lifting. Bree loved hearing the enthusiasm in Kirk's voice as he shared his life's passion with her. She *knew* how he felt. She'd experienced her own near-euphoric rushes when she'd had the opportunity to see a rare piece of ancient art.

Kirk walked around the hole, then pointed down at a particular section. ''I've been quarrying fossils from that spot, getting a better idea of the nature of the rainforest that existed right where we stand, oh, sixty-four million years ago.''

''Give or take a million?''

Kirk did a double take at her, then grinned. The morning sun cast gold on his profile. ''Give or take a million? Closer to sixty-four point one.''

Only a scientist would pin it to ''point one,'' she thought, amused at his analytical nature.

Damn, she was going to miss him. An adventurer, a scientist and one hell of a rugged-looking hunk. Guys like this were rare, as rare as the artifacts they both revered. She'd never shared a mutual love of the ancient world—whether it be sixty-four million years ago or first century B.C.—with anyone. Probably never would again. Every single moment with Kirk counted...every single moment she'd hold in her heart forever.

Even those insane moments last night when she'd pretended to be Robbie's sister. Kirk, who was quite the storyteller she'd discovered, wove tales to guests about how Robbie had flown Bree out as a "surprise fill-in." How Kirk, Robbie and Bree had spent their childhoods in Washington state together, doing everything from skydiving to once spending a day lost in the forest near the Canadian border.

And Bree had smiled politely and nodded, secretly wishing she'd really had those adventures with Kirk.

Although, she had to admit, their dashing out of the mansion this morning before anyone else was up felt like an adventure. Kirk had asked Bree to join him on errands, plus a quick visit to the excavation site. After they'd ensured that Val was still comfortable with plenty of food, in the back of the trailer—which was nicely hidden in a far corner of the massive backyard behind a guest cottage—Bree had been thrilled to split mansionville. Otherwise, she'd have spent the morning stuck in bridesmaid hell as Alicia and her girlfriends got their hair, nails and other girly-girl stuff done for tonight's wedding.

Wedding.

Bree didn't even like to think of the word. It was a wall slamming down between her and Kirk, forever.

The sooner she left, the better.

And it would be soon. George had promised to meet her and Val back at the mansion by noon and then she'd be away from this forevermore. With the plans set, Bree had left another phone message for Grams, explaining where she was in Denver and not to worry, Bree and Val would be home soon.

And Kirk was going to explain Bree's absence tonight by saying she'd been called back home, an emergency.

"This hole might be my big breakthrough," Kirk said exuberantly. He stood wide-legged, his muscled arms crossed over his chest. There was power in that stance, a forceful masculinity that made Bree acutely aware of her own sexual nature.

Yes, the sooner she left, the better.

"Because?" Bree asked, wanting to hear Kirk explain it again. To hear that passion in his voice, to hear how his dreams fired his soul.

"Because..." He strolled around the dirt periphery, "these fossils could potentially reveal the K-T boundary I told you about, which would be a *major* scientific coup—the culmination of my lifelong quest."

He glanced up at her and shrugged, the boyishness returning. "But as yet, we haven't found anything to prove it. Although last week, we dug up that ancient stone with the peculiar engraving."

Bree's pulse notched higher. "Ancient stone?" She flashed on Kirk mentioning it that first night at the lodge.

"Got a message that one of my assistants took it back to the museum for safekeeping until we figure out the appropriate curator to contact."

"Wish I could have seen it," Bree said. "That's the kind of ancient art I want to see in Europe…" She'd skip the part about taking the Orient Express. She had a lot to clean up, resolve. There was a chance she'd end up with no money, again. Just as she needed to let go of Kirk, she needed to let go of her dreams to travel overseas. For now, anyway. Someday, she'd figure out how to fulfill that dream…

Kirk looked at Bree, wondering what cloud had just passed over her thoughts. He wished he could take her in his arms, murmur that everything would be okay.

Damn if he didn't ache for her.

It was more than simply wanting to comfort her. Every single time he looked at her, he wanted to crush her into his arms, devour her soft lips, savor her scent, caress her sweet, strong femininity.

He wanted to make her his own.

Crazy thoughts. Or were they?

"We could swing by the museum," he suggested. "I could show you that stone."

"There's no time," Bree murmured.

No time…time's running out. He should act now, tell her what lay in his heart before it was too late.

"That's all right," Bree continued. "Some day, when I get to travel the world, I'll see a lifetime's worth of ancient engravings."

"Right," Kirk said, mesmerized by her lips. Had he ever noticed before how they parted when she spoke, how her tongue flicked out to wet her bottom lip. "Right," he repeated, "that's your dream."

"Just as yours is discovering the K-T boundary."

"Yes, that…and to have roots, family, children."

Bree flinched slightly. Had he mentioned this before? "So that's why you're getting married…"

"Absolutely," he said quietly. "I was a lonely kid. Early on, I swore I wouldn't grow old alone, too. Having a family, having roots, is like having air to breathe. I *need* it." *Did Bree need it?*

Bree nodded slowly, her heart sinking. "Having a family and roots is, at this time of my life, downright suffocating," she admitted. "Except for a few years in Laramie, I've spent all my life in a town that has less people than were at your rehearsal dinner. I yearn to explore the world, see what's out there, with nothing tying me down."

"Nothing…or no one?"

Bree looked away, avoiding the look in Kirk's eyes. He looked so…disappointed. Sad.

Or maybe she was just projecting her own sorrow onto him. Because they'd just stumbled on the real reason the two of them could never expect more than this brief encounter they'd shared.

He needs roots, I need to be free.

"Nothing or no one?" Bree turned and started walking back to the car, not wanting Kirk to see the tears in her eyes. "Same thing," she whispered.

"YOU'RE THE CHEFS from Paradis?" asked Alicia, walking up behind the family butler, Errol, who'd just answered the front door.

Louie, never at a loss for words, was struck speechless at the vision of shiny blond hair and the prettiest, poutiest face he'd ever seen. Damn if she wasn't wearing shorts, too, and here it was January. Well, it was sorta warm enough to wear shorts, he guessed, but more than likely she wanted to show off her lean, tan legs.

Show, don't touch?

In a flash, he knew this was the kind of uptight, privileged broad who needed a bad boy to loosen her up, show her what living was *really* about.

"Parrot what?" asked Shorty.

Louie shot Shorty a shut-up look. Looking back at the butler and the broad, Louie plastered his best I'm-your-guy smile on his face. "That's right. We're the chefs." He picked a piece of lint off the starched white jacket he was wearing, courtesy of one of the two real chefs he and Shorty had nabbed outside this fancy mansion. He congratulated himself on thinking to ditch his pinkie ring in the van—no chef would wear somethin' like that.

"And you're—?" Louie asked, meeting the blonde's blue-eyed gaze.

"Alicia," she said.

A-leesh-a. Louie liked the way it sounded. Frothy, like whipped cream.

"Follow me," she said, pivoting neatly on her little lace-up white sandals and mincing across the shiny marble floor.

"You know it," Louie murmured, motioning for Shorty to follow.

A few minutes later, Alicia was gesturing into the grandest kitchen Louie had ever seen. Bigger than the kitchen at Antonio's, the Italian family restaurant in Jersey that nearly took up a frickin' block. From the ceiling hung every conceivable size and shape of shiny copper pots and pans. A large butcher-block table, big enough to sleep on, sat in the middle of the room. Damn, there was even a fireplace and couch at the far end.

This was fine and dandy, but Louie wanted to see more of the place...check outside where the girly and the bull might be. Thanks to the vehicle registration in that Kirk dude's van, Louie had found this home...which he figured was where he'd find Kirk's friends, too.

"You're not listening to me." The blonde stood stiffly in front of Louie, her slender arms folded tightly across her chest. Her nostrils flared delicately, indicating her displeasure.

Oh, yeah, she needed loosening up, bad. "Sorry, ma'am," he said. "I was listening, but got distracted by your beauty." It was an old line, but one worth dusting off at moments like this.

She raised her elegant chin a notch, her blue eyes glistening, betraying her pleasure at the compliment. "It's my wedding day," she said softly, taking a step back.

Too softly. *Dame doesn't seem real sure about that.*

One of those princess types who's marrying for the wrong reasons. He'd seen it before.

"Shame," he murmured huskily, inching closer. "A beauty like you, taken off the market." He let his gaze rake from her pretty pink-painted toes to her pouty pink lips. "There should be a law." He was so close, he smelled her fancy perfume, felt the sweet heat off her overpampered body.

Red flooded her cheeks. "You shouldn't be speaking to me like this." She stepped back again.

He inched closer. "No, I shouldn't. But around you, I lose control."

They were backed into a kitchen alcove, next to the pantry. Louie edged against her, forcing her to step into the darkened pantry, where her sweet perfume mingled with the scents of clove and cinnamon.

"I'll scream," she whispered shakily.

"No, you won't," Louie said huskily, placing one hand on the wall behind her. "Because you like me."

She raised her hand to slap him, but he caught it midair. Intertwining her small, soft fingers with his, he gently held her hand against the back wall.

He looked her over, taking his time, letting his gaze linger on the crotch of her neatly pressed shorts, imagining her sweet little cleft with its soft ringlets of hair that probably smelled like lilacs.

He raised his gaze to her prim cotton blouse, eyeing her breasts. Small and round, the kind that filled a man's hand nicely.

He met her eyes. A bright, glistening blue. "I could

take you right here," he said thickly, speaking so close he felt the warm puffs of her breath against his lips. "I could pull down those pretty little shorts and have my way with you, here in the pantry, your family right outside..."

She was breathing hard, her breasts straining against her blouse.

Oh yeah, he had her pegged. This was one of those dames who'd never indulged her lustiest fantasies, who'd never been bent over a table, who'd never begged for it...

He released the hold on her hand. "But I won't." He took a step back, gave her a hot look filled with even hotter promises, then turned to leave the pantry.

"Wait!" she said, nearly choking on the single word.

He cocked a look over his shoulder.

"Why...why not?"

"Why not what?" he asked, knowing damn well what she was asking.

She straightened, fluffing her fingers through her hair. "Why not take me?"

He smiled to himself, shifting to his "lover boy" best behavior. "Because I don't take," he said, lowering his voice to a sultry growl. "I *give*. And I only give when the lady asks for it." *Nobody's ever turned you down, doll, have they?*

He turned and left the pantry, smiling to himself. That was a fun diversion...now he had to find Mr. Money Bull.

"MR. DUNMORE?" asked Errol.

Kirk was staring out the library windows at the massive tent in the backyard where he'd be married tonight. Alicia offered what he fundamentally wanted...what he'd spent a lifetime wanting...but Bree...ah, Bree...she'd wound her way around his heart and he wondered if he'd ever be the same.

He'd just returned from meeting with George, who at this moment was hidden behind a guest house on the edge of the property, working with Bree to load the bull into George's truck. Within minutes, Bree and Val would be safely on their way to Chugwater, Bree forever out of Kirk's life.

"Call me Kirk," he reminded the butler, turning to look at the older gentleman.

"Something wrong, sir?"

How could he explain that his heart had been torn in two on the day of his own wedding? "No," he lied.

"Then, Mr. Ivey is here, sir."

George Ivey? He should almost be on his way to Chugwater with Bree and Val. "Where is he?"

"At the front door, sir."

Kirk rushed out of the library, across the marble foyer to the front door, where George stood, his forehead furrowed with worry.

"The I-25 excavation site," George whispered frantically, gesturing wildly. "You gotta stop them!"

Kirk pulled George outside, closing the door behind them. "Stop who?"

"The construction crew. One of the volunteers just called me on my cell. She dropped by the site to check on the dig, and overheard the foreman telling the crew to *fill* the hole! Seems that section of the highway is done, and they want to clean up, move on."

"We had a verbal agreement! They were going to give us notice so we could finish the dig!" Kirk dragged a hand through his hair.

George gave his head a disbelieving shake. "Damn, Kirk, they got us in a catch-22. We're invited guests at that site, nothing more. But you're good with people—maybe you can go down there, ask for a time extension!"

"Right." Kirk paced a few feet, then turned to George. "I'll speak to the foreman, hell, take it up with the mayor, the senator if I have to. I'll remind them this one spot could hold the key to an extraordinary scientific discovery. All we need is a week or two more…" Damn, he'd have to convince Alicia to postpone the honeymoon. She'd be irked, angry that the "old hole" had disturbed her plans.

Kirk patted his pockets. "Good. I have my keys. My car's parked around the corner. I'll let Errol know I'll be right back."

Kirk opened the front door a notch. "Where's Bree?"

"Here." She walked up behind George.

"Go with George," Kirk ordered. "Go home." He turned away, but not before he saw the flicker of hurt in her eyes. "George will explain."

He pushed open the front door, hating to turn his back on her, but they both had to move on, lead their own lives...

Across the foyer, he saw a flash of white at the door to the kitchen. A chef.

The guy turned and looked directly at Kirk.

Louie.

Kirk slammed shut the door, and shot a look at Bree. "They're here. Inside the house."

"Who?"

"Them!"

She paused. "The thugs?"

"Right. You two, get back to the truck," Kirk ordered. "Wait ten minutes before leaving. They don't know where you're parked, you'll be safe."

He started jogging toward his car, parked just around the corner of the house. Over his shoulder, he gave Bree a last look. The last time he'd ever see her. "I love you," he mouthed.

A fast jog and he reached the car. Jumping into the driver's seat, he started the ignition.

The passenger door opened.

Cold dread filled him as he looked over, expecting to see Louie staring at him over a pointed gun.

Instead, he looked into those familiar gray eyes, glistening with courage.

Bree jumped in and shut her door. "I'm going with you."

He shoved the gear into Drive. "Damn it. I wanted you to stay with George. You'd be safe with him."

Too late to argue. Every second counted. He stepped on the gas, peeled out toward the side street.

"But you love me," Bree said matter-of-factly. "And I love you. I'm not leaving you now. We're going to face this together."

Kirk turned right onto the street, tires squealing, and punched the gas. He glanced in his rearview mirror.

Following them was the "wedding-gift" van, with two white-clad chefs in the front seat.

And between them, Alicia.

"Oh, God," exclaimed Bree, looking over the seat at the scene behind them.

"I know. They got Alicia," said Kirk, clenching his jaw.

"No," said Bree, her voice shaking. "That's my Grams's truck behind them!"

"Your grandmother!" he yelled.

"I told her the address…she probably saw me, your car…"

"Wonderful. And she joined the caravan." Kirk blew out a pent-up breath. And he'd thought the fiasco in Nederland was like a Marx Brothers movie. Hell, that was tame in comparison.

Racing down the street, trees and houses blurring in his peripheral vision, he forced himself to think clearly.

Okay, at this moment, this caravan will follow you wherever you go…

And then he knew the best place to lead everyone.

"I'M DIALING 911," said Alicia, pulling her silver-and-pink cell phone out of her shorts pocket.

"Like hell." Louie, keeping one hand on the wheel, grabbed at the phone.

Alicia jerked away from Louie, accidentally thunking Shorty in the head with the phone.

"Ow!" Shorty yelled.

"Give me that frickin' phone!" Louie yelled at the same time, the van swerving as he kept one eye on the road while reaching for the object.

Alicia dropped the phone down the front of her blouse.

Louie smacked the wheel. "Oh, cute move, Bonbon. Gonna make me go fishin', eh, *before* I get to the Keys?"

"Keys?" she asked, pressing her hand to the spot between her breasts, "protecting" the phone.

"Louie's dream is to buy a fishing business in the Keys," offered Shorty.

"Shut up, Shorty." Louie pumped his fingers in a give-me gesture to Alicia. "Give it up."

"No," Alicia said primly, tightening her hold on the lump between her breasts.

Where types like Ms. Pouty got their attitudes, Louie would never understand. Well, he'd nip this little game, fast. He pulled out his gun.

Alicia squealed. Her eyes widened, but she didn't look frightened. She looked…excited.

"Don't shoot 'er, Lou!" Shorty yelled. "'Member what that kid said about society's illnesses!"

After this frickin' cell-phone incident, Shorty definitely lost his Keys visitation rights. Keeping his eye on the car ahead of them, Louie barked, "Where's that fiancé of yours going?"

"Probably to that big ol' hole he's so proud of," Alicia answered. "With that tall ol' girl he *claims* is Robbie's sister—but when I called Robbie to check on his leg, I found out he doesn't even *have* a sister." Alicia made an indignant, huffing sound.

"Big ol' hole—where's that?" Louie repeated, ignoring the rest. When women turned green, Louie turned off.

"It's an excavation site off I-25 and Hampden," Alicia explained. "You can see it from the freeway."

"Does he have a cell?"

Alicia blinked as though that was the dumbest question in the world. "Of course."

"Call 'im. Tell 'im we don't want trouble, just the bull. Tell 'im we got guns."

"The bull?" she simpered in a disinterested voice, more interested in fumbling with her top. "The phone's stuck in my bra."

"Then take *off* your frickin' bra and *call* 'im." Louie scratched his neck. This starched fabric was chafing him. No wonder chefs got so cranky.

After more fuming and fumbling, Alicia announced, "I can't get it off with my blouse on, and I *never* take off my clothes in public!"

That did it.

Louie yanked on the wheel, pulled the van over and

slammed on the brakes. A pickup truck swerved to miss them, blasting its horn.

"What the hell you doin', Lou?" Shorty yelled, smashed up against his passenger window.

Louie looked at Alicia. "You. Bra."

Her glossy pink lips pursed. "Why, I never—"

"Don't tell me, sister, 'cause it's written all over you that you've never. Now take off the bra."

"No!" She crossed her arms tightly under her chest.

"You're a frickin' nuisance. Worse than Shorty."

Shorty's mouth dropped open, but he didn't say anything.

Alicia small chin quivered. "You *drag* me out of my house, *force* me to ride in this van, now you're *ordering* me to take off my clothes..."

"Oh, you wish," muttered Louie, checking her over. He wasn't the kinda guy to rip off a girl's clothes, unless she was begging for it. Well, Alicia had already spilled where Kirk and girly were heading, so Louie decided his best move was to dump his difficult passenger.

"You, outta here," he said to Alicia. He opened his door. Gripping her arm, he dragged her with him as he hopped out of the van.

"You oaf! Let go of me!" She wiggled a little, bopping him a few times with a semiclosed fist.

Oh, yeah, all fluff and no struggle. He definitely knew this type. Loud, incensed...but loving every moment.

With a light spank on her butt, he gave her a helpful boost toward the sidewalk. "Run along now."

She spun around, her pouty pink mouth uttering an incredulous gasp. "*Nobody* orders me around!"

"Yeah? Well, I just did." He started to get back into the van.

"I'm calling 911," Alicia said in a shaky high voice, reaching down her blouse top. "I know Kirk's license plate number. I'll tell the police how you kidnapped me, stole my fiancé's van, threatened me with a gun, ordered me to strip…"

She had a serious strip fantasy. "I've been threatened by worse than you, Bonbon," Louie said, now back in the driver's seat. He leaned out, grabbed the door handle, ready to shut the door.

"And I'll say they can find you at I-25 and Hampden," she yelled.

Louie halted. Who the hell said blondes were more fun? He jumped back down and pointed at his opened door. "Get back in the van—"

She did a little twirly move, then started to run away in her laced-up high-heeled sandals. It was like watching a fairy princess try to be a jock. Louie sprinted after her, catching her as they ran onto the lawn of the house he'd parked in front of.

Alicia whirled around. "Let go of me!" The phone dropped out of her other hand.

They both dived for it, falling onto the grass, their bodies scrambling and lunging, their hands flailing.

Finally, the phone in his hand, Louie rolled over on

top of Alicia, crushing her against him as he pinned both her hands to the ground. They were gasping for breath, their faces flushed.

"Get off me," Alicia whispered hoarsely, the hollow at the base of her throat pulsing wildly. Her chest heaved against his as she sucked in ragged breaths. Dark heat flickered in her eyes.

Instinctively, his knee forced her legs apart.

Her gaze turned hungry.

He bent his head, hesitated, then branded her with a rough kiss, his tongue plunging deep into her sweet, wet cavern. Her body thrashed beneath him, her pelvis thrusting hard against his.

He ripped his mouth off hers, sucked in a sharp breath, then pushed himself off her. Standing over her, he stared at the sight of her sprawled on the lawn.

She panted through swollen red lips. The top buttons on her blouse had popped open, revealing her lacy bra. Over the top her breasts swelled, one pebbled nipple emerging. She arched herself toward him, her eyes asking...

"I don't think you're getting married today, Bonbon," he said in a low, husky tone. "Now get back in the van. I got business to take care of."

10

KIRK SWERVED off the Hampden exit, turned a sharp right and gunned it to the middle of the construction site, a cloud of dust in his wake. After slamming to a stop, he jumped from the car and jogged to the hole.

Filled.

Except for what he'd quarried, his painstaking research was buried. Gone.

Furious, he strode toward the foreman, a tubby guy with a bright orange-and-blue hard hat with Go Broncos emblazoned on it.

Bree unfolded her six-foot frame out of the passenger side of the car, coughing from the haze of dirt, and glanced toward the filled hole.

No wonder Kirk was stomping toward the foreman. This confrontation was going to get messy. She was clueless how to help, but at least she could be here, nearby, as support.

Those thoughts had barely crossed her mind when a red pickup truck barreled onto the construction site, knocking over several large plastic barrels before sideswiping a tractor.

Metal shrieked.

Sparks flew.

Everyone stopped, looks of horror on their faces as they watched the red pickup lurch to a stop.

The driver's door flew open and out hopped a white-haired woman, dressed in jeans and a brown leather flying jacket. She did a quick look around, spied Bree, then sloshed through dirt and mud puddles in her cream-colored boots, crying, "My precious grandbaby! Your Grams is here to save ya!"

Kirk, who'd barely had the chance to express himself to the foreman, stared at the two women. So this was Bree's grandmother. The source of Bree's wild, unconventional genes.

Bree ran to her and they hugged, amid crying and laughing and no small amount of cussing.

The foreman sighed heavily, wiped his brow, and looked at Kirk. "Friends of yours?"

"Sort of." This construction-site fiasco was getting complicated enough without adding his own life drama to it.

Instead, Kirk gave his head a shake and faced the foreman, ready to argue about the filled-up hole. "About that hol—"

Crash! Crunch! Fwop-fwop-fwop...

A shiny black Mercedes-Benz zigzagged onto the construction site, barely missing the barrels and tractor, but doing a dead-on job of bouncing squarely into a pothole and blowing a tire, before fwop-fwop-fwopping in a semicircle as though unsure what to do next.

Everyone watched the damaged Benz as though it were the next act in a wacky circus.

The foreman sighed again, even more heavily, causing his beer gut to expand slightly. "More friends of yours?" he asked drolly.

"Sort of," Kirk said again. "Now about that ho—"

"You got more 'sort ofs' than anybody I've ever known," the foreman interrupted, his tone bland as though he just couldn't work up the energy to get miffed at anything.

To tell the truth, Kirk had run out of miffed, too. The hole was covered—what was he going to do? Make them redig it and charge the cost to the museum? Besides, he was suddenly bone-tired exhausted. He'd done more strange things in the past twenty-four hours: picked up a stray bull, stripped for strange women, been tied up, jailed, shot at...

And fallen in love.

How could he be mad over a hole when he was madly, hopelessly in love?

And it had all started with picking up a girl and her bull on a dark mountain road. If life hinged on defining moments, that one had changed his life forever. Oh, it had been followed by chaos and confusion and moments of gut-wrenching anguish, but because of that moment, his life was forevermore changed...

Because for better or for worse, he'd found his true soul mate, Bree.

Euphoric, reckless sensations ripped through him.

Joy, so intense it bordered on anguish, filled his heart. So *this* was how it felt to be in love.

The Mercedes-Benz shuddered to a stop. The doors flew open. From the driver's side stumbled a woman wrapped in a satiny blue robe with matching blue slippers with fluffy little pom-poms on the toes. From the passenger door slunk a sullen-looking boy in slacks, a pullover sweater and a mismatched pair of loafers. Charging from the back seat was a larger-than-life older gentleman, a worn field coat thrown over a pair of plaid pajamas, wearing a pair of scuffed cowboy boots.

The older woman stormed toward Kirk, shrieking, "Kirk, darling, George told us we'd find you here! Oh my Lord, oh my Lord, gangsters have kidnapped our innocent little Alicia!" The woman wrung her manicured hands together, sobbing hysterically. "Our little girl, your fiancée, traumatized on her own wedding day!"

The foreman cocked Kirk a look.

"Sort of," Kirk murmured, figuring that answered just about anything the guy might want to ask.

The grandfather, muttering a string of cuss words, followed the woman. His white hair stood out as though electrified, and he had an unnatural look in his eye that said he'd kill the first sonofa-whatever who crossed his path.

The foreman stayed put, motioning to his men to do the same.

The only one not yelling was the sullen brother,

who hung back near the Benz, a why-am-I-here? look on his face.

Kirk stiffened, waiting for the grandfather to smack someone or something, when Kirk's shiny white van—his "wedding gift"—reeled onto the scene, slamming to a stop just before it broadsided the Benz.

The foreman, obviously stunned by the escalating sequence of events, just stood there, his mouth open.

"Those are the gangsters," Kirk explained calmly to the foreman, as though explaining to a child why the sky is blue. "With my kidnapped fiancée." Kirk knew these thugs were more bluff than dangerous, but he didn't have the energy to explain that, too.

The two chefs descended from the van, both brandishing guns, the tall one dragging a blonde with him.

All three of them headed straight for Kirk. Which, counting Alicia's mother and grandfather, made a total of five people zeroing in on him.

"I gotta go," muttered the foreman, his motor skills kicking in. He backed up several steps. "Sorry about the hole."

Kirk smirked. The hole. "Hey, man," he said, "we both did our best." And suddenly, he meant it.

Because at this moment he *got* it. Nobody ever knows what lesson a life experience has to offer because it's all a gamble. Whether it be a relationship, a job, some damn hole—sometimes you win, sometimes you lose.

But if you're willing to learn the lesson, then you're always a winner.

Right now his newfound winner theory was being put to the test as the taller thug, waving a gun under Kirk's nose, growled, "Turn over the bull and nobody gets hurt."

Alicia, standing next to the thug, her top unbuttoned and pink lipstick smeared all over her face, whispered, "Kirk, for God's sake, give him what he wants!"

Kirk blinked at Alicia—he never could figure her out—then shifted his gaze to Louie. Maybe life was a gamble, but Bree's future was at stake.

"Over my dead body," Kirk said, meeting Louie's gaze dead-on. Tarl Cabot would be proud.

Louie raised his gun a notch, pointing it directly between Kirk's eyes.

Bree screamed, followed by a chorus of screams from Alicia, her mother, even her brother who'd finally decided to say something. The grandfather took a step toward Kirk, his eyes pleading for Kirk to give the thugs what they wanted.

Kirk had always thought that, at the brink of death, one's life flashed before one's eyes.

Now he knew that wasn't true. What flashed in front of his eyes was the disappointment that he'd never made love to Bree, never experienced the lifetime of joy they could have shared.

An ear-splitting, prolonged shriek punctured his near-death fantasies.

At first Kirk thought it was his mother-in-law again, then realized it was a police car, followed by three more, lights flashing, sirens screeching. They halted mere feet from this insane gathering that had to be the wackiest cross-section of society ever assembled on a construction site.

''Everybody freeze!'' yelled a harsh masculine voice over a bullhorn.

TWO HOURS LATER, Bree sat next to Kirk on the bench in the holding cell, trying to avoid his I've gone-to-hell-in-a-handbasket look. She bit her bottom lip, trying not to admire his tortured face, his chin roughened with just enough stubble to add to his drop-dead, hunky ruggedness.

No man had a right to feel so bad and look so damn good.

Yeah, she shouldn't be thinking such thoughts right now, but hell, considering what they'd been through, she'd *earned* the right to appreciate him, full tilt. And with every appreciative thought, fresh waves of sizzling desire swept over her, teasing her with what could have been.

What could have been if only…if only…

The tap-tap-tap of footsteps sounded.

Alicia, in the company of several officers, waltzed down the cement walkway between the cells, wearing a flower-printed sarong number. She wore a bright fuchsia flower stuck behind her ear and carried an oversize straw beach bag under one slender arm.

''Aloha!'' she yelled to the group, who were divided among different cells. The family was grouped in one large holding cell, the thugs sequestered in a more cramped one across the aisle.

No one answered. Not even the bored-looking cop standing next to her, keys jangling in his hand.

"I've paid *everyone's* bail!" Alicia squealed proudly, holding her hands up in the air in some kind of victory gesture.

"Even ours?" asked a glum Louie, his chef's outfit smudged with dirt after the fracas at the construction site.

"*Especially* yours," Alicia said, lowering her voice to a sultry whisper. Rolling back her shoulders, Alicia turned back to everyone.

"I have an announcement," said Alicia, her cheeks nearly as pink as the flower behind her ear. "The wedding's off."

Alicia's mother gripped her chest and groaned.

"Oh, Mommy, it's okay," said Alicia offhandedly. "I figure let's just have everyone over, announce there's been a change in plans, then have us a big ol' party."

Alicia looked at Kirk. "Kirk, honey…" Her voice turned oozy soft. "We both wanted the same thing so bad. Children, family. After our lonely childhoods, we thought we'd struck gold when we met each other and realized we wanted the same thing. Only problem is…the passion we felt was for our *dreams,* not each *other.*"

Kirk started to say something, then shut his mouth

and nodded. Obviously he knew exactly what Alicia was talking about.

"And besides," Alicia added, "it's obvious you love that girl, the one you claim is Robbie's sister."

Bree's cheeks flamed hot. Kirk had mouthed he loved her, and she'd said the same to him, but she'd figured it was one of those "we might die so let's go for the gusto" kinds of things. Although, deep inside, she knew she'd meant it, soul-deep meant it, when she'd uttered those words.

And maybe it was the same for Kirk?

Her heart swelled. *He loves me.*

"And as for me," Alicia said coyly, batting her eyes at Louie. "I'm in love with this big bad hunk of a guy who showed me what passion and dreams and…well, we'll leave the rest of it out…what life is really about."

Alicia's mother uttered another shriek.

Ignoring her mother's outburst, Alicia smiled triumphantly. "Louie and I are staring life over in the Florida Keys, where we plan to start a fishing business!"

A loud thunk.

Everyone dropped their gaze to the family cell. Alicia's mother had collapsed on the bench, still clutching her chest. "For God's sake," she murmured pitifully, "somebody get me a triple martini, straight up, twist. Alicia's running away from home again. Thought she'd outgrown this in her teens, but guess not…"

"Besides the emergency martini," said Kirk, "I have another emergency request."

In silence, everyone looked at him.

He turned to Bree, started to drop to one knee, then changed his mind and remained sitting. "I like being eye level with you," he whispered.

He cleared his throat. "Bree," he said, his eyes glinting that luscious azure blue that turned her insides liquid. "Will you marry me?"

Marry? Thoughts collided in her head. Yes, he was the man of her dreams. The man she wanted to explore the world with, share adventures with, delve into the planet's ancient art and history...and every step of the way, they'd love each other with a passion she never dreamed possible. But...

Roots.

Family.

Children.

Weren't those the very things Kirk yearned for? The things he wanted desperately, every bit as much as discovering the K-T boundary?

That look on Kirk's face tore her apart. That sparkle in his eyes, asking her to say yes.

Bree swiped at the corner of her eyes, hearing the oohs and aahs of people who thought she was overcome with emotion. Well, she was overcome...totally, irrevocably, weak-in-the-knees overcome.

But not blind to the future.

"I've spent all my life waiting to escape Chugwater," Bree whispered hoarsely. "Waiting for the chance to see the world, explore ancient art, maybe even ride the Orient Express…'' She rolled back her shoulders uneasily, fighting a sick, tangled feeling in her stomach. God, she loved this man.

But would love diminish, even die, if she gave up her dreams? If not for her, surely for him…he yearned for the very thing she wanted to escape.

Through a mist of tears, she met Kirk's gaze. ''No, Kirk, I can't marry you.''

''VAL!'' Bree ran to the bull, who was munching oats, tethered to a large boulder in the center of a cleared area at the heart of the labyrinth-in-progress being constructed at the museum. She wrapped her arms around his head and shot Kirk an appreciative look. ''You took care of him, just like you said you would. Thank you.''

Kirk smiled, a little sadly, memorizing those dimples he'd grown to love. It had been a short drive here from the jail, but a long ride in his heart. He felt good having taken care of Val, and despite the chaos he and Bree had weathered, he'd ultimately taken care of her, too. Although he'd wanted to take care of her for the rest of her life as well, he'd had to accept her refusal graciously. Sometimes, he'd learned, two people might be in love, but they disagreed on its very nature.

''Well, it's really George you should thank. I told him to hide Val here, at the museum, in the center of this Minotaur and the labyrinth exhibit,'' Kirk said. ''No one is allowed into this section because it's under construction…and considering the exhibit is about a bull—the half man, half bull Minotaur—nobody even blinked an eye that George quietly led Val into here.''

As Alicia had said she'd take care of transportation for her mother, brother, Louie and Shorty, it was just the four of them—Kirk, Bree, Grams and Alicia's grandfather—in the center of the labyrinth exhibit.

Grams looked around. ''Pretty fancy,'' she mused. ''Back in Chugwater, we'd tear down this wood and build us a home.''

Kirk grinned at her. ''Well, when the exhibit closes, I'll recommend that's what we do.''

The grandfather harrumphed his approval. ''Smart planning, m'boy.'' He glanced at Grams. ''With your truck out of commission after hitting those barrels and a tractor, I'd be happy to give you a lift back to Chugwater.''

''Well, now,'' Grams said, her voice sounding almost girlish, ''that'd be right gentlemanly of you.''

''And I'll keep tabs on how the truck repair is going,'' the older man added. ''When it's ready, please allow me to pay the bill and return it to you.''

Grams started to hesitate, but Bart pressed his point, as well as pressing her hand, Kirk noticed. ''It's the least I can do,'' he whispered gruffly, ''and I want to do it.''

Seeing Grams's cheeks shade to a full-blown blush, Kirk turned to Bree to give the two older folks some privacy.

"Still want to see the stone I told you about?" he whispered.

Bree's pulse pumped harder. "The ancient stone with the engraving?"

Kirk nodded and positioned her closer to the boulder to which Val was tethered. "Look down into the center of the rock," he instructed. "To protect the artifact, and make for easy viewing, we set it within the rock, the opening covered with Plexiglas."

Bree stared into the sand-colored rock, its opening roughly two by two. Lights overhead pinpointed a rough-edged chunk of stone with a smeared dark etching, parts of the drawing filled with faint reds and yellows.

A memory sharpened in her mind.

"Good…Lord…" she breathed.

"Like it?" Kirk asked.

"Like?" She shot a wide-eyed look at Kirk. "Do you know what this is?"

He paused. "No. We've contacted several curators who specialize in ancient art, but none has had a chance to visit Denver yet."

"I saw a picture similar to this in a book," she said, barely able to speak she was so awestruck. "A drawing of a bison around thirteen thousand years ago, in a cave in France. But nothing like this has been unearthed in this part of the world…until now."

She looked back at the stone, blinking with incredulity. "Look at the red and yellow," she whispered. "Those were made from chunks of red and yellow ochre.'' She tilted her head, observing the drawing. ''Wonder what he—or she—was drawing?''

''The first signs of humans in this area were approximately eleven thousand years ago,'' Kirk explained. ''Maybe they were drawing a mammoth or a horse…''

Bree beamed at Kirk. ''I love how our understanding of ancient history meshes.'' She almost said more. How their passions, their interests meshed too…but to say that only intimated the other ways they meshed. But all that didn't matter because fundamentally, they were polar opposites. *He wants roots, I need freedom.*

She turned to Kirk, tears burning her eyes, hoping he thought it was because of his monumental discovery, not the pain in her heart. ''Do you realize you discovered a critical piece of ancient art in your excavation site? Maybe you missed some clues to the K-T boundary, but you gave the world a treasure from the past, a message from people thousands of years ago.''

She choked back a laugh and hugged Kirk tight. ''Oh, my valiant scientist,'' she murmured in his ear. ''How many times have I overhead you say you wish you could live up to the heroism of that Tarl Cabot fellow, but I think *he* should be the one wishing to be as great a hero as you.''

Kirk cradled her in his arms, pausing for a beat. ''Well, if heroes can have wishes,'' he whispered, ''I wish I hadn't lost you.''

Epilogue

"I NOW PRONOUNCE YOU husband and wife," said the minister, smiling at Grams and her new husband, Alicia's grandfather, Bart Hansen. To the crowd assembled on folding chairs in a tree-shaded portion of old Mr. Connors's pasture, the minister announced, "I'm pleased to introduce Mr. and Mrs. Bart Hansen."

Everyone applauded as Grams and her husband kissed...so long and passionately, some of the guests giggled.

As Grams and Bart walked down the rose-petal-strewn aisle between the chairs, Bree, the maid of honor, stepped forward and took Kirk's, the best man's, arm.

During the entire service, it had taken all of Bree's willpower not to stare at Kirk. Damn, he looked more handsome than ever. Tan, rugged, and what a tux did to that man should be illegal. But despite his elegant attire, a slight hint of stubble shadowed his face and Bree couldn't help but wonder if he'd done that for her benefit. He knew she loved that *Raiders of the Lost Ark* look on him—was he teasing her, just a bit?

"You look beautiful, Bree," Kirk murmured, as

they continued walking arm-in-arm down the aisle.
"You dress down, *and* up, very nicely."

She smiled up at him, her insides caving in a little
at his azure eyes. Kirk had seen Bree in plenty of
rough-and-tumble clothes, but never "gussied up like
a lady" as her Grams would say. As maid of honor,
Bree wore a long teal chiffon dress her grandmother
had picked out, with a neckline scooped too low for
Bree's taste, but Grams had insisted Bree flash "some
of her goods." Bree decided not to mention that she'd
once been willing to flash all her goods in a bar in
Nederland, but that had been a goodwill gesture only.

And although Bree had argued *not* to have her hair
"dolled up" Grams had insisted her grandbaby wear
her hair in a frothy, curly "do" with a few baby roses
added for effect.

When Bree had looked in the mirror, she'd been
surprised how pretty she looked. She'd even blushed
a little, amazed how a few additions could turn a
down-home girl into a sophisticated woman. It was
like *My Fair Lady* in Chugwater, Wyoming!

But to see Kirk's expression, and the effect Bree
was having on him, turned her knees jelly-loose. She
clung tighter to his arm, determined to keep her balance, stay upright. Damn, this man still got to her,
big-time. His smoldering eyes and powerful masculinity speared her heart with a pain both sharp and exquisite. She'd missed him, terribly, but she'd never
admitted it to anyone, not even her Grams.

Instead, Bree had spent the last few months cleaning up the misunderstandings surrounding the "alleged" theft, while deciding to not sell Val to any breeders, even Bovine Best. She'd also started her own consulting business to local ranchers. Bree did everything from grooming and feeding livestock to giving classes on how to breed and raise Brahmans. She wasn't going to be rich overnight, but she figured within a few years she'd save enough money for her dream trip to Europe.

"Let's take a detour," Kirk murmured, as they reached the end of the aisle.

His voice sent tremors through her, from her toes to the roses adorning her hair. Bree sucked in a shaky breath, meaning to say something sophisticated like, "Yes, lovely, let's..." but all that came out was, "Uh-huhhh."

Kirk steered her across the Connors's field toward a fence, over which hung Val's head, watching the two of them approach. Bree swore Val was smiling...

Kirk stopped and put his hands on Bree's shoulders. His gaze traveled over her before settling on her eyes.

Kirk had missed those gray eyes. So big, so full of emotion, so ready to see that big world she was aching to discover.

"Bree," he said gently, caressing her shoulders. "Remember that engraved stone you identified, the one I'd found at the excavation site?"

"Of course! It was in all the papers. I read that it's currently on display in New York at the Metropolitan."

"Yes, it's on loan to several museums before it re-turns to Denver. After New York, it's being shown in London, Paris, Rome…" He took a deep breath. *Here goes.* "I was wondering if you'd like to visit those places, see the stone again…"

Questions burned in her eyes. "I could just wait until it returns to Denver."

He waved her words aside. "Why root yourself here and wait? Let me put it more bluntly. I have two tickets to London, where I've made arrangements to travel, with a guest, on the Orient Express through Europe…and I'm bringing a stack of historical ro-mances if there's any extra time for reading."

Bree nearly strangled on tears of joy. Europe, the Orient Express, seeing ancient art…and to top it off, he'd even thought of her favorite type of reading ma-terial…as though she'd want to read while sharing a train ride with this man.

But…why was he offering her everything *she* wanted, but not what he wanted? No relationship could survive on such terms. She dragged a trembling hand through her curls, causing a tendril of hair to tumble down her cheek. "But…roots, family, chil-dren," she said softly.

He toyed with her tendril of hair, gently tugging on it, urging her a bit closer. "Maybe our roots will al-ways be planted throughout the world," he whispered huskily. "Or maybe we'll find some special spot, someday, where roots make sense." He glanced over at the wedding party, then at Val. "And we already have a family…maybe someday we'll add to it, too, if we feel the need…or desire…''

She read the urgency in his gaze, felt her insides flash with fire and hope. He was offering a compromise…a lovely, workable compromise…and if she read that look in his eyes correctly, he was offering more. ''Are you asking me to…?''

Heat smoldered in his eyes as he leaned closer, his lips brushing hers as he whispered hotly, ''Marry me, Bree. Let's explore the world through our love.''

''Marry you,'' she repeated, her resolve melting as his kisses grew more feverish. ''A small ceremony,'' she whispered, her breaths ragged with desire.

He nibbled at the corner of her mouth. ''Untraditional,'' he said huskily, ''something unique that's just you and me…''

''And Val,'' she added as Kirk's lips seared a hot path down her neck, lingering there to kiss the pulsing hollow in her neck.

''Of course,'' he murmured. ''Val will be our best man.'' Kirk raised his head, his blue eyes flaming. ''So will you marry me?'' he asked again, his voice deep and dusty.

She nodded exuberantly, her heart wild with need for him, for their life together.

''Say it, Bree.''

A sob of release escaped her lips. The desire, the love she'd held a bay these past few months finally burst free. ''Yes!'' she cried, wrapping her arms around Kirk's neck.

Colleen Collins

Can't Buy Me Louie

HARLEQUIN®

TORONTO • NEW YORK • LONDON
AMSTERDAM • PARIS • SYDNEY • HAMBURG
STOCKHOLM • ATHENS • TOKYO • MILAN • MADRID
PRAGUE • WARSAW • BUDAPEST • AUCKLAND

Dear Reader,

Can't Buy Me Louie started as an idea for a "road story" sequel to *Let It Bree* where a down-on-his-luck gangster—Louie—is stuck on the lam with a spoiled, rich princess. As I told my editor, imagine a young Goldie Hawn à la *Private Benjamin* on the run with a young Robert De Niro. The good girl with the oh-so-yummy bad boy.

I have to admit it was hard letting go of the hero of this book, Louie Ragazzi. He's a tough-minded, soulful gangster whose dark, sizzling looks made being bad so deliciously good. Maybe I can't buy me Louie, but I'll sure remember him for a long, long time.

To read about my upcoming books, and enter contests for prizes, please visit my Web site at http://www.colleencollins.net.

Enjoy!

Colleen Collins

Books by Colleen Collins

HARLEQUIN DUETS

HARLEQUIN TEMPTATION

Don't miss any of our special offers. Write to us at the following address for information on our newest releases.

Harlequin Reader Service
U.S.: 3010 Walden Ave., P.O. Box 1325, Buffalo, NY 14269
Canadian: P.O. Box 609, Fort Erie, Ont. L2A 5X3

To Keith Jones, fellow Sag and good friend

Acknowledgments:
Marrying Sam, my "Key West contact"
who generously answered my questions about the
region, and Shaun Kaufman for his legal expertise,
Beatles music and unflagging goodwill.

1

LOUIE HAD BEEN in his share of holding cells, but never while dressed as a chef.

Hell, white wasn't even his color, he thought, fighting the other, more somber, thoughts that had been banging around his skull the last few hours, ever since he'd been hauled in by the police from that frickin' construction site. Thoughts like how he could lose years of freedom for attempted kidnapping alone. Top that off with possession of a weapon, aggravated motor-vehicle theft...and whatever else these rich people trumped up...and his view of the world could have bars across it for the rest of his life.

Louie rubbed his eyelids with his thumb and forefinger. He'd made a lot of mistakes over the last few days, but his biggest was reeling Bonbon into the van. With her phone-in-the-bra and lawn-wrestling antics, they'd lost valuable time. If he hadn't taken her, he'd have made it to that damn construction site at least ten minutes earlier, which would have given him time to force Kirk, one way or another, to give up the location of Mr. Money Bull.

But nooo, Louie had to take Missy Bonbon along on the ride, which was his fatal mistake.

Bye-bye bull. Bye-bye to his dream of the fishing business in the Keys. Hello prison.

Click-click-click.

Louie stopped rubbing his eyes. He'd know that sound anywhere...it was the crisp, uptight sound of a pair of heels marching to her own drummer.

"Aloha!"

Yeah, and that was the voice that went with those heels. Louie dropped his hand and stared through the bars at Miss Bonbon.

She looked as though someone had tightly wrapped her in a beach towel. A bright orange, flowered, body-revealing beach towel that clung to her pert breasts, slightly flared hips, tight ass.

She made a man want to lie on a beach towel for the rest of his days...

She blinked at Louie, playing with a big pink flower stuck behind her ear. Her green eyes sparkled excitedly.

Green eyes? He distinctly recalled their being blue earlier. He'd heard of women changing their hair color often, but eye color?

She shifted a glance at the two cops who'd accompanied her and who were now talking to each other, then shot a wink at Louie.

He frowned. *Now* what was she doing? Signaling him? In front of *cops,* in a *jail?* Louie had been around his share of crazy dames, but Alicia had just taken first prize. Waltzing around with cops, dressed in sprayed-on towels, giving him I'm-gonna-get-you-outta-here looks.

Jingle-jangle.

Louie dropped his gaze to the set of keys one of the cops was holding. It appeared *somebody* was getting out. And *soon*.

Louie shifted his gaze to the larger cell directly across from where he sat. Most of the people in it were from Alicia's family, which he had figured out from their assorted conversations. Now they sat quietly, their expressions ranging from dazed to stunned.

Hell, he'd only spent a few minutes with her and had experienced those things!

Seemingly oblivious to the fact that no one had responded to her aloha greeting, Alicia squealed, "I've paid *everyone's* bail!" She held her hands up in the air in some kind of victory gesture, a big straw basket dangling from one of her arms. Louie noticed she'd gotten a manicure since their earlier van escapade. Her fingers were tipped in a bright orange color to match the flowers on her wrap-around towel.

"Even ours?" he asked glumly. Yeah, like he'd ever see the other side of bars.

"*Especially* yours," Alicia answered, her voice dropping to a husky, sultry range that hit him like a hot bolt of lightning.

He looked at her, seeing that same look of dark heat in her eyes as when they'd been grappling on the lawn. "My lawyer and I ensured all charges were dropped, except the police were a little fussy about your illegally possessing that gun you were waving around at the construction site. So, because of that, the judge has set some special conditions on the bond…''

Special conditions? His insides tensed as he held Alicia's gaze. He doubted she could even boil water, but she'd definitely cooked up something with that judge. And here Louie had thought her skills ranged from petulant to pouty, but it appeared Bonbon could also be an efficient deal maker.

As long as it was in her favor, of course.

''I have an announcement,'' Alicia continued, her voice returning to that high, articulated tone cultured dames typically used. ''The wedding's off.''

She shot Louie a look, her cheeks a hotter pink than that big, exotic flower stuck behind her ear.

What was she thinking? Maybe her wedding was off to that other dude, but she was making a *big* mistake if she was setting her sights on Louie. Maybe he'd had three wives, but bottom line, he was a one-man show—no baggage—and he'd let her know that in no uncertain terms as soon as he got out of here.

A loud groan distracted him.

He looked at the family cell where the big broad clutched her chest, her eyes rolling heavenward.

''Oh, Mommy, it's okay,'' said Alicia offhandedly, adding they'd just tell everyone there'd been a change in plans.

''Do you know how many people have already flown in? Aunt Kay's family, Uncle Shaun, the Kaufmans…'' Her mother kept staring heavenward, a glazed look in her eyes as she continued reciting names.

Alicia made a dismissive motion with her hands, saying people could still enjoy the party.

Party? Did she always try to turn hassles into special events?

The way she turned near-lifetime prison sentences into special conditions?

Louie started pondering again what the hell those special conditions could be while Alicia murmured things to her former fiancé about how they weren't meant to be together.

She breaks things off easily, Louie mused. The engagement. The wedding. *All I need to do is give her a good reason to break it off with me, too.* The thought brightened his darkening mood. All he needed to do was toss her a little disappointment, hell, tell her she looked as though she'd gained a few pounds, and she'd scamper back home.

Louie glanced at the former fiancé, Kirk, wondering if the guy knew all along he and princess weren't meant to be together. Louie could've told Kirk this from the moment he'd laid eyes on the woman. *She wants hot and dangerous, pal, not easygoing and reliable.*

Suddenly, Alicia turned and batted her eyes at Louie. "And as for me," she said coyly, "I'm in love with this big bad hunk of a guy who showed me what passion and dreams and...well, we'll leave the rest of it out...what life is really about."

Louie's mind went on red alert. *She's in love? One kiss, and she's in love?* He hated to think what happened if a guy got to first base with her. He'd tell her she'd gained a few pounds *and* he only dated red-heads.

Smiling triumphantly, Alicia swung her gaze around the room, announcing loudly, "Louie and I are starting life over in the Florida Keys, where we plan to start a fishing business!"

A loud thunk.

At first Louie thought that was his heart crashing to the floor before he realized the big broad across the way had collapsed on the bench, begging for a martini.

Make that two, he thought. Alicia had fantasies of starting *her* life over in *his* dream world, the Keys? The two of them starting a fishing business? She needed to renew her membership to reality.

Louie continued staring at Alicia, ignoring the next event in that family cell where that Kirk dude was asking the girly to marry him…hell, Louie knew those two were meant for each other after that little tango they did while they'd been tied up.

He kept his gaze on Alicia. He was cool under fire, and this piece of fluff wasn't going to shake him up. Within minutes, Louie was gonna be a free man, informed of some "special conditions." He'd listen—after all, Louie could be a polite sorta guy when he had to be—then he'd take Bonbon aside and tell her she looked chubby, that he had a thing for redheads and the Keys were off-limits.

He smiled to himself, imagining her running back home on those pretty little pampered feet, the click-click-click of those high-heeled sandals fading into the distance.

CLICK-CLICK-CLICK. "Louie, hon, wait up!"

Hon? Louie kept walking away from the police station, not looking back. Just because she'd paid his bail didn't mean she'd bought *him.* But it appeared she thought differently, because, despite his giving her the cold shoulder while the cops were going through the release procedures, Bonbon was now running after him, calling out sugarcoated names, ready to *cling* to him.

And Louie Ragazzi didn't go for clingy types unless *he'd* paid for dinner and *he* was in the mood.

His cohort Shorty was huffing and puffing to keep up, but he knew better than to complain about Louie walking too fast. Probably Shorty had seen how Bonbon's put-on only made Louie more pissed-off. And one thing Shorty had learned these past few days was not to irritate Louie more than necessary, especially when Louie's dark mood was turning downright black.

"Lou, hon!" Click-click-click. "I'm not wearing running shoes, you know!"

As if she ever has. Louie rounded the corner of the police station, determined to get out of sight of those massive glass front doors so no cop would oversee the little confrontation he planned on having with Bonbon.

He strode down the sidewalk for several more feet, glancing at the crisp blue sky through the bare branches of the trees overhead, then turned abruptly and collided with a flash of orange and pink.

"Oh!" squealed Alicia, running into him.

A searing pain shot through his left big toe and a sharp elbow wedged in his solar plexus. Unsure whether to wince or try to gulp another breath, he opted to grip her wrists and simply hold her in place. God knew what else she'd step on, punch or accidentally elbow if he let her go.

"Sorry," Alicia whispered, her words hot and minty against his cheek. "I didn't mean to step on your foot."

"You and your frickin' stilettos," he murmured roughly. He breathed in a lungful of air, fresh and cold and filled with her scent. An exotic perfume that smelled like spicy peaches.

Yeah, that was her all right. A spicy peach. A package of creamy, pampered sweetness filled with sizzling need.

A hot rush of sensations swept over him, overriding the physical pain, leaving him unsure if he was more aroused or angry. Damn, he never should have thought of peaches. Now all he was aware of was the woman in his arms, all soft on the outside, ripe on the inside.

Stay angry. You gotta move on, get back to Jersey, figure out how to make enough dough to get to the Keys.

Now that he was free, he never wanted to chance a life behind bars again. Maybe he'd be scraping by, only dating one lusty broad at a time, but he was going to own that fishing business in the Keys if it killed him.

He released his grip. "We gotta talk," he said gruffly.

Clunk-clunk-clunk.

Alicia's mother rounded the corner, joining the impromptu gathering.

"Alicia, darling," she said, catching her breath, "we must talk about this little problem with your running away…" She stopped and panted a little while fanning herself with her bejeweled hand. "I knew you should have stayed in therapy longer."

A young man, blond and lanky and sulky—undoubtedly Alicia's brother—sauntered around the corner next. He stopped, checked out the scene, then looked at his Rolex as though timing this next dramatic event in the ongoing chaos in the life of his family.

"Oh goody," Alicia said, looking over Louie's shoulder. "There's our cab."

Louie looked behind him. Sure enough, a red-and-white cab was pulling up to the curb. He looked back to see Alicia talking animatedly to her mother.

"Louie and I are taking a cab to the airport, so here's the keys to my car—"

Louie and I? "No, we're not," he cut in.

Alicia, rummaging about in that straw monstrosity that appeared to be a purse, ignored his outburst as she extracted a jangling mess of keys and handed them to her mother.

"Darling," the mother said, "you're overreacting, just the way you did as a teenager. There's no need to run away. Just come home, spend a day at the spa, and let's you and I plan a shopping trip to Paris or Rome…"

Mama was pretty good with all this mother-daughter posh talk. Louie decided to back off for a moment and let her handle this. *She'd* convince Alicia to stay, and he'd provide emergency backup if needed.

"No," Alicia said, her voice taking on that clipped tone he recognized meant she was determined to get her way. "I'm going with my lover and that's that."

"Lover?" The mother gazed incredulously at Louie. "But he's so…so…"

Time for the emergency backup. "Bad, disgusting, downright filthy," he filled in. "Plus I've been married three times." He cocked a look at Alicia. "But, to set the record straight, I've never been her lover."

"What do you call what happened in the pantry?" Alicia snapped, her eyes flashing. "Or on that stranger's front lawn?"

The mother's mouth, which had dropped open on his "married three times" line, gaped even wider. "On a *stranger's* front lawn?" She blinked rapidly.

But the pantry was okay? Louie gave his head a shake. Time to split, get back to reality. "How much dough you got, Shorty?"

Shorty, fidgeting with his box of cigarettes, said, "Uh, thirty, maybe forty bucks?"

"Give it."

Shorty handed over a wad of bills and some loose change.

Louie tucked the money into his pockets while strutting toward the waiting cab. "We'll figure out tickets when we get to the airport." He made a gesture toward Shorty to follow.

"I'm the surety on your bail!" yelled Alicia. "I can turn you in for breaking any of the special conditions on that bond!"

Louie stopped in his tracks, turned and leveled her a look. "First, never, *never* yell at me—'*specially* in front of a police station. Second, the cops already informed me of those frickin' special conditions. No carrying firearms, no liquor." He swiped the air with his hands, as though rubbing away the words. "Neither's on me, so I'm clean, I'm free and I'm *outta* here." He continued heading toward the cab.

"And there are other special conditions!" Alicia yelled.

Louie halted, turned and stared at her. "What'd I say about yelling?"

She stood there alone—it appeared her family had fled, probably when she started yelling—her legs slightly spread, her slim arms folded tightly under her breasts. It was getting chilly out here, but as usual, Bonbon seemed oblivious to the weather in her zeal to expose as much skin as possible. Amazing how she had the bucks to buy all the clothes she wanted, but seemed to prefer short shorts and Hawaiian gear in the dead of winter. She'd never get away with this in Jersey, where it could get bone-cold unbearable instead of this breezy chilliness that Colorado called winter.

He continued to stare at Alicia, observing how the sunlight shimmered and glinted off her blond hair, giving her a halo effect.

Some angel.

She was being a devil and he didn't take this kind

of "do what I say or else" treatment from anybody, especially some dame.

She swiped hair out of her eyes and refolded her arms. "Sorry for yelling," she mouthed, adding a roll of her eyes as though this was the stupidest conversation she'd ever had in her entire life. She minced toward him in those ridiculous high-heeled sandals, stopping a few feet from where he stood. "And there are other special conditions," she repeated, modulating her voice.

"Excuse me?" he said icily, closing the space between them. He was so close, he could count the smattering of freckles across the bridge of her pert nose.

"Now, Lou," muttered Shorty, "don't blow—"

"Shut up," Louie growled to Shorty, not breaking eye contact with Alicia. "*What* other special conditions?" he snarled.

Alicia looked at Louie in his white, still sort-of starched chef pants and top. Smudges of dirt covered him from the fracas at the construction site. His raven hair, which before had been slicked back, was unkempt, a lock hanging provocatively over his brow. And he had such a downright evil look in his dark eyes, it was all she could do to remember how to breathe.

Damn, she'd never been this excited before in her life.

"Don't play games with me, Bonbon," Louie growled. "You play with me, you play with fire."

She'd never had a man say no to her. Whether it be a boyfriend giving in to her whims or a stepfather placating her with money. Her mother had often said Alicia's biological father had been a strong-willed, opinionated man. Alicia figured she got those traits from him—and if he hadn't died when she was four, she probably would have learned how to deal with a man saying no.

Instead, she'd grown up with a mother who fretted over Alicia instead of disciplining her. And two stepfathers—or technically ex-stepfathers, she guessed— who, on the whole, seemed more interested in her mother and the family money than in trying to be fill-in fathers.

Looking into Louie's burning eyes, Alicia realized he wanted her to be afraid of him. And she thought about feigning it, looking scared, but the truth was she'd soon have him wrapped around her little finger, just like any other guy.

He just didn't know it yet.

She eyed a jagged white scar above his eyebrow, wondering what dangerous, bad thing he'd done to get that. She shuddered involuntarily before speaking.

"I'm not playing games," she whispered. She scrunched her face. "Okay, maybe a little." Damn, she never made such confessions. Well, if she was on a confessional roll, she might as well explain further. "Yes, I'm playing a little with you because…" She licked her trembling lips. *Say something sassy, cute. That gets guys every time.* "Because my free bird will fly away without me."

Louie emitted a sharp bark of laughter. "*Your* free bird? Baby, you need a reality check. Nobody, especially no *dame,* is going to clip these wings." He leaned forward and whispered hotly in her ear, "What happened between us was *fun,* Bonbon, not love."

He pulled back, solidifying his rage in a cold, challenging gaze.

But instead of growing indignant or defiant, her eyes moistened with emotion. Her chin quivered.

For a moment, Louie felt like a dog for what he'd said. Maybe he didn't always treat people with respect, but he tried to treat ladies decent-like, not purposefully hurt them. And even if he knew he was only having "fun" with a lady, he never threw that brutal truth in her face.

He might be a gangster and a ladies' man, but one thing he prided himself on was that Louie Ragazzi wasn't a cad.

As though she knew his guard was down, she batted her dewy eyes and whispered demurely, "I'm sorry."

Oh yeah, plunge the guilt in deeper. "No problem." He looked around, shrugged, avoiding those teary green eyes. "Let's just call it a day."

Alicia liked the way he avoided looking at her, his head bent a bit boyishly. Had she pierced Louie's Achilles' heel? The knowledge empowered her to say what she wanted, point-blank.

"Louie," she said, lightly touching his hand. "Here's the truth, no more games. I'm *asking* you to go to the Keys. *All* expenses paid. You have a dream, and after the hell I've gone through planning this now-cancelled wedding, I *desperately* need a vacation."

"Lou," Shorty chimed in. "All expenses paid? Dat's a good deal—"

"Shut up."

"And," Alicia said, upping the stakes, "I'd like to help finance that fishing store you've always dreamed about."

"*Store?*" He snorted. "I'm not opening up some catch-and-release Neiman Marcus, Bonbon."

"I have two airfare tickets, first-class, to the Keys," she countered.

"I'll take Shorty," Louie answered brusquely, his tone sounding anything but happy with *that* choice.

Alicia picked up on her advantage. "We'll buy Shorty a ticket to wherever…"

"Jersey," Shorty said.

Louie shot him another shut-up look.

"Hey," yelled a voice.

They all looked over at the cabbie, who was leaning against the hood, smoking a cigarette.

"I don't mind taking a break while the meter's running," he said, plumes of smoke escaping with his words, "but how long you people plan to chat out here? I got another pickup after this airport run."

"We're coming!" she called out sweetly, mincing toward the cab.

Shaking his head, Louie followed. This little peach had gotten to him, but he had to get back in the driver's seat. Tell her who was boss.

"Oh!" squealed Alicia, looking over her shoulder at Louie. "And I also bought you some clothes! Some real cute Hawaiian shirts and shorts…and a bunch of flip-flops!''

No way in hell he'd wear flip-whatevers. Reaching her, Louie grabbed Alicia's elbow and steered her away from the door. "Enough's enough," he said huskily. "Give me the tickets. Shorty and I are going to the Keys, not you."

Alicia smiled sweetly, too sweetly, and dug into her purse. Instead of tickets, she extracted her pink-and-chrome cell phone. "The other special condition I started to tell you about?" she said, punching a number into the keypad. "You're not to have contact with the victim…"

"What victim?"

Alicia batted her eyes. "Me." She made a silencing motion with her hand. "Shh, I'm calling the judge…"

He yanked the phone out of her grip, punched the end button and pinned her with a fierce gaze. "Give me the tickets. As I said, *Shorty* and I are going to the Keys."

Alicia's chin tilted up. "I'll call the authorities and say those tickets were stolen. You'll pull up to the unload passenger zone and be loaded right into a police car."

Louie's chest brushed against her breast as he sucked in an angry breath. "Then Shorty and I will leave you here, find our way back to Jersey."

Stealing a few precious moments, Alicia pretended to pull a piece of lint off his chef's jacket. "How old are you, Louie?" she whispered. She guessed thirty-four, thirty-five. "How many years are you going to waste in Jersey, being a bad guy, saving up for a dream that might never come true?''

She was hitting low, but hitting the truth from the painful look that shadowed his face.

His fingers ran up her arm, gripping her elbow. ''You're a brat.''

Alicia shrugged nonchalantly, even though her heart was pounding mercilessly at the sight of his fiercely dark eyes boring into her. She dropped her gaze to his sullen mouth surrounded by all that coarse, black stubble. He was wild and bad and everything she'd never had…but wanted. Her stomach did a funny clench, the contraction working its way down between her legs. ''And your point is…?''

Louie took a deep breath and expelled it. Raking a hand through his raven hair, he growled, ''Get in the cab.''

2

"WHERE'S YOUR ROOM?" asked Louie, sliding the hotel magnetic card in the slot on his room doorknob. The green light blinked on.

"This is it," answered Alicia, standing behind him.

Louie paused, turned slowly around, the card in his hand. "What?"

Alicia pointed one manicured nail at the door. "This is my room."

Louie gave her a cool once-over, from her orange-tipped toenails peeking out from those high-heeled orange sandals, up that body-molding towel number to her pretty green eyes that looked at him with wide-eyed innocence.

Yeah, right. She was about as innocent as the devil.

Louie lowered his voice as a young couple exited their room next door. "I thought you were getting *two* rooms."

The couple, in matching blue polo shirts, leaned against the wall, giggling and nuzzling each other before going for a full-tilt kiss. Honeymooners, thought Louie. Head-over-heels stupid for each other, looking at life like it was a sunrise, all bright and happy and endless.

Poor suckers. They don't know it's a one-dimensional picture that rips and tears when you try to walk into it.

After the couple finally disentangled enough to walk down the hallway, Louie settled his gaze back on Alicia. "Thought it was going to be *two* rooms," he repeated, "one for you, one for me."

While she'd been registering downstairs in the lobby at this ridiculously fancy Key West resort, he'd waited next to the elevators. At the time, he'd thought it a good idea to put a little space between them. Since the jail, he and Bonbon had been damn near soldered together. Plus, after her "I'm in love" announcement to her family back in Denver, he needed to help her understand he wasn't boyfriend—or worse, husband—material.

But now he wished he'd stayed by her side while she registered so he could have ensured they got separate rooms. After one hell of a week chasing a damn bull, he was now in the Keys with nothing to his name but a wad of bills, a wrinkled and dirty chef's outfit, an old T-shirt and his boots. At this very moment, Louie's greatest wish was to head outside, suck in some of that Key West ocean air, and find something to warm his gut and someone to warm his bed.

Someone lusty, busty, who wasn't polishing the words *I do* in her vocabulary.

"Would you believe I couldn't get two rooms because they're full up?" Alicia said, one slim eyebrow rising with her voice.

"Try again."

"I love you?"

He leveled her a no-nonsense look. "After one kiss?"

"We could squeeze in some more, test my theory."

He stared at her pink, pouty lips. Hot need coiled tight within him as he recalled how delicious she'd tasted, how her body had arched greedily against his.

Chill. This broad has special conditions attached to everything. Your bond, her body. One more kiss and you're going to end up in some chapel, for worse than anything better.

"We're not lovers," he growled. "I've told your mama, and now I'm telling you *again*. Whatever fantasy trip you're on, it's time to take a detour."

Alicia's green eyes did that moistening thing again. Man, she had a bag of tricks bigger than that straw purse she lugged everywhere.

"I know you're a one-man show," she whispered, repeating the very term he'd used to describe himself. She started to say something else, but changed her mind. "Can we go inside, please, and not have this intimate discussion in a public hallway?"

He eased in a breath, taking in her peachy scent with the air-conditioned air that flooded this place. She'd been willing to do it on a stranger's lawn, but didn't want to discuss issues in an empty hallway?

"I don't want to take it inside," he said, "until we've cut to the chase. After a week with Shorty, I need lots of breathing space. If we're stuck in this room together, we're roommates only." He was glad finally to be rid of Shorty, but he envied the guy being free, on his own, even if he was winging his way back to Jersey.

"Don't think of me as a roommate," Alicia whispered, her eyes glistening. "Think of me as being liable for your bail, so it's practical that you and I stay in the same room."

That did it. "You think I'm going to skip bail? What kind of fool do you take me to be?"

"You're raising your voice." She glanced up and down the empty hallway. "Can we please go inside to continue this discussion?"

Louie angrily swiped his card through the slot again. The green light blinked and he shoved open the door.

"Even if I *managed* to shake you loose," he growled as Bonbon breezed past him, "you'd be *speed-dialing* numbers on that phone of yours faster than a one-fingered NASCAR driver." He shut the door.

Ignoring his outburst, she minced into the room a few steps and halted. "See," she said sweetly, "it has two beds." She gestured toward the two queen-size beds, both covered with shiny tropical-print bedspreads that almost matched Alicia's towel-dress. "One for you, one for me."

Pampered types always switched gears like this. Sugary observations totally unrelated to the topic at hand. In other words, she was letting him know she wasn't pursuing their previous discussion. And if he wanted to pursue it, it would be less painful to bang his head against a wall.

He glanced at the beds. *One for you, one for me.* That's probably how her life had always been, always plenty to go around. Everybody got one, at least.

Growing up dirt-poor in Jersey with five siblings, he'd shared beds with two or three kids at a time, an experience Bonbon would find surreal.

But even after all these years, it was still painfully real to Louie. Growing up on leftovers and hand-me-downs, his earliest prayers were that he wouldn't end up poor, dependent on others—the latter reinforced by seeing how the tire company owned his father and how the demands of a large family owned his mother. By the time he was twelve, Louie was determined that nothing or nobody would ever own him.

"This bed's mine," he said, pointing to the one closest to the door. If he needed a break from Bonbon-ville, he could make a fast exit, check out the ocean view, envision his boating business.

"And I'll take *this* bed," Alicia said, tossing the straw monstrosity and a big, tan Gucci bag onto the bed closest to the window.

He glared at the bag. When the cabbie had dropped them off at the airport in Denver, Louie had been surprised when the guy had also unloaded that fancy piece of luggage from the trunk. Alicia had explained that the cabbie had picked up her "Goo-chi" from her butler, who'd filled it with some clothes Alicia had requested for the trip. Clothes that included Hawaiian-print shirts and "flip-flops" for Louie.

The Atlantic would have to freeze over before he'd wear Hawaiian *anything* or *flip-flops,* whatever the hell those were. Plus, the entire flight here he'd been irked that he'd lost his black leather jacket, which, as far as he knew, was still in that Kirk dude's impounded van. Not that a leather jacket came in all that handy in the Keys, but maybe in some over-refrigerated room he'd have slouched it on sometime. After all, it was a lusty-babe magnet.

Alicia turned her back to Louie and pulled back the drapes. Outside was the faint hum of traffic, an occasional high-pitched squeal from someone partying early.

He looked out the window. Despite the circumstances, he had to admit he felt damn glad finally to be here, his dream business so close. No more tough guy. Louie was on his way to being a legit businessman. He made a mental note to start talking better, drop the wise-guy lingo, 'cause one day soon he'd have that fishing business and be dealing with customers.

His thoughts were distracted by the late-afternoon sunlight spilling brightly into the room, casting a golden sheen over Bonbon's form. Overhead, a rotating fan swirled, lightly lifting wisps of her blond hair. She looked like a peach all right. With all those orange and cherry colors in her dress and the honeyed pink of her skin, she looked all ripe and tasty.

His gaze skimmed down her body, pausing on the teasing fullness of her breasts and how they bulged provocatively against the sides of her dress. The sun seemed to gravitate there, too, the rays burning hotly around the curves as though massaging the mounds that lay beneath that towel number. Louie imagined his hands being the sun, hotly stroking her, heating her silky skin, dipping into that towel and firing her desires…

His gaze slid down her back, over her high, compact ass, down to the slit in the fabric between her legs. The damn sun had beat him to the punch again, the sizzling light seeping through, outlining the taut shape of her thighs and offering a provocative glimpse of the apex between her thighs.

Louie ran a hand across the scrub on his face, thinking about how long it'd been since he'd been with a woman. Too long. Typically, after a rough job—and even if he'd failed to get the bull, this last week had been *rough*—he rewarded himself with a lusty entrée. Nothing like a little hot sin to burn away life's troubles. But with Bonbon, a little sin meant a lifetime sentence, so he'd let his troubles simmer, postpone the reward.

She suddenly turned around.

He jerked up his gaze.

Too late. He caught her self-satisfied smile.

"Always check out your *roommates?*" she purred.

"Just window shopping," he murmured huskily. "Not buying."

She tossed back her hair with one hand, the sunlight catching flecks of silver and gold in her hair. "I should have asked—are you married now?" she asked, a little frown pinching her face.

"No."

"Lucky girl."

Sassy. Well, he deserved a comeback after his wise-crack about not buying. Although it surprised him Bonbon could give back as good as she got. He bit the inside of his cheek, not wanting to smile. Not wanting her to know she'd just notched several points of respect in his book.

But she must have caught the look on his face because her body posture suddenly changed. As though she were relaxing. Her shoulders slumped a little and she shifted her weight to one leg, causing one nicely rounded hip to jut out as a lazy, simmering look crossed her features.

She's not just relaxing.

Alicia slid one foot to the side, opening wider that slit of light between her legs.

She's heating up. Raising the stakes.

He held her gaze, determined not to let his slip. Determined not to let on that that little between-the-legs view made him want to howl. But he refused to give in. If a kiss equaled love, he'd be in big trouble to try more. "We should—"

But the rest of the sentence stuck in his throat as he watched her hands slide teasingly up her torso, those slim orange-tipped fingers feathering a little underneath her mounds. "We should what?" she asked softly, her eyes glistening.

Damn if he knew. Should something. But whatever he'd started to say seemed like a lifetime ago.

She jutted out that hip a little farther. One of her fingers inched up, almost pointing the way to her nipple which he could clearly see was hardening, straining against the fabric.

"Should..." Even though his mind knew better, his body roared what Louie should do. *Should toss you on the bed, rip that towel off and give you want you want.*

"Should leave, get something to eat and drink," he muttered, or tried to. His voice was husky, strained. The sound of a man losing the fight.

She undoubtedly saw the look of doom on his face, sensed his quandary, felt her edge.

Her hands inched up the sides of her breasts, brushing the sides of the mounds, moving up her long, creamy neck, tunneling into her hair. "It's so hot in here," she murmured.

As though on cue, a drop of sweat broke loose from his brow, trickled slowly down the side of his face. It wasn't hot, it was an inferno. Heat that couldn't be quelled by the humming air-conditioning or the swirling fan.

He was trapped, sweating, watching her hands as they fluttered down again to her sweet, long neck. Her fingers played with a spot on her bare chest, that expanse of creamy skin above the edge of that strapless dress.

"You're right," she said, suddenly dropping her hands to her sides. "We should go out for something to eat and drink."

Go out?

Oh yeah, that'd been *his* suggestion. "Right," he croaked.

Desire, hot and greedy, pooled in his gut. He shifted his stance, trying to get comfortable.

"We could get something sweet and icy with little umbrellas in them."

Sure. Whatever. "I need to wash up." *Splash ice-cold water on my face, sober up from this sensory binge.*

"Okay," she said, mincing across the rug in those ridiculous high-heeled contraptions to the large rectangular mirror over the wicker dresser against the right wall. "I'll freshen up out here." Leaning over to look at her reflection, she stuck out her rump, lifting one sandaled foot for balance.

He stared at that round bottom, glazed with sunlight, poised in the air. To hell with sobering up. He wanted to get drunk on her. Cross this room in two steps, yank off that towel and take her, fast and hard, right there on the dresser.

But it's what she wanted.

And she was accustomed to always getting what she wanted. Nobody had to tell him, he could *see* it.

And if he gave in, her next outfit wouldn't be a towel outfit. It'd be a bridal gown.

For a moment, he had the crazy thought that he should turn himself in, call the judge and confess he was with the "victim," maybe even say he was holding her hostage, say anything to prove he was violating one of the special conditions of that frickin' bond. Hell, he'd be a lot safer behind bars in Denver than sharing this room with her in Key West.

He gritted his teeth. No, he had to win this game.

Had to. He was in the Keys, free, so damn close to his dream. He'd pull it together, figure out how to raise the dough to buy his fishing business. Louie always figured out how to solve the problem.

Besides, Bonbon was doing everything in her power to own him, and *nobody* owned Louie Ragazzi. Never had, never would.

"Can't do it, baby," he murmured huskily.

She glanced over her bare shoulder, her eyebrows rising in a question. "Can't…?"

"Can't do drinks," he said, heading to the bathroom. "No liquor, no firearms, remember? Part of my special conditions."

Can't do drinks, can't do you. Liking the feel of being in the driver's seat again, he headed into the bathroom and shut the door behind him with a crisp click.

ALICIA BIT her bottom lip, staring at the closed bathroom door, listening to the gush of running water and splashing sounds. It sounded like a bull moose was in there.

An angry bull moose who'd just cut her off, stormed away, put a wall between them.

No guy's ever walked away from me like that.

Her heart thudded dully, painfully. She sat down on her bed and played her fingers along the satiny bedspread, wishing her life were as seamless and smooth.

I shouldn't have teased him.

That sexy routine in front of the windows had been spontaneous, inspired the moment Alicia turned around and saw the way Louie was looking at her, his eyes hooded, simmering with carnal need.

Then, as though a curtain had lifted, rays of sunlight had streamed through the window and penetrated his dark armor. And for a golden, suspended moment, she'd seen a different Louie. His arrogance fell away, replaced by a look of tender yearning and need that filled her with a giddy warmth.

Because in his gaze, she suddenly felt more than she ever had before with a man. Felt beautiful, outrageously desirable. She'd ached to close the space between them, to know the real Louie…

To make love.

And she knew it was in her court to do something because this was the guy who wanted two rooms. Insisted they were roommates.

And when he'd tried not to smile after her brazen retort, her insides had turned to mush. He looked so boyish with that kicked-up grin, that wicked glint in his eye, she'd decided to go for it.

That's when she'd mentally locked on a video of Britney Spears. Alicia was no Britney, but guided by the visual playing in her brain, she did a demure rendition of the diva's finger-teasing, hip-thrusting movements. If Britney could do that for a video, seen by millions of guys, Alicia had figured she could do a toned-down version for *one* guy. One guy who needed a little encouragement to do something sweet and good in life.

But her spontaneity had backfired. Louie had turned her down. Said no. And he'd stomped away from her, all bluster and brashness, shoving the world away at an arm's distance.

Alicia leaned back, propping her weight on her elbows, suddenly exhausted from the last few days' events. She stared up at the rotating fan, its lazily circling blades whirring silently, the air pulsing with their beats, going in endless circles...

Suddenly, that's how she felt about her own life. Running in endless circles...

Had she made a mistake to run away?

But this time it was different than when she'd been a teenager. Back then, she hadn't known where she was running to. This time she did. This time, she'd run to a place to be with the man who'd shaken up her world, who, she sensed—especially in the last few minutes—was more than he wanted to reveal. She'd run some*where* this time, and she didn't want to leave.

Not yet.

She lowered her gaze and stared at the bathroom door. *Maybe I should tap softly, whisper that I'm sorry, make a few teasing remarks about those turquoise boots.* She smiled to herself, liking this idea. It had always worked in the past. Play a little, kid a guy out of his bad mood. Games like that turned men to putty.

She frowned. *Bad idea. Louie doesn't do "putty."* One thing about him, a person didn't have to guess his intentions. He could be taken at face value.

Face value. Sure can't say the same about me.

A pain pierced her as she reflected on her manipulations. Not that she hadn't been aware of them before. Buying gifts whose price tag was really the relationship. Passing compliments to appease, not praise. Things she'd grown up seeing her mom and her socialite friends do. It was part of the fabric of their world, being extraordinarily gracious and pleasing, like politicians to the elite.

But she'd never really questioned that behavior…until now.

Because for the first time, Alicia realized with a sickening feeling that although she wanted Louie's love, she'd played the game too hard. And he'd responded in kind.

She heard his rough words in her ear again. *What happened between us was* fun, *Bonbon, not love.*

She sat up, clutching the edge of the bed, and stared forlornly at the closed bathroom door. More splashing sounds. He didn't need to close the door, but he'd wanted to. It was a barricade between the two of them.

She glanced at her reflection in the mirror over the dresser. Funny, even if her insides were topsy-turvy, at least on the outside she was having a great hair day. She tried to smile at her own joke, but it didn't feel very amusing.

She leaned forward, peering into the mirror. Well, maybe her hair looked great, but that expression in her eyes was anything but…she had that hazy, lost look that made her green eyes appear darker, the way the sea looks when a storm is brewing.

And she recalled how ten years ago, at sixteen, she'd always had that lost look. Her friends used to tease her about it, and she'd play along, but deep down she'd *felt* it. It had been like a gnawing in her soul that kept ripping open a lonely space wider and wider.

It started after her mom's second husband, Sam, had left for good. She hadn't been that close to her stepdad, but with her mother and brother always gone, and her preretirement grandfather constantly traveling on business, Sam's departure gutted the house for Alicia. Sure, the place was filled with *things,* but it lacked the warmth of people.

So, with her brand-new driver's license, she'd jumped in her Bimmer and driven to a lodge outside Taos, New Mexico, where she'd stayed for four days. There'd been scurrying maids, meandering guests and she hadn't felt so lonely. The second time she ran away, she drove all the way to Los Angeles where she crashed with a friend attending UCLA. She'd loved the babbling students, loud parties.

After a third runaway to Las Vegas, her mother had put her foot down and insisted Alicia go into therapy. But the psychologist seemed distant, cold, and Alicia had felt lonelier than ever. So she'd stopped going. But, surprisingly, she'd also stopped running away.

Until yesterday.

Alicia glanced back at the bathroom door, hating the feeling that Louie had run away, too. From her.

The water abruptly shut off in the bathroom.

The door creaked open.

She opened her mouth, ready to speak sincerely about how sorry she was, apologize for her Britney

Spears moment, maybe explain a little about her run-away past....

But instead, her mouth dropped open. With great effort, she closed it and swallowed dryly.

He stood there, water beading his black unruly hair, his neck still wet. He'd shed the chef's jacket and wore only a tight black T-shirt that tucked into those white, starched chef's pants.

He stared her down as he tugged off his shirt, stripping it off in one, brusque movement.

Her heart pounded so hard, she had the crazy thought it would rip loose of her body and careen around these walls. She licked her suddenly quivering lips, unable to do anything but stare, wide-eyed, at his naked torso.

Oh my...oh my...oh myyyy...

The words in her head kept repeating themselves, spinning faster and faster, competing with the ffop-ffop-ffop of the overhead fan. Outside, someone squealed.

She was pretty sure it was someone outside. Or maybe she'd just internally detonated.

But Louie's eyes remained cool, unchanged, not a flicker of anything being different with her. Good. She hadn't lost control...yet.

Her gaze dropped to his chest and she froze, spell-bound, unable to look away. He was...*magnificent.* Louie wasn't very tall—maybe five-nine—but that chest belonged on a six-footer. Massive. Muscular. His skin had a warm coppery sheen, and her mind raced with what he did outdoors without a shirt on.

Run? Swim? Omigawwwd, make love at high noon on a blanket?

Black hair rushed thickly down his chest all the way from his collarbone to the bottoms of his pecs. The unruly carpeting then tapered to a line that swirled teasingly down his ridged abdomen before disappearing into the waistband of his pants.

He stepped toward her.

Her palms went clammy.

And as he continued to look at her with a stern, unsettling gaze, his arms suddenly lashed out as he tossed the black shirt onto his bed. "Can't wear that damn thing," he grumbled.

She surreptitiously wiped her moist palms against the bedspread. Good. He was pissed about the shirt, not her. "What's wrong with it?" she asked, her voice rising precariously high. She closed her eyes for a moment, willing her overloaded libido to get a grip.

"I've been wearing the damn thing for two days, can't stomach wearing it another minute. But no bar will let me in without a shirt."

So it appeared he was willing to break the "no alcohol" part of his special conditions, after all. "We could have a drink here," she suggested, gesturing limply toward the minibar.

He grimaced as though she'd just suggested they sip Shirley Temples. "Forget that. I didn't travel all the way to Key West to stay holed up in a hotel room. I want to walk the streets, smell the sun lotion, feel alive again." He looked around the room. "Do fancy places like this leave shirts or something for people to use?''

Alicia shook her head no. Biting her bottom lip, she hesitated, then said softly, ''I, uh, have some shirts you can wear.''

One interested eyebrow cocked before his face shut down in another grimace. ''I'm not wearing some *flower*-printed shirt.''

''You'd look like Jimmy Buffet.''

''Jimmy who?''

She paused. ''Lots of men wear flower-printed shirts in these hot, exotic locales.'' Hot. Exotic. She meant to take a calming breath, but ended up making a smacking sound as she half sucked in a mouthful of air.

''You okay?'' Louie actually looked concerned.

She nodded, or tried to. It was more of a head wobble. ''Huh-huhhh,'' she answered, not sure what she meant, but feeling the need to respond.

He frowned. ''Thought you were primping while I was washing up.''

''Do I look that bad?'' she blurted, suddenly riddled with anxiety. ''It couldn't be my hair!''

''No, you look a little pale, a little…''

They stared at each other for a long moment, the only sound the quiet hum of the air-conditioning and the fwop-fwop of the overhead fan. The look in Louie's eyes softened, shifting from an angry black to a velvety gray. The way storm clouds start to dissipate when blown by the wind.

"You look like a little girl, Bonbon," he finally murmured.

Alicia straightened, as though sitting a bit taller made her seem more adult, more a woman, but inside she knew he'd pegged her. She felt small, little... seriously out of her league.

"I know you don't like the shirts, but if you toss one on, we can see Key West, get that drink," she said, hearing the forced cheer in her voice and realizing it sounded bizarrely like her mother.

He started to say something, stopped, then shrugged in resignation. "Where are they?"

Despite her trembling legs, she managed to stand and walk to the end of her bed where she'd tossed the Gucci bag. It took her a small eternity to open the damn thing with shaking fingers, but finally she did. Pulling out one of the milder prints, a shirt with light yellow flowers, she held it up.

He frowned and crossed the room to her.

She stared at his chest the entire way, gripping the shirt as though it were a life raft.

"Let's see it," he said gruffly, taking the shirt out of her hand. He held it up, rolled his eyes, muttered something about wifey number two, then shrugged into it.

She rummaged through the bag, mainly so she wouldn't stare as he buttoned the shirt over that mouthwatering chest, and extracted a pair of flip-flops. "And here's a pair—"

"No."

She blinked. "But those boots...your feet will be

so...so hot.'' Like me. Hot and needy and on the verge of a hormonal meltdown.

He stared at the shoes as though aliens had just delivered them from Planet X. ''I don't wear bright blue plastic doodads on my feet.''

''They're flip-flops, not doodads—''

''*No.*''

She looked him over. Turquoise boots, white bulky starched pants, Jimmy Buffet shirt. He was a fashion disaster, but she knew better than to utter a single word.

He positioned himself in front of the mirror in a wide-legged stance and tunneled his fingers through his damp hair. Alicia held her breath. He looked like Antonio Banderas dressed in clothes from three different movies.

''I'm ready for that drink.'' Louie dropped his hands and leveled her a look. ''That is, unless a certain woman has itchy fingers to place a call that I'm breaking the terms of my bond.''

Alicia was suddenly preoccupied with smoothing her dress, avoiding his penetrating gaze. ''Maybe,'' she said nonchalantly, picking a mysterious piece of lint off the fabric, ''that woman will be a different woman tonight. One who's forgotten what those silly terms are.'' She straightened and looked him right in the eye. She dropped the false, cheery tone and added solemnly, ''One who's sorry she's been such a pain in the butt and wants to just enjoy a hassle-free evening out.'' *Who wants to be with you...who wants to share more than this damn room.*

She grabbed her straw bag and headed for the door before he saw the emotion filling her eyes. "I'll wait out in the hallway for you."

"Bonbon?"

She stopped, feeling Louie's low, throaty voice as much as hearing it. She barely glanced at him over her shoulder. "Yes?"

He held up a twenty-dollar bill. "I'm paying."

Maybe he'd had those wives, but he sure played up the "one-man show" all right. Always needing to be in control. Must have been hell on his ego having her bail him out, fly him out here, pay for the room.

"Sure. One for you, one for me," she murmured, opening the door and stepping into the hallway.

3

ALICIA STARED at the No Sniveling sign hung crookedly over the cash register behind the Green Parrot's bar. The words were painted on a piece of driftwood, as though a person could be shipwrecked, stripped of their worldly goods, down for the count—but hey, no sniveling.

She hadn't sniveled, murmured or even talked to Louie during their walk over here from the resort. They'd both been in their own worlds, observing the street jugglers, dive shops and gingerbread conch houses that filled the palm-lined streets of Key West. Louie had paused at several charter boat companies and she'd stood quietly by, observing flickerings of wistfulness cross his face.

Watching him, she'd wondered how he planned to finance his dream. He didn't seem to have a stash of money he could draw on. Otherwise, he'd have called someone, made arrangements to have it wired or transferred. And she seriously doubted he'd do something illegal to get the money. Despite his shifty past, she sensed he wanted to put it behind him. Otherwise, wouldn't he have returned to Jersey with Shorty, which seemed to be their home base?

Alicia would gladly give him money—after all, she had that hefty trust fund—but she knew that was asking for one of his sullen, dark looks. Maybe another closed door. He'd made it clear he didn't want her money. In fact, he seemed to resent that she had it! She'd never met a guy who felt that way about her family's wealth. Most guys had liked the perks of dating a rich girl. Well, except for Kirk. He hadn't been like that.

And Louie.

Funny, she'd never thought of the two of them as having anything in common.

So, without money, Louie was stuck in his dream world without the means to make the dream come true. The thought saddened her.

Still gazing at the No Sniveling sign, Alicia took a sip of her drink. Typically, she ordered a glass of champagne or chardonnay, but after seeing the signs around this bar—See The Lower Keys On Your Hands & Knees and Maybe We're Not For The Culturally Elite, But We're Certainly For The Culturally Deprived—she'd decided to shed her elite ways and be daring, different.

Otherwise she risked standing out like an orchid in a cacti garden.

So when the bartender had suggested a "spine-tingling drink" called the End of the World she went for it. It had doubled her pleasure when Louie flashed her a you've-got-to-be-kidding look.

She liked shaking him up, not being what he expected.

Alicia's eyes watered as the first discharge of the End of the World exploded in her mouth. This wasn't alcohol. This was jet fuel. It fired its engines and blasted through her brain, annihilating every cell in its path. Blinking rapidly, she forced herself to swallow, wincing as the liquid flamed its way down her throat.

She raised her hand to her mouth and coughed. *Spine-tingling? More like brain-melting.*

"How's your drink?" asked Louie.

Determined to be cool, she straightened and rasped, "Fine."

He cocked one eyebrow. "Disappointed it doesn't have one of those little umbrellas?"

"No," she whispered hoarsely. *Disappointed it doesn't come with a fire extinguisher.*

While Louie watched her, an amused look on his face, she bravely wrapped her burning lips around the straw and took another sip. She wanted to prove to him she was no wuss. She could sit in a dive bar, drink concoctions that could propel the space shuttle into orbit and not utter one itsy-bitsy snivel.

She stared at the mirror behind the bar as the second sip took off from the launch pad that was formerly her tongue. She fluttered her eyelids, blinking back the sting of tears, and held onto the bar. Catching her reflection, she realized her lips were no longer pink-glossed, but a ghastly red.

She glanced at the slushy crimson drink. What did this stuff do? Stain anything it came into contact with?

Making a mental note not to touch her face, chest or neck, Alicia grabbed a cocktail napkin and, after pretending to fan herself, surreptitiously wiped the tears from the corners of her eyes.

But as she was dabbing her right eye, she caught Louie's reflection in the bar mirror. He was staring at her, his amused expression replaced with a tender look. Just like the kind he'd given her back at the hotel room. The man was two men rolled into one. On the outside, the tough guy. On the inside, a regular mush. Not that he'd given her free access to Mr. Inside, but she'd glimpsed it several times through his dark armor.

Then it hit her. *He has the same problem I have. People view him as a one-dimensional bad guy just as they view me as a one-dimensional princess.* And maybe she and Louie had given in to that, played the game, because it was an easy way to protect their real selves.

She shifted her gaze from the mirror to Louie.

"You okay?" he asked, his voice deep, dusty.

"It's the drink," she said, gesturing to the curvaceous glass that looked as though it was filled with fruit juice and not jungle fire. "It's…painful." No sniveling. "But good," she added quickly. *Sort of like being with you.*

"You're crying."

"I'm teary. There's a difference."

He frowned. "Your eyes…" He squinted. "They were blue when I first met you, now they're green."

"I had on contacts that first day. Not to see, but for effect. You know, like putting highlights in my hair."

"So green is real?"

"Yes."

His gaze dropped to her breasts.

"They're real, too."

"How's it going?" The fortysomething bartender paused in front of them. His tan, lined face was the kind of craggy-handsome that had seen better days, but the sparkle in his eye said there were plenty of good ones left. He was wiping a glass, a spiraling tattoo of barbed wire around his bulging biceps.

"Drink's good." Louie took another sip of his whiskey, the glass sparkling with stray sunlight from the windows.

"Good," she seconded weakly.

The bartender's mouth kicked up in a devilish half grin as he observed her. "So you're a virgin, huh?"

She did a double take. "I beg your pardon?"

He nudged his head, indicating the drink. "Your first End of the World?"

How many can a human being endure? "Yes, my first." She coughed. "And my last."

"Then I'll take your picture, put it on our End of the World Wall of Shame."

Alicia waved her hand in front of her face, not wanting her teary eyes and fire-engine-red lips to be documented for all time.

Too late. The bartender whisked an instant camera from underneath the bar, positioned himself smack in front of her, and said, "Just say yesss!"

A blinding flash obliterated her vision.

"Thanks," she muttered, wondering when she'd be able to see again. Weepy, dyed red and now blind.

Good thing she was having a great hair day. At least something was going right.

"Am I in the picture?" asked Louie.

She heard, more than saw, the bartender yank out the film and tear it off. "It's still developing…looks like I got your hand. Hey, you want a picture of the two of you?"

"No," Louie snapped.

Alicia blinked, her vision clearing. She could see the bottles behind the bar, a green neon exit sign hovering over what must be a back door, make out the Green Parrot logo on the bartender's pec-straining shirt. "No," she echoed softly, giving in to just a bit of sniveling. But, damn it, Louie's "no" had hurt. Had she been so difficult that he didn't want to remember her at *all?*

She took another sip of her drink, realizing it didn't taste so hot on the third sip. Or was this the fourth? She took another and let it loll about in her mouth, savoring its icy sweetness. Hmm, it was starting to taste pretty tame. Maybe the End of the World wasn't so bad, after all.

Louie held out his hand, palm up, and the bartender gave him the photo. Alicia slid a glance over Louie's shoulder. In the picture she had a bug-eyed look, her neon-red lips pursed into a lopsided O. She squinted. Were her lips *swollen?*

She sucked in a quiet gasp. *I look like Goldie Hawn in that movie where she OD'd on collagen.*

"*Sure* you don't want a picture of the two of you?" the bartender asked again.

"No!" snapped Alicia, ignoring Louie's double take.

Louie was quiet for a moment. Then he asked, "What's your name, pal?"

"Keith."

Louie handed back the picture. "Here's the photo, Keith, but do me a favor. Don't display it. It doesn't do the lady justice."

Alicia's insides did a funny clench. Normally, she'd think such a comment meant a man liked her. But Louie seemed so determined to be a one-man show...

"No problem." Chuckling good-naturedly, Keith set the picture under the bar top. "Staying in the Island City long?"

"Don't know," mumbled Louie before downing another sip.

"I've been here twenty-five years," continued Keith, putting a bowl of fish-shaped crackers in front of them. "Moved here in the seventies when it was a regular brawl on the streets most nights. Mainly shrimpers in a drunken frenzy." He chuckled. "Now the frenzy is tourists' motor homes and sport utilities competing for parking spaces." He glanced down the bar. "Be right back. Got a few regulars to take care of." He moved down the bar toward a rotund guy wearing a paint-splattered muscle shirt, his arm slung around a woman in a palm-frond hat.

Feeling warm and fuzzy, Alicia looked around the room, swaying a little to the rhythmic beat of an old Beatles tune playing on the jukebox. She hummed along with the words about hiding love away. A young couple in the corner were making out, the girl's bare feet on the table. A basset hound sat underneath another table, at the flip-flopped feet of his master, staring around the bar with a woebegone expression. Scents of ocean air and French fries wafted past.

Alicia hadn't felt this peaceful in she couldn't remember how long. Funny, this *was* starting to feel like a vacation.

Her gaze swept across the scratched wooden floor, scattered with cigarette butts, to Louie's boots.

No, *boot*.

He'd shucked the other one, along with his sock. His bare foot dangled, the toes twitching to the beat of the music.

She smiled to herself. *Told him those boots would be too hot.* It might be January, but Key West was balmy, humid. She didn't dare utter a word. Louie liked being always in control, always right. She'd let him keep thinking that...

He held up his almost-empty glass, signaling Keith for another whiskey. "Want another drink, Bonbon?"

"No, I'll just nurse this one for the next decade." She smiled at Louie, dipping her head back and forth to the music. "It's nice to be here," she said lazily.

He stared at her for a long moment, as though seeing her for the first time. "It *is* nice," he agreed. "Key West is heaven on earth. My dream come true. Well, almost true."

She waited, a bit taken aback by the tone of his voice. He sounded...*happy*. "'Almost' meaning until you get your fishing business?"

"Yeah." He nodded a thank-you to Keith as he freshened Louie's drink.

After Keith left, Alicia asked, "Why the Keys?"

"This place has memories…" He swirled the amber liquid in his glass, a distant look in his eyes. "When I was nine, during Easter break, my family caravanned down here from Jersey. We camped out for several days, spent our time fishing and laughing and playing in the surf. I never forgot how magical it felt, how happy we were. It was the family I'd always wanted. And I spent more time with my dad on that trip than ever before. He taught me how to fish down here—that's where my dream of a fishing business started." He took a long sip.

She imagined a nine-year-old Louie with his family and wondered what he'd been like as a kid. Surely not as repressed and macho as he was now. Then a word he'd said hit her. "Caravanned?"

He tapped a finger against the side of his glass in time to the music. "My family was impulsive. On a whim, we'd go to the Jersey shore. Or Long Island. But sometimes my dad would get a bug to do something adventurous, call his brothers, and bada bing." Louie snapped his fingers. "There'd be several families, ours and usually my uncles', piled into cars with tents and suitcases tied on the roofs. We'd drive in a caravan to some spot. Once we drove all the way to the Canadian border. Another time to North Dakota 'cause Uncle Marty decided we kids needed to see Mount Rushmore. But my favorite trip, hands down, was to the Keys…"

Alicia liked how Louie's face relaxed as he talked. It made his ruggedness less edgy, more...noble.

Funny, she'd never thought of him as noble, but the guy had a combination of strength and smarts—and from that wistful moment recalling his family, a deep-seated gentleness—that leaders displayed. And she should know, what with all the executives and local politicians who'd paraded in and out of her life growing up. If Louie hadn't taken a shadier path, he could have been one of them.

He frowned. "What're you thinking?"

She leaned closer, inhaling his masculine scent. "You could rule the world," she whispered.

"I think you've had enough to drink." But the glint in his eyes betrayed his pleasure at the compliment.

She grinned and toyed with the idea of complimenting him some more. Swaying a little, she opened her mouth to speak...

Slam!

She could feel the bar reverberating under her fingertips.

Alicia looked past Louie. A man's beefy hand, weighted with enough gold bracelets and rings to start a small jewelry store, lay fingers-spread on the bar top next to Louie. She wrinkled her nose at the sting of cheap cologne.

"You're an easy guy to find, Lou," said a rocky voice. "Lost your touch?"

Louie slowly turned, his body preventing Alicia from seeing more than the guy's bald head and an arm that could double for a side of meat.

"How are ya, Rings?" Louie said, his voice low, even. "What brings you to Key West?"

The man laughed. A gravelly sound that lacked mirth. "Why, you, Lou!" He slapped Louie on the back. "I flew here special to kill you."

All the liquid fire she'd sipped turned to ice in her gut. She glanced at the mirror and sucked in a gasp. The guy was leaning into Louie, holding a gun dead-level with his chest!

She jerked up her gaze. Keith stood about ten feet away, his back turned to them. He was hunched over, talking quietly on a cell phone. He needed to help them, damn it, not chat on the phone!

"Let's take it outside," the man said under his breath.

"Let me get my boot on," Louie answered calmly.

"You ain't pulling a fast one on me." The man glanced past Louie at Alicia. "You. Put his boot on 'im."

"I don't know her," Louie said. "Leave her outta this—"

"Give me a break." The man chortled. "Your pal Shorty spilled everything. In plenty of time, too, for me to catch a flight down here, welcome you properly to the rest of your brief life."

Alicia swallowed, hard. So Shorty had blabbed about her and Louie flying to Key West. If this guy was hot to shoot Louie, he probably was hot to bump off Louie's new sidekick, too. Sheer, black fear swept through her.

"Put his boot on 'im," the man repeated icily to Alicia.

She sagged off the stool, and didn't stop until she was sitting on the hard floor. Vaguely aware of the stench of stale liquor and bleach, she picked up the turquoise boot. Louie was wriggling his big toe. Was he signaling her to do something?

Heavy footsteps distracted her. She peered through Louie's legs. Across the room, just inside the door, two sets of shiny black shoes came to a halt.

"Hey, officers," called out Keith. "Here to make sure we're behaving?"

She glanced up in time to see Rings ease his gun into the pocket of his Bermuda shorts. A trickle of perspiration escaped her hairline, inched painfully down the side of her face.

"You won't be so lucky next time," Rings growled to Louie. He headed past them, away from the officers, toward where she remembered that green exit sign.

Alicia stood, her knees wobbling too much to get back onto the bar stool, so instead she leaned against it and watched Keith nudge his head toward the back door, indicating to the officers that the guy who'd just slipped out was the one to follow.

After the cops left, Keith headed over to Louie and Alicia. "I saw that guy pull a gun, so I called the cops. Police station is three doors down...whenever we have trouble, those suits are here within minutes."

"Thanks," Louie muttered. "I owe you, pal."

Keith shrugged. "No problem. We get squirrelly types in here all the time. I used to wrestle knives out of people's hands, but I'm getting too old for that. Now I just slip in a call to the cops—got their number on auto-dial. That creep is probably in cuffs by now.'' He looked at the bills Louie had tossed on the counter and pushed them back. ''On the house.''

''Thanks,'' Louie answered, his face tight, controlled. He looked at the front door. ''We should split.''

''Hey,'' Keith said, ''you guys have a place to stay?''

''No,'' Louie said.

''Yes,'' Alicia said at the same time.

Keith gave them a knowing look, then checked his wristwatch. ''Listen,'' he said, ''in about twenty minutes, my friend's taking some people out on his catamaran to Dry Tortugas National Park, around seventy miles from here. I could give him a buzz, see if he'd give you a lift. You can camp cheap at the park. Three bucks a night.''

Louie waited a beat, then nodded his go-ahead.

Keith pulled out his cell and punched in a number.

Alicia leaned toward Louie and whispered, ''Let's go back to the hotel—''

''No.''

''Why?''

''Rings. He's slick, may have given the slip to the cops. If he found us here, he'd find the resort, too. How much money you got on you?''

''None!''

''Keep your voice down.''

She rolled her eyes. ''None,'' she whispered, enunciating the word. "I left my purse back at the hotel, like you asked." Well, he hadn't *asked*. He'd *ordered* her to leave behind that "straw monstrosity." "This is great," she added. "I have no clothes, no money, no cell phone, no makeup…"

God. *No makeup*. She blinked at her reflection in the mirror, wondering what she'd look like au naturel.

"Don't sweat it, Bonbon."

"You're one to talk," she huffed. "You don't have to put on your face every morning. I'm going to look washed-out, hideous…" She looked again at her reflection, wondering what Goldie Hawn looked like without mascara, lipstick, blush. Probably like Judi Dench.

Alicia sighed heavily. Maybe she was vain, but she was not stupid. If going back to get her straw monstrosity meant risking their safety, well, there were worse things than looking like the English actress.

Louie's attention was diverted to Keith, who had finished his call and was leaning over the bar, talking in a hushed tone. "Head down Whitehead toward Mallory Square. Jerry will be waiting next to one of the sunset acts, Dominique the Catman, which you can't miss. I told Jeremy how you're dressed so he can spot you."

"But lots of guys wear these flower-printed shirts," muttered Louie.

"Yeah, but not turquoise boots. I told Jerry to have some flip-flops ready so you can be more comfortable."

Louie slid a glance at Alicia, who smiled sweetly.

A few minutes later, after Louie had assured Alicia that Rings wasn't stupid enough to hang outside the Green Parrot waiting for them, they hightailed it down Whitehead.

"Can't you walk any faster?" Louie grumbled.

"These aren't running shoes," she huffed, pumping her arms to keep up. "Plus I'm not used to speed-walking after drinking."

Louie stopped. When she caught up, he bent over and scooped her into his arms. Cradling her tightly, he continued walking down the street.

"You can't carry me all the way there!"

"Like you're so fat. I've lifted bags of flour that weigh more than you."

He was strong. Although she could have guessed that after that glimpse of his muscled chest. She locked her arms around his neck—better to hold on and be helpful, right?—and inhaled his salty, masculine scent. Feeling a little drowsy, a little aroused, she sank into his embrace. She was definitely in sync with Louie now. It was the two of them against the world.

"As soon as we get to the park," Louie huffed, "you're going to call Mama and have her wire you money so you can fly back home."

She sliced a gaze up at his hardened profile. "Huhhhmmmm," she murmured. Yeah, he liked being in control, being right.

She'd let him keep thinking that....

4

―――――――

"HERE'S TWO honeymooner specials," said the guy who referred to himself as Marrying Jerry, handing two filled plastic bags to Louie.

Marrying Jerry, Keith's pal, owned the catamaran that had whisked Louie and Alicia out of Key West to safety on this tropical island—the Dry Tortugas National Park and campground—an hour-plus ride from Key West. Thanks to Keith's phone call, Louie and Alicia had slipped onto this "romantic cruise" with two just-married couples to this island for what Jerry called a sexy sunset. Afterward, the boat, minus Louie and Alicia, was returning to Key West.

Just Louie's luck that the guy who saved his and Bonbon's skins ran a frickin' *wedding* service. In the past, Louie had judiciously avoided taking dames anywhere that even *hinted* of ever-after, even his ex-wives. No overly romantic movies or dinners, no syrupy "I love you's." Not that Louie didn't treat ladies well, he just made triple sure they knew where the line was drawn in the sand.

And here he was standing in the sand with Bonbon, talking to a guy whose first name appeared to be Marrying.

I should've encouraged Rings to shoot me back at the bar.

"Thanks, pal," Louie muttered. These honeymooner specials were heavy—what the hell did newlyweds need on a tropical island? "How much I owe you?"

The guy waved off Louie's comment. "Dude, I owe Keith *mega* for saving my butt more times than I care to remember. Some times I *can't* remember, if you get my drift. Giving you a lift and some honeymoon supplies is nada. Besides, I keep bunches of these supplies on board in case any honeymooners get the urge to camp out, do the *Bohemian rhapsody,* if you get my drift."

He winked, accompanied by a clicking sound with his teeth. Then he glanced over at the couples, who were giggling and cuddling down the beach.

"Gotta vamoose," he continued, returning his attention to Louie and Alicia. "They paid for the sexy-sunset tour, then a ride back to Key West for a sightsee of what I call 'honeymoon hottie spots.'" He motioned to the bags Louie was holding. "They should have everything you need, including water. There's a phone booth at the campsite, another outside the visitor's center at the fort. I'll be back tomorrow evening, same time, for a lift back to Key West."

Louie nodded. Phones. Good. He should whisk Bonbon over there now to call Mama, but considering it'd be dark in a few hours his priority was to set up camp. But first thing tomorrow morning, he'd have

Alicia exercising her dialing finger. Meanwhile, he needed to plan how he'd shake Rings. "Thanks."

"Over there's the self-serve station to reserve a camping spot." Marrying Jerry pointed toward a metal box about forty feet away. "Great place, man," he said in an awe-filled voice, followed by that clicking sound. "Brought my old lady here a few times myself."

"Thanks *again*," Louie said, wondering when this guy was gonna split.

"Be cool and stay hot!" Marrying Jerry called out, wiggling his fingers in a two-fingered wave as he walked away.

"Sure thing," Louie said, watching their escort head back to his clients. The guy wore a bright red-and-blue-flowered shirt, a pair of cutoffs and a pair of red flip-flops.

Louie gave his head a shake, wondering if it was the sun or the booze that burned off men's macho cells down here in the Keys. Did they overindulge some night and wake up with a hangover and a hang-ten attitude?

Will never happen to Louie Ragazzi. I keep my drinks neat, my women dirty, my dream pristine.

Liking the sound of that, he smiled and turned to Alicia.

Who was staring off into the distance, her pretty face puckered with confusion. "Is *that* the hotel?" she asked, gesturing toward a towering building of red bricks that loomed at the far end of the island. She fisted her hands on her hips. "That has to be the *ugliest* resort I've ever seen."

After a beat, Louie said, "It's a historical monument, not a hotel."

"What?"

"It's the Jefferson Fort. A prison during the Civil War, named a national park in the early nineties. Weren't you listening to Marrying Jerry's spiel on the way out here? Or the campsite he just pointed out to us?" Damn, now he was saying "Marrying Jerry" as though it were a real name. He made a mental note to stop saying the marrying part—the word made him edgy.

Alicia's red-tinged mouth formed a little O of surprise. Tilting her head, as though that gave her a better view of the fort, she said, "Sorry, I didn't hear what he said just now—I was checking out the—" She waved dismissively toward the fort. "On our way here, I was busy talking to one of the girls who just got married. Do you know how inexpensive it is to get married on the beach in Key West?"

"No. And don't care." He turned and started trudging toward the self-serve reservation machine. "Let's get our camping spot."

He marched through the sand toward the machine, hearing Bonbon's little huffs and puffs behind him. When she shrieked, he glanced over his shoulder and saw her teetering and waving her hands frantically before regaining her balance.

"You should lose those heels," he grumbled.

"Aren't those boots hot?" she countered, blowing a strand of hair out of her eyes.

"No." Like he'd admit it.

A few minutes later, he stood in front of a two-by-three metallic box with numbered slots. He peeled off three one-dollar bills. "Pick a number."

"Why?"

"We reserve a camping site by the number," he said, pointing to the numbered slots. "The instructions say each number corresponds to a number painted on the site's picnic table."

Alicia gazed over the array of wooden picnic tables chained to different palm trees scattered around the small island. A white-bellied bird swept low, making a kii-kii-kii sound.

She looked up and flinched. "After those honeymooners leave, are we the only ones here?"

Louie looked around. "Only humans, anyway. But as Marrying—" Damn. "—as *Jerry* said, tourist boats start arriving first thing in the morning."

"Well-l-l," she said, playfully digging the toe of her shoe in the sand, "I'd like a room with an ocean view, room service, king-size bed, fireplace and a minibar." She grinned, her white teeth near-dazzling in the sunlight.

"You've never camped before, have you?"

She rolled her eyes. "I was *joking*."

"You didn't answer my question."

She made a noise that registered high on the sanctimonious scale.

"Great, a camping virgin," he murmured under his breath. It was going to be a long night.

She fisted her hands on her hips. "Before today, nobody ever called me a virgin. I wasn't even called a virgin when I *was* a virgin!"

She tilted her head, the sun playing wicked tricks with her hair as it sparked glints of gold and silver. Louie recalled tunneling his fingers into that silky mass of hair when he'd pinned her to that lawn...

His gaze dropped, traveling over her body the way a car takes a dangerous dip in the road. *Nobody ever called her a virgin?* Images of her naked, writhing in the throes of passion, seared through his brain.

"Are you listening?" asked Alicia.

"Huh?" he said, meeting her gaze.

"I said, two."

The word *two* turned lethal in his brain as he recalled how her two breasts strained against her dress. Two nicely rounded, perky breasts...the kind that filled a man's hands *just* right. Damn, he'd been too long without...and now here he was spending the night on a deserted island with Bonbon and her two—

"Two what?" he croaked, forcing himself to maintain eye contact.

She looked peeved. "Our campground number. I picked two."

Two. Right. He needed to ice his thoughts before he got in over his head with Bonbon. *Tonight is about survival, safety and planning the next steps in this crazy run-for-your-life fiasco. You take this side-trip into a hotter zone and you'll be in big trouble.*

"I heard you," he muttered defensively, neatly folding the bills and stuffing them, one by one, into slot number two. The last bill was particularly stubborn, forcing Louie to reinsert it several times, each thrust jacking up his testosterone level.

After damn near shoving in the last bill, Louie wiped the sweat off his brow and looked around. "Okay," he said hoarsely, "let's find campsite two." Avoiding Bonbon's eyes, and anything else Bonbonesque, he picked up the honeymoon supplies and started trudging through the sand toward the campsites.

They migrated from table to table, Alicia huffing behind him, occasionally emitting little shrieking noises that triggered flurries of overhead chirpings. Tropical breezes swirled around them, enveloping them with scents of flowers and ocean.

"How much farther?" Alicia asked breathlessly after a few minutes.

"There's only *eleven* tables," he said. "Buck up."

She gasped indignantly, muttered something about Sherman's march to the sea, then continued her huffing and puffing.

Louie was more than a little impressed with the Sherman comment. He'd labeled her as knowing how to shop and mix mimosas, but it appeared she knew some Civil War history, too.

As a kid, he'd been on the far side of academic, but one summer he'd devoured Shelby Foote's *The Civil War* trilogy. It had been more dramatic than any detective novel, his typical choice of book, maybe because it told real stories of real people struggling for survival. And at fourteen, Louie had related to that kind of struggle. And on a deeper, gut-deep, painful level, he'd wrestled with how a country could fight to abolish slavery, yet over a hundred years later people like his dad could be owned by a tire company.

"Look, look, look!" squealed Alicia, pointing a manicured nail at a table. "Table two!"

Louie paused, rubbing his cheek against his shoulder to catch a drop of sweat. Sure enough, there was their table, a big number two painted in black on its surface. A corded hammock, tied between two neighboring palm trees, swayed slightly with the ocean breezes. In the distance a pelican flew low over the water, dipping its bill into the surf.

Oh yeah. Louie envisioned sleeping in that hammock, rocked to sleep by these fragrant tropical winds, waking up to a glorious sunrise.

A nice reprieve while he figured out what to do about Rings.

"What's this piece of metal doing nailed to the tree?" Alicia was peering into what looked like a flat, shiny square of pewter.

Louie tossed the bags onto the table. "Don't know."

"Is it a mirror?" Alicia peered intently into it. "If I tried to put my makeup on with this, I'd look like a circus clown. Oh my Gawd!"

"Bonbon, forget about the makeup—"

"No!" she squealed. "Look at the sunset! It's better than a postcard!"

Louie stopped rummaging through the bags and turned. The sun, a molten ball of fire, hovered at the very edge of the world, flaming the horizon with pinks, oranges and gold.

"*That* makes any bad day good," he murmured, dropping what he was doing and heading straight for the majestic sight.

Moments later, he stood at the edge of the water and sucked in invigorating lungfuls of ocean air. Waves crashed gently in the distance, wide-winged birds wheeled overhead.

This is paradise, baby.

The muted sounds of laughter from Jerry and his honeymooning couples floated from down the beach.

And in the blink of an eye, time parted, bringing back memories to Louie of his family frolicking at the seashore on that long-ago Keys trip. In his mind's eye, Louie could see his father's face, the lines of worry hidden beneath a tan, laughing boisterously as though he didn't have a care in the world.

Before that trip, he'd never seen his father act like that. Open, relaxed, happy.

The memory disappeared, replaced again by the distant laughter.

And for an excruciating instant, Louie realized what life is. Not about dog eat dog. But about simple, happy moments that are taken for granted. And then one day, a person wishes those moments were real again, not fading images that tease the mind and weigh on the soul.

Louie blinked back a rush of emotion.

"It's beautiful, isn't it?" said Alicia, who'd walked up to stand beside him.

"Yeah." He pretended to scratch the side of his face, shielding himself from her seeing that he'd just been sucker punched by the past.

Seemingly unaware of his mood, she headed to the water, her bare feet leaving glistening imprints in the wet sand. The colors of her dress bled into the fiery sky, her slender form a sharp silhouette against the blazing sun.

And for a moment, she looked as though she were walking into his dream...becoming part of it.

She looked over her shoulder. "This feels good! Like a big, warm bath."

He nodded, amused at her reaction. He had no doubt she'd been ready to complain about the cold water and how it sloshed around her legs, but she was discovering that being outdoors could feel pretty damn wonderful.

Picking up the hem of her dress, she swished her way through the tide, giggling. The sun, again her lover just as back in the hotel room, gilded her with a honeyed glaze. Alicia didn't look human anymore. She looked...magical. Her skin radiated light, as though the sunlight had seeped through her skin and glowed in her veins. And when she giggled, Louie felt as though someone was feather-tickling his libido.

These boots are getting awfully hot.

He slipped them off and tossed them behind him.

"Wade in! The water's delicious!"

The way she said "delicious" sent shock waves of

sizzling heat through him. And despite his determination to be in control, to be a one-man show, his damn feet betrayed him as they started wading through the shallow water toward her, heading into the sun, mesmerized more by the beauty between it and him.

"Isn't it wonderful?" Alicia called out, holding higher the edge of her towel-dress.

His sexual frustration peaking, he halted a few feet from her. "I'll watch the sunset from here—"

She cut him off with a squeal. "Something brushed my leg!"

A sea monster. Come here and let me protect you. "Probably seaweed," he called out in a strained voice, some sane—or insane—part of him holding onto being a gentleman.

"I think it's time for me to get back to shore." She began marching toward him as the tide swirled around her thighs. Fighting the current, she stopped and swayed, her body leaning precariously forward.

Splash!

She toppled over, headfirst into the water.

Louie rushed forward as she popped back up, drenched from head to toe, sputtering water.

Next to her, he wrapped an arm around her back and tugged her forward, the water churning around their calves.

"Play time's over," he said gruffly, his tone hiding the fact that she'd just scared the bejesus out of him. This wasn't Coney Island. This was a frickin' piece of coral reef in the middle of nowhere. If she did something stupid, like wade out too far, she could be sucked into the sea in the blink of an eye.

He held her tightly as they walked back to the shore. Behind them, the sun sank into the horizon. In front of them, their shadows merged into one.

"I feel so dumb," she whispered.

"My fault. I shouldn't have let you wade out so far…" *I could have lost you.*

"Guess I could have seen the *real* end of the world," she said a bit too lightheartedly, shivering.

They reached solid ground—well, solid sand. Louie paused, then released his hold on her. "Forget it. You're okay, that's what matters."

She fluttered her hand to her hair.

"You look fine."

Her eyes widened.

"Great," he corrected. "Looked great even when you were falling."

He'd been with princesses before. Knew how to flatter with the best of them. But something about the yearning on her face, the need for approval, stung him. Problem with women, especially beautiful women, was the world made them feel their natural beauty was inadequate. They had to buff and shine and shellac it until it was damn near artificial. If he had his way, she'd always look the way she did at this moment. Fresh, unadorned, a little tousled.

She blinked at him, dots of water shiny on her face. Her towel-like dress, which had conformed nicely to her body before, now clung to it, leaving little to the imagination.

He quickly returned to her face. "Let's get you back to camp." Heading in that direction, he began unbuttoning his shirt. "You'll need to strip out of that wet dress. You can wear my shirt. It'll cover you…" Sort of. "…and it's dry." He hoped there was something else she might wear in one of those honeymooner bags, but he seriously doubted it.

Reaching their picnic table, he tossed the shirt onto the big painted two. "I'll stand over there—" he pointed to a palm tree a few feet away "—to give you some privacy."

He looked at her and paused. She was staring at his bare chest, her face flushed. Then she met his gaze, her eyes wet pools of sparkling sea-green.

The scent of salt from the ocean grew pungent. The air was hot, steamy…and the incessant breezes didn't do a damn thing to cool his skin.

"Take off your dress," he whispered, "before…" *I lose control. Make love to you right here, on the sand.* "Before you catch a cold."

They studied each other a little longer than was necessary. He shouldn't be allowing this to happen. "We can't go there," he said in a husky voice.

"Why not?"

"You're not like that." Yeah, she was cute and flirtatious, but she wasn't the kind of woman you took to bed and ravaged, then dropped off to fly home, never to see again.

"I could be that way tonight."

He shook his head. "No, I can't…"

What in the hell was he saying? He wanted her so

bad, his whole damn body ached. He almost laughed at himself. Tough lover-boy Louie, stuck on an island with a babe who was about to strip off her dress, and he resisted sampling the goods? This was a first.

He turned and blew out a silent breath. First thing in the morning, he was leading Bonbon straight to a pay phone. He toyed with just marching her there after she put on his shirt, but he didn't want to take the chance they might be roaming around this desolate area in the dark. What if Bonbon wandered into the ocean again?

Staring at the opposite end of the island, he saw the tiny figures of Jerry and his gang heading back to the catamaran. Louie returned Jerry's wave.

His gaze shifted to the left.

There, reflected in that piece of metal nailed to the tree, he could see the hazy image of Bonbon's naked body. Her ivory form bending this way and that, shimmering like an oasis. Dark desires, disturbing in their neediness, reverberated through him.

"I'm dressed," she finally said. "Well, halfway dressed, anyway."

He turned. The shirt hung to the top of her thighs, the mild yellow flowers paling against her golden, tangled hair and sun-kissed skin. She was starting not to even look like Bonbon anymore, but like some kind of dream-soaked island babe.

Louie's gaze dipped to her legs. Long, lean killer legs. The shirt billowed slightly, like an invitation.

"It's getting late," he whispered irritably, clenching his fists as though that helped him contain his needs. "Let's make a fire, eat, go to bed."

Go to bed. If he wasn't being such a damn gentleman, he'd gladly skip the first two and do the last.

TEN MINUTES LATER, Louie had laid out all their worldly belongings on the picnic table. A blanket, two of those instant fire logs, a sleeping bag, matches, flashlight, two jugs of water, assorted bags of food and two pairs of flip-flops.

What was it with this part of the world and flip-flops?

But the pièce de résistance was a pint of whiskey, which Louie had set to the side, in a place of honor.

"What's this?" Alicia said, picking up a bag with two fingers.

"Jerky."

"Oh."

"Haven't you ever eaten it?"

She wrinkled her nose. "I think I would have remembered."

"How about fruit?" he asked sarcastically.

"Of course," she answered. "Best to eat it before noon, though."

No, it's best to roll over and eat something else before noon...Louie tapped his fingers on the table, wishing he didn't feel so restless, so damned pent-up. It didn't help that he had a wispy blonde running around in half an outfit.

"I'll take the hammock tonight," he announced. "You can have the sleeping bag. One for me, one for you," he said, repeating the words she'd used back at their hotel room.

She stared at the sleeping bag, then looked around. "And I'm sleeping where?"

"On the sand." He ripped open the bag of jerky.

"I don't think so."

"What's the problem?"

She opened her arms wide, indicating the vast area of the island. "This is the wilderness. Wild beasts come out at night."

He blinked. "What wild beasts?"

"Spiders. Wild boars. Bears."

How did her mind work? "I don't think there's wild boars or bears here."

"So there *are* spiders!" She wrapped her arms around herself and dead-eyed the hammock. "I want to sleep there, off the ground."

"*I* want the hammock," he responded tightly. "You'll be safe in the sleeping bag, on the sand." *Away from me.* "Anyway, spiders don't like sleeping bags."

She blinked at him. "How do you know?"

"Everyone knows that. Everyone who's ever been in a sleeping bag, that is." He would bet his future fishing business she'd never seen one of those before, either.

Sure enough, she was eyeing the bag like a foreign object. "Really?"

He nodded, suddenly preoccupied with rummaging through the bags of food.

"You're lying."

Nobody called Louie Ragazzi a liar. Even when he was lying. But before he could respond with something snappy, she spoke again.

"I can tell when you're lying. Your voice sounds…hollow."

"Hollow? What the hell does that mean?"

"Means you're lying and I get the hammock."

She was good. Real good. Well, the night was still young…he still had plenty of time to get his way.

"When do we talk about Rings?" she asked for the umpteenth time.

"Let's start a fire, then eat," he said, ignoring her question. His past, and why Rings wanted Louie dead, would be lousy dinner conversation. "Going to be dark before we know it." The sky had deepened to a deep purple with wisps of pink and gold the only reminders of the sun.

He picked up the fake log, one of those prefabricated numbers laced with chemicals. "There's some driftwood in that campsite," he said, gesturing to pieces of bleached-out wood stacked in the neighboring grill. "Bring some back here."

She didn't move.

"Please."

She scampered off, the edge of her shirt rippling with a breeze. He started to pick up the box of matches when she bent over to pick up the driftwood, giving him the view of a lifetime.

His mouth went dry, and he wondered who he was kidding by playing nice guy tonight of all nights. He pulsed in every vein. The warm breezes singed his skin.

He wanted her so bad, his damn body was on the verge of exploding.

He grabbed the bottle of whiskey, unscrewed the top, and tossed back a long, deep drink as he watched her scampering back, smiling over an armload of driftwood.

"Drinking already?" she said, reaching their site. She dropped the driftwood next to the fire pit.

He didn't answer. Instead, he took another healthy swig. "Okay," he rasped, "I'll light the log. You lay out the blanket to sit on." Images of her bending over again blasted through his brain. "No, I'll do it," he added quickly.

After lighting the fire, he folded the blanket in half and laid it in on the sand. Then he tossed the sleeping bag onto the blanket. "Sit there, use the bag as a backrest."

She smiled appreciatively. "You're such a gentleman."

If you only knew. Rather than look at her, he stared into the fire. The flames crackled, their tips licking the deep blue sky. In the distance, the solitary evening star kept winking at him as though knowing the dilemma he was in.

He crouched down and handed Alicia the bottle. "Care for a drink?" She sat with her legs folded back primly, the shirt *just* covering her hips.

"What is it?" she asked.

"Whiskey. A lot tamer than The End of the World."

She accepted the bottle and took a sip. After handing it back to Louie, she patted the blanket next to her. "Sit," she whispered. "Let's eat by firelight."

He hesitated, then sat cross-legged next to her.

She giggled. "This is just what I asked for."

"My sitting next to you?"

"No, silly. Remember earlier when I said I'd like an ocean view, room service, a king-size bed, fireplace and a mini-bar?"

"You memorized the list?"

"No, it's what I always request at a hotel."

"It's not what we had at that fancy resort."

"No, they only had that one room available. But tonight, I got everything on the list."

He cocked an eyebrow. "Room service?"

"Well, you did offer me a drink of whiskey. And you laid out the bags of food on the blanket for me to help myself."

"There's no king-size bed."

"That hammock's pretty big."

"That's mine. You get the sleeping bag. One for me, one for you, remember?"

And she flashed him a look, full of simmering need and promise, that said he'd just lied again.

5

IN THE DARKNESS, Louie sank into the hammock, his body conforming to its gentle swaying. Warm, ocean-soaked breezes stroked his naked chest, arms, face. In the distance, waves crashed softly, rhythmically, lulling him to sleep…

Sleep. He hadn't had a good night's sleep in…hell, he couldn't remember. In the last year, he was always on edge, working some stressful job, feeling lousy about the man he'd grown up to be.

There was a time when he didn't think about what he did for a living. Money was money. Then, a year ago, during a Sunday-night dinner with his mother, he realized he didn't feel so good about himself. Oh, he felt good that he gave his family cash to help them out every month. Felt good helping his mother with her house repairs.

But he didn't feel good about *himself.* He could never talk about his work, although his mother and siblings knew damn well what he did—he saw it in their furtive glances, heard it in their unfinished questions. But that night at dinner, it hit Louie how he was scraping bottom, doing things he couldn't share with those closest to him, and he was glad his father hadn't lived to see what his son had become.

After that, Louie had agreed to one last job, the bull one, because he thought it would be the golden key to going straight and owning his fishing business in the Keys.

And here I am, in the Keys, with zero dough to back that dream.

He blew out a gust of air. *Turn off your thoughts. Listen to paradise.* Nearby, waves crashed and rolled, over and over, the soothing sound easing his mind. Yeah, tonight he'd earned a good night's rest. Maybe he'd blown the bull deal, maybe he barely had a cent to his name, but he was falling asleep under the stars, smack in the middle of a tropical wonderland.

Life still had its sweet moments…

He closed his eyes…

"There's something in my sleeping bag!"

He opened his eyes. "Go to sleep, Bonbon."

"How can I sleep when I'm on the ground with the spiders and you're on the hammock?" She huffed something under her breath, followed by a flurry of thrashing and rustling sounds.

He stared up at the stars, envying that they were millions of miles away. He'd thought she'd calmed down about this hammock thing after their meal, complete with swigs of whiskey, next to the fire. The dinner even more enjoyable every time Louie'd sneaked peeks at her long, lean limbs curled underneath her.

Post dinner, he'd checked out her sleeping bag in the flickerings of the dying fire. After announcing the bag was bug-free, he'd laid it out on the blanket for her to get into. Then he'd ambled over to the hammock, ready for a night of peace and quiet...

"Eeeek! I felt something!"

He released a weighty sigh. "I checked the bag before you got inside," he reminded her, forcing himself to sound reasonable, calm. "There are no spiders."

"It's a scorpion, then! Or a...a gerbil."

How *did* her mind work? To hell with reasonable and calm. "There are no bugs, or gerbils, on this island!"

"Then what do the birds live on? Fish only? I don't *think* so!" More rustling and thrashing about, punctuated with an occasional "Why does everything happen to me?"

A moment of eerie calm descended. Blessed quiet, touched only by the hush of distant crashing waves...

"I want to sleep with you!"

He should have known it was a false alarm. "We've had this talk before—"

"Not sex, *sleep!*" She muttered something about men's egos. "I want to be off the ground, out of bugland."

"This hammock's not big enough."

"It's plenty big for the two of us!" More mumbling. "Where's the flashlight?"

"Somewhere on the table."

"Help me find it."

"Why?"

She heaved a long-suffering sigh that could compete with any tropical wind. "So I can find my way safely to the hammock."

"It's farther to the table than it is to the hammock," he snapped. Damn. That might encourage her. "Just get back into your sleeping bag."

"No."

Was her voice growing closer?

"You're hogging the best seat in the house," she said sulkily.

He stared into the darkness. Was that pale blotch her? "It's not a seat, it's a—"

"Don't correct me! I want to live through the night, if you don't mind."

Live through the night? A spicy peachy scent teased his senses. Yeah, she was standing right next to the hammock, probably with her fists on her hips, glaring at where she assumed he lay.

He imagined her there, the shirt falling loosely to her thighs...the breezes lifting the hem...

His palms itched to feel underneath that shirt, touch her bare skin. She was so close, all he had to do was reach out and...

"No," he croaked, as much to himself as to her.

After a beat, her soft voice said, "You have that hollow sound again..."

She knew he was lying. Okay, so he wanted her, *bad*. But damn it, this was *not* the kind of woman to have hot, unbridled, jungle sex with. Not unless he wanted a hot, unbridled, jungle wedding, too. He could see it now. He and Bonbon on a tropical beach, the "sexy sunset" behind them, Marrying Jerry doing that two-fingered wave and saying, "I now pronounce you two to be..." Louie squeezed shut his eyes. *Argghhh.*

The peachy scent wafted closer. "If you don't let me sleep with you," Alicia whispered, "I'll call the judge instead of my mother in the morning, say you're violating your special conditions—"

In a flash, Louie rolled over, his feet hitting the cool sand. He reached into the darkness until he touched something soft. Her shoulder. He grabbed hold and tugged her close, his arm snaked tight around her back.

He tried not to think that if he felt her back that meant her shirt was shoved above her naked tush...

He inched his face forward until he felt puffs of warm breath from her lips. He hovered there, angry and aroused, his lips brushing hers. Abruptly, he slid his mouth across her salt-tinged cheek until he nudged a soft earlobe.

"Cool it, baby," he whispered hotly, "I don't react well to threats."

Her body tensed. "I'm not threatening—"

"Don't pull that crap on me," he said. "You're a spoiled brat who's threatening me to get her way. Tell you what. Call the judge. He'll have the cops pick me up and I'll get free transportation to a secure jail, which is a hell of a better deal than figuring out how to shake Rings on my own."

His hand cupped the small of her back, her skin hot, moist underneath his fingers.

"I'm sorry," she whispered, her lips moving against his neck.

"You should be."

"I'm scared."

"Join the club."

"*You* get scared?"

"I'm human, too." Too human. He pressed his fingers harder against her back, holding them in place so they didn't drift down over that curvaceous, naked bottom…

"Human?" She giggled softly. "Thought you were my guardian angel."

"Baby, I lost my wings a long time ago…"

Guardian angel?

Wings?

This conversation had taken a wrong turn. Next they'd be having one of those touchy-feely talks that women liked to have in the dark.

He released his hold on her and stepped back, the breezes almost chilly as they collided with the hot sweat on his body. "Let's check your bag again, get you tucked back into bed," he growled.

"Can we negotiate?"

"No."

"Please?"

Man, if anybody had a "never say die" attitude, it was Bonbon. What was he thinking? Yeah, he could march her back to her sleeping bag, do the bug check again, but he could see this little drama repeating itself all night long.

Time to try another tactic.

"Doll," he said, pumping sincerity into his voice, "we've had a hell of a day. For me, a hell of a week. You got to be as dead tired as I am. Let's go to bed."

"I've had a hell of a week, too, you know. I almost got married."

Like he was going to get sucked into chatting about the M-word at a time like this. "Let's go to bed," he repeated, fighting hard to keep the warm fuzzy in his voice.

"Let's." She placed her small hands on his chest. "I promise we'll only sleep. No hanky-panky."

The way she said hanky-panky, all sweet and a little achy, made his skin prickle.

"I'll stay on my side of the hammock," she whispered.

His groin tightened. "I don't think it's a good idea—"

"Oh, we'll be fine," she said cozily, obviously sensing her advantage. She evaporated into the darkness. "I'll get the blanket. I'll wrap myself up in it, like protection, you know?"

Like protection. Like he didn't have any even *if* they were planning on doing the horizontal rumba.

But we're not *doing* anything, he reminded himself, scraping his hand across his face. Plus, she'd have the blanket for "protection." And he was still wearing these damn chef's pants. Toss in his underwear, and there were *three* sets of protection—what could go wrong?

Damn, he was already buying in to her sleeping with him…

This is going to be a long night. Long long long…

"I'm back!" Muffled noises. A series of soft creaks. She was on the hammock, just where she'd wanted to be all along.

She was good. Really good.

Well, tomorrow she'd be on her way back to Denver, out of his life forever. He stepped forward, felt the taut cords of the swinging bed.

"I'm on the far side, just get in," she whispered.

It was like her frolicking in the ocean all over again. Just out of reach, her sun-kissed body tormenting him. And his feet had betrayed him as he waded toward her like a man whose rock-hard willpower had been pulverized into ash.

No part of my body will betray me tonight, he assured himself as he rolled cautiously onto the hammock. It swayed as he settled in. The blanket touched his bare chest, the texture rough against his skin.

"Comfy?" she whispered.

"Sure."

"Sleepy?"

"Don't start—"

"You're so defensive! Sheesh, just checking how you're doing."

"I'm sleepy," he grumbled. He stared up at the sky. *Oh, to be a distant star.*

"Good," she whispered. She moved a little, adjusting the blanket. As she got comfortable, she made little needy, mewing sounds deep in her throat.

He felt himself go hot and rigid.

Finally, she stilled. "Nighty-night," she whispered cheerily.

"G' night."

She giggled softly. "Don't let the bedbugs bite."

Oh, that would be the least of his worries...

ALICIA'S EYELIDS fluttered open. She blinked, wondering who'd repainted her Antoinette-pink bedroom ceiling...then realizing the overhead color—a sharp, clear blue—was the *sky*.

The island. Louie. Hammock. It came back in bits and pieces.

She shifted to get up.

And froze.

Underneath her shirt, a hand covered her left breast.

A very large, very warm hand.

Her heart kicked up a notch.

She slid a sideways look. Louie lay curled next to her, his brown, carpeted chest swelling with each sleeping breath. One hand was underneath her shirt, his other rested against her blanket-covered hip.

She shifted her gaze. Although her bottom half had managed to remain covered, a teeny part of her rump stuck out of the blanket—a beige curve streaked with rays of sunlight.

She glanced at the rest of his body. He still wore those chef's pants, now hopelessly wrinkled and dirt-streaked, but they were still *on*.

Which meant they hadn't...no, surely she'd remember...

She thought back. Her last memory was an exchange of good-nights before falling asleep. Add that this morning he was still partially dressed, so obviously nothing had happened…

Except at some point his hand had found her breast. And the way it lay on her, it felt…comfortable. Not sexual. Not really.

Oh yes, really…

Desire, like liquid heat, trickled into her veins. And her nipple, eager to get into the act, blossomed to full, erect attention underneath his palm. Instinctively, she arched, just a little, and her nipple eased itself between two of his splayed fingers, their hard surfaces damn near squeezing her ever-hardening tip.

Holding her breath for fear she'd start panting, she glanced at Louie's face again, amazed at his relaxed, innocent countenance. Not a flicker of desire. In fact, he looked peacefully protective, a sleeping man watching over a woman he cared about.

She paused, pondering that look.

Could he really feel that way about her? Wanting to protect her, love her, be the man at her side?

Maybe the protecting part, but the rest was pure Alicia fantasy. But since her mind had gone there, and he was here, so what if she fantasized a bit? It was hardly a sin to dream of what she wanted for a few precious moments.…

She closed her eyes and released a slow stream of pent-up breath, selfishly savoring the intimacy of being held by Louie, sharing his bed. Imagining a lifetime of this, waking up in the safety of his arms, a sheltered place untouched by the world's petty problems.

Untouched by loneliness.

The last thought made her heart clench. Well, that's how it was in her life back home. Lonely. Even surrounded by her mother's socialite friends and hangers-on, she'd felt this way.

But not with Louie.

Alicia slitted open her eyes and slowly, oh so slowly, rested her hand very gently on his jaw, her fingers barely touching his warm, stubbled face. She tilted her head slightly, studying how a lock of raven hair fell over his relaxed, unlined brow. And over his eye, there was that small, jagged white scar. A distant memory he still wore on his face. What else had happened in his past to make him this tough, guarded man?

Her gaze shifted to his mouth. His full, sensuous mouth.

She frowned. *A mouth that's probably sucked face with hundreds of women.*

A jolt of jealousy shot through her as she fought images of those faceless women who'd greedily received Louie's love. They'd probably gotten the full banquet treatment and Alicia, like Cinderella with her stepsisters, had barely snacked on an appetizer before it'd been yanked away.

Jealousy morphed into a raging moment of self-pity.

He'll never kiss me again. He'd come on to her in

the pantry, and then on the lawn, and after taunting her with a deliciously wicked taste of his passion…

Nothing.

His hand wouldn't even be touching me intimately right now if he was awake.

Alicia shut her eyes, aching to have him as the real thing. If he only realized that beneath their physical attraction—and she *knew* he had major hots for her—there was more. It wasn't easy to articulate, but just as she knew she'd run *to,* not *from,* a place this time, she also knew she'd met her match.

Met her man.

Yes, it was crazy being on the run for their lives, some gangster named Rings on their tails, *camping out* for God's sake…and yet, she and Louie made sense. *If he'd only realize that between his feelings for his family and dreams, and my need to have my own family and roots, we're like two people searching for the same home.*

His hand twitched, slightly squeezing her breast, then relaxed again.

Ever so casually, she slipped him a peek.

His eyelids flickered slightly. His tongue ran across his bottom lip, then he frowned. Sleepily, he slid a look at her hand on his jaw, then down at her shirt, under which he still cupped her breast.

Then down to that flash of rump, pink and golden in the morning light.

Before he looked back up, she closed her eyes, forcing herself to breathe in and out. Gently. Evenly. *Like I'm asleep, lying here totally unaware he's touching my breast.* She *hoped* she looked innocent, a look she'd never really practiced in the mirror.

They remained frozen in place, but Alicia knew darn well their minds were whirling with heated possibilities. One shift of a hand and...

But no-o-o.

She felt Louie, with painstaking slowness, inch his big, hot male fingers off her breast. Then he touched her hand that rested on his jaw, laying his fingers on top of hers for the briefest of moments, before gently pulling her away.

She opened her eyelids a millimeter, observing him through her lashes. He looked at his hand that had been on her breast, studying it as though it didn't belong to him. Then he rubbed his fingertips together and held them to his nose.

Damn if he didn't close his eyes and inhale, deeply, the way someone might sniff a flower. He opened his eyes and the sunlight slanted across them and Alicia saw how they glittered with a smoldering intensity.

He wants me.

Dropping his hand, he moved cautiously into a sitting position, catching himself whenever the hammock swayed. He braced his arms on either side of him, his chest heaving deep breaths, as he stared out at the ocean, his back to her.

Take me! I'm right behind you!

But he continued staring at the distant ocean, his brown, muscled torso blocking her view.

Well, no use pretending to sleep anymore...

Alicia feigned a little yawn and stretched, purposefully wriggling a little bit to shake the hammock. When Louie turned to look at her, she blinked "awake" and smiled at him. "Morning."

"Morning."

She propped herself on one elbow, the hammock rocking slightly. A bird swooped overhead, chattering.

"Sleep well?" Louie asked.

"Yes. You?"

"Very well, yes." His dark eyes flickered heat. Sunlight fell in dappled gold across his chest, burrowing into the dark mass of chest hair.

Pin a gold earring on the man, and he'd look like a wicked pirate.

Shipwrecked on a deserted island. A dark, bad-boy pirate, a not-so-innocent fair maiden. The state of Florida would have to rename this place Pleasure Island...

Glancing over her shoulder, Alicia surreptitiously pressed her suddenly moist palm against the blanket. "No tourist buses, yet."

"Yeah, we're still alone."

Their eyes locked, and she swore they were breathing in unison.

"You know what we have to do?" he finally said, his eyes narrowing behind a screen of black lashes.

Electricity crackled along her skin. Oh...yesyesyes.

"No," she whispered shakily. "Tell me."

"We have to call your mama."

6

"STAY COOL, be hot," Jerry called out to several couples who were heading toward the metal reserve-a-campsite box on Dry Tortugas.

Louie felt sorry for the guys, all wearing Hawaiian shirts with color-coordinated flip-flops, obviously victims of the burned-off-brain-cells syndrome. The guys carried matching "honeymooner special" plastic bags while trudging dutifully behind their just-marrieds.

Okay, so Louie was wearing one of those flower-printed shirts himself, but it was that or go bare-chested. Anyway, the shirt was wrinkled and dirty, which proved his macho cells were intact.

And if he thought too long about how this shirt looked on Bonbon, he *knew* his macho cells were fully functioning.

Turning back to Louie and Alicia, Jerry made that clicking sound with his teeth. "You two wanna stay for the sexy sunset?"

"No," Louie answered. "We need to go—plane to catch." He shifted the plastic bag from one hand to another. Minus the food, logs and water, all the "honeymooner" supplies fit easily into one sack.

"Flight, eh?" Jerry said with a smile. "Next stop on the honeymoon?"

"No," Louie snapped. How could a man be in the wedding business and look so damn happy?

"Well, I got your bag from Keith, just like you requested." After a neat one-eighty on his flip-flops, Jerry started heading to the catamaran that was docked a few feet away.

Louie paused. "What?"

But Jerry, bobbing his head to some unheard tune, kept walking toward the boat.

Louie shifted his gaze to Alicia. "What's he talking about?"

She stood a few feet in front of Louie, blinking prettily at him over her tan shoulder. Louie checked out her posture, wondering if she was slouching like that to stay within the shrunken—thanks to yesterday's dip in the ocean—boundaries of her now dry towel-dress.

Or slouching out of guilt?

Oh yeah, she's hiding something. He could read people as good as any shrink. And right now Bonbon was easier to read than a flaming-red stop sign.

"What'd you do?" Louie asked.

"What'd *I* do?" she squeaked, her voice rising with her eyebrows.

That cinched it. Her little cultured act always got shaky when she was up to no good. Somehow, she'd contacted Keith which wasn't a sin in itself…but *why* she'd contacted him was a question that tasted bad—'specially because she hadn't mentioned anything to Louie.

Besides the why, he couldn't figure out when, either. He'd been sitting right next to her at the Green Parrot, heard every word she'd said to Keith and they'd never once discussed anything about luggage. Hell, the guy didn't even know where her luggage was…

No, Bonbon had pulled this *after* that. Louie shoved his mind into reverse…

This morning, after they'd rolled out of that hammock, and she'd shrink-wrapped herself into the dry towel-dress, he'd escorted her to a nearby phone booth. He'd stood smack next to her while she placed a collect call to her mother in Denver. While the phone was ringing, Louie had taken the receiver and, when a man answered, asked for Alicia's mother. Informed Mrs. Hansen wasn't home, Louie asked who was speaking and was told Alexander. Covering the receiver, Louie had mouthed the name to Alicia, who'd mouthed back, "My brother."

Satisfied Bonbon hadn't pulled a fast one, Louie had given the phone back to her and listened while she chattered about being safe in Florida, well, except for "island spiders." In the middle of explaining how they ran rampant at night, she'd sucked air down a wrong pipe and gone on a coughing jag.

And Louie—the gent—had trotted the forty-or-so feet back to their campsite, poured a plastic cup full of water and brought it back to Princess Storyteller.

Oh yeah, he got what had *really* happened. In those

few minutes he'd played water boy, she'd screwed him over.

He recalled how she'd slowly drunk the water, peering at him over the rim of the glass. Those green eyes glistening...and he'd thought she was flirting with him again.

Louie needed to do a rehaul of his male ego. She hadn't been flirting, she'd been *gloating*.

After finishing off the water, she'd licked her plump lips, chirped *"Ciao!"* to her brother, then hung up and told Louie this amazingly detailed story about her brother logging onto a computer while they were on the phone and booking her on a 9:05 p.m. Key West-to-Denver direct flight that very evening.

Nine-oh-five. What a little actress.

"So," Louie said, wishing to hell he had some cigarettes so he could bite off their filters. "You didn't ask your brother to call the airport. You had him call Keith."

Sucking in a self-righteous breath, she opened her mouth to speak.

"Can the story," Louie growled. "Answer the question."

She snapped shut her mouth, blinked, then dipped her head in the affirmative.

"And," Louie continued, "there's no plane reservation."

She dipped her head again.

"What'd you think you were accomplishing, Bonbon?" He started edging toward her. "Buying time?"

She did a half nod, her lips parting as though she wanted to say something.

He moved closer.

So close, he could count the freckles across the bridge of her pert, sunburned nose. He leaned in and whispered, "Thought you'd learned by now, Bonbon. You mess with me, you mess with trouble."

Her tongue darted along her bottom lip. "My intention," she whispered shakily, "never was to 'mess' with you."

Louie looked over her shoulder at Jerry, who was busy checking something on the boat. Louie shifted his gaze back to Alicia. "Then what the hell was your *intention?*"

She swallowed, hard. "To get my bag and purse from the hotel room."

Louie nodded, slowly. "You could have had your brother help with that *and* make your plane reservation."

"But..." She gestured with the hand that gripped her sandals by the straps, while she shuffled one of her flip-flopped feet in the sand. "I don't want to leave you alone. I want to help you."

He snorted. "I can't shake Rings if I have you hanging on me, Bonbon. You're not help, you're a liability."

He swerved away from that hurt look in her eyes to again check out Jerry, who was waving them to come aboard. "When we get onto the boat," Louie said, "you're getting out that pretty cell phone of yours from that straw-monstrosity purse and calling

Mama. And don't start that crap about calling some judge or the police. No funny business, got it?''

"Got it.'' She offered a wobbly smile.

"Let's go.'' Louie started trudging through the sand toward the boat, knowing in his gut that ordering Bonbon to behave was like waving a red flag at a bull.

"STAY COOL, be hot,'' Marrying Jerry called out as Louie and Alicia headed from the dock toward Key West.

Louie waved over his shoulder at Jerry, who stood under a street lamp wiggling his signature two-fingered salute. "Wonder if he ever just says 'good-bye,''' Louie muttered.

Those were the first words he'd spoken to Alicia in over an hour.

She glanced at Louie, who wore the same menacing scowl he'd had ever since she'd confessed to not making her plane reservations. A scowl that had deepened when, on the boat ride home, she'd discovered her cell phone battery was dead.

After that, it had been a long, painfully quiet ride back to Key West. If Marrying Jerry hadn't belted out a few songs about tequila and women, the only sounds would have been the roar of the motor and the splashing waves.

"Let's find a phone before Rings finds us,'' Louie said, stopping in the midst of an endless flow of people along the beachfront sidewalk. Sea breezes picked up scents of suntan lotion and perfume. The bustle of

Key West was to their left, the silent ocean to their right.

"First," Louie said, scanning the crowds. "I'll call the airport and reserve a flight home for you, then you'll call Mama and give her the flight info. I'm not letting you screw it up this time, Bonbon. Let's go."

They continued weaving their way through evening crowds. Ahead, a guy wearing shorts decorated with cigarette-smoking happy faces juggled shot glasses and a bottle of vodka. A palm-frond hat, filled with an assortment of bills, lay at his feet.

"Here we go," said Louie. Gripping Alicia's elbow, he guided her to an open-air phone booth. Next to it sat a woman with long black hair and a sandwich board that read Madame Manisa, Psychic Readings $15. Several sticks of incense burned at the woman's feet, the wisps of smoke fading into the night air.

Madame Manisa shifted her heavily made up eyes to Alicia.

Alicia smiled weakly, wondering if the woman took plastic. What Alicia would give to know her future—specifically the next few minutes of it. A kid with a boom box skated past, the Beatles tune "Help!" blasting, which further aggravated her need to stop Louie from putting her on a plane.

But no matter what she wanted, desperately wanted, Alicia had the sinking feeling he was going to get his way this time.

She hated to think of him alone in Key West with that jewelry-store wannabe chasing him. Except for some pocket change, Louie had no money—how'd he expect to survive in the jungle without credit cards?

Digging in her heels—not an easy task in flip-flops—she halted. "Can we talk for a moment?"

Louie shot her an irritated look. "Sorry, I'm fresh outta chitchat." He tugged her into the booth, where he picked up the receiver and shoved in several quarters.

"We could use one of my credit cards," she continued, trying not to think how squishy tight it was in here, how their bodies pressed together. "We could fly anywhere. Paris. Rome."

"Right. And I have a passport tattooed on my—"

"New York, then." Damn, the man smelled good. Musky and masculine. "L.A."

Shooting her a you've-got-to-be-kidding look, Louie growled, "Gotta clean this up with Rings. Wouldn't matter if I hitchhiked to Fargo, he'd follow me."

"Then let me stay with you. You don't have any money and I can help."

With the receiver wedged under his chin, Louie eyed the flow of people up and down the sidewalk. "No."

She raised her chin a notch. "I refuse to go."

"Tough."

She'd offer sex, but *knew* that wouldn't work. Once this guy made up his mind, he was like a wall—thick and immovable.

But not dense. Oh nooo. He was sharp. Calculating. She'd have to be slick to get her way.

Slick and sweet.

"Okay," she said, pouring some sugar into her voice. "The truth is, I can't run from the place I ran *to*. Even if you make me fly away, I'll just hop on another plane and return." And in her gut, she knew she'd do just that. "Then you'll have two people chasing you. Me and Rings." She smiled sweetly and batted her eyes, hoping to coax a smile out of Louie the Wall.

"Great," Louie grumbled. "Two-for-one special."

Forget slick and sweet. She opened her mouth to say something slick and snappy, but Louie started talking.

"Operator," he said into the receiver, "connect me to Delta airline reservations."

He covered the receiver with his hand. "I'll call your mama and tell her you're planning a return trip."

"Now look who's threatening to make phone calls!"

"Reservations?" he said coolly into the receiver, ignoring Alicia's outburst. Without breaking eye contact with her, he said, "Yeah, I want *one* ticket, *one*-way, Key West to Denver tonight."

That man needs to learn to love another number. Alicia made a great show of looking away, her only comeback to his brazen what're-you-gonna-about-it stare.

In the throng of passersby, a fleshy woman, her breasts spilling out of her halter top, giggled loudly as she did a little dancing step alongside a ruddy-faced guy wearing a Hogsbreath T-shirt. The couple, obviously indulging the Margaritaville life, laughed and kissed.

Wish I'd kissed Louie one more time. Not that Alicia would let the stubborn control-freak *know* that, but it didn't stop her wishing for it. She'd tasted his hot, I'm-gonna-take-you kiss on the lawn that had ended as quickly as it started. Before he forced her to leave Key West, it would be sweet to taste something different, something to remember, like a steamy, lingering kiss…

The kind of kiss she'd halfway expected this morning in the hammock. The way he'd inhaled her scent with that simmering look in his eyes, she'd have sworn the man wanted it as bad as she did. She'd never met a guy who placed such a value on self-control. Which left her wondering whether to be irked or impressed.

The woman's giggles brought Alicia back to the present. She watched the woman dance away, her laughter fading.

While glancing back at the meandering pedestrians, Alicia suddenly caught a clear view of the restaurant across the street, a windowless shacklike structure decorated with flashing beer signs. Its interior and sidewalk tables were well lit, beckoning partyers with false sunlight before the real thing rose again in paradise.

At one of the outside tables, sipping a drink, sat a man. His bald head like a fleshy beach ball.

Rings.

Alicia's insides contracted.

She glanced down at the sidewalk and stared at the pool of light on the cracked cement. Damn. This phone booth was under a street lamp.

If I caught a look at Rings through this crowd, did he do the same?

Don't panic. She slowly lifted her gaze and turned, stiffly, toward Louie. Her eyes watered as she stared at the scratched names of lovers on the metal wall of the phone booth. Tiger Lovs Melody 1999.

"Rings," she whispered hoarsely, staring at the names, crazily wondering why Tiger didn't know how to spell *love*.

Louie remained engrossed in his phone conversation.

She gulped in a fortifying breath, catching the pungent scent of incense.

"Rings," she whispered again, pressing her shoulder against Louie's, trying to peer through the meandering tourists to catch another glimpse of the restaurant. But a sea of Hawaiian-print shirts, bare fleshy arms and tank tops blocked her view. For all she knew, Rings could have left, was on his way over here, fingering that pistol...

"That flight works—" Louie frowned at Alicia and covered the mouth piece. "Bonbon, stop flirting and get me a credit card."

She tapped her flip-flop hard, several times, against Louie's booted toe. If the man thought *that* was flirting, he'd been alone too long. "Rings," she said in a guttural voice she didn't recognize.

His face tightened. "Where?"

"Across the street."

"Did he see us?"

"Maybe."

"Hell." Louie hung up the phone. "Let's split."

Hand in hand, they merged with the crowd, drifting along like pieces of human flotsam. Someone sloshed beer on Alicia's foot, but she barely registered the cold assault as she sneaked a last peek over her shoulder.

The restaurant seat was empty.

"He's gone," she whispered, hearing the growing hysteria in her voice.

"Stay cool, be hot," Louie said, picking up his pace.

She choked back a laugh. "You pick funny times to play comedian."

"Near-death brings out the best in me. Here." He turned sharply, forcing her to make an abrupt right with him down a stubby walkway.

The unexpected movement caught her off guard. She stumbled forward a few feet, dropping her Gucci and straw bags, losing Louie's grip. As she staggered, fighting for balance, she heard a shrill, wheezy party whistle before she tripped and pitched forward.

As a patch of dirty cement reared up to meet her, she realized that sound was from *her*.

Big hands gripped her waist.

Louie's face appeared.

A blur of green and purple.

WHOMP.

She was lying on a narrow strip of soft sidewalk, gasping for air, her vision black as night.

No, she was staring into Louie's hair. And it wasn't a soft sidewalk, it was *Louie's body.*

She pulled back her head and stared into his pain-filled eyes. "I'm sooo sorry—"

"Get...off...me," he wheezed.

She rolled sideways, her butt making contact with the warm, sticky cement. Shrubbery and bougainvillea lined either side of this narrow walkway. *So that was the green and purple.* Several feet away, tourists paraded along the same sidewalk she and Louie had just been on, their forms shadowing the entrance to this walkway.

Glancing down, she nearly shrieked at the sight of her dress scrunched up to her midriff, the only thing between her and God a pair of bikini fuchsia-pink undies.

A catcall pierced the air.

Tugging down her errant dress, she scrambled to her feet and snatched her bags that had tumbled a few feet away. "Rings is going to be part of that tourist procession any moment," she said on a rush of air. "Can you get up?"

"My...ankle." Louie muttered an expletive.

She glanced behind her.

The walkway led to a white Victorian building with what looked like a lighthouse behind it, both of them highlighted with pinpoints of pink, green and red lights. A hanging sign on the Victorian porch said Lily's Lighthouse Inn.

Alicia stretched her hand to Louie. "Take my hand."

Surprisingly, he did as told.

"Stand on your good foot, pull yourself up."

Leveraging himself with the aid of her hand, Louie stood.

"It'd be stupid to go back to the sidewalk and try to walk, so we're going inside this place," she whispered. The Victorian house had a short set of stairs to its porch. "We've got a few steps ahead of us. Lean on me. I'm stronger than I look."

"Tell me something I don't know."

As though in a three-legged race, they did an awkward hopping-walking while lugging bags up the stairs, across the narrow whitewashed porch and through the beveled-glass French front doors.

As the door closed behind them, Louie glanced over his shoulder.

"Any sign of—?" whispered Alicia.

"No."

The girl behind the desk, wearing a tie-dyed T-shirt dress with strings of coral necklaces, looked at them as though hopping, wincing people were nothing out of the norm in Key West.

"Can I help you?" she asked.

"Yes," Alicia said, snuggling a little closer to Louie. "My groom and I would like a room."

He groaned.

"Darling," Alicia cooed, glancing at a wicker loveseat between the registration desk and front door. "Why don't you sit there while I check us in?"

"One for you, one for me," Louie growled, hobbling toward the seat.

"Oh, newlyweds!" the girl said, typing something into a computer. "You're in luck. We have one room available, in the lighthouse—the Guiding Light Room." The girl giggled. "There's no light anymore, but Lily's a soap-opera nut so there you have it. The room's *awesome* for a wedding night. *Very* romantic. Folklore says Captain Josiah, the infamous Captain J, once stayed there. Some people think the eerie groans are his ghost, but really it's just the metal contracting at night."

"Probably ticked his bachelor pad turned frou-frou," muttered Louie.

"Sounds great," Alicia said, raising her voice to drown out Louie. She dropped her bags and traipsed to the desk. "And we'd like a bottle of champagne—Taittinger, preferably—and two flute glasses." She smiled over her shoulder at Louie. "Just like you asked for, honey. Two glasses. One for you, one for me."

He rolled his eyes.

"Fill out this registration form," the girl said. "And I'll need an imprint of a credit card." The girl picked up a phone. "We don't have room service, but I'll call the corner liquor store and have some champagne delivered. Can you write down that brand again?"

"Certainly," Alicia chirped, scribbling Taittinger at the top of the registration form.

The girl leaned over and spelled out the letters to whoever was on the other end of the phone. "They just got married," she added, then paused. "Oh, let me ask." She looked at Alicia. "What's your last name?"

Alicia blinked. "Rigatoni."

"Hammock," Louie said at the same time.

The girl looked at Alicia, then Louie.

Alicia coughed. "Hammock. Right, it's Hammock. I'm, uh, starved, thinking of dinner. Rigatoni. My favorite. Little spumoni for dessert and life just doesn't get much better than that!" She plastered a big fake smile on her face.

The girl blinked, then returned the smile. "No problem," she finally said. "There's a phone in the room. Lots of places deliver." She spoke back into the receiver. "For the champagne, deliver it to the lighthouse, for a Mr. and Mrs. Hammock."

LOUIE PLOPPED down on the bed in the Guiding Light Room, swiveled his body and let his head drop back onto a soft, lacy pillow. He'd managed to hobble up the spiraling iron staircase to the top of this lighthouse room, a feat he never wanted to repeat as long as he lived.

He swiped at his brow, grateful for the open window that let in breezes from the ocean. The yellow light from an overhead bulb highlighted the curve of the walls and it struck him he'd never been in a round room before. *Unnerving not to see corners.* Like not knowing the rules. Not that he cared about them, but it was always good to know which ones you were breaking.

He did a quick inventory. Just enough room for the

bed, a door he figured led to the bathroom, a few pieces of white wicker furniture, and an oversize white claw-foot bathtub smack in front of the window.

He hadn't seen this much white since his first communion.

He sucked in another lungful of salty ocean air. He hadn't felt like talking while navigating those steps. It had been enough of a test to hop and breathe. But now he wanted to ask the question that had been on his mind.

"Rigatoni?"

"Huh?" Alicia sashayed into the room, breathing normally, as though the trek up the staircase was a mere jaunt.

What did she do to stay in shape? Speed shop?

"Oh, *Rigatoni*." She tossed her Gucci bag on the floor. "It's your last name, right?"

"Rigatoni—" he winced as a pain flashed through his ankle "—is a *pasta*."

She did an empathy wince. "We need to get that boot off." She headed toward the bed and pointed to his left foot. "This one?"

He nodded.

She wrapped her orange-tipped fingers around it and gently tugged. "That's what it said on your plane ticket," she said with a grunt as she pulled.

Cool air assailed his foot. He'd run out of socks, so he'd been wearing these damn boots barefoot. He wriggled his toes. Free at least. "Said what?"

"Rigatoni."

He stopped wriggling. "It said *Ragazzi*. Louie Ragazzi." Next she'd think his middle name was ravioli.

She held up the boot, the turquoise almost matching her eyes. "Your last name's Ragazzi?"

"Yes."

"Oh, that's right. I knew that when you were booked. Just forgot." She tossed the boot onto the floor. "Ragazzi. Sounds like a gangster's name." Her eyes widened. "Oops. Sorry."

"Former gangster," he muttered. Couldn't believe he was talking about this, openly, to a blue-blooded dame in a round white room. Plus, here he'd successfully avoided taking women anywhere that even *hinted* of ever-after—even the ex-wifeys—and he ends up with one in a bridal-white room on his "wedding night."

If any of the guys back home heard about this, they'd accuse Louie of going soft.

Alicia was tugging off his other boot. "I was thinking that's how it is."

"How what is?"

"That what you've done in the past is...in the past." She smiled, tossing the second boot in the general vicinity of the first. "I'm thinking who I was is in the past, too."

For a moment, they shared a look. Her Caribbean-sea eyes, the color of his dreams, momentarily took him away from his bad mood the way a ship rides the waves away from life's problems.

She broke their locked gaze and looked at his foot again. "Oh," she said, elongating the word until it sounded like the saddest sound in his sorry life. "Your poor ankle."

"I'll be okay."

"It's a little swollen." Alicia touched it, her fingertips cool against his skin. Then she looked up at him with big, dewy eyes. "That's why I ordered the champagne. There'll be lots of ice in the bucket."

"You ordered champagne for the *ice?* Don't joints like this have ice machines?"

"We're in a *lighthouse.*"

Good point. But he didn't want to give it to her.

"Hungry?" she asked.

"Yeah."

"I'm starved. We should order food soon." She was running her fingers lightly along his ankle, the heat from her fingers seeping through his skin. "That hurt?"

You kidding? "No."

She gave a little squeeze. "This?"

Hurt me more. "No."

She squeezed again. "This?"

He flinched, then glowered at her. "Doll, let's cool the pain-threshold search."

"Sorry," she whispered apologetically. "Did I squeeze too hard?"

Maybe it was the way her voice blended sensuously with the sea breezes, or maybe he'd been without too long, but the damn question was giving him a hard-on.

"I was squeezing to check your ankle, which isn't broken, by the way. Just wrenched. Same thing happened to me at a debutante ball when I slipped in my heels on a marble floor. We'll elevate your foot, wrap it in ice, you'll be as good as new in no time."

He grudgingly appreciated her somewhat-qualified prognosis. To be honest, he also appreciated her fast thinking, getting the two of them inside this joint. Hell, even thinking fast enough to say Rigatoni instead of her real last name was good. Real good. Her never-say-die attitude had probably done just that...saved their lives.

"Thanks." He smiled at her, the first one since they'd left the island.

"For what?"

"For saving our butts."

Her face lit up. "You're welcome," she said, her face softening. "I was curious—why did you say our last name was hammock?"

Our last name. She was pushing the envelope, but he didn't feel as riled up as he normally got. Hell, bottom line, they were in this together—it didn't get more committed than that in Louie's world.

"It was the first thing that came to my mind," he answered, liking how the overhead light burnished a golden spot on Bonbon's hair. "If we registered under one of our real names, we might as well send out a written invitation to Rings for a visit."

Louie didn't want to elaborate on how, by now, Rings no doubt had their whereabouts narrowed down to a few blocks. At this very moment, he was probably on a pay phone, calling local lodgings, checking if an Alicia Hansen or Louie Ragazzi were registered. From experience, Louie knew lodgings wouldn't divulge the name on Alicia's credit card. At most, they'd check the registration and confirm a Mr. and Mrs. Hammock were here.

Alicia was sitting on the edge of the bed, leaning over so far he had a Grand Canyon view of her breasts. "Why is Rings after you?"

"Bad deal," Louie murmured, transfixed by the sun-kissed tone of her skin, the swollen curve of her mounds.

"Bad deal?"

"Laundering scheme. Rings took the heat. I had nothing to do with it, but Rings obviously thinks differently. Bad guys have ways of holding grudges..." He dragged his hand through his hair. "Let's talk about something else." For the moment, they were safe. He needed a rest.

"Okay," Alicia said. "Want me to order dinner? What would you like?"

I'd like to touch you again. Louie's hand flinched, as he recalled waking up with it cupped on her soft breast. Recalled how her hardened nipple pressed teasingly between his fingers.

"You're kneading the bedspread," Alicia whispered.

"Wha—?" He looked down, caught himself rubbing a tuft of chenille between his thumb and forefinger.

Knock-knock-knock.

"It's bubbly time!" Alicia stood, tugged on the

hem of her shrunken dress as though that did any good, and headed to the door.

A few minutes later, Louie was lying on the bed like a man of leisure, his wrenched ankle—wrapped in an ice-filled towel—elevated on one of those lacy pillows, a glass of fizzy in his hand.

It was a mind-opening role reversal for him. He was used to being the strong one, the dame the liability. But here he and Bonbon were, their roles reversed as she took charge. And even with a wall phone next to the bed, she hadn't once threatened to call some judge or cop.

Yeah, the lady was changing before his eyes. Except, he guessed, in her credit-card I'm-going-to-save-you mentality. It smacked of ownership to Louie, but he'd cross that issue when he came to it.

"To your ankle," Bonbon said, clinking her glass against his. She sat perched on the side of the bed.

"And to the lady who saved our skins." He took a swig. The chilled, frothy liquid slid down his throat real smooth-like.

"Omigawd!"

He jerked his gaze to the door, imagining Rings standing there, a pistol aimed between Louie's eyes.

Door's closed. And he distinctly remembered Bonbon locked it.

He swerved his gaze to the window, half expecting to see Rings hulking there, like a bat morphing vampire-like into a killer.

But through the window, Louie only saw the dark sky, glittering with stars.

He looked back at Alicia, who was sitting ramrod straight, staring across the room at a mirror on the wall.

"Look at me!" she rasped, patting her hair. "I look like…like…Goldie Hawn in that movie where she fell off the yacht and ended up poor and pathetic!"

"*That's* what you just yelled about?"

She blinked rapidly. "Yes! Why didn't you say something?"

He downed the rest of his champagne, needing to blot out the images of Rings. After swallowing, he said hoarsely, "You look fine." Where was that No Sniveling sign when a man needed it?

"*Fine?* I look hideous!" She looked at the mirror as though it were her worst enemy. "My face is all splotchy pink, my dress looks like an old dishrag, and my hair's matted and tangled!"

He was surprised she knew what a dishrag looked like.

"Look on the bright side," he said, motioning for Alicia to refill his glass. "Your lips aren't all swollen and red anymore."

"No, they're just dry and peeling…" She poured more champagne. Too fast. The froth rapidly filled his glass and started to spill over.

Alicia leaned over and sucked off the spilling foam. Then she leaned back and ran her tongue along her lips, missing a bit of froth on the corner of her mouth. "It'll take all my makeup and *then* some to do damage control!"

Easing in a long, slow stream of air, Louie stared

at the touch of white foam on her lip that added a touch of naughty to her wildly natural look. It was going to take him hours to recover from the froth-sucking maneuver.

"Bonbon," he said gently. "You don't get it, do you?"

"Get what?"

"You're more beautiful *without* all that goop."

"I am not—"

"Women like you," he interrupted, "think they're not beautiful unless they're slathered with war paint. Men like a woman who's *comfortable* in her own skin."

"Comfortable?"

"Let me put it this way. Give me a woman who's just rolled out of bed—naked, tousled, no makeup— any day over some magazine cover."

"Even if it was Cindy Crawford on a magazine cover?"

"Cindy who?"

She narrowed her eyes. "Good try. I'd buy that if you were an alien who'd just landed on the planet."

"Okay. Uncle. Even if it was Cindy Crawford, who I bet doesn't look at *all* like she does when she's been painted and airbrushed and whatever else they do to make women look abnormally perfect."

"Yeah," Alicia murmured, "without all that stuff, she probably looks like Judi Dench."

"What?"

"Nothing."

He downed half the glass in a single sip. *We*

wouldn't be having this absurd conversation if I'd made love to her before now.

And as he swallowed, relishing the liquid's chill, he wished they'd made love this morning in the hammock. Wished he taken her there, outside, the ocean breezes caressing them, the ocean waves crashing in the distance.

"So you like how I look?" she said softly, her voice barely a whisper.

"Yeah." He swallowed back another sip. "A lot."

And in that instant, he no longer cared about small actions having big consequences. A kiss equaling a wedding was downright stupid considering everything they'd gone through. They were a man and woman who'd weathered a hell of a lot these past twenty-four hours, and he was worried her favorite tune was the Wedding March?

He had better things to worry about.

He fingered a wisp of her golden hair, letting his fingers trail down her cheek before they cupped her elegant little chin. "Come here, baby," he murmured huskily.

Alicia paused, then leaned forward, her sun-kissed face so close he could smell the sea and wind in her hair, the scent of champagne on her lips. He recalled how those lips had kissed, how they'd tasted. Like this bubbly concoction they were drinking. The first sensation light and sparkling, then warming as it swirled in the mouth, until it burst with small explosions of heat everywhere it touched...

He drew her to him, his mouth almost touching that

little piece of errant froth on the corner of her plump, pink mouth...

"You know what we have to do first," she whispered, her breath hot against his cheek.

"Tell me."

She narrowed her gaze, eyeing him through her lashes. "Order dinner."

7

"ORDER...DINNER?" Louie repeated, his face going slack.

Alicia leaned over and picked up the receiver from the white wall phone next to the bed. "Yes, dinner. Aren't you hungry?" she asked, knowing damn well what he was hungry for.

Well, he'd have to wait.

During all of her flirtations, innuendoes and literally crawling into bed—well, hammock—with him, the guy had acted as though she were more off-limits than Site 51 or whatever that top secret military base in Nevada was called. A girl with a more fragile ego would have given up by now.

Not Alicia.

No, she was only beginning.

It was time for him to get a taste of how it felt to have the carrot dangled without getting even a little itsy-bitsy nibble. It was time for her to up the stakes, make Mr. Control lose a little of his.

Time for her to make Louie jealous.

She punched in the number for Information and asked for the Green Parrot.

"Why are you calling there?" asked Louie.

"Calling my personal shopper."

He flashed her a confused look.

"Hello, Keith?" she said, putting a little extra ooze into her voice. "How's the tattoo?"

She paused while the girl on the line said she'd go get Keith. Meanwhile, Alicia figured, this break gave Louie time to remember the sexy, spiral barbed-wire tattoo that wrapped around the bartender's bulging biceps.

"Hello?" said Keith in his easygoing rock-bottom voice. A Bonnie Raitt song played in the background.

"Hi!" Alicia chirped. "It's me!"

"Who's 'me'?" asked Keith.

"Sure, you can call me your little End of the World as long as you never, ever display that picture of me." She giggled conspiratorially.

"Oh, it's *you*," Keith finally said. "How's it hanging, Sweet Lips?"

"I'm, uh, it's hanging fine." She nonchalantly scratched a little spot under her breast.

Louie made a sound like an engine chugging to life.

"Hey, I picked up your bags at the resort, gave them to Jerry like your brother asked. He didn't have to leave that tip with the resort manager to thank me, by the way. I don't mind helping people—figure what goes around, comes around."

"Well," she said, lowering her voice to a simmering range, "aren't you the gracious gentleman..."

In the background, Louie muttered something about "slathering it on."

"By the way," she continued, ignoring him,

"we're back in Key West, staying in the Guiding Light Room at Lily's Lighthouse—"

"Great place," Keith said. "You two know how to do it sexy."

"Sexy, really? Why, thank you." She fluffed her fingers through her hair, purposefully avoiding Louie's eyes.

"Hang on a minute," Keith said, "Gotta take care of a customer."

She heard the clunk of the phone being put down. Bonnie Raitt blasted louder accompanied by clinking of glass and a woman's high-pitched giggle.

"Oh, so, you'd like to, uh, hear about my vacation?" Alicia said into the receiver. Darting a look at Louie, she mouthed, "He wants to hear about the island."

Louie mouthed, "Why?"

"Guess he's interested in me—I mean us."

"Why aren't you mouthing anymore?"

"So," she said, speaking loudly into the receiver, "the native island experience was really, really fabulous. I fell in the ocean, ate high-fat nuts and slept in a hammock."

From the corner of her eye, she saw Louie's frown deepen.

"Mmm, I'd have roughed it sooner had I known tropical sea breezes could feel better than a silky, hot bath…" She squirmed a little as though the memories were more than she could stand.

"Hey, Sweet Lips, I'm back," said Keith. "Gonna

have to cut this short, more customers just came in. Anything I can do you?''

''Well, aren't you sweet for asking,'' she said, brushing her hand across her forehead. ''Think you could do me some takeout?''

''*Do me?*'' whispered Louie. ''What kind of call is this?''

''You mean…place an order?'' asked Keith at the same time.

''Yes, yes, that's it,'' Alicia said. She shot a look at Louie, who glowered at her like the devil himself.

Hot damn. The man was jealous.

''Sure, I'll order something from the Meteor Smokehouse,'' Keith said. ''Owned by my boss, so I can get you a discount, too. You like hot and spicy barbecue?''

''*Love* hot and spicy,'' she said. ''The hotter and spicier, the better.''

The bed shook as Louie leaned forward, keeping his foot elevated. ''*Now* what are you two talking about?''

''Chicken? Pork? What's your desire?'' asked Keith.

Alicia cupped her hand over the receiver and whispered to Louie. ''We're talking barbecue. What's your desire?''

''For you to get off the frickin' phone.''

''But,'' she said, batting her eyes innocently, ''I need to get our order in first.''

''Then get it in,'' he snapped.

''You must be *awfully* hungry,'' Alicia turned her

head a little so Louie wouldn't catch her smiling, then continued speaking into the receiver, "What do *you* recommend," she sucked in a long breath, then expelled it slowly as she uttered his name. "Keeeeith?"

"Minnie's green beans are killer," he answered matter-of-factly, obviously clueless to the drama on the other end of the phone. Or maybe he'd seen and heard just about everything tending bar at the Green Parrot, so a slightly bizarre phone conversation was nothing. "Their barbecue meats are dynamite—I dig the chicken."

"Oh, *yes!*" Alicia enthused, à la Meg Ryan in the infamous *When Harry Met Sally* diner scene. "Give me some of *that!*"

The bed shook again.

"Corn bread with jalapeños?" Keith continued. "Meteor calls them 'mouth-melting.'"

"Mouth-*melting?*" She slicked her tongue across her bottom lip. "Oh yeah, need that, too. And for dessert, I'd love something sweet and decadent—"

"Thought you liked spumoni," Louie muttered.

"Key lime pie?" Keith suggested.

"Perfect," she purred. "Make that two pieces. One for him, one for me."

After she hung up, she looked at Louie, whose ruddy face had the biggest, baddest scowl she'd ever seen.

"You don't look so good—your ankle still hurting?" she asked innocently.

"No," he snapped.

"Oh, that's good," she said, standing, wriggling a

little to adjust herself into the shrunken dress. "That ocean did a wicked number on my outfit. On me, too. I feel all sticky and dirty." She looked up and met Louie's eyes. "How do you feel?"

Damn if the man wasn't fingering tufts of chenille on the bedspread again. It gave her no little sense of power to know she'd expertly dangled a very succulent carrot just out of reach of those macho, masculine lips…

Feigning nonchalance, she rambled on, "I was thinking how delicious a hot, soapy bath would be— we've been wearing these same clothes *forever,* plus all that camping-out stuff we endured…"

"Don't pawn that bath line on me, too," Louie grumbled.

"What?"

"I heard you telling Keith how those tropical breezes were just like…" He mimicked her voice. "'…a silky, hot bath.'"

"You were listening to *every* word?" Bat-bat-bat.

Louie pressed his lips together, his dark eyes blazing.

"I'll go check out the tub." Alicia sashayed across the room, adding a little extra oomph to her walk.

When she reached the tub, she bent over—very, very slowly—to look at a white wicker basket nestled next to one of the porcelain claw feet. "What have we here?" She rummaged about among its containers. "Shampoo, soap, body lotion and…" Her voice trailed off as she fingered several foil-wrapped packages.

"And what?" asked Louie.

Her fingers moved onto a small book tucked in a corner of the basket. She tilted her head and read the cover. "And a biography of Captain Josiah, it appears, right next to some bubble bath."

"I don't do baths."

She straightened and looked at Louie where he lay sprawled across the bed, one foot elevated on a white, lacy pillow. He was finishing off his glass of champagne.

"White frilly foot pillows, champagne...but you don't do baths? Who invited you?" Bat-bat-bat.

A red hue crept up his neck. "That's different."

"Well, you can do a bird bath in the bathroom sink or a body bath in this tub. Your choice."

He glared at her over the rim of his glass. "Body," he finally said.

"Good choice," she murmured. She turned on the tub faucet. "We'll take turns. After you're through, I'll drain the water, then run another bath for *moi*." She sat on the edge of the tub, wriggling her fingers in the water as she adjusted the temperature. "Tea for two," she sang lightly, recalling a song her mom used to hum, "and two for tea..."

Alicia twisted the white handle marked H, increasing the rush of heat into the water. "One for you," she continued singing, "and one for me..."

KNOCK-KNOCK-KNOCK.

Louie sat in the tub, his foot—sticking out of the bubbles—wrapped in a fresh ice-filled towel and propped on the sloping edge of the tub. His mood was considerably better after sinking into the liquid warmth—hadn't hurt to be doted on by Bonbon either, who fussed over everything from the temperature of the water to wrapping his foot *just* right.

"I'll get it!" Alicia said as she minced to the door. Forget that her shrunken dress looked more like a wrinkled handkerchief, he had to admit the lady still had class.

And not just high class, Louie thought, but a class unto herself. The type of woman who was above and beyond the generic lusty-babe variety he'd previously fantasized about. A fantasy that now seemed too predictable, too boring.

"Uh, Mrs. Hammock?" said a teenage kid standing at the open door. He held a large plastic bag.

Alicia giggled. "Yes, that's me! Mrs. Hammock!" She leaned one hand against the doorjamb, and even from behind, Louie could see that that emaciated dress was having a hell of a time containing her breasts.

That poor kid was clutching the bag for dear life. He cleared his throat and started talking to her chest about the food tab.

Louie took another swig of champagne, observing Bonbon's effect on the opposite sex. As Alicia handed the boy some money, thanking him, damn if the kid's face didn't flame redder than his hair.

I know how that kid—and probably Keith—feels. Hot, bothered, losing control.

Louie took another chilly sip, wondering if he'd been so afraid of losing control that he'd blown it by pushing her away every time she'd hinted, flirted or downright propositioned him. He, Louie Ragazzi, had *never* blown it with a woman before, but this time he'd bet every last cent of his pocket change that he had.

Why in the hell had he played up his die-hard macho side? To prove, just as he had with his former wives, that he's a one-man show?

Yeah, he thought glumly. *That's exactly why.*

Hell, if the angel of death were to appear at this very moment and announce it was Louie Ragazzi's last day on earth, his first regret would be that he'd never made love to Alicia.

The door shut and she carried the bag to the tub, bringing with her savory scents of barbecue.

Alicia set the bag on the floor next to the tub. "There's no table in the room, so we'll make it a picnic," she announced.

He'd smirked before at her domestic skills, but it appeared she had serious picnic-assembly talents. She laid a towel on the floor, organizing cartons of food on one side. On the other, she set out the paper plates and arranged the plastic knives, spoons and forks next to a fanlike display of paper napkins.

She handed Louie one of the napkins. "You can dry your hands on this, then dip into the food whenever you get the urge."

Dip. Urge. She was on her knees, which were spread just far enough apart that he caught a glimpse of creamy thigh.

Thighs that spread a little wider as she reached to

open a white carton. "Oooh, these must be Minnie's green beans!" She picked one up and crunched on it. Closing her eyes, she chewed with such relish, he swore he wanted to eat nothing but green beans for the rest of his days.

Then the green-bean vixen licked her oily fingers as she moaned softly. "Mmm...I'm *so* bad eating this greasy food."

"Give me some." Louie held out his hand.

"Nice social skills," Alicia teased. "What do you want?"

You. "Meat."

She lifted the plate of ribs and he helped himself to a fat, sauce-drenched piece. He tore into it like a jackal, washing it down with champagne—the combination of hot sauce and bubbly reminding him of Bonbon.

"Oh, look at these corn muffins!" she said, breaking one open. Steam rose, yeasty and succulent. "Want a bite?" she said, holding half toward him.

He'd barely growled "yes" before half a muffin was tucked into his mouth. He chewed, damn near overwhelmed with the warm, crumbly texture.

He watched her delicate fingers pick up a rib. After holding it up and observing it as though deciding where best to dive in, she nibbled a little on the end. Then, with a tug of her head, she tore off a strip with her pristine white teeth.

Louie probably could have handled that, but when she sucked the barbecue sauce off her fingers, making deep-in-the-throat primal sounds of appreciation, he went rock-hard.

Thank God for bubble bath.

He purposefully avoided looking at her while he finished eating because, although he prided himself on being able to juggle multiple tasks at once, eating while in erotic pain was beyond his powers.

A few minutes later, Alicia exclaimed, "Oh, let's read the story of Captain Josiah!"

"What, a bedtime story already?" Louie asked, tossing another stripped-bare rib bone onto the growing stack.

"For you," Alicia said with a wink, "a *bath*time story." After pushing aside the food items and wiping her fingers on a napkin, she pulled a book out of the basket and showed its cover to Louie.

A swashbuckling pirate stood spread-eagled on the hull of a ship, the wind whipping back his black mane, his bronzed, bare chest glistening with sweat under a fiery sun.

"Is that a knife between his teeth?" asked Louie.

Alicia peered closer. "Yes, I believe you're right." She sucked in a shaky breath that made her breasts bulge over the top of her pathetic dress. "What a man, huh?" Big, dewy green eyes met his. "Looks sort of like you."

Louie fought the urge to put one of those plastic picnic knives between his pearly whites.

She opened the book. "Listen to this!" She began reading. "'A monstrous coal-black beard covered his face from the eyes down. Before attacking a vessel, he stuck lighted cords—dipped in saltpeter and lime-water—under his hat, which he used to ignite powder in cannons. The sight of him boarding a ship, smoke curling around his raven head, terrified sailors. Many ships surrendered before battles even began." She paused, shaking her head. "Can you imagine? Surrendering just at the sight of someone?"

Louie looked at her, noticing how her blond hair shimmered with hidden streaks of gold, as though it'd stolen light from the day.

Could he surrender at the sight of someone?

"Oh, listen to this," she said enthusiastically, pressing her finger at a line on the page. "He was ruthless in war and with women, winning at both."

Yes, I could surrender, Louie thought. Because in his heart he knew he already had.

She continued reading to herself, absorbed in the book. Before this moment, he'd never seen her so intensely involved with something outside of fretting about her makeup or worrying about spiders in a sleeping bag. But her concentration while she read was different, *intimate.* He was observing her lost in the secret world of her imagination.

"Bonbon?"

She looked up, a distant look in her eyes. "Huh?"

"What are you reading?" he asked. *Let me into your world.*

"Right. What am I reading." She lowered her head and read softly. "In 1718, after shooting out the beacon at a lighthouse on a section of coast now known as the Florida Keys, Captain Josiah—called Captain J by his crew—stayed there with some of his men, looting ships that wrecked on the coral reefs." Alicia looked up at Louie. "That has to be *this* lighthouse!" she whispered excitedly, looking around. "Imagine. Captain J, in this very room."

She went back to reading. "Shortly thereafter, he kidnapped a prominent landowner's wife, the beautiful Lady Georgiana, and made her his captive. She was never seen again, although eye witnesses claimed she rode the high seas with Captain J, sometimes donning the gear of pirates and fighting by his side in battle."

Alicia looked up, frowning. "Wearing men's clothes? Fighting with fuses in my hair? I don't *think* so."

She returned to the page. "Later, stories circulated that Lady Georgiana and Captain J settled down on a plantation in Argentina where they lived out their lives in wealth, surrounded by their children. Oh!" Alicia's lips moved silently as she continued reading.

"What?" Damn, he was getting sucked into this story.

Alicia looked up with moistened eyes. "They married on her deathbed, minutes before she died of yellow fever."

He and Alicia stared at each other for a long moment and, for a crazy instant, Louie imagined spending his days with her, until the very end when the angel of death made an appearance. Except this time, Louie would have no regrets.

Alicia tucked the book back into the basket, then

stood and looked down at Louie's foot. "How's the ankle?"

"The same as the rest of me."

She arched a questioning eyebrow.

"Inflamed. Aching."

He couldn't hold back anymore.

He reached out and gripped her wrist, gently pulling her closer to the tub. "You're my captive, my beautiful lady," he murmured.

Alicia's breath broke as she felt her cheeks grow warm. The breezes flitting in through the open window did little to disperse the suddenly thick, saturated air.

"Your Lady Alicia," she whispered, loving the sound of it. Loving more that he'd embraced the fantasy of the lady and the pirate.

"I want…" Louie tightened his grip as his words burned into silence.

Alicia wet her lips and stared at him, the electricity of his touch unknotting her will to play any more games. Whatever reasons she'd had to hold back, to act as though she didn't care, melted in the fire of her desire.

"Yes," she whispered.

He released his hold on her, even while the simmering look in his eyes still held her captive. "Take off your dress."

Through the window, the stars burned holes in the sky, fiery colors that mirrored her smoldering need. She lifted the hem of her dress, just a little, enjoying how his eyes devoured every exposed inch of her flesh. Then she ran her fingers up her torso, along the sides of her breasts before hooking her thumbs into the elastic that held up the strapless dress.

He stirred restlessly in the water, his massive, hairy chest glistening with soapy bubbles.

Alicia turned around, slowly, until her back was to him. Then she pulled the dress over her breasts, catching her breath as the onslaught of cool air made her nipples pucker. She slid the dress the rest of the way off and stepped out of it.

"Turn around."

She did, the only thing between her and Louie her pink bikini underwear.

He emitted a primal sound, like a wounded animal. "Take off your panties."

She tugged on the thin elastic strap.

"Slowly."

She paused, then inched the underwear down, finally kicking the piece of fabric aside. She straightened.

"Oh, baby," he murmured, his eyes taking her in. "You're more beautiful naked than with clothes on."

She'd never had a man say words like that to her before. Not in that awe-filled tone, as though she were the first woman to burrow under his skin, right down to his soul.

"Come here," Louie murmured, holding out his hand. "Get in."

"Walk the plank?" she said lightly, not wanting him to see that she was shaking. She'd teased and taunted him plenty before now, but all that bravado suddenly felt false, as whoever she'd pretended to be slipped away, leaving her stripped down to her very essence—a woman aching to love and be loved.

She gave him her hand, and he lifted it to his lips, brushing her fingertips with a kiss. "You're trembling," he said gently. "Do you want to stop?"

"No!"

A wicked grin slow-danced across his full, masculine lips. "That's my Lady Alicia," he growled. "Speaking her mind." He kicked off the towel wrapped around his ankle and dropped his foot into the water. "Get your sweet self in here."

She looked at the water. "Your foot—"

"Is still achy, but better. Plus it doesn't want to get in the way."

She smiled, then lifted one foot to step inside the tub, but Louie caught it before it touched the water and gently positioned her heel on the side of the cool porcelain.

"Comfortable enough?" he asked.

She nodded. She stood, one foot on the floor, the other poised on the tub, opening a view of her most private self to him. It felt deliciously wanton to be so exposed to a lover. Wanton…and safe.

Safe in a way she'd never felt before with a man.

He looked at her appreciatively, then leaned forward and blew puffs of air on her cleft, his warm breaths caressing, teasing her. Instinctively, she tipped her pelvis up, her body aching for more…

"*Now* get in," he murmured.

He guided her as she stepped into the warm, sudsy water. She started to sit, but his rough hands held her thighs. "No. Stand."

Balmy gusts of wind blew in through the window, bringing scents of the sea and the distant twittering of birds. She closed her eyes, relishing the sensuous breezes on her face and the sensation of Louie's fingers trailing up her calf, along her thigh. When he skirted her sex, she shuddered a gasp.

"Hold that thought," he said huskily, taking the bar of soap from the ledge of the tub. He moved the soap in a leisurely tour of her body. Over her hips, in frothy circles on her tummy. And when he dipped lightly between her legs, she shivered as desire pooled like liquid heat in the core between her thighs.

"Turn around," he said.

She did.

And he repeated the same ministrations to the backs of her thighs, up to her bottom which he lovingly sudsed and rubbed before slipping the soap into her crevice where he rhythmically stroked, back and forth, pausing only to sluice warm water over her, rinsing away the soap, before his fingers returned to massage her.

Searing need engorged her as she moved in tandem with his hand, her hips involuntarily rotating with his motions. Shifting her foot a little to the side, she widened her stance, giving him more access.

He halted.

"Don't...stop...!"

He chuckled. "Don't plan to. Turn back around."

She did and he leaned forward, his lips kissing one thigh, then the other, before running his tongue up to her tangle of curls and kissing her *there*.

Alicia gasped, holding onto the window ledge for

support as his tongue masterfully slid into the sensitive folds. Tension, hot and needy, coiled tighter within her. She was barely aware of his chest hair tickling her legs, the gentle sloshing of the water in the tub that mimicked the distant waves. All sensations coalesced into a white-hot need where his lips nibbled and licked and suckled...

And when he moaned, the deep guttural sound vibrating intensely against her, she couldn't wait any longer.

Slipping onto her knees in the warm water, she leaned over and plucked a foil packet from the basket. Brushing aside suds, she saw his erection under the water. Rigid, hard, the tip almost breaking the surface. Opening the packet, she slid the sheath onto him, the slick water aiding her motion.

Blood hammered through her as she positioned herself over him, letting his hardened member barely touch her opening. There she hovered, gyrating gently, teasing...

"Don't...stop," he growled savagely.

"Don't plan to," she whispered hotly, sinking herself slowly onto him.

Louie's breath tore loose as she leaned forward, searing her mouth to his as her velvety warmth tightened around his aching flesh. Then, straightening, she gently rocked, raking her incendiary fingertips across his jaw, chest, arms, burning his skin with her touch.

He stroked her breasts, wet and full in his palms. "Beautiful, so beautiful," he murmured, bending forward to suckle a hardened, dusty-pink tip.

Her hands tangled in his hair and she held him

fiercely in place while she grazed one nipple, then the other, across his lips. Then, with a guttural moan, she pulled back and, clutching the sides of the tub, thrust hard along his shaft.

Gritting his teeth, he held himself still, wanting to make it last, make it good. Then, slowly, he rocked her, his body urgent, driven, fighting not to lose control. But when she sobbed his name, her insides convulsing, he grasped her buttocks and buried himself deep in her hot, slick cavern.

Warm water splashed over them, onto the floor, their rhythm escalating, surging with every thrust. When she braced her hands on his legs and let her head fall back with a prolonged wail, he thrust one last time, then relinquished himself to wave after wave of scalding pulsations.

Moments later, Alicia lay on top of him, their bodies partially submerged in the slick, soapy water. Their heartbeats pressed together, he stroked her damp hair and stared out the window at the night sky. In the distance, he could see faint streaks of color on the horizon, the last dying light of the day.

He recalled how, as a kid, he'd look out his bedroom window and mourn the setting of the sun. But tonight, a grown Louie didn't regret its loss. Because, for the first time in as long as he could remember, he felt complete. Joined. And even with the impending nightfall and its dark isolation, he knew he was no longer a man alone.

8

___

ALICIA BLINKED open her eyes and stared overhead at an expanse of white. Who'd repainted her Antoinette-pink bedroom ceiling?

Sleep-heavy breathing and a warm, muscled thigh against the back of her leg brought her to the present. This wasn't her bedroom back in Denver…it was the lighthouse room in Key West.

She smiled to herself. Which should be repainted fire-engine red after last night's passionate encounter.

She burrowed a bit into the warm covers, indulging herself in sizzling memories from last night. Louie lathering her body with slow, sensuous strokes. Their bodies, slick and wet and needy, making waves in the bathtub. And, afterward, Louie meticulously toweling her off, making the act of getting dry the most inventive foreplay she'd ever experienced.

They'd darn near raced to bed after that, where they'd made love again. Prolonged, sinewy love…

And afterward, when they'd lain in each other's arms, Alicia had sleepily watched the sky through the open window and played with names for the color of moonlight. Pure, she'd finally decided, the way it is with new beginnings.

Louie stirred, his strong body nestling closer behind her. She shimmied her butt, just enough to park it into a masculine alcove of heat and muscle. Then she paused, listening to his rhythmic breathing, feeling his warmth, and savored the moment.

And to think that all those years she'd ached to find love, even thinking she'd stumbled on it a few times. What she'd experienced in the past, compared to what she felt with Louie, was like the difference between a zircon and a diamond. Other men had been attractive, polished...but none had the depth, the fire of Louie. He was the real thing, dark side and all.

She smiled to herself. Even the moon—with its pure light—had a dark side.

He stirred again. A muscular, hairy arm draped lazily around her, the fingers finding her breast. Her nipple beaded under his touch.

"Mmm." He eased his lips to her earlobe, which he suckled between his teeth.

"Good morning to you, too," she whispered, her voice catching as his hot breath singed the sensitive hollow behind her ear.

"I remember waking up before with my hand on your breast," he murmured huskily, gently rolling her nipple between this thumb and forefinger. Sizzling need shot through her.

"I remember, too," she whispered.

His hand stilled. "You were awake on the hammock when my hand—?"

"I'll only answer if you continue what you were doing."

He squeezed her breast, drawing his fingers up to her nipple. He gave it a gentle tug.

She groaned. "Yes...I was awake."

"You *brat.*" His removed his hand and spanked her bottom playfully.

"Brat?" She giggled. "Why Louie Ragazzi, you tough talker you."

"So you were awake, eh? And faking it?"

She wriggled a little against him. "I've never faked it with you. Well, except for yesterday morning, when I pretended to be asleep..."

"And what did you think *pretending* being asleep would get you?"

His hand now rubbed her bottom with slow, sensuous strokes, bringing back memories of his soapy exploration of her body last night. "Figured if you knew I was awake, bada bing, you'd be up and out of there."

"Bada bing?" His hand stilled again. "What—you talkin' Jersey now?"

"I ain't talkin' nuttin' until that hand gets back to work."

The way he paused made Alicia doubt few women had taken on Louie in a battle of the wits. Oh, no question he'd had his share of—what'd he call them? *Lusty babes?*—but how many had sexually challenged him by using their tongue to form complete sentences?

As though in response, Louie chuckled. A husky, rumbling sound full of sex. After giving her bottom another playful pat, he trailed his callused fingertips in lazy, round circles over her flesh.

She closed her eyes and shivered as a dusting of goose bumps rose on her skin.

Needing to be closer, she took his hand and wrapped it around her as she turned and snuggled against him. Moving down a bit, she burrowed her face in a cushion of chest hair, inhaling his familiar masculine scent spiked with a touch of last night's bubble bath.

Impulsively, she flicked her tongue along some sleek strands, their taste salty on her tongue and she recalled other tastes, textures from last night...

"So, Miss Bada Bing, you seem quite chipper this morning. Sleep well?"

She scooted back up, meeting his sleepy-eyed gaze. His eyes had softened, their color warm and inviting like hot chocolate. "Like a baby."

"You are a baby," he murmured. "A very spoiled, very sexy baby." He kissed the tip of her nose, and she felt his hardness pressing against her thighs. It flitted through her mind that they'd run out of condoms.

His teasing fingers traveled up her side, traced her collarbone, her jaw. "Your skin is so soft," he growled. "Softer than the leather on that jacket I lost in Denver..."

"Don't get too romantic on me," she whispered. "Next you'll be telling me I smell better than your mama's ravioli."

"And you kidded me about *my* sense of humor."

"Near-death brings out the best in me," she said, repeating his line.

He pulled back slightly, his eyes clouding over as he stared deeply into hers. At that moment, she swore she saw something she'd never thought she'd see in Louie—fear.

For her?

"Louie—?"

"Shh." He wrapped his arms around her, silently entreating her to move closer. After a moment's hesitation, she sank against him, and he breathed a heavy sigh of relief as he cradled her close.

For this minute, Louie thought, *she's safe*.

For this minute, he could shelter her, protect her…but what about the minutes, hours, days to come?

He nestled his chin into her soft hair, experiencing an onslaught of emotions that were foreign to him—contentment, joy, a burning desire that had nothing to do with the flesh.

And then he knew. If life were perfect, he'd keep her in his arms for always. It's where she belonged.

I need her in my life.

Before now, he'd prided himself on being his own man—a one-man show. Even when he'd been married before, he'd viewed himself that way. But that theory was shot to hell because, in some rock-deep part of his soul, he knew her stubborn, passionate belief in him brought out his potential. Made him complete.

How had he gotten through life alone before now? He couldn't imagine going through the rest of it alone.

The rest of it.

A cold knot formed in his stomach.

If she wanted to live, *he* was the liability. The irony didn't escape him that he'd thrown that very word in her face, accused her of being the liability. But now their roles were reversed. With Rings out for blood, Louie needed to get Alicia out of harm's way.

Frustration tensed his jaw as he gently gripped her shoulders and pushed her away. Not too far, not yet.

"You can't stay here."

She stiffened. "Why?"

"Rings has to be dealt with. You need to leave."

Alicia looked into his face, trying to decipher his darkened expression. In the awkward silence that followed, she wondered when their world, warm and loving mere moments ago, had turned alien, forbidding.

Like the dark side of the moon, she thought.

She sat up and pulled the sheet around her, suddenly not wanting to be overly exposed. "We're in this together."

"No, I'm in this alone."

She shook her head, furious at his pigheadedness. "Don't give me that one-man-show line again."

Her gaze caught something in his eyes she couldn't decipher—hurt?—before they cooled into black, fathomless pools. "I didn't say that. I said you can't stay here."

She fought a rising hysteria. "You *need* me."

He thrust his hand through his hair, then said in a tired voice, "If you stay here, you'll die. Don't fight me on this. You'll lose."

"We're in this together—"

"Alicia..."

Hearing her name for the first time from his lips stopped her. She'd always been "Bonbon" and sometimes she'd actually wondered if he'd forgotten her real name. But now that he'd said it—in a tone rich with warmth, tenderness—she had the crazy anticipation he was going to say something to turn all this around, return them to that loving cocoon they'd created in this room, this bed.

Her heart lurched. *He's going to tell me he loves me.*

"Alicia..." He leaned forward and buried his face in her hair. "Go home," he said, his voice almost inaudible.

Her stomach plummeting, she pressed her forehead against his roughened cheek, swore she felt him tremble.

Then she pulled back, wrapping the sheet tighter around her. "Can I say something?"

He waited a beat, his face etched in anguish, then nodded.

"Hear me out." A gust of ocean breezes swirled through the window and around them, a reminder of the outside world. The place Louie would roam, hunted by Rings. "You're stuck here with no money. I still have some cash, and enough credit cards to fund anything you need."

The look in his eyes shifted. "I can't be bought."

She slammed her hand on the bed. "Oh, good grief. I'm not trying to *buy* you, I'm trying to help you."

"Is there a difference, Bonbon?"

Back to Bonbon, are we? "You are so pigheaded!"

She swiped a hair out of her eyes. "How are you going to survive in that jungle out there?"

"A person doesn't need credit cards to survive in the jungle."

"You are so full of it!" She had a few choicer descriptions, but bit her tongue. Instead, she sat taller, waiting for him to argue, yell, go full-tilt Italian on her. And she was ready to confront his macho maneuvers, issue by issue. Damn it, she knew what was best for him!

But he surprised her by instead gently touching her hand. And when he spoke, she had to strain to hear.

"Honey, don't take this so hard," he said, his voice hoarse, the way grief sounds. "My wanting you to leave is for your sake. Rings is like a rabid dog, foaming at the chops to get to me. I don't want you in the way."

His thumb gently rubbed her skin, his touch almost more unbearable than his words. And she thought how he'd also touched her, deep down inside, in a place where his caresses would never fade.

Her heart pleaded with him even as her mind cursed him. She understood what he was saying. He was concerned for her safety. But didn't he realize she could stay *and* remain safe?

"One more option," she whispered, her pain so great she knew if he didn't listen, she'd toss aside her pride and beg the man to hear her out.

He gave his head a shake. "Never say die, eh?"

"Let me stay in Key West. I'll rent a room in some out-of-the-way place where I'll wait for you." Louie started to speak, but she kept talking. "Besides the credit cards—forget the jungle, we're talking survival in the *city*—I also have a substantial trust fund—"

"Don't go there—"

"Because after you get Rings off your tail," she said, her words gaining speed before he cut her off, "my trust fund can finance your fishing business." There. She'd said it. Offered him the whole package— a sanctuary, support, his dream…

And herself. Her love, devotion. Forevermore.

Outside, birds chattered, waves crashed. Sunlight sifted into the room, a buttery rectangle on the floor, inching its way to them, its warmth just out of reach.

Louie shook his head. "No."

"But—"

"No." He got up, his body brown and muscled, and headed to the bathroom. "I'm going to the restroom, wash my face, then get dressed. After that, we'll make plane reservations. I'm not the one you should be worrying about."

"I'll be fine," she murmured, but he'd already crossed the room and shut the door.

And here I am again, facing a closed door. Louie's put up his wall. Subject closed.

She rolled back her shoulders. Sure, somehow, she'd be fine being alone again. She'd made her peace with it her entire life, hadn't she?

She listened to the distant crash of waves and thought how the future would be. The days sifting into one another like sand to the sea, and one day Louie's face would fade from her memory along with the sound of his voice, the glint in his eye. And on that day, she'd try to resurrect him in her mind's eye and fail. He'd be gone…

Except one thing. One thing would never fade, never die, for the rest of her life.

The memory of Louie's love.

LOUIE LEANED his hands against the cold porcelain sink and stared at his reflection in the mirror. "You stupid bastard," he muttered.

So smart, wasn't he, being the tough guy all his years. Thinking one day he'd change, embrace the good life, be the good man…only to discover he's blown it because the past isn't some hazy memory that fades into nothing.

The past can hunt you down, make you pay for your sins. Hold you back from the dreams of your future.

He jerked the knob on the faucet. Cold water rushed down the drain.

Just like his dreams. Down the drain.

You stupid bastard. He cupped his hands under the rushing water and sank his face into the chill, wishing it could freeze him senseless. Isolate the pain that gutted him so he could chip it off like a piece of ice, not feel the remorse of screwing up his life…

Of losing Alicia.

That was the worst of it. Losing the best thing that had ever entered his sorry life, and all because of his own stupidity. If he could turn back time, he'd make different choices, be a different man. One without the dirty baggage that forced him to choose a woman's life over her love.

If only he'd not let poverty—and the fear of being enslaved like his dad—choose his path. He had the sick feeling he'd spend the rest of his life playing ''if only'' over and over in his mind.

A pounding sound distracted him. Someone knocking?

Louie lifted his head, straining to hear over the rush of water. Yeah, someone knocking at the front door. Followed by a voice calling out something about ''breakfast.''

Right. This joint is a bed-and-*breakfast.*

Alicia's voice. ''Just a minute…!''

He imagined her throwing something on, mincing those killer legs to the door, some dumbstruck kid blushing and stuttering at the vision of this disheveled beauty who'd obviously just rolled out of bed…

Louie scooped more water into his hands, but barely felt its cold as hot thoughts of last night filled his mind. Her sinfully curvy, pink body peeking through frothy suds. How she arched her back, crying out his name at the moment of her release…

Gritting his teeth, Louie splashed more cold water on his face.

Then he jerked the faucet off, stilling the rush of water, and grabbed a plushy white towel. Staring at his sorry mug in the mirror, he wiped it while shifting his weight from one foot to the other, testing his ankle. A little sore. He'd manage.

After tossing the towel on a rack, he opened the door.

A tense silence shrouded the room.

The first thing he noticed was Alicia's open Gucci bag on the bed, one of her numerous Hawaiian-print shirts hanging out of it. His gaze darted around. Her makeup pouch lay on the chenille bedspread...a lipstick tube on the floor.

Then he saw the room door, slightly ajar, with its view of the top of the iron spiral staircase that led to the bottom of the lighthouse.

Cold, black fear lodged in his gut.

Rings.

Louie strode outside, looked down the spiraling stairwell.

Empty.

He strained to listen.

Silence.

He tore down several steps, jutting his head over the railing, looking down. Nothing nothing nothing.

He stopped and slammed his hand against the metal railing, the tinny sound reverberating through the lighthouse.

She's gone.

Thoughts crashed through his mind. Maybe Alicia, pissed at Louie's pigheadedness, had taken a walk. Maybe something was wrong with breakfast and she returned it to the front desk.

He jogged back up the few stairs to the room, dismissing the thoughts. *Alicia wouldn't leave this room without telling me why.*

It had to be Rings.

He's taken her somewhere. Get dressed, find them.

Louie crossed to the Gucci bag and pawed through

its contents, shoving aside clothes, a long gold necklace chain, some men's briefs.

He grabbed a pair and held them up. Tiger-striped. A flash of puzzlement, then gut-deep remorse. Wasn't that like Bonbon, planning her romantic getaway even if the guy didn't know what was in store.

He stepped into them, berating himself for her not knowing what else was in store. *If only I'd cut her loose in Denver. Or demanded she return the moment we landed in the Keys.*

Louie snatched a pair of shorts and a shirt—a swirl of gaudy flowers—and put them on. He started to race out the door, then paused.

No, think. Think!

Blindly following anything that looked like a clue would waste time. He could spend hours out there, wandering, while she was being...

A wash of sweat chilled his skin.

Don't go there.

He paced the room. *Where in the hell would Rings take her?* The creep could have just stayed in the room, shot them point-blank. Louie glanced at the still-open door. One exit, the stairwell. Jackass stupid to commit a crime with only one long escape route.

He imagined Rings dragging Alicia down those stairs. Probably clamped something on her mouth so she couldn't scream for help.

If that bastard hurts her, I'll kill him.

Louie paced again, scrubbing his hand across his face. Key West was dense with party-goers...a guy pushing around an abducted woman would stand out. They had to be nearby...

Brring-brring-brring.

Alicia?

Louie raced to the phone, every cell in his body on alert.

Maybe she's calling from the registration desk, saying something princesslike about the food or the wait staff. I'll give her hell, tell her to get her butt back here.

He picked up the receiver. "Talk to me."

"I was thinkin' the same thing." A deep, malevolent chuckle. "Got your girl."

Rings.

"Where is she?"

"Took her out for breakfast."

Rings knocked on the door. I was only a few feet away. Damn it to hell. Louie squeezed shut his eyes, swallowing back a bitter taste. *Should've kept the door open. Should've never let her out of my sight.*

"Let her go," he growled. "She has nothing to do with you and me."

"Oh she has *plenty* to do with you and me," taunted Rings. "She's bait. Insurance you'll meet me."

Louie heard a rhythmic pounding over the phone, a background noise that mimicked the same sound in the room. Hammering from some nearby construction site.

He plugged his free ear with his finger, concentrating on the conversation. "Where is she?" he repeated.

"In your backyard. Wanted to make it easy for you."

Easy for you, you bastard. Louie strode toward the

window, stretching the cord with him. It jerked taut and he stopped, ten feet shy of the tub. Through the window, all he saw was endless sky.

More hammering, the sharp sounds competing with the throbbing roar of blood in his ears.

"Tell me where," Louie barked. He didn't dare drop the phone, go and look out the window. If he left Rings hanging, literally, who knew what the scum would do.

Every second counted…

"She's all cozy in a romantic little corner," Rings continued, "tucked between shrubbery and an old life-guard station. Perfect spot for lovebirds to be killed."

Louie glanced at the clock on the nightstand. Eleven o'clock. "I'm yours, Rings. Let her go."

Rings chuckled. "She knows too much."

She could finger Rings to the authorities. "Hear me out," Louie countered, buying time, "I said I'm yours. Just one condition—"

"Shut up," Rings snapped. "I'm sick of chitchat. Get your ass down here. Outside the lighthouse, you'll see a line of palms that lead to the beach. Follow those. When you get to a row of bushes with big or-ange flowers, there's a break in the shrubbery you can pass through. The lifeguard station will be to your right."

Click.

Louie hung up the phone, blew out a gust of breath.

He'd had near brushes with death before, but it had always been his problem to figure out. But this time, he didn't give a rat's ass about his own skin. Nothing mattered except Alicia. He had to get to her.

Have to save her.

He stepped into a pair of flip-flops, seeing her face in his mind's eye. That sassy smile, those big, dewy green eyes. In a dark, tangled place in his gut he knew if anything happened to her, he'd never recover. Hell, he'd thought before that he loved her? It was more than that.

She was sacred to him.

He looked around the room, seeing what he could use as a weapon. Plastic knives and forks were piled by the tub. He tore across the room and grabbed one of each. About as useful as sticks and stones, but better than nothing. He shoved them into his pocket, scanning the room for anything else.

Bathtub, mirror, twisted sheets…

Bang-bang-bang. The hammering pounded out the passing seconds. Ticking off precious time…

Her Gucci bag.

Louie returned to it, groped its contents until his fingers touched cool metal. He extracted the long, thick necklace and gave it a sharp tug. Stronger than it looked.

Like Alicia.

Hold on, baby. Keep your wits, stay strong. That was often the fine line between life and death.

Stuffing the necklace into his shorts pocket, he headed to the door.

9

LOUIE TORE DOWN the lighthouse stairwell, cursing every step of the way. At the damn flip-flops that kept sliding underneath his feet, at the endless stairs, but mostly at himself for Alicia's life being on the line.

Regret stabbed through him. If only he hadn't left Alicia alone, if only he'd second-guessed Rings, if only, if only...

His foot slipped and he lurched forward, grabbing the cold metal handrail. "Damn shoes," he growled, resuming his flight, his pounding steps counterpoint to the muffled, repetitive hammering from outside.

Finally, he hit the bottom step. He raced through the lighthouse door to outside.

Sunlight momentarily blinded him. He shielded his eyes, catching his breath as balmy ocean breezes swirled the air.

"Follow the line of palm trees to the beach," he murmured, recalling Rings's instructions.

Louie blinked as he looked around. The whole damn world was filled with palm trees...

But there was definitely a string of them to his left, their fronds slashing the air with passing gusts of wind. And they headed toward the ocean, just as Rings had indicated. Louie headed in that direction, the flip-flops slapping against the sidewalk.

Shrieks of seagulls mixed with the incessant pounding as he followed the trees. Ahead, he saw where the palms terminated at a rock wall that blocked his view of the ocean.

Where's the frickin' green bush Rings talked about?

When Louie finally reached the last palm, he knew. Where the rock wall ended, a mass of green began. Two walls, essentially, delineating where one property ended, another began.

Louie veered toward the green, which turned out to be ten-foot-high trees planted into a series of wooden troughs laid side by side, which formed a natural privacy fence between beachgoers and someone's property.

He glanced over his shoulder, seeing that this property was a fancy home that neighbored Lily's Lighthouse. Sunlight glistened off windows that comprised the back wall of the house—windows that provided sweeping views of the Atlantic. Clustered behind the house were several lawn chairs and a red-and-white striped umbrella.

What were Rings's next instructions? Something about going through a break in the bushes.

Louie walked briskly along the green barricade, the scent of the orange flowers sweetly surreal. The foliage was dense. Impenetrable. No damn openings.

What in the hell was Rings talking about?

Louie reached the last wooden trough, which butted against a wooden fence that ran west, marking the property line on that side of the home. He looked around, penned into the backyard, bounded by this fence, the dense green wall, the line of palms.

Bam-bam-bam. The hammering pounded his skull. *Damn you, Rings. Your lousy directions are eating up precious minutes.*

Louie looked back at the house, a good sixty feet away, but close enough for anyone standing at one of its windows to see the trespasser. For the first time in his life, Louie hoped to God someone would see him, call the cops.

Hell, he'd have called the cops himself before he left the lighthouse but he had no doubt it would have only wasted time. Trying to explain the bizarre situation to the cops, dancing with their questions…they probably would've written him off as one of the hundreds of wacko calls the Key West police got every day.

Louie stared at the massive wall of green and orange, which shuddered with gusts of wind.

Need to retrace my steps, check again for a break.

Louie marched back along the line of trees, slogging his way through the sand, cursing Rings for playing hide-and-seek. When he reached an area where splintered light seeped through some broken branches, he stopped.

Louie blew out a pent-up puff of air. *If this is a passage, I'm Saint Anthony.*

Willing to battle for sainthood, he shoved his weight against the opening, which gave way to his weight. He pushed forward. Branches scratched his face, arms, legs as he tore his way through.

Finally, he fell free, cool breezes assaulting his body.

He swiped his hand across his face, barely registering a streak of blood across his palm. *Where's the lifeguard station?*

There.

A dome of carved wood, dingy blue, hovered above another hedge forty or so feet to his right. He jogged toward it, realizing if the dome was at eye-level, the structure had to be located down a decline. Probably built in a nook where there was once a private beach.

Perfect place for a killing.

His toe caught in the strap on top of the flip-flop and he stumbled. Cursing, he caught himself and continued. In the distance, on the far side of the station, he saw the frame of a building in progress—had to be the source of all that damn hammering.

Reaching the hedge, he eyed its length. Twenty or so feet.

He had no option but to go to one end or the other.

Rings was undoubtedly down below, watching, waiting for Louie's entrance.

If there could be good news, it was that Rings would not be stupid enough to shoot Louie the instant he came into view. Rings had to know that up here, Louie was still visible to that fancy house with all the windows...

Bad news was Louie wasn't visible once he descended to the lifeguard station.

Reaching the end of the hedge, Louie sucked in a fortifying breath and turned the corner.

Below, approximately thirty feet, Alicia sat in the sand at the base of the station steps, leaning against one of its cement-anchored stilts. Waves crashed and ebbed nearby.

He noticed her hands were behind her. *She's probably tied to a post, scared to death that the tide will rise before she's freed.*

Louie detected a strip of tape over her mouth. Her feet were bare, her orange-tipped toes rising and falling as she tip-tapped her soles against the sand.

Too hot for her to rest her feet.

Cold adrenaline rushed Louie's arteries.

Rings, you bastard. Taking away her shoes, knowing the sand burns like hell underneath her feet, tying her where the tide could rise, drown her. *You sick, sadistic bastard.*

He shifted his gaze to the shade at the top of the lifeguard station and saw the bottom half of Rings's body sitting on a wooden bench, his pasty legs sticking out of a pair of khaki shorts. Behind him, the surf rose on its white knuckles and battered the shore.

"Come on down," called Rings, waving his gold-weighted hand at Louie. In Rings's other hand, he pointed a gun at the back of Alicia's head.

Louie half stepped, half slid down a sandy decline toward the structure.

Reaching level ground, he walked slowly toward Alicia, his gaze darting between her and Rings.

Closer, he saw how her green eyes sparkled, twice as bright with the sheen of nervousness.

He halted at her feet. They stared at each other with an intensity that was almost tangible.

"Hold on, baby," he murmured.

Rings stood and chuckled, an unpleasant sound. "Oh, she's holding," he said, sauntering down the steps and stopping in front of Louie.

Rings's bald head shone pink under the sun. Buried under sagging eyelids were dark eyes devoid of light. "Nice to see ya."

"Glad you think so," Louie answered, darting a look at Rings's gun. Ruger .22 automatic. He raised his gaze while pressing his forearms against his sides, feeling the exact location of the plastic utensils in one pocket, the bulk of necklace in the other. "Let her go."

Rings snorted. "We already had this conversation."

"She won't talk."

"Bullshit."

Hammers pounded, pounded.

"I'm a lucky guy," said Rings, his eyes shifting toward the sound, then back to Louie. "One or two gun shots will blend in real nice with that hammering."

One or two? Was Rings undecided about killing Alicia?

"She doesn't want trouble," Louie said calmly, catching the rise and fall of her feet, like a pendulum, in his peripheral vision. *Time. We're running out of time.* "She just wants to go home, back to Denver. Let her go—you'll never see or hear from her again."

Rings's fat lips curled into a fake smile. "Do I look stupid?"

"No. You're a real smart guy. Got me to meet you."

Rings paused, nodded, his imitation smile almost looking real.

Guess nobody ever flattered him in prison. "You're also too smart to kill a rich girl whose family will spend every last dime to hunt you down."

"That what they're doin' to you? Huntin' you down?"

"Me?" Louie laughed sharply. "They could care less about me. Hell, even my own family has written me off."

A sadness stabbed Louie as he realized how true that statement was. Just past Rings's head, he saw the ocean swell and retreat to the sea…the way Louie had undoubtedly retreated in his family's memories after years of witnessing his quiet deceit. He hated that this would be his final realization. That he'd wasted years of family. Years of love.

"So she's a rich bitch, eh?"

Louie refocused on Rings. "Yeah," he said, wishing he could slam a right hook into the bastard's face.

"Her family'll never find me."

"You've been in the slammer too long. The universe isn't expanding, it's shrinking. Even the filthy rich can't hide anymore."

Staccato raps from the construction site punctured

the air. When they stopped, Rings spoke in a low, ominous tone. "When they find her body, they'll never make the connection to me."

Louie's gut curdled at the word "when."

"Witnesses saw her with me at the Green Parrot," he countered calmly. "And the cops got an ID on you, and your gun, that day. She shows up dead, your mug will get more media attention than Tom Cruise."

Rings's face collapsed into a dark frown. "You sonofabitch."

"Let her go and this sonofabitch is all yours."

Rings huffed a breath. "Okay, smart-ass. Get over there and untie her."

Louie took a step toward Alicia, meeting the sad look in her eyes. *She just heard me trade my life for hers...and I'll never get to tell her it's the best deal I ever made.*

He crouched down next to her, catching a whiff of her familiar scent. Maybe he'd wasted years of his life, but he wasn't going to waste these last moments.

He wasn't going to die a loser.

As Louie craned his neck to peer behind her, his face blocked by hers from Rings's view, he whispered, "I love you."

She stirred, her eyes glistening.

He checked out the silver duct tape wound around her wrists and the post. Her fingers waggled to him, and he reached over and touched them. *Good-bye.* Then he tugged on the seam of the tape. It pulled free, but not completely. He tugged again, ripping it almost loose.

Louie glanced at Rings. "You got something to cut this tape?"

"How come you tell me I'm smart, then treat me like I'm stupid?" Rings walked across the sand to them.

"I don't have anything to cut the tape, that's all," answered Louie. As he looked back at her bound wrists, he caught a flash of her orange-tipped toes burrowing into the blistering hot sand.

"Use your teeth," Rings barked, standing in front of Alicia.

At first Louie thought wind had kicked up sand…then realized it had been Alicia's shapely legs kicking sand into Rings's face.

As Rings yelled, raising his hands to his eyes, Louie's reflexes went on autopilot.

He lunged at Rings, one hand flailing for the gun. He knocked it loose and dove for it, his fingers barely touching warm metal before Rings landed on his back, the impact ripping air out of Louie's lungs.

"Give me the gun!" Rings screamed.

Gripping it with one hand, Louie shoved his other into his pocket. "Do I look stupid?" he rasped. With a violent twist, he turned and jerked his knee into Rings's crotch.

As Rings bellowed, Louie tossed the knife in Alicia's direction, hoping to God it fell close enough so those magic feet could scoot it to her fingers.

As Rings coughed and rolled over, Louie saw Alicia painstakingly tapping the knife with her toes.

She'll never get it to her hands without help.

Louie glanced behind him. Rings was writhing about, clutching himself. Louie surged forward, grabbed the knife and threw it—it landed inches from her fingers.

Damn.

He started to scramble to his feet when a mother of a truck slammed into his back and he flew forward, a sharp pain tearing through his ankle. As he slammed into the sand, he watched the gun sail into the air, flashing silver in the sunlight, and hit the ground.

Digging his way across the sand on his elbows, Louie grabbed for it just as Rings kicked it free. It skittered wildly, stopping at the edge of the surf.

Mustering all his strength, Louie surged to his feet and ran toward the gun, fighting the pain in his ankle. Neck and neck with a screaming Rings, Louie threw himself on top of the object, the cold surf hitting his face like pellets.

Hands gripped his throat before thundering water roared in his ears, obliterating his vision. He swung wildly, made solid contact with flesh. Rings's hold loosened.

Louie lunged for freedom.

Staggering to his feet, he spat salty water and gasped for air. Water burned his eyes. Blinking, he scanned the area for Rings...

And saw Alicia, standing at the edge of the water, waving her hands as though she were about to take flight. "Behind you!" she screamed.

Ducking his head, Louie shoved his hand into his

pocket and turned. Tugging the necklace tight, he yanked it around Rings's neck.

Rings howled like a madman, clawing at the chain, salt water bubbling from his nose and mouth.

"You sonofa—" he sputtered before toppling over.

10

"MORE ICE?" asked Alicia, swirling the champagne bottle in the bucket.

Louie leaned back on the bed in the lighthouse room, his foot elevated on one of the white lacy pillows, a glass of frothy champagne in his hand. "If you pack any more ice around my ankle, it'll freeze."

"Good idea," Alicia murmured. "It'd stop you from taking off."

"Nothing could stop me if you were in trouble."

Alicia smiled, feeling happy and sad and anxious all at once. Her emotions were so twisted together, they were almost indistinguishable. In just the same way, the horrifying and exhilarating experiences of today were bound together—experiences she and Louie hadn't had a chance to discuss since the insanity of the abduction, the showdown at the lifeguard station and the subsequent wrap-up with the police.

They'd been back in the room long enough for her to order champagne, get Louie's foot propped up, pay the delivery boy.

And now it was finally time to celebrate that they were alive.

She raised her glass. "To..." Her hand trembled.

The glass shook. She sucked in a ragged breath. "If you hadn't tossed that picnic knife—" she suddenly said, the words sticking in her throat. *I wouldn't have made it to the shore, warned you about Rings.*

She stared down into the bucket of ice, which looked like the white, churning ocean. Her vision blurred as she remembered Rings's gold-encrusted hands shoving Louie's head under the waves.

Something warm touched her. She lifted her gaze and saw Louie leaning forward, his hand on hers.

"It's okay," he murmured.

"When I saw you walking down to the lifeguard station, I thought Rings would shoot you right then." She swiped at the corner of her eye. "And I'd be tied up, helpless, watching you die."

"It's okay, baby—"

"I barely remember running to that house," she whispered. After she and Louie had dragged Rings out of the water and bound his hands and legs with the remaining duct tape, they'd rummaged in his pocket and found a cell phone. Soaked, it hadn't worked and Louie had yelled for her to run to the house and call the cops.

Then there was the scream of sirens. Being driven to the police station. Someone handing her hot coffee in a chipped cup. Questions. Later, a woman officer saying Rings matched the description from several tourists who'd been held up at gunpoint. Louie must have mentioned Keith, because someone said he was on his way to give a statement about what had happened at the Green Parrot.

Then Alicia and Louie had shared a surreal taxi ride home through streets crowded with tan, laughing people who acted as though life was one big don't-worry-be-happy party.

"Alicia," Louie said, distracting her. "It's over." He squeezed her hand. "We're here, safe. That's all that matters."

He raised his glass to her. "Let's finish that toast. Here's to the good things in life, like those killer legs of yours. When I called them that before, I had no idea how true it was." With a wink, he took a sip.

She smiled despite her mood and joined him in the toast. It had been sheer impulse on her part to kick sand in Rings's face. She'd figured if it backfired, well, Rings was going to kill them anyway.

Louie set his glass on the nightstand. "Never thought I'd develop a taste for the bubbly, but it goes down mighty smooth…one of those acquired tastes, I guess." One side of his mouth kicked up, and she thought how white his teeth were against his bronze skin. "Like the taste I acquired for you…"

He slid his hands up her arms and gently pulled her toward him.

For a fleeting moment she hesitated, her eyes searching his face, torn between wanting to sort through the terror they'd shared while also desperately needing his solace.

"Louie, I—"

He touched his forefinger to her lips. "Shh. Come here."

She set aside her glass and sank forward, bridging the space between them.

And as she drew closer, she eased in a long breath and took in Louie's familiar scent as though she could absorb it, make it part of her being. As his essence mingled with hers, a warmth flooded her body and she realized her emotional turmoil was melting and she was finally feeling alive again.

Her lips lingered against his as she savored the heat of his skin, felt a silken strand of his hair against her brow, sensed his life pulse beating.

The very air thrummed with their arousal.

She lightly touched her tongue, almost secretly, to the underside of his lip. "Louie," she whispered, urgency straining her voice, "kiss me."

He didn't kiss her.

He captured her, plunging his tongue into the womb of her mouth with the fiery affirmation of their being alive.

Her fingers tunneled into his hair and she held on for dear life as she fully tasted his hot, wet kisses, entwining her tongue with his, devouring his passion with an unbridled need that bordered on maniacal.

Louie's lips slipped across her cheek, and he nuzzled her neck, his breath hot in the crook of her neck. "Alicia," he murmured, "my dear, sweet Alicia."

Her head fell back and she panted as he pressed his lips along her neck, collarbone. Tiny bursts of flame ignited beneath her skin, following the path of his kisses.

He raised his head and cupped her face in his hands. "I love you, baby."

When he'd told her before, she'd been physically unable to speak. But now that she could, the words burst from her heart. "Oh, Louie, I love you, too." And in that moment, she felt as though she had come home.

She'd never feel lost again.

Louie smiled, amazed at what he saw on Alicia's face. A trusting sweetness that made his heart ache. He wasn't a man who was often at a loss for words, but right now he was speechless, staring into the shining eyes of the woman with whom he'd fallen in love.

No, the women. Alicia may have seemed one-dimensional in the beginning, but since then he'd discovered she was really a mix of different women. One opinionated and willful, a spirit who refused to be broken. Another sweetly innocent, who believed with the heart of a child. Another so unabashedly erotic, he could be aroused to the point of pain.

And he loved this complex, challenging woman. Undeniably so, but...

"There's something I have to say," he began, not sure how to shape his thoughts.

Her mouth opened into a little O, but she didn't say anything.

"I'm a man of honor." Hell, he hadn't even known he was going to say that until he heard himself say the words. But it was true. Or, it was true in that he was driven to be a better man. One who could hold

360 Can't Buy Me Louie

his head high with the world, with his family, with his woman.

An honorable man who would make his father proud.

"I think we need some more champagne," Alicia said, breaking the silence. She pulled the bottle out of the ice bucket and topped off their glasses. After settling the bottle back into the bucket, she said, "Please. Continue."

He took a sip, then said, "I have no money, no worldly goods to offer you. No future to promise." Damn, this was hard. He took another sip.

So did Alicia.

They sat in silence, the only sound an occasional bird chirping as it soared past the open window. He closed his eyes, wishing the balmy breezes swirling through the room could carry away his worries...

But life was never that simple.

He opened his eyes. "When my situation improves, I'll have things to say to you."

She blinked. *"Improves?* I thought we were celebrating your life—our lives—being in damn good shape! We're alive, Rings is in jail, this very moment is our new beginning." She chewed her bottom lip as though stopping herself from saying more.

Gone was the joy Louie had seen on her face only a few moments ago. Now her eyes glistened with a sadness that tore at his heart.

"Baby," he murmured. He reached over and circled her slim arm with his fingers. "I need to make my way in the world. That's all. After that, we can be together." He tightened his hold on her as though he could will her his strength, make her understand.

She shook her head. "I have everything you need to make your way in the world—"

"Don't go there, Bonbon."

"But I must!" Standing, she broke loose of his hold and paced a few feet from the bed before turning back to him. "I have money in my trust fund to finance your fishing business, help us settle down here in Key West. We can be together, have a fresh start—"

"No."

"Why not?" She shrugged to the room as though an audience of spectators were in agreement with her that this was the stupidest man ever to grace the planet.

"Because I can't be owned." It was the rock-hard truth at the core of everything else in his life. He'd spent years and years not wanting to be shackled to anyone or anything the way his father had been. He'd seen what that could do to a human being, how it imprisoned their character, weakened them despite their strengths. He'd learned as a kid that if a person can't stand on their own two feet and face the world freely, they might as well be dead.

"Alicia, you and I come from different worlds. We never talked about your wealth or how your family came into it, but I'll wager you never witnessed a person being tied to something that drained them of their self-respect. My father…"

He thought of his father's hatred for his job, the disrespect he endured, all for the sake of a paycheck.

Louie's mother had begged her husband to quit, but after twenty-plus years at the tire factory, he'd said he didn't have the skills to work elsewhere and was too old, too tired to start fresh.

But rather than explain his past, Louie simply said, "I don't want anyone, or anything, to own me."

She held open her arms, as though showing him she had nothing to hide, only the purest of intentions. "For God's sake, I don't want to own you! I want to support you, be your partner. I'm offering you what you need to start a new life…"

He raked his hand through his hair. "And you'd get a new life with a man who'd compromised himself. *Half* a man. I couldn't do that to you. Or to me."

"Half a man?" She dropped her hands. "Or a one-man show?"

Their gazes locked before she turned away from Louie and started quietly packing her bag.

"HERE'S YOUR CHANGE," Louie said, handing the boy several bills. "And take a candy." He nodded toward a coconut-shell bowl he kept next to the cash register filled with brightly wrapped sweets.

"Cool!" The kid starting pawing through the goodies.

Louie grinned, thinking how his dream of owning a fishing business had started when he was about this kid's age, years ago when Louie's family had caravanned here to Key West.

Now, all this time later, Louie Ragazzi was halfway to fulfilling that dream. He ran Louie's Lures, a postage-stamp-size rod-and-reel shop on the Key West harbor walk. And in a few years, he hoped to have enough for a down payment on a boat. Until then, he worked part-time as a crew member on several local sportfishing charter boats to earn more money.

"Tell your dad that's a great pole for handling sailfish and marlin." Louie nodded at the fishing rod the boy had purchased, which Louie had been holding for the kid's dad who'd visited the shop earlier. "And when you go out, wear hats. The sun down here fries brain cells. Trust me, I know."

The kid flashed Louie a grin as he plucked a blue gumball from the bowl.

Louie chuckled to himself, thinking how he'd once groused about the Florida sun burning off men's macho brain cells, as though it were a bad thing. But now that he'd learned how comfortable it was to wear Hawaiian shirts and flip-flops in sweltering humidity, he'd decided the eradication of macho cells was an excellent thing.

"Thanks, mister," the kid chirped, stuffing the gum into his mouth. The boy half skipped away from the counter to the front door of Louie's store just as a woman entered.

Tan, long limbs and a mass of sun-streaked hair paused in the open doorway. Sunlight fired the tips of her locks, giving her a halo effect. Then she closed the door and minced toward him, walking expertly in a pair of orange flip-flops, her pink sundress rippling with her movements.

Alicia.

His mouth went dry. His heart plummeted.

Impossible. Five long months ago she'd left that lighthouse room, never to be heard from again. Didn't *want* to be heard from again. Louie had gotten that message loud and clear when he'd called her in Denver a few weeks later and been told Ms. Hansen was unavailable.

She walked straight to the counter and put her hands on the smooth glass countertop, under which were displayed a variety of fishing lures. "I'd like to apply for the job advertised in the paper," she said matter-of-factly. "An assistant shopkeeper for Louie's Lures."

No hello. No thanks for kicking me out of your life five months ago. Okay, he didn't deserve her falling all over him for how he'd treated her, but "I want to apply for a job" didn't cut it.

"Alicia, what're you doing here?"

"Didn't you advertise in the paper for an assistant?"

For a moment, he felt lost in those green eyes, remembering how they sparkled like sunlight on the sea. "Yes, but—"

"I'd like to apply. I can keep inventory stocked, work the cash register—"

"Where the hell have you been?" *And why are you acting so normal?* Louie was so floored by this ghost from his past, he was holding on to the damn counter to keep himself steady.

She blinked innocently. "Living here in Key West."

"You live in Denver."

"Yes, my family lives there. Is this part of the interview?"

"Hell, yes." *She still smells like spicy peaches.*

"Well, I did visit them. But after a while, I returned."

Visit? He'd made her leave. Yet she'd come back. "Why?"

"Let's just say I wasn't overly attached to the terms of the trust fund. My mother wanted me to marry someone of my 'social class.'" Alicia shrugged as though it were a trite issue, but the look in her eyes said it had been far more than that.

"And you let them do that?"

"Do what?"

"Take away your trust fund?"

"I don't have the legal control. Anyway, they didn't take it *all* away. Just a big chunk of it." Her mouth twisted. "Okay, most of it." She raised her elegant little chin a notch. "Do you ask everyone applying for the job such personal questions?"

"Hell, yes." He shrugged. "You're the first applicant." His gaze dipped. Her sun-pink skin and freckled nose told him she spent time outdoors. Taking walks on the wharf? Riding in a boat?

Is there another man?

"Tell you the truth, I don't care about the trust fund," she said. "Bottom line, you can't sleep with money. Can't marry it. Can't have kids with it. Money offers cold comfort if your heart is elsewhere."

Doesn't sound like there's another guy.

"Besides…" She leaned forward and looked up at

Louie through a screen of lashes. "The only time I really wanted to use that trust fund, it cost me what I prized most in life..."

The sound of her voice resonated through him, hitting a deep chord. *I lost what I prized most, too.* It still hurt. Like a raw, gaping wound that would never heal.

"Where have you been living? What are you doing?"

She splayed her fingers on the counter and he noticed her nails were unpolished. "I'm renting a room. And I've worked as a waitress—"

"Waitress?"

"That didn't work out so well," she said morosely. "They were awfully fussy about food being served while it was still hot." She flashed him a can-you-believe-that? look. "After that I worked as a maid at a motel—"

"You? A *maid?*" That was harder to believe than her slinging lukewarm food to customers.

"Hey," she countered, "it's a great way to stay in shape. But when I saw this ad yesterday for a shop assistant at Louie's Lures, I figured this job was *much* more my style..."

More her style? Was she stuck in Key West, needing a job? Here his heart was pounding, his palms sweating like he was some lovesick, crushed-out teenager...and maybe Bonbon was simply needing his help, not him?

Well, what did he expect after he sent her away? That she'd come crawling back, begging him to love her forevermore? Hell, he didn't have the good sense to take her up on that when she asked him before—only a fool would ask again.

And Alicia was no fool.

"So," she finally said, breaking the silence, "how did you build your business?"

He realized he'd been standing here for a small eternity, staring at her. He'd seen those plump, pink lips move, but the words had escaped him. "What?"

"Your business. How'd it come about?"

He looked around his empire, a room barely twenty by twenty, packed with fishing gear. "I saw this place for sale soon after..." *After you left. Those first few days were sheer hell, my world gutted.* "I got some odd jobs on the harbor and saved almost enough for a down payment. Shorty loaned me the difference, and I sealed the deal. After opening Louie's Lures, I started working on some charter fishing boats. Got old closing this place every time I worked a boat, so I placed the ad for an assistant to manage Louie's Lures while I'm on the ocean."

She smiled. "I'd make a good assistant."

He paused, his heart splintering. He couldn't maintain the facade any longer.

"I'm dying here," he blurted. He thrust a hand into his hair, his mind and heart in an uproar. "Standing here talking to you, acting like we never..." Images of her naked body bent beneath him seared through his mind. *What are we, Alicia? Is it too late?*

Damn counter was a wall between them.

He headed around it, stopping a foot or two in front

of her. His heart surged painfully in his chest as he faced her. "Seeing you," he said in a rough murmur, "makes me feel alive again. I thought if you stayed, I'd only be half a man. I was wrong. It was losing that you made me less..."

Alicia's breath caught in her throat. These past months had felt like years as she struggled with the heartache and hopelessness of losing the only man she'd ever loved. How often had she wondered what it would be like to see him again? And now she knew. Every fiber of her being ached to hold him, embrace him fiercely, never let him go...

But she couldn't fall blindly into something with Louie again. Not until she'd spoken her truth.

"I learned some things while we were apart," she said, her voice low. She wet her lips and searched his gaze, vaguely aware of the tangy ocean breezes encircling them. "You thought if I funded your way, you'd feel owned. I thought about that for weeks, and I think I finally understand." She eased in a calming breath, as though that could temper her pounding heart. "If I'd stayed, you would have been unhappy...and, knowing I was the cause, I would have been unhappy, too. We would have been two miserable people..."

The rest of her speech evaporated as she stared into his dark, emotion-filled eyes.

"I learned something, too," he said, stepping closer. "I grew up hating how my dad was trapped at his job, how he felt enslaved, owned. But you know what? It had nothing to do with his being owned. What trapped him was his *pride*."

Louie stared down into her eyes for a long time. "What trapped me was my pride, too," he said. "I thought being independent made me strong, but when I lost you…" He gave his head a shake. "I realized I'm dependent on you in ways that have nothing to do with money. That love isn't about boundaries— being a damn one-man show—but choosing to be part of something bigger, better."

Trembling, she stepped closer. Her voice emerged breathless, scarcely audible. "Choose now."

And in a swirl of movement, he crushed her into an embrace, nearly knocking the breath out of her. She choked back a startled laugh, unable to contain her soaring joy. "Louie, oh God, how I've missed you—"

A rough kiss drowned the rest of her words and she sank against him, pressing herself against the familiar comfort of his warm, solid body. He kissed her hard, with a hunger that matched her own, pausing to murmur huskily, "No more missing…no more apart," before his mouth again seized hers.

After a moment he pulled away, gazing at her with so much love, tears sprang to her eyes. She drew in a ragged breath. "My trust fund…well, what's left of it…"

"I thought I'd name the boat Bonbon."

A slow smile lifted her lips. "Candy would melt out there on the ocean, under that hot sun…"

He wound his hands in her hair, his black eyes smoldering. "Maybe we need some ice, then." He pulled her to him, brushing his lips against hers. "Let's order some champagne," he said, his voice a throaty rumble, "two glasses..."

"One for me, one for you," she murmured, succumbing to another kiss, one of many for the rest of their lives.

* * * * *

She's hip, she's cool and her world has been turned upside down by love! Harlequin Flipside™ is coming in October 2003.

Turn the page for a sneak preview of this new romantic comedy line...

1
___

IT WAS A BAD DAY for a wedding.

Francie Morelli gazed down the red-carpeted aisle toward the altar, where her handsome husband-to-be, all smiles and nervous perspiration in a black Armani tux, awaited her arrival, and knew this with a certainty.

Though unlike him, Francie wasn't nervous, just panicked. The kind of panic you get when you can't catch your breath or feel like you might throw up.

Okay, so maybe she was a teensy bit nervous.

Though she'd done the wedding thing twice before and knew what to expect. Not that she had ever actually made it all the way to the altar and said her "I dos."

And it didn't look as though she would get that far this time, either.

Swallowing with some difficulty at the dangerous thoughts going through her mind, she tried to ignore the "Run, Francie, run!" mantra currently playing to the tune of "Burn, Baby, Burn," the disco song so popular in the seventies.

The choice of music was a bad omen. Burning in hell was a definite possibility if she didn't go through with this wedding, which was probably the lesser of the two evils, because she knew Josephine Morelli's punishment would be far worse.

The devil had nothing on Josephine Morelli.

Through her blush veil, she could see her mother, hands locked in prayer and supplication, pleading with the Almighty to give her daughter the courage to go through with the ceremony this time. The older woman's tear-filled eyes—Francie knew there were tears because her mother liked to make a good showing at public events (funerals were her specialty)— were fixed on the massive gold crucifix hanging above the altar, as if by sheer will alone she could command God to do her bidding, as Josephine had commanded Francie so many times before.

Fortunately for the world at large, God seemed to have a stronger backbone than Francie.

A hushed silence surrounded her, as those in attendance waited to see if she would actually go through with the ceremony. Aunt Flo was biting her nails to the quick, while Grandma Abrizzi had her rosary beads clacking at top speed.

Francie's sixteen-year-old brother, Jackie, had taken perverse delight in explaining that several of the male guests, her uncles in particular, had placed bets on the outcome of today's event. The odds were five to one that she would never see her wedding night.

Not that Francie had anything in particular against matrimony. It just wasn't right for her. She had no desire to become an extension of a man, with few interests of her own, except family and meddling in her children's lives.

Meddling, like marriage, was another one of those *M*-words that Francie hated—*meddling, marriage, menstruation, menopause, Milk of Magnesia*—Josephine's remedy for every childhood ailment. No, *M*-words were definitely not good. She'd have to remember that the next time she dated, if there was a next time. At the moment, that seemed remote... *remote, redundant, ridiculous.*

She would not allow her mother to bully her again.

Standing beside Francie, John Morelli clutched his daughter's arm in a death grip, trying to keep her steady and on course. But she knew, just as he did, that it wouldn't. She was in collision mode and there was no way to avoid it.

Still, he had to try. His wife would expect no less. And John, like most of the Morellis, wasn't going to buck Josephine's wedding obsession. Not if he wanted a moment's peace.

Francie's toes began to tingle—a surefire indication that flight was imminent. She wiggled them, hoping and praying the urge to flee would pass. If not, the white satin shoes she wore, like Dorothy's ruby slippers, would whisk her away from the solemn occasion, to her favorite place of refuge, Manny's Little Italy Deli, where she knew he would be waiting for her with a pastrami on rye and a large diet cola.

Okay, so stress made her hungry!

Her roommate, Leo Bergman, suitably armed with a packed suitcase and a train ticket to an as-yet-unknown destination, would also be there to offer moral support and a stern lecture. Leo was almost as good as Josephine when it came to offering opinions and advice that no one wanted, only he did it with a bit more finesse.

Patting his daughter's hand reassuringly, John leaned over and smiled lovingly.

"Don't be nervous, *cara mia*. Soon this will be over and you'll be married and settled down. It's the right thing to do, you'll see. And it will make your mother very happy. You know how she's waited for this day."

The second coming paled by comparison!

Francie adored her father and wanted to agree with him; she wanted that more than anything. But words of reassurance stuck in her throat like oversize peanuts, and all she could offer up was a gaseous smile and a deer-in-the-headlights look.

"I'm sorry, Pop, but I don't think I can go through with this. I'm just not ready to get married. I'm not sure I'll ever be ready."

John's eyes widened momentarily, then he looked down the long aisle to where his wife was sitting in the first pew, the smile on her face suddenly melting as she noticed his resigned, worried expression.

"Your car's out back. I gassed it up, just in case, and left some money in the glove box."

Warmed by the gesture, Francie kissed her father's cheek. "I love you, Pop. Thanks! I hope Ma doesn't give you too bad a time of it."

Then she turned and hightailed it out of the church and into the warm September sunshine.

COMING NEXT MONTH

HARLEQUIN® flipside

#1

STAYING SINGLE by Millie Criswell

"Engaging men" are lining up for Francesca Morelli, thanks to her interfering mother! She's arranged three weddings so far for her twenty-nine-and-pushing-it daughter. Unfortunately, all three have gone off, uh, *without* a hitch, because the only vow Francesca's taking is to stay single! That is, until former best man Mark Fielding steps onto the scene.

#2

ONE TRUE LOVE? by Stephanie Doyle

Corinne Weatherby believes everyone has just *one* true love. Okay, so the one she's picked is a shallow, inconsiderate womanizer—nothing a good breakup scene can't fix. There's a drama queen lurking just below her financial-controller surface. Her "I'm leaving you!" will turn the boy around. But her office buddy Matthew overhears her performance and decides to go for it, determined to prove *he* is her real one and only.

Clever, witty and unexpectedly romantic!

HFCNM0903

HARLEQUIN® *Blaze*™

"(NO STRINGS ATTACHED) battle of the sexes will delight,
tantalize and entertain with Kent's indomitable style. Delicious!
Very highly recommended."
—*Wordweaving.com*

"(ALL TIED UP) is hot, sexy and still manages to involve
the reader emotionally—a winning combination."
—*AllAboutRomance.com*

"With electrifying tension, creative scenes and…seductive
characters, Alison Kent delivers a knockout read."
—*Romantic Times* Book Club

Find out why everybody's talking about Blaze author Alison Kent
and check out the latest books in her gIRL-gEAR miniseries!

#99 STRIPTEASE
August 2003

#107 WICKED GAMES
October 2003

#115 INDISCREET
December 2003

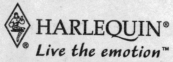

HARLEQUIN®
Live the emotion™

Visit us at www.eHarlequin.com

HBGG

Is your man too good to be true?

Hot, gorgeous AND romantic?
If so, he could be a Harlequin® Blaze™ series cover model!

Our grand-prize winners will receive a trip for two to New York City to
shoot the cover of a Blaze novel, and will stay at the luxurious Plaza Hotel.
Plus, they'll receive $500 U.S. spending money!
The runner-up winners will receive $200 U.S.
to spend on a romantic dinner for two.

It's easy to enter!

In 100 words or less, tell us what makes your boyfriend or spouse a true romantic
and the perfect candidate for the cover of a Blaze novel, and include in your submission
two photos of this potential cover model.

All entries must include the written submission of the contest entrant, two photographs of the model
candidate and the Official Entry Form and Publicity Release forms completed in full and signed by
both the model candidate and the contest entrant. Harlequin, along with the experts at
Elite Model Management, will select a winner.

For photo and complete Contest details, please refer to the Official Rules on the next page. All entries
will become the property of Harlequin Enterprises Ltd. and are not returnable.

**Please visit www.blazecovermodel.com to download a copy of the Official Entry Form and
Publicity Release Form or send a request to one of the addresses below.**

Please mail your entry to: **Harlequin Blaze Cover Model Search**

In U.S.A.	In Canada
P.O. Box 9069	P.O. Box 637
Buffalo, NY	Fort Erie, ON
14269-9069	L2A 5X3

No purchase necessary. Contest open to Canadian and U.S. residents who are 18 and over.
Void where prohibited. Contest closes September 30, 2003.

HARLEQUIN® *Blaze*™

HBCVRMODEL1

HARLEQUIN BLAZE COVER MODEL SEARCH CONTEST 3569 OFFICIAL RULES
NO PURCHASE NECESSARY TO ENTER

1. To enter, submit two (2) 4" x 6" photographs of a boyfriend or spouse (who must be 18 years of age or older) taken no later than three (3) months from the time of entry: a close-up, waist up, shirtless photograph; and a fully clothed, full-length photograph, then, tell us, in 100 words or fewer, why he should be a Harlequin Blaze cover model and how he is romantic. Your complete "entry" must include: (i) your essay, (ii) the Official Entry Form and Publicity Release Form printed below completed and signed by you (as "Entrant"), (iii) the photographs (with your hand-written name, address and phone number, and your model's name, address and phone number on the back of each photograph), and (iv) the Publicity Release Form and Photograph Representation Form printed below completed and signed by your model (as "Model"), and should be sent via first-class mail to either: Harlequin Blaze Cover Model Search Contest 3569, P.O. Box 9069, Buffalo, NY, 14269-9069, or Harlequin Blaze Cover Model Search Contest 3569, P.O. Box 637, Fort Erie, Ontario L2A 5X3. All submissions must be in English and be received no later than September 30, 2003. Limit: one entry per person, household or organization. **Purchase or acceptance of a product offer does not improve your chances of winning.** All entry requirements must be strictly adhered to for eligibility and to ensure fairness among entries.

2. Ten (10) Finalist submissions (photographs and essays) will be selected by a panel of judges consisting of members of the Harlequin editorial, marketing and public relations staff, as well as a representative from Elite Model Management (Toronto) Inc., based on the following criteria:

Aptness/Appropriateness of submitted photographs for a Harlequin Blaze cover—70%
Originality of Essay—20%
Sincerity of Essay—10%

In the event of a tie, duplicate finalists will be selected. The photographs submitted by finalists will be posted on the Harlequin website no later than November 15, 2003 (at www.blazecovermodel.com), and viewers may vote, in rank order, on their favorite(s) to assist in the panel of judges' final determination of the Grand Prize and Runner-up winning entries based on the above judging criteria. All decisions of the judges are final.

3. All entries become the property of Harlequin Enterprises Ltd. and none will be returned. Any entry may be used for future promotional purposes. Elite Model Management (Toronto) Inc. and/or its partners, subsidiaries and affiliates operating as "Elite Model Management" will have access to all entries including all personal information, and may contact any Entrant and/or Model in its sole discretion for their own business purposes. Harlequin and Elite Model Management (Toronto) Inc. are separate entities with no legal association or partnership whatsoever having no power to bind or obligate the other or create any expressed or implied obligation or responsibility on behalf of the other, such that Harlequin shall not be responsible in any way for any acts or omissions of Elite Model Management (Toronto) Inc. or its partners, subsidiaries and affiliates in connection with the Contest or otherwise and Elite Model Management shall not be responsible in any way for any acts or omissions of Harlequin or its partners, subsidiaries and affiliates in connection with the contest or otherwise.

4. All Entrants and Models must be residents of the U.S. or Canada, be 18 years of age or older, and have no prior criminal convictions. The contest is not open to any Model that is a professional model and/or actor in any capacity at the time of the entry. Contest void wherever prohibited by law; all applicable laws and regulations apply. Any litigation within the Province of Quebec regarding the conduct or organization of a publicity contest may be submitted to the Régie des alcools, des courses et des jeux for a ruling, and any litigation regarding the awarding of a prize may be submitted to the Régie only for the purpose of helping the parties reach a settlement. Employees and immediate family members of Harlequin Enterprises Ltd., D.L. Blair, Inc., Elite Model Management (Toronto) Inc. and their parents, affiliates, subsidiaries and all other agencies, entities and persons connected with the use, marketing or conduct of this Contest are not eligible to enter. Acceptance of any prize offered constitutes permission to use Entrants' and Models' names, essay submissions, photographs or other likenesses for the purposes of advertising, trade, publication and promotion on behalf of Harlequin Enterprises Ltd., its parent, affiliates, subsidiaries, assigns and other authorized entities involved in the judging and promotion of the contest without further compensation to any Entrant or Model, unless prohibited by law.

5. Finalists will be determined no later than October 30, 2003. Prize Winners will be determined no later than January 31, 2004. Grand Prize Winners (consisting of winning Entrant and Model) will be required to sign and return Affidavit of Eligibility/Release of Liability and Model Release forms within thirty (30) days of notification. Non-compliance with this requirement and within the specified time period will result in disqualification and an alternate will be selected. Any prize notification returned as undeliverable will result in the awarding of the prize to an alternate set of winners. All travelers (or parent/legal guardian of a minor) must execute the Affidavit of Eligibility/Release of Liability prior to ticketing and must possess required travel documents (e.g. valid photo ID) where applicable. Travel dates specified by Sponsor but no later than May 30, 2004.

6. Prizes: One (1) Grand Prize—the opportunity for the Model to appear on the cover of a paperback book from the Harlequin Blaze series, and a 3 day/2 night trip for two (Entrant and Model) to New York, NY for the photo shoot of Model which includes round-trip coach air transportation from the commercial airport nearest the winning Entrant's home to New York, NY, (or, in lieu of air transportation, $100 cash payable to Entrant and Model, if the winning Entrant's home is within 250 miles of New York, NY), hotel accommodations (double occupancy) at the Plaza Hotel and $500 cash spending money payable to Entrant and Model, (approximate prize value: $8,000), and one (1) Runner-up Prize of $200 cash payable to Entrant and Model for a romantic dinner for two (approximate prize value: $200). Prizes are valued in U.S. currency. Prizes consist of only those items listed as part of the prize. No substitution of prize(s) permitted by winners. All prizes are awarded jointly to the Entrant and Model of the winning entries, and are not severable - prizes and obligations may not be assigned or transferred. Any change to the Entrant and/or Model of the winning entries will result in disqualification and an alternate will be selected. Taxes on prize are the sole responsibility of winners. Any and all expenses and/or items not specifically described as part of the prize are the sole responsibility of winners. Harlequin Enterprises Ltd. and D.L. Blair, Inc., their parents, affiliates, and subsidiaries are not responsible for errors in printing of Contest entries and/or game pieces. No responsibility is assumed for lost, stolen, late, illegible, incomplete, inaccurate, non-delivered, postage due or misdirected mail or entries. In the event of printing or other errors which may result in unintended prize values or duplication of prizes, all affected game pieces or entries shall be null and void.

7. Winners will be notified by mail. For winners' list (available after March 31, 2004), send a self-addressed, stamped envelope to: Harlequin Blaze Cover Model Search Contest 3569 Winners, P.O. Box 4200, Blair, NE 68009-4200, or refer to the Harlequin website (at www.blazecovermodel.com).

Contest sponsored by Harlequin Enterprises Ltd., P.O. Box 9042, Buffalo, NY 14269-9042.

HBCVRMODEL2

eHARLEQUIN.com

Your favorite authors are just a click away
at www.eHarlequin.com!

- Take our **Sister Author Quiz** and
  we'll match you up with the author
  most like you!

- Choose from over 500
  author **profiles!**

- Chat with your favorite authors
  on our **message boards.**

- Are you an author in the making?
  Get advice from published authors
  in **The Inside Scoop!**

- Get the latest on **author appearances**
  and tours!

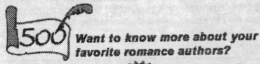

*Want to know more about your
favorite romance authors?*

Choose from over 500 author profiles!

**Learn about your favorite authors
in a fun, interactive setting—
visit www.eHarlequin.com today!**

INTAUTH

If you enjoyed what you just read,
then we've got an offer you can't resist!

Take 2 bestselling
love stories FREE!

Plus get a FREE surprise gift!

Clip this page and mail it to Harlequin Reader Service®

IN U.S.A.	IN CANADA
3010 Walden Ave.	P.O. Box 609
P.O. Box 1867	Fort Erie, Ontario
Buffalo, N.Y. 14240-1867	L2A 5X3

YES! Please send me 2 free Harlequin Duets™ novels and my free surprise gift. After receiving them, if I don't wish to receive anymore, I can return the shipping statement marked cancel. If I don't cancel, I will receive 2 brand-new novels every month, before they're available in stores! In the U.S.A., bill me at the bargain price of $5.14 plus 50¢ shipping & handling per book and applicable sales tax, if any*. In Canada, bill me at the bargain price of $6.14 plus 50¢ shipping & handling per book and applicable taxes**. That's the complete price—what a great deal! I understand that accepting the 2 free books and gift places me under no obligation ever to buy any books. I can always return a shipment and cancel at any time. Even if I never buy another book from Harlequin, the 2 free books and gift are mine to keep forever.

111 HDN DNUF
311 HDN DNUG

Name	(PLEASE PRINT)	
Address	Apt.#	
City	State/Prov.	Zip/Postal Code

* Terms and prices subject to change without notice. Sales tax applicable in N.Y.
** Canadian residents will be charged applicable provincial taxes and GST.
   All orders subject to approval. Offer limited to one per household and not valid to
   current Harlequin Duets™ subscribers.
® and ™ are registered trademarks of Harlequin Enterprises Limited.   DUETS02

HARLEQUIN®
INTRIGUE®

Our unique brand of high-caliber romantic suspense just cannot be contained. And to meet our readers' demands, Harlequin Intrigue is expanding its publishing schedule to include **SIX** breathtaking titles every month!

Check out the new lineup in October!

MORE variety.
MORE pulse-pounding excitement.
MORE of your favorite authors and series.

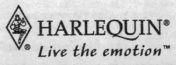

HARLEQUIN®
Live the emotion™

Visit us at www.tryIntrigue.com

HI4T06T

You like
Harlequin Duets™

You'll LOVE

HARLEQUIN®
flipside

It's fun, witty and full of insightful moments you *know* you can relate to!

"It's chick-lit with the romance and happily-ever-after ending that Harlequin is known for."
—*USA TODAY* bestselling author Millie Criswell, author of *Staying Single*, October 2003

"Even though our heroine may take a few false steps while finding her way, she does it with wit and humor."
—Dorien Kelly, author of *Do-Over*, November 2003

Don't miss the exciting launch next month!

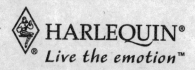

HARLEQUIN®
Live the emotion™

Visit us at www.harlequinflipside.com

HFDUETS

With the sun pouring down its warmth, she surrendered fully to Kirk's kiss, the first of a thousand kisses, a thousand dreams, from which she never wanted to escape because she'd finally found her home, her own special roots, in his love.